visions

ALSO BY
LISA McMANN

Don't Close Your Eyes
Includes *Wake*, *Fade*, and *Gone*

Cryer's Cross

Dead to You

FOR YOUNGER READERS

The Unwanteds series

visions

Includes *Crash*, *Bang*, and *Gasp*

LISA McMANN

SIMON PULSE
NEW YORK   LONDON   TORONTO   SYDNEY   NEW DELHI

SIMON PULSE

An imprint of Simon & Schuster Children's Publishing Division

1230 Avenue of the Americas, New York, New York 10020

This Simon Pulse paperback edition November 2015

Crash text copyright © 2013 by Lisa McMann

Bang text copyright © 2013 by Lisa McMann

Gasp text copyright © 2014 by Lisa McMann

Cover photograph copyright © 2015 by Mark Owen/Getty Images

SIMON PULSE and colophon are registered trademarks of Simon & Schuster, Inc.

For information about special discounts for bulk purchases, please contact Simon & Schuster Special Sales at 1-866-506-1949 or business@simonandschuster.com.

The Simon & Schuster Speakers Bureau can bring authors to your live event. For more information or to book an event contact the Simon & Schuster Speakers Bureau at 1-866-248-3049 or visit our website at www.simonspeakers.com.

Cover designed by Karina Granda

Interior designed by Mike Rosamilia

The text of this book was set in Janson Text.

Manufactured in the United States of America

2 4 6 8 10 9 7 5 3 1

Library of Congress Control Number 2015948993

ISBN 978-1-4814-4850-5

These titles were previously published individually by Simon Pulse.

ISBN 978-1-4424-0592-9 (*Crash* eBook)

ISBN 978-1-4424-6629-6 (*Bang* eBook)

ISBN 978-1-4424-6632-6 (*Gasp* eBook)

CONTENTS

crash

One

My sophomore psych teacher, Mr. Polselli, says knowledge is crucial to understanding the workings of the human brain, but I swear to dog, I don't want any more knowledge about this.

Every few days I see it. Sometimes it's just a picture, like on that billboard we pass on the way to school. And other times it's moving, like on a screen. A careening truck hits a building and explodes. Then nine body bags in the snow.

It's like a movie trailer with no sound, no credits. And nobody sees it but me.

Some days after psych class I hang around by the door of Mr. Polselli's room for a minute, thinking that if I have a mental illness, he's the one who'll be able to tell me. But every time I almost mention it, it sounds too weird to say. *So, uh, Mr. Polselli, when other people see the "turn off your cell phones" screen in the movie theater, I see an extra five-second movie trailer. Er . . . and did I mention I see stills of it on the billboard by my house? You see Jose Cuervo, I see a truck hitting a building and everything exploding. Is that normal?*

The first time was in the theater on the one holiday that our parents don't make us work—Christmas Day. I poked my younger sister, Rowan. "Did you see that?"

She did this eyebrow thing that basically says she thinks I'm an idiot. "See what?"

"The explosion," I said softly.

"You're on drugs." Rowan turned to our older brother, Trey, and said, "Jules is on drugs."

Trey leaned over Rowan to look at me. "Don't do drugs," he said seriously. "Our family has enough problems."

I rolled my eyes and sat back in my seat as the real movie trailers started. "No kidding," I muttered. And I reasoned with myself. The day before I'd almost been robbed while doing a pizza delivery. Maybe I was still traumatized.

I just wanted to forget about it all.

But then on MLK Day this stupid vision thing decided to get personal.

Two

Five reasons why I, Jules Demarco, am shunned:
1. I smell like pizza
2. My parents make us drive a meatball-topped food truck to school for advertising
3. I haven't invited a friend over since second grade
4. Did I mention I smell like pizza? Like, its umami*-ness oozes from my pores
5. Everybody at school likes Sawyer Angotti's family's restaurant better

Frankly, I don't blame them. I'd shun me too.

----

*look it up

Every January my mother says Martin Luther King Jr. weekend gives us the boost we need to pay the rent after the first two dead weeks of the year. She's superpositive about everything. It's like she forgets that every month is the same. Her attitude is probably what keeps our business alive. But if my mother, Paula, is the backbone of Demarco's Pizzeria, my father, Antonio, is the broken leg that keeps us struggling to catch up.

There's no school on MLK Day, so Trey and I are manning the meatball truck in downtown Chicago, and Rowan is working front of house in the restaurant for the lunch shift. She's jealous. But Trey and I are the oldest, so we get to decide.

The food truck is actually kind of a blast, even if it does have two giant balls on top, with endless jokes to be made. Trey and I have been cooking together since we were little—he's only sixteen months older than me. He's a senior. He's supposed to be the one driving the food truck to school because he has his truck license now, but he pays me ten bucks a week to secretly drive it so he can bum a ride from our neighbor Carter. Carter is kind of a douche, but at least his piece-of-crap Buick doesn't have a sack on its roof.

Trey drives now and we pass the billboard again.

"Hey—what was on the billboard?" I ask as nonchalantly as I can.

Trey narrows his eyes and glances at me. "Same as always. Jose Cuervo. Why?"

"Oh." I shrug like it's no big deal. "Out of the corner of my eye I thought it had changed to something new for once." Weak answer, but he accepts it. To me, the billboard is a still picture of the explosion. I look away and rub my temples as if it will make me see what everybody else sees, but it does nothing. Instead, I try to forget by focusing on my phone. I start posting all over the Internet where Demarco's Food Truck is going to be today. I'm sure some of our regulars will show up. It's becoming a sport, like storm chasing. Only they're giant meatball chasing.

Some people need a life. Including me.

We roll past Angotti's Trattoria on the way into the city—that's Sawyer's family's restaurant. Sawyer is working today too. He's outside sweeping the snow from their sidewalk. I beg for the traffic light to stay green so we can breeze past unnoticed, but it turns yellow and Trey slows the vehicle. "You could've made it," I mutter.

Trey looks at me while we sit. "What's your rush?"

I glance out the window at Sawyer, who either hasn't noticed our obnoxious food truck or is choosing to ignore it.

Trey follows my glance. "Oh," he says. "The enemy. Let's wave!"

I shrink down and pull my hat halfway over my eyes.

"Just . . . hurry," I say, even though there's nothing Trey can do. Sawyer turns around to pick up a bag of rock salt for the ice, and I can tell he catches sight of our truck. His head turns slightly so he can spy on who's driving, and then he frowns.

Trey nods coolly at Sawyer when their eyes meet, and then he faces forward as the light finally changes to green. "Do you still like him?" he asks.

Here's me, sunk down in the seat like a total loser, trying to hide, breathing a sigh of relief when we start rolling again. "Yeah," I say, totally miserable. "Do you?"

Three

Trey smiles. "Nah. That urban underground thing he's got going on is nice, and of course I'm fond of the, ah, Mediterranean complexion, but I've been over him for a while. He's too young for me. You can have him."

I laugh. "Yeah, right. Dad will love that. Maybe me hooking up with an Angotti will be the thing that puts him over the edge." I don't mention that Sawyer won't even look at me these days, so the chance of me "having" Sawyer is zero.

Sawyer Angotti is not the kind of guy most people would say is hot, but Trey and I have the same taste in men, which is sometimes convenient and sometimes a pain in the ass. Sawyer has this street casual look where he could totally be a clothes model, but if he ever told people he was one, they'd be like, "Seriously? No way." Because his most attractive features are so subtle, you know? At first glance he's really ordinary, but if you study him . . . big sigh. His vulnerable smile is what gets me—not the charming one he uses on teachers and girls and probably customers, too. I mean the warm, crooked smile that doesn't come out unless he's feeling shy or self-conscious. That one makes my stomach flip. Because for the most part, he's tough-guy metro, if such a thing exists. Arms crossed and eyebrow raised, constantly questioning the world. But I've seen his other side a million times. I've been in love with him since we played plastic cheetahs and bears together at indoor recess in first grade.

How was I supposed to know back then that Sawyer was the enemy? I didn't even know his last name. And I didn't know about the family rivalry. But the way my father interrogated me after they went to my first parent-teacher conference and found out that I "played well with others" and "had a nice friend in Sawyer Angotti," you'd have thought I'd given away great-grandfather's last weapon to the enemy. Trey says that was right around the time Dad really started acting weird.

All I knew was that I wasn't allowed to play cheetahs and bears with Sawyer anymore. I wasn't even supposed to talk to him.

But I still did, and he still did, and we would meet

under the slide and trade suckers from the candy jar each of our restaurants had by the cash register. I would bring him grape, and he always brought me butterscotch, which we never had in our restaurant. I'd do anything to get Sawyer Angotti to give me a butterscotch sucker again.

I have a notebook from sixth grade that has nine pages filled with embarrassing and overdramatic phrases like "I pine for Sawyer Angotti" and "JuleSawyer forever." I even made an *S* logo for our conjoined names in that one. Too bad it looks more like a cross between a dollar sign and an ampersand. I'd dream about us getting secretly married and never telling our parents.

And back then I'd moon around in my room after Rowan was asleep, pretending my pillow was Sawyer. Me and my Sawyer pillow would lie down on my bed, facing one another, and I'd imagine us in Bulger Park on a blanket, ignoring the tree frogs and pigeons and little crying kids. I'd touch his cheek and push his hair back, and he'd look at me with his gorgeous green eyes and that crooked, shy grin of his, and then he'd lean toward me and we'd both hold our breath without realizing it, and his lips would touch mine, and then . . . He'd be my first kiss, which I'd never forget. And no matter how much our parents tried to keep us apart, he'd never break my heart.

Oh, sigh.

But then, on the day before seventh grade started,

when it was time to visit school to check out classes and get our books, his father was there with him, and my father was there with me, and I did something terrible.

Without thinking, I smiled and waved at my friend, and he smiled back, and I bit my lip because of love and delight after not seeing him for the whole summer . . . and his father saw me. He frowned, looked up at my father, scowled, and then grabbed Sawyer's arm and pulled him away, giving my father one last heated glance. My father grumbled all the way home, issuing half-sentence threats under his breath.

And that was the end of that.

I don't know what his father said or did to him that day, but by the next day, Sawyer Angotti was no longer my friend. Whoever said seventh grade is the worst year of your life was right. Sawyer turned our friendship off like a faucet, but I can't help it—my faucet of love has a really bad leak.

Trey parks the truck as close to the Field Museum as our permit allows, figuring since the weather is actually sunny and not too freezing and windy, people might prefer to grab a quick meal from a food truck instead of eating the overpriced generic stuff inside the tourist trap.

Before we open the window for business, we set up. Trey checks the meat sauce while I grate fresh mozzarella into tiny, easily meltable nubs. It's a simple operation—our winter truck specialty is an Italian bread bowl with spicy mini meatballs, sauce, and cheese. The truth is it's delicious, even though I'm sick to death of them.

We also serve our pizza by the slice, and we're talking deep-dish Chicago-style, not that thin crap that Angotti's serves. Authentic, authschmentic. The tourists want the hearty, crusty, saucy stuff with slices of sausage the diameter of my bicep and bubbling cheese that stretches the length of your forearm. That's what we've got, and it's amazing.

Oh, but the Angotti's sauce . . . I had it once, even though in our house it's contraband. Their sauce will lay you flat, seriously. It's that good. We even have the recipe, apparently, but we can't use it because it's patented and they sell it by the jar—it's in all the local stores and some regional ones now too. My dad about had an aneurysm when that happened. Because, according to Dad, in one of his mumble-grumble fits, the Angottis had been after our recipe for generations and somehow managed to steal it from us.

So I guess that's how the whole rivalry started. From what I understand, and from what I know about Sawyer avoiding me like the plague, his parents feel the same way about us as my parents feel about them.

Trey and I pull off a really decent day of sales for the middle of January. We hightail it back home for the dinner rush so we can help Rowan out.

As we get close, we pass the billboard from the other side. I locate it in my side mirror, and it's the same as this morning. Explosion. I watch it grow small and disappear, and then close my eyes, wondering what the hell is wrong with me.

We pull into the alley and park the truck, take the stuff inside.

"Get your asses out there!" Rowan hisses as she flies through the kitchen. She gets a little anxious when people have to wait ten seconds. That kid is extremely well put together, but she carries the responsibility of practically the whole country on her shoulders.

Mom is rolling out dough. I give her a kiss on the cheek and shake the bank bag in her face to show her I'm on the way to putting it in the safe like I'm supposed to. "Pretty good day. Had a busload of twenty-four," I say.

"Fabulous!" Mom says, way too perky. She grabs a tasting utensil, reaches into a nearby pot, and forks a meatball for me. I let her shove it into my mouth when I pass her again.

"I's goo'!" I say. And really freaking hot. It burns the roof of my mouth before I can shift it between my teeth to let it cool.

Tony, the cook who has been working for our family restaurant for something like forty million years, smiles at me. "Nice work today, Julia," he says. Tony is one of the few people I allow to call me by my birth name.

I guess my dad, Antonio, was actually named after Tony. Tony and my grandfather came to America together. I don't really remember my grandpa much—he killed himself when I was little. Depression. A couple of years ago I accidentally found out it was suicide when I overheard Mom and Aunt Mary talking about it.

When I asked my mom about it later, she didn't deny it—instead, she said, "But you kids don't have any sign of depression in you, so don't worry. You're all fine." Which was about the best way to make me think I'm doomed.

It's a weird thing to find out about your family, you know? It made me feel really different for the rest of the day, and it still does now whenever I think about it. Like we're all wondering where the depression poison will hit next, and we're all looking at my dad. I wonder if that's why my mother is so upbeat all the time. Maybe she thinks she can protect us with her happy shield.

Trey and I hurry to wash up, grab fresh aprons, and check in with Aunt Mary at the hostess stand. She's seating somebody, so we take a look at the chart and see that the house is pretty full. No wonder Rowan's freaking out.

Rowan's fifteen and a freshman. Just as Trey is sixteen months older than me, she's sixteen months younger. I don't know if my parents planned it, and I don't want to know, but there it is. I pretty much think they had us for the sole purpose of working for the family business. We started washing dishes and busing tables years ago. I'm not sure if it was legal, but it was definitely tradition.

Rowan looks relieved to see us. She's got the place under control, as usual. "Hey, baby! Go take a break," I whisper to her in passing.

"Nah, I'm good. I'll finish out my tables," she says. I glance at the clock. Technically, Rowan is supposed to quit at seven, because she's not sixteen yet—she can only work late in the summer—but, well, tradition trumps rules sometimes. Not that my parents are slave drivers or anything. They're not. This is just their life, and it's all they know.

It's a busy night because of the holiday. Busy is good. Busy means we can pay the rent, and whatever else comes up. Something always does.

By ten thirty all the customers have left. Even though Dad hasn't come down at all this evening to help out, Mom says she and Tony can handle closing up alone, and she sends Trey and me upstairs to the apartment to get some sleep.

I don't want to go up there.

Neither does Trey.

Four

Trey and I go out the back and into the door to the stairs leading up to our home above the restaurant. We pick our way up the stairs, through the narrow aisle that isn't piled with stuff. At the top, we push against the door and squeeze through the space.

Rowan has already done what she could with the kitchen. The sink is empty, the counters are clean. The kitchen is the one sacred spot, the one room where Mom won't take any garbage from anybody—literally. Because even after cooking all day, she still likes to be able to cook at home too, without having to worry that Dad's precious stacks of papers are going to combust and set the whole building on fire because they're too close to the gas stove.

Everywhere else—dining room, living room, and

hallway—is piled high around the edges with Dad's stuff. Lots of papers—recipes and hundreds of cooking magazines, mostly, and all the Chicago newspapers from the past decade. Shoe boxes, shirt boxes, and every other possible kind of box you can imagine, some filled with papers, some empty. Plastic milk crates filled with cookbooks and science books and gastronomy magazines. Bags full of greeting cards, birthday cards, sympathy cards, some written in, some brand-new, meant for good intentions that never happened. Hundreds of old videos, and a stack as high as my collarbone of old VCRs that don't work. Stereos, 8-track players, record players, tape recorders, all broken. Records and cassette tapes and CDs and games— oh my dog, the board games. Monopoly, Life, Password, Catch Phrase. Sometimes five or six duplicates, most of them with little yellowing masking-tape stickers on them that say seventy-five cents or a buck twenty-five. Insanity. Especially when somebody puts something heavy on top of a Catch Phrase and that stupid beeper goes off somewhere far below, all muffled.

We weave through it. Thankfully, Dad is nowhere to be found, either asleep or buried alive under all his crap. It's not like he's violent or mean or anything. He's just . . . unpredictable. When he's feeling good, he's in the restaurant. He's visible. He's easy to keep track of. But on the days he doesn't come down, we never know what to expect.

We climb those stairs after the end of our shift knowing he could be standing right there in the kitchen, long-faced, unshaven, having surfaced to eat something for the first time since yesterday. And rattling off the same guilt-inspired apologies, day after day after day. *I just couldn't make it down today. Not feeling up to it. I'm sorry you kids have to work so hard.* What do you say to that after the tenth time, or the hundredth?

Worse, he could be sitting in the dark living room with his hands covering his face, the blue glow from the muted TV spotlighting his depressed existence so we can't ignore it. It's probably wrong that Trey and Rowan and I all hope he stays invisible, holed up in his bedroom on days like these, but it's just easier when he's out of sight. We can pretend depressed Dad doesn't exist.

Tonight we breathe a sigh of relief. Trey heads into the cluttered bathroom, its cupboards overflowing with enough soap, shampoo, toothpaste, and toilet paper to get us through Y3K. Thank God our bedrooms are off-limits to Dad. I peek into my tidy little room and see Rowan is sleeping in her bed already, but I'm still wired from a long day. I close the door quietly and grab a glass of milk from the kitchen, then settle down in the one chair in the living room that's not full of stuff and flip on the TV. I run through the DVR list, choosing a rerun of an old Sherlock Holmes movie that I've been watching a little bit at a time over the past couple of weeks, whenever I get a chance. Somebody else must be watching it too, because it's not cued up to the last part I watched. I hit the slowest fast-forward so I can find where I left off.

Trey peeks his head in the room. "Night," he says. He dangles the keys to the meatball truck, and when I hold out my hand, he tosses them to me.

"Thanks," I say, not meaning it. I shouldn't have agreed to only ten bucks a week, but I was desperate. It's not nearly enough to pay for the humiliation of driving the giant balls. "Where's my ten bucks?"

"Isn't it only eight if one day is a holiday?" He gives me what he thinks is his adorable face and hands me a five and three ones.

"Sorry. Not in the contract." I hold my hand out for more.

"Dammit." He goes back to his room for two more dollars while Sir Henry on the TV is flitting around outside on the moors in fast mode, which looks kind of kooky.

Trey returns. "Here."

I grab the two bucks from him and shove all ten into my pocket with my tips. "Thanks. Night."

When he's gone, I stop the fast-forward, knowing I went too far, and rewind to the commercial as I slip the keys into my other pocket, then press play.

Instead of the movie that I'm expecting, I see *it* again.

It flashes by in a few seconds, and then it's gone. The truck, the building, the explosion. And then back to our regularly scheduled programming.

"Stop it," I whisper. My stomach flips and a creepy shiver runs down my neck. It makes my throat tighten. I pause the recording and sit there a minute, trying to calm down. And then I hit rewind.

Ninety-nine percent of me hopes there's nothing there but a creepy giant hound on the moor.

But there it is.

I watch it again, and I get this gnawing thing in my chest, like I'm supposed to do something about it.

"Why does this keep happening?" I mutter, and rewind it again. I hit play and it all flies by so fast, I can hardly see it. I rewind once more and this time set it to play in slow motion.

The truck is yellow. I notice it's actually a snowplow, and the snow is falling pretty hard. It's dark outside, but the streetlamps are lit. The truck is coming fast and it starts angling slightly, crossing to the wrong side and going off the road. It jumps the curb spastically and jounces over some snow piles in a big parking lot, and then I see the building—there's a large window—for a split second before the truck hits it. The building explodes shortly after contact, glass and brick shrapnel flying everywhere. The scene cuts to the body bags in the snow. I count again to make sure—definitely nine. The last frame is a close-up of three of the bags, and then it's over. I hit the pause button.

"What are you doing?"

I jump and whirl around to see Rowan standing in the doorway squinting at me, hair all disheveled. "Jeez!" I whisper, trying to calm my heartbeat. "You scared the crap out of me." I glance back at the TV with slow-motion dread, like I've just been caught looking at . . . I don't know. Porn, or something else I'm not supposed to look at. But it's paused at a sour cream commercial. I let out a breath of relief and turn my attention back to Rowan.

She shrugs. "Sorry. I thought I heard Mom come up."

"Not yet. Not for a while."

She scratches her head, the sleeve of her boy jammies wagging against her cheek. "You coming to bed soon? Or do you want me to stay up with you?"

Her sweet, sleepy disposition is one of my favorites, maybe because she can be so mellow and generous when she just wakes up. I suck in my bottom lip, thinking, and look at the remote control in my hand. "Nah, I'm coming to bed now. Just gotta brush my teeth."

She scrunches up her face and yawns. "What time is it?"

I laugh softly. "Around eleven, I guess. Eleven fifteen."

"Okay," she says, turning to go back down the hallway to our bedroom. "Night."

I look at the TV once more and close my weary eyes for a moment. Then I turn it off and stand up, setting the remote on top of the set so it doesn't get buried, and carefully pick my way to the bathroom, and on to bed. But I don't think I'll be sleeping anytime soon.

Five

Five minutes later and Rowan's breathing sounds like she's asleep again. I wish I could just drift off like that. Instead, I lie here watching the wall opposite the window, where faint pulsing light from our restaurant sign beats out a song nobody knows or hears.

The movie theater. The billboard. Now TV commercials. What could be next? Ten minutes crawl by. Fifteen. And I may as well get up and get it over with.

I slip back out to the living room and cue it all up again, staring at the TV like I'm in some kind of weird hypnotic zone, not seeing the movie at all. I rub my bleary eyes and hit slow play, and it's there like before. A few seconds later there's the close-up of the three body bags, and then it's over and the commercial starts.

I rewind to see if I can pause the scene on the body bags close-up, which I hadn't really noticed before in the regular-speed version. It's like a hidden frame at regular speed, too fast for the human brain to comprehend.

I hit the slow-play button and then wait for it, and pause it at the exact right moment. It's a slightly blurry shot, but it's obvious what I'm looking at. I scan the picture, noting that one of the bags isn't zipped up all the way. The plastic is folded over at the top corner, and the head of the dead body is exposed. I'm strangely drawn to it out of curiosity, rather than repulsed by it.

I squint for a better look. And then my heart bangs around in my chest and I lean forward, get down on the cluttered floor, and crawl to the TV to get a better look.

And then I suck in a scream.

The dead face belongs to Sawyer Angotti.

I scramble to my feet and stumble back to the chair, grab the remote, and hit the power button so many times I actually turn the thing off, then on, then off again before my brain can compute that I've gotten rid of the image from the TV.

My heart won't stop freaking out inside my chest. "No way," I whisper, as if that will take away the scene I just saw. "No way, no way, no way."

I pinch my arm to make sure I'm not having a nightmare, and it hurts, so I think this is real. I pace in the narrow carpeted space that isn't covered by hoards of junk, talking to myself, trying to calm down. But I can't.

Why am I seeing this?

What the hell is going on?

I go back to the remote and turn the TV on, flinching and shuddering as I delete the movie. Then I delete a bunch of other stuff that Rowan will kill me for, but I can't help it. I need to get these images away from me. I need to get this scene off my TV, off my billboard, out of my local theater, and make it go away.

When I hit the power button again, I'm enveloped in darkness, and I can't stop thinking about dead bodies lying in wait under Dad's piles of junk. It's like a nightmare, only I'm not asleep, my mind playing tricks on me. I skitter to my room and get into bed where it's safe, pulling my blankets up to my chin and hugging my pillow. My Sawyer pillow.

I toss and turn, checking the clock every few minutes. Willing my mind to go blank, willing myself to go to sleep, which makes it even more impossible. I have this ridiculous urge to call Sawyer to make sure he's alive, but tell myself I'll be mortified at school tomorrow if I do that. I mean, I just saw him alive this morning! There's no way he could be dead.

After a while I hear Mom coming up the steps. She

clatters in the kitchen, and then I can hear her moving things around in the living room, probably throwing junk away. A while later she makes her way to her bedroom, where she and Dad will sleep until nine thirty or ten, and then she'll get up and do the restaurant thing all over again, with or without my dad.

Eventually, I calm down. Sometime after two I drift off, the vision following me into my dreams.

Six

Six a.m. comes fast. We three kids all stupidly get up at the same time every morning—hey, old habits are hard to break; besides, we miss each other *so much* after literally hours of being apart. Automatically Rowan and I kick ourselves loose from our blankets and race to the door. I whip it open, and there's Trey emerging from his room. Expertly, and almost quietly, we jostle and shove each other in the packed hallway as we jockey for the first slot in the bathroom. Trey shoves his butt against my hip and throws me off balance, knocking me into Rowan, who almost pitches a whole stack of Christmas cookie tins over—holy shit, what a racket that would be! I swallow a snort and Trey strikes a triumphant Gaga pose in the bathroom doorway before sliding in and closing the door. It's kind of like we live in that *Silent Library* game show and we're all trying to be superquiet while competing to win at a ridiculously noisy challenge, which makes everything so much more hilarious.

But once I have a minute to remember what happened last night, the fun evaporates and I start getting this recurring wave of nausea. I can't handle the thought of breakfast right now, so I pocket a granola bar for later. After an hour, when I'm waiting for Rowan to finish her makeup so we can go, I cautiously flip on the TV, hoping I can find the news and not a creepy encore of last night. Thankfully, there's just some morning talk show. No mention of explosions or body bags. No weird vision taunting me.

Trey slips past me and flies down the stairs two at a time without saying good-bye. We'll see each other at school. We're in the same lunch and sculpting class—which we of course elected to take because why the heck not bring our pizza-crust-making skills to a new level with clay? The other day I was making a plate on the potter's wheel and nearly threw it up into the air when I was daydreaming about Sawyer.

My stomach clenches again.

Sawyer. Body bag. Is he dead already?

In the hallway outside the bathroom, I jiggle the door handle and whisper as harshly as I can, "Hurry up, Rowan!"

Finally she comes.

. . .

We ease out of the alley in the meatball truck. Today's trip to school is brought to you by two chicks with big balls. Har har. Rowan flips down the mirrored sun visor and puts on lip gloss, then fusses with her hair. A minute later she sighs and snaps the visor back up, slouching into the seat like she's given up on her looks for the day. She's been fussy about her looks a lot lately. I think she's got a crush, but I don't say anything. She pulls out her phone and takes a picture of herself and then studies it. I smile and focus on the road.

Traffic is busy, making every block agonizingly slow, and I'm hitting almost all the lights red. I tell myself not to look at the billboard as we pass, and almost manage it. But I steal a glance at the last second, and there's no Cuervo . . . just the crash. At school we park in the back of the lot, which is the only place the truck fits.

I sprint through the parking lot to the school, hugging my book bag and avoiding icy spots, leaving Rowan behind. Inside I speed walk to my locker and look down the hall like I always do, to where Sawyer is usually standing, hanging out with his friends, some of whom are my former friends.

I stand on my tiptoes, straining to see through the crowd.

At first I don't see him, but then, thank the dogs, there he is in his usual spot. How weird is it that I feel my eyes well up with tears of relief for a second? He glances my way, and I almost duck, but realize at the last moment that that would look even more stupid than me staring, so I quickly turn my head and stare into my locker, blinking hard.

And then my respiratory system checks in, reminding me to breathe before I pass out. Sweat pricks my scalp. I whip my hat off and slip out of my jacket, and then try to smooth down my flyaway hair in the little mirror I have inside my locker door.

I want to start walking to class, but my legs are still a little too weak to keep me from tripping down the hallway. The whole time I'm standing here, all I can think about is how Sawyer isn't dead. This vision thing scared the living crap out of me for no good reason. These crazy scenes I'm seeing are meaningless. So I guess there's maybe something wrong . . . with me.

All I know is that it can't be a mental illness.

Not like depression. Not like hoarding.

Please . . . it just can't be like those things at all.

Seven

I don't look at the billboard. I don't turn on the TV.
I don't go to any movies. For a week, I keep my head down,
go to school, go to work, do homework, go to bed. Still,
every morning at school I look over at Sawyer to make sure
he's alive.

He always is.

Five reasons why I love a guy who won't talk to me:
1. In first grade he always let me be the cheetah
2. He's kind to people, even the unpopular ones,
    and if I ever really needed him, I bet he'd
    help me
3. He isn't gross
4. He's soft-spoken, under the radar, but

somehow everybody seems to know and
like him
5. He volunteers at the Humane Society on
Saturday mornings

Do I think Sawyer has something against my family?
Sure, he has to. But he's not *mean* to me—he just ignores
me most of the time now. Still, when we were forced to
pair up for a science project in ninth grade, we talked
almost like normal, which gave me so much hope it practically killed me after the project was over and things went
back to the way they were.

I don't get it. I'm just not really into the drama of this
whole family-rivalry thing. It stresses me out. I'm guessing
he's not into it either, because we never talked about it. We
never discussed seventh grade and what happened. Now
I sort of appreciate that about him, because it could have
started a big fight, and we could have ended up having a
major problem. And I know that if classmates began taking
sides, he'd win epically.

Outside of forced projects, we steer clear of one
another, because obviously I'm not going to follow him
around. Much. It's not like I don't have other shit to do
besides moon around after a boy. I mean, I watch him,
though. Like, all the time, but I'm not a creep or anything. And I eavesdrop. That's how I know about him

volunteering at the Humane Society. I really hope one day I'll get over him. Sometimes I think I'm past it all, but then he does that smile and reality hits.

Saturday morning, on our way into the city for the lunch rush, I make Trey drive past the Humane Society to see if Sawyer's car is there. It is. I don't know why I keep worrying about him when ignoring all of this is what I really want to do, but I can't shake that image of his dead face from my mind.

"What's going on with you?" Trey asks after a while.

"Just tired," I say automatically. It's the stock answer in our house whenever we don't want to talk. Everybody understands tired—nobody questions it, nobody tries to talk you out of it.

But Trey knows me better than anybody. "Why don't you ever do anything for fun?"

I snort. "When?"

"Mom will give you nights off for stuff. You know that."

"I . . . don't have anything else to do."

"You could go see a movie—"

"No," I say.

Trey glances at me at a stoplight as we near our destination. I stare straight ahead. I can't look at him or he'll know something's wrong. I focus on the construction crews along the side of the street hanging up banners for a spring flower show at the conservatory. In that instant, all the banners, as far ahead of us as I can see, change.

I suck in a breath. The banners now advertise dead Sawyer Angotti's face.

"What's wrong?" Trey asks. His voice is concerned.

"Nothing," I say. I lean down and pretend to rummage around in my purse. "Seriously. I just need more sleep."

"I don't believe you."

I don't know what to say to that. Besides, it's time to park the balls and feed some hungry people.

Every time I hand food out the window to the customers, I catch the long line of banners out of the corner of my eye and see Sawyer's dead face. "Go away," I mutter.

A customer looks at me, taken aback.

"Oh, no—not you," I say. "I'm so sorry." Great, now I'm insulting customers and talking to the banners. No mental illness here.

I keep my eyes closed for the ride home.

Eight

Back at the restaurant for the dinner rush, Dad is in the kitchen with his chef jacket on, which is a good sign. Trey and I exchange a glance and Trey calls out, "Hey, Pops."

Dad looks up and smiles. "How's my boy?" His voice booms. It always has. He's been startling innocent children for as long as I can remember. Luckily, Trey did not inherit that trait. "Did you have a good day? Where'd you end up? Any other trucks out in this weather?" He can never just ask one question when he's feeling good.

I let Trey handle him and keep walking, grabbing a fresh apron and tying it around my waist on my way to the hostess stand.

"Hey, Aunt Mary," I say. She's my dad's sister. She

reaches for me and air-kisses my cheek, then squeezes my upper arm and shakes me like she's been doing since I was a little girl.

"So beautiful!" she declares loudly. "You have your father's face."

Yeah . . . uh . . . thanks. That's not, like, a weird thing to say to a girl or anything. I smile and ask, "Is it busy? Where's Rowan?"

"Tables seven and eight—a ten-topper. Rowdy bunch of hooligans. Maybe Trey should help her."

I try not to scowl. Aunt Mary still lives in the last century. "I'm sure she and I can handle it fine. Trey's doing deliveries tonight. He's talking to Dad."

Aunt Mary gives me a knowing look.

We never discuss Dad's little "problem" with anybody. It's this huge secret everybody knows but nobody talks about. Nobody's allowed in our apartment. Nobody who knows us personally asks why. Just invoking Dad's name is enough to stop Aunt Mary from pressing the issue. Talk about power. The guy who does the weirdest shit has all the power.

I grab a pen and an order pad, head into the dining room, and catch Rowan's eye. She gives me a stricken look and points with a sideways nod to the big group. I look, and my heart sinks. It's a bunch of kids from school, looking like they're all on one giant, icky date. With a glance I see three guys who have tortured Trey in one manner or another since middle school. Two of the girls, Roxie and Sarah, used to be my friends in elementary school, before the cliques formed. Roxie was even upstairs for my sixth birthday party, back before the formation of the psycho's dump.

I get the status from Rowan and help her bring out the drink orders. I smile politely at anyone who catches my eye. I am not here to socialize. I am here to serve as their nanny and slave, clean up when they make a huge sticky mess of sodden sugar packets, hot-pepper water glasses, and clogged parm shakers, and smile gratefully as I watch them not leave a tip. And I will promptly dismiss it from memory the next time I see them, when they call out in the hallway, "Hey, Jules, how are the big balls treating you?" Because that is what we Demarcos do to survive and pay the bills. And we do it well.

"Oh, hey, Julia," Roxie says. I don't remind her that I've gone by Jules since third grade.

And I do not call her Roxanne in return. "What can I get for you, Roxie? Or do you guys need a few minutes to decide?"

Half of them haven't acknowledged me at all, and the other half give each other that smirky, *Hey, we should probably check out the menu* look, and no one answers my question. I stand a moment more, and then say, "So, you need a few minutes?"

"Yeah," a couple of them say.

"I'll stop back. If you decide before I get here, just flag me down."

Silence.

"Okay, great." I walk away feeling like a big bucket of stupid. My face gets hot. I hear the order-up bell, so I make a beeline for the kitchen to grab food for Rowan.

Trey is headed my way. I put my hand out. "Don't go out there," I say, and that stops him. I give him a sympathetic smile.

"Who's here?"

"Assholes. Don't worry, we've got it covered for now. I'll let you clean up after them."

"Awesome," he says, rolling his eyes, but I know he's grateful. It's not like Trey needs anybody to protect him, but with Dad in the kitchen tonight, none of us want any trouble out on the floor. And with that cast of bigots out there, there would most certainly be trouble. Trey turns around and starts helping Casey, the dishwasher, while I grab the pizza and spaghetti for table four and head back out.

Over at the group-date table, I see straw wrapper carcasses all over the floor. "What sounds good tonight?" I say, perky. I hold my order pad so they get a clue that it's time.

"Angotti's sounds good," one jackass says, "but they're closed."

I look up sharply. "On a Saturday night? Why, did something happen?"

The guy shrugs.

I stare. Why on earth would Angotti's be closed? Angotti's never closes. There has to be a family tragedy for that to happen.

"Um . . . ," Roxie says. "Hello . . ." She waves her menu in my face and I look at her, my stomach twisting. "We'll have two large pepperoni pizzas and a supreme. Thin crust." She hands me her menu.

I picture Sawyer Angotti's dead face staring back at me where my grandfather's face is.

"We don't have thin crust," I say in a weird, wispy voice that doesn't even sound like me. The table wavers. I glance over at Rowan, then back at Roxie. "I have to go," I whisper.

I drop the menu on the table and take off. As I pass Rowan I say, "Can you help them? I think I'm going to be sick," and I just keep going, running now, through the kitchen, out the back door, calling out, "Ma, help out front, please," before the door closes. I suck in a cold breath of air and hang on to the door handle before I go into the apartment stairwell and run up, bumping against stacks of stuff on my way to the living room. I grab the TV remote, turn it on, and pick up the phone, but my hand is shaking and I don't know the number. I can't think.

On TV is a gardening show. I pause and play, and it's still the show.

I drop the remote in the chair and whirl around. "Phone book," I mutter. I look around the room at all the junk, no idea where to start. My chest floods with panic. "Where's the fucking phone book? God! I hate this stupid place!" I start whipping through four-foot piles of magazines looking for a phone book, knowing there are probably no fewer than fifty of them in this room, yet not a single one shows its face. I go to the little desk drawer, and it's jam-packed with paper clips. I can't even slam it shut, it's so full. I pinch my eyelids, trying not to cry in frustration. Just trying to breathe and think.

And then the TV sound goes off, all on its own.

Nine

I look over at the TV screen, and there it is. Only this time it's a longer clip.

The snowplow crosses to the wrong side of the street, careens up over the snow pile and curb of the parking lot, almost getting airborne, and lands, bouncing. Not slowing down. I see the building for a split second, the big long window, and then the crash and the explosion. Bricks and glass go flying.

And then there's a new part: The building catches on fire, and through the dark smoke, I see the structure as if we are fleeing from the scene, and we're panning wide. It's a three-story. A striped awning hangs precariously from a part of the wall that is still intact. And then everything is gone, and I'm watching a commercial for bug spray.

"What do you want me to do about it?" I yell at the TV. "I'm just a kid! Leave me alone!"

I stare at the phone in my hand, and my head clears. I dial 411. "Melrose Park," I say, my voice shaking. "Angotti's Trattoria." A moment later I get the automated number, and push to dial direct.

It rings.

Five times it rings, like bells tolling for the dead.

And then it stops ringing, and a man's voice announces, "Angotti's."

I am stunned and can't speak at first. I clear my throat and realize I don't know what to say. "Um, are you . . . I mean, how late are you open?"

"We're actually closed to the public tonight for a family wedding reception. Really sorry about that. We'll be open again tomorrow, eleven to eleven."

"Oh." I breathe out a relieved sigh into the phone, and then curse myself. "Okay, eleven to eleven. I—I was just checking. Thanks." I want to ask, *Is Sawyer alive?* I want to ask, *Are you sure it's not a death in the family?* But my heart is stuck in my throat.

And then the man says, "Jules?"

Shit. I'm a terrible liar when confronted. "Yeah," I say.

"It's Sawyer."

"Oh. You sounded . . . older."

His voice turns quiet, like he's trying not to let people

hear. "Why the heck are you calling the restaurant?"

"How did you know it was me?"

"Caller ID says 'A. Demarco.' And by your voice."

I answer with another little breathy noise that I think probably sounds like a dog panting. He recognized my voice.

"So why . . . ?" he asks again. "Are you trying to spy or something?" he says, like he's starting to wind up. "If so, you're not very good at it. I can't believe your parents are making you do this."

"No, Sawyer," I say. "That's not why . . ." I can hardly talk. I'm so relieved to hear his voice.

"So, what, you want a reservation?" He laughs sarcastically.

"No," I say in a firmer voice, "and stop accusing me of stupid things. I just heard from a customer that you guys are closed tonight. And—" I grip the top of my head with my free hand, hoping that'll help me think of a lie. "And . . . you guys never close. So, ah, I just wanted to make sure you were okay." Crap. I barely get the words out when I hear footsteps coming up the steps, and I remember the disaster I left Rowan with downstairs.

Sawyer doesn't answer.

"I'm sorry," I whisper. I hang up the phone and whirl around as my mother opens the door and peeks in at me.

"Are you sick? Rowan said you were pale as a ghost."

She comes up to me and presses the back of her hand against my forehead.

I give her a weak smile. "I'm okay now. I guess I forgot to eat lunch today. And I got dizzy there for a minute. But I had some juice and a sandwich. Sorry about that." I'm saying sorry a lot lately.

"No fever. You just rest for a bit," she says. "Dad's cooking, I'm helping Rowan. Mary's here. We're covered. You need a break." She smiles at me. "Go watch some TV."

I glance at the TV, still on. "Thanks," I say.

She closes the door and disappears. I hear her stepping unevenly down the stairs, and I wonder how she takes it. The hoarding. How she doesn't crack, being married to him.

And then the phone rings right next to me and I nearly hit the ceiling. I look at the caller ID and wait for the name to come up.

It's Angotti's Trattoria.

Ten

I panic. Did he hit the call button on his caller ID by accident? If I answer, I'll look desperate. What does he want? I'm sure it's a mistake, and I imagine the awkward conversation that would follow.

Hello?

Um . . . oops. Wrong number. Hit "last call" by mistake.

Okay, bye.

Yeah. Bye.

Weird. Awful. After six rings, it stops.

I wait a minute more, and then scroll through the caller ID list. Stare at his number, then reluctantly hit delete, and it feels like the breakup we never really had. But if Dad sees that, he'll freak.

And then I go back to the TV.

I rewind the show to the commercial, and just like last time, the scene appears. I watch it over and over in slow motion. There's the snowplow, the parking lot, the building with the window just before the crash. This time I pause the scene here. There are blinds on the big window, but they are open. I see shapes—people's upper bodies. And hanging light fixtures.

The upper half of the building looks like an apartment. There are several smaller windows up there, all curtained, but I can tell lights are on. I can't make out what the words on the building say—they are mostly cut off from the frame. I go to the next frame, and the next, and the next. I can't figure out why everything has to explode—why the truck doesn't just crumple instead.

When I get to the newer part, with the fire and the wider shot, I pause again and stare at the TV. There are a few cars in the parking lot, but they are hard to make out in the dark. The only distinguishing feature I can see is the awning that's dangling there from the explosion. I can't even tell what color it is because of the smoke and shadows and the snow, but it definitely has wide stripes.

Like a restaurant awning would have.

An Italian restaurant.

I sigh deeply and squeeze my eyes shut, massaging the lids. I've been avoiding this thought, not wanting to face it. But nothing else makes sense. I don't remember ever being behind Angotti's before. We just never go there, for obvious reasons. But I think the vision is showing me the back of their restaurant. From memory, I can only picture the front of it, but even now, as many times as I've been past it, I don't remember if they have an awning out front that might be a matching counterpart of the one in the vision. I don't remember if there are apartments above the retail shops on that street or not. I can picture their sign and logo no problem—that part's etched into my brain. But the other details . . . I just don't know. I watch it to the end, and then turn off the TV and sit in the dark and think.

All I know is what I've been avoiding all along. These visions, or scenes, or whatever they are, are getting more and more frequent, and showing up in more places all the time. Obviously Sawyer isn't in a body bag. So either that means I'm insane, or it means this hasn't happened yet. I am seeing the future, and the only reason I can think of for why this is happening is that I'm supposed to do something about it. The vision is badgering me, trying to get my attention.

I guess I'm supposed to warn them, those nine people, even though I don't know who eight of them are, and get them out of there. All by myself.

Either that or I'm the biggest nutcase in the history of this family.

• • •

After a while I get my notepad and a pencil and I turn the TV back on. I don't have to go looking for the scene now—it's right there. I pause it at the wide shot where I have the best view of the whole building, searching for any street signs or other landmarks. I argue with myself. Truthfully, I don't even know if this place is in Melrose Park, or in Chicago, or even in the United States. But instinctively, I know where it has to be if there's going to be a dead Sawyer Angotti in a body bag outside.

I sketch the back of the building—what's left of it, anyway. Then I shove the sketch in my pocket, turn off the TV, grab my coat, and head downstairs. I pause before opening the door and look out the window.

The pizza delivery car is gone. I debate—if I go inside the restaurant, I'll have to wait tables. I look at the meatball truck and there's no question—I can't be seen in that tonight, lurking around. I call Trey's cell.

"What's up?" he says.

"Where are you?"

"On the way back. You feeling okay?"

"Yeah, fine—just needed some air. Can I do deliveries?"

He's quiet for a second, and I know he's trying to figure out why I'm asking. "Is this, like, your 'getting back on the horse' moment?" He's not joking. I almost got robbed—and who knows what else—last time I delivered. And even though it was a really weird situation and crime is normally not that bad here, I haven't wanted to do deliveries since then.

"Yeah, I guess it is."

"Okay," he says. I can tell he's not sure.

"I'll be fine. It was just a fluke. I need to do this to prepare for the Super Bowl tomorrow, 'cause I'm helping you. I just decided."

He hesitates. "Just make sure you do what I told you if anything happens."

"I will, I promise." I smile. He told me to kick 'em in the meatballs. "You're the best."

"I know," he says. "Now, go check the next order and make sure it's a good neighborhood—I'm pulling into the alley now."

"Got it." I hang up and go into the restaurant. I see the delivery bag on the warming shelf by the door, check the address to make sure I know where it is, and without anybody noticing me, I grab it and meet Trey at the car.

He gives me a weird look. "Is it in a good neighborhood?" he asks.

"Yeah," I say, showing him the ticket. "I'll be safe." I look him in the eye so he knows I'm not lying. "I have my phone and my keys." I show him how I stick the keys between my fingers so I can punch and gore somebody's eyes out. "And my meatball kicker," I add, wiggling my boot. I am seriously prepared.

He seems satisfied. "And Mom and Dad are good with this?"

I open my mouth to say yes, but I can't lie to him, so I just close it again.

He shakes his head at me and sighs. "Just go. Pizza's getting cold."

"Thank you." I hop in the car as he turns to go inside.

"If anything happens to you, they'll blame me," he calls out. "Do you really want that guilt hanging over you?"

I smile a little so he knows I heard him and close the door, drive down the alley. My mind is not on getting robbed. I head straight to Angotti's and pull down the side street, into the back parking lot.

When I stop the car and take a good, long look at the building in front of me, I don't need the sketch in my pocket to confirm it.

This building is going to explode.

Eleven

But when? And what am I supposed to do, wander around telling people to stay away from Angotti's because it's gonna blow?

I point my headlights at the building, and with the aid of the streetlights and building lamps, plus the light coming through the restaurant windows, I stare at it, thinking about the scene I've watched dozens of times.

There's the evergreen-and-white-striped awning, solidly attached above the back entrance. The windows above, definitely an apartment—probably where Sawyer and his parents live, just like our family. There's a glow up there, maybe from night-lights or a hallway light left on while they work the wedding reception.

I look into the wide restaurant window and see happy

people at the tables, but all I can think about is the truck crashing into them and the glass flying. I see Sawyer walk past like a blur, but I know that walk, that flip of his head, that easy, tossed-off smile that charms all the teachers. Not me—only the crooked, real smile charms me. I think about it, think about him, and my stomach quakes so hard that an aftershock runs down my thighs.

I swallow hard. "Don't die," I whisper. But I don't know how to save him.

In my head I check off everything that's supposed to be in this picture. The only things I don't see are the light fixtures hanging down over the window tables. But they probably had to hook them up to the ceiling to change the seating arrangement for the special event. And I realize that probably means it won't happen tonight, at least. A shuddering sigh escapes my throat, and I realize I've been so tensed up, I barely have a neck anymore. I drop my shoulders and take a breath, trying to shake it off.

I glance at the pizza next to me, knowing I've got to get it delivered before the customer calls to complain— that would make Trey freak out. I take one last look at the building. Even faded, the black words painted on the side are clear without the veil of snow: "Angotti's Trattoria, est. 1934." A year before ours. They've always been a step ahead of us, and we've been chasing them ever since.

I look for one last glimpse of Sawyer, but he's

nowhere to be seen, and then drive out of the parking lot to deliver this pizza. Luckily, the roads are good and I hit almost all the lights green. I call Trey and get his voice mail. "I'm on the way back. No problems."

Biggest lie of the century.

In the middle of the night the vision runs through my dreams. I startle and sit straight up in bed, wide awake, with one thought on my mind. Snow. "Oh my God," I say. "Don't be so stupid, Jules." In the scene, it's snowing.

In her bed, Rowan lifts her head off the pillow, and I can see her sleepy face scrunch up, confused. "Huh?"

I glance at her, but my mind is occupied. "Sorry. Go to sleep."

Obediently, she drops her head back on the pillow and is asleep again a moment later. I sneak out to the living room, move a pile of newspapers from the desk chair, and flip on the computer, hoping the sound is on mute like it's supposed to be. It takes forever, but finally the page loads. I dim the screen light and search for the weather forecast.

When I find it, I pull up the extended forecast and all I can do is stare. There's a chance of snow nine out of the next ten days.

"Wow. That's just great." I'm so disgusted I turn the computer off without shutting it down properly, which would really piss Rowan off. And then I just sit there in the dark, wondering how much time I have to solve this life-or-death puzzle.

And wondering how I'm going to convince people who hate us that I'm trying to save their lives . . . because I saw a vision. A vision of their restaurant, which supposedly my family has hated for generations, exploding.

Yeah, that's going to be easy.

Twelve

When I get up in the morning, I hardly have time to think about it, because today is one of the busiest Sundays on the pizza delivery calendar. Super Bowl.

Mom and Dad and Rowan go to mass. Trey and I won't go anymore out of protest—if the church won't accept my brother, they can't have me, either. Mom and Dad support our decision. I wish they'd join us. But old habits are hard to break, and their religious fear runs deep. They'll come around eventually, I think—I mean, we don't really talk about it. They're not horrible like some parents. But it still hurts Trey. Rowan wants to stay home in protest too, but they won't let her until she's sixteen, and then she can decide.

But I don't have time to think about that, either.

Trey and I get our homework done and meet Tony in the restaurant at ten to start making dough and chopping vegetables. My mind wanders as we work in silence, everybody a little sleepy this morning. I wonder if Sawyer is doing the same thing as I am today.

Sometimes I picture him and me working in a kitchen together like this, and we'd be laughing and flirting and leaving sweet little messages to each other on the cutting board in words made from green pepper slices. And I hate when I do that, because it hurts so much when reality comes crashing down on my little scene. It always does. I wish I could stop liking him. God! I just can't. I pulverize the hell out of a mushroom and have to put my knife down for a minute before I cut all my fingers off.

"Everything okay over there?" Tony asks. "I feel sorry for your cutting board. He didn't mean anything by it."

I grin. "Yeah, everything's great." I shake my hands, letting the anxiety flow out of them, and pick up the knife again.

Angotti's is bigger and has more employees than we do. I think Sawyer has two older brothers, but Sawyer is the only one left living at home, and I'm not sure if his brothers still work there. All I know is that Sawyer doesn't have to work quite as many nights as I do, because

I overhear him at school talking about places he's gone. Dances he's been to. Parties, and stuff like that. But I bet he's working today.

I shouldn't say I *have to* work as much as I do. Mom would give me a night off anytime if I asked. But I don't have a life or really many friends—no close friends, anyway, unless you count Trey. So I figure I may as well earn some tips for college, because there won't be enough money to go around for all three of us.

Today I'm actually kind of excited to work. It's my first Super Bowl doing delivery. I remember last year Trey was insane. Our cousin Nick—Mary's son—helped out as a backup driver like he does sometimes. This year, the backup driver is me. Last night, after my successful delivery, I told my mom I was ready. She was a little skeptical, but I think I convinced her I'm fine, so she called Nick and told him he had the night off, which he seemed really happy about.

So they need me. By the time Mom, Dad, and Rowan get down to the restaurant after mass, the phone is ringing off the hook with big preorders for later.

It's funny—sometimes I see how it is at fast-food restaurants and on those reality cooking shows when the aspiring chefs are slammed and yelled at constantly. Everybody's running around, not communicating, and it's supertense. Usually somebody's barking out orders—and everybody hates that guy. Here at Demarco's we sort of go into superhero mode when we're slammed, and it's really pretty fun. Today, Trey and I play a game to try to get Rowan to laugh when she's on the phone, because if we can really get her going, she'll snort. "Hey, Trey, do you wanna see—" I say.

"Harry Potter?"

"No—"

"Boobies?"

I crack up, and Tony shakes his head and gives a reluctant laugh, but Rowan stays concentrated on her phone order. She's always been wound up pretty tight, and it takes a while to get her loose enough. Apparently today is not that day. By the time the lunch crowd dwindles and we're all in the kitchen stocking up supplies and making boxes and chopping more veggies, Rowan is answering call after call, ignoring us while we're making dumb "dot-com" and "that's what she said" jokes after every twelve-inch meatball sub order she reads back.

Yet, in the back of my mind, I'm agonizing. Wondering if tonight is the night.

When it's time to start, we get serious. "I'll take the east-side deliveries," I say to Trey. "I know the streets better." I lean against the door with my first loaded-up pizza sweater—that's what Tony calls the insulating bag.

Trey shrugs, distracted by the crap ton of orders that

are piling up. "That's fine. We need to move it. Don't speed, but don't linger."

"I know," I say. "I'm heading out." With a wave, I push out the back door into the cold, snowy afternoon. I try to drive by Angotti's every chance I get.

Thirteen

The afternoon flies by. Mom keeps up with the few tables in the dining room, and Rowan stays in the back pulling pizzas out of the oven, cutting them and boxing them up, keeping watch out the back door so she can see us coming and run them out to us so we don't have to park and come in for our next load.

The slick roads are slowing us down. I'm not afraid to drive in snow, but it's frustrating when customers don't understand that weather is a factor in how fast we get the food out. But the upside is that the later into the evening we get, the drunker the customers get, and for most of them that means they tip more.

I manage to drive by Angotti's twice even though I really don't have time, and everything looks okay inside. If the crash is going to happen tonight, there's nothing I can do about it. And somehow, in the midst of all this driving and thinking today, I realize that I absolutely *do* have to do something about this. I have to tell Sawyer. Because what if this vision thing is not just a big weird nothing? What if something really happens to him? To all nine of them? How's that going to make me feel for the rest of my life? It would be worse to do nothing and feel horrible forever than to say something and make a temporary fool out of myself. And, hell, maybe I am nuts. Maybe I just need to do that one over-the-edge cry-for-help thing that'll get my illness noticed and give me the treatment I apparently need. That's what all the experts say on TV, you know. Here's my big blaring chance to be heard.

I head toward Traverse Apartments, which is across the street from where "the incident" happened on Christmas Eve. My thoughts turn to that night, that walk through the shadows of the apartment complex trying to find 93B, that prickly feeling at the back of my neck and the sweat that came out of nowhere when I heard pounding feet and felt the guy grab my coat.

It all went really fast. The guy shoved my pizza bag up at my face and slung his arm around my neck, staying behind me so I couldn't see him. He ripped my little money belt off me and shoved me into a snowy bush, face-first. And then I heard a click of a knife by my ear.

I couldn't even scream—my throat was paralyzed. My whole body was paralyzed. I was so scared I couldn't even react to wipe the burning snow from my face. I was like some stupid bunny in the street when he sees the lights of an oncoming car and waits for a tire tread to hit him in the face.

I heard a door slam and a rush of footsteps as apparently some stranger came flying out of one of the buildings and tackled the guy. They rolled around while I scrambled to wipe the snow off my face, and the mugger managed to get up and get away. The stranger chased after him, and I never saw either one of them again.

I wasn't hurt, and I wasn't much help to the police. It had been really dark, and I didn't get a look at the mugger's face, didn't really have a concept of how big a dude he was. The police guessed it was probably a random incident— some meth addict who needed money for supplies and was waiting for anybody to come along.

I shake away the memory and squint at the signs in this complex until I find the right building and a parking spot nearby. I don't give myself time to get nervous, I just grab the warmer bag, zip out of the car. I jog up the three steps to the building and nearly wipe out on a slick spot right by the door, where a bunch of icicles must drip during the day and make a big ice patch on the step at night.

When I grab the door handle to steady myself, it swings open hard, right at me, knocking into the corner of my pizza bag and sending it sliding off my gloved fingers just as somebody plows out of the building into me, more startling than scary.

Out of instinct I reach out as I fall back, my focus on catching the pizza bag rather than on how I'll land, and it's one of those slow-motion moments where everything is blurry, my hands won't move where I want them to, and my body is going in the opposite direction from the way I want it to go. Meanwhile, whoever plowed into me is now tripping over my leg and falling too . . . and his shoulder or arm or something takes my precious red bag with it.

My elbow takes the worst hit when I land, then my back, and my head smacks on the cement, but I'm wearing a hat so it's cushioned, thank the dogs. The wind rushes out of me and I lie there for a moment trying to get it back, stunned. Immediately I think it's another attack, but there's no menacing feeling here. A second later I'm sure it's just an unfortunate collision.

"Shit," I hear. "I'm sorry."

I try to sit up, and flames shoot through my arm, tears of pain and frustration over the lost merchandise and lost time starting to sting. My pizza bag rests upside down in the snow about five feet away. I close my eyes. "Shit," I echo. My brain rushes to calculate the time wasted. At least forty minutes before I can get back here again with a fresh pizza. Maybe thirty-five . . .

"Are you okay?"

I freeze as it registers: I know that voice. And now I can't speak at all, because Sawyer Angotti is tossing his empty pizza bag aside and kneeling on the icy step next to me. And I'm furious.

Five reasons why I, Jules Demarco, am furious:

1. The pizza I was ten feet away from delivering properly is now something only Trey would eat

2. My stupid wenus* is broken and hurts like hell

3. It's a snowy Super Bowl Sunday and I'm already running forty-five minutes behind

4. Some loser (even though I'm in love with him) wasn't watching where he was going, and I'm the one who has to suffer for it

5. That loser just delivered *his* pizza without consequence, and also? Does not have a broken wenus

"I'm fine," I manage to say. Embarrassed, I ignore the pain, roll away from his outstretched hand, and get

---

*look it up

to my feet, holding my sore elbow close to my side. I reach out and gingerly pick up my pizza bag. I close my eyes once again and swallow hard. The inside of that box will be pretty gross right now. I don't want to think about it.

"I'm really sorry—I was in a hurry . . ."

It's true that he's being ridiculously nice about this. I almost wish he weren't. If he were a jerk about it, I could stay furious a lot longer.

"Me too," I confess with a sigh. "I was already off balance from the ice when you barreled through the door." *Shut up, shut up,* I tell myself. Now I'm mad at myself for taking part of the blame. *What the hell, Jules?*

It's love! I cry back to myself. *How can I help it?*

I hate you, I say to inner Jules. *Hate. You.*

Sawyer cringes when he sees how not-floppy my bag is. "Oooh. Been there. Sorry. I really am," he says. He dips his head and looks into my eyes.

"Yeah. Thanks." I've dropped a few pizzas in my day. "Not the best day for it, but there it is." All of a sudden I sound like my dad talking about the weather. I drop my eyes because I can't stand to look at him being nice, knowing what I know.

"Want me to pay for it?" Sawyer comes to life and whips out a wad of tips from his pocket, and all I can do is stare at him.

"Who *are* you?" I say, almost under my breath, but he hears me, and I see his lips twitch.

"I'm just a clumsy guy," he mutters. "I hope your parents don't freak out."

I narrow my eyes, not sure if he's just concerned about me dropping a pizza and getting yelled at, or if there's another layer there. "They won't," I say slowly. "Why would they? And put your money away. It's fine. It happens. Trey will eat it."

He laughs then. "So would I. You sure?" He looks at me, eye to eye again, and I remember his lashes from a long time ago when we were forced to share a library table doing research. His lashes are superthick, superlong, deep brown, complemented by the green of his irises. Every blink is a sweeping drama, a sexy ornament, a mating ritual. Dear dog, I'm so hopelessly pathetic, I'm grossing myself out.

I nod stupidly.

He shoves the money back in his pocket, and we just stand there, silent and awkward. Finally he says, "Need me to call in the reorder for you?"

That wakes me up. "Shit," I say again, and dig wildly for my phone. "No. But that would definitely make my parents freak out, if that's what you're going for."

He grins. I dial and turn away so his ropy eyelashes don't distract me. "We have a situation," I say when Rowan answers. "There's a pie down at Traverse

Apartments. Repeat: A pie. Is down. Reorder stat."

"Jules!" she says. "We don't have time for that."

"Calm it down, yo," I say, gingerly stretching out my sore arm to see if it still works. "I'll be back in fifteen so you can load me up. . . . I don't know what else to say. It happened. There was ice. Sorry."

She sighs. "Fine. Just get here."

"Roger that." I hang up and turn back to Sawyer, who is still smiling.

"Is something funny?" Now I'm back to almost furious again. I start walking to my car.

He shrugs. "It must be fun to work with you."

"Oh yeah, I'm a real hoot," I say, opening my car door and knocking my boot on the runner.

"I think you guys . . . you and Trey, and your little sister—"

"Rowan," I say automatically.

"Rowan," he says with a nod. "It's cool you all get to work together. I'm stuck with the proprietors." He says the last word with sarcasm.

And that's the moment when I picture him at the hostess stand at his parents' restaurant, by the jar of suckers, and that's when I remember the phone call, and that's when I see the body bag in my mind's eye. My mouth opens slowly, as if it's deciding whether to say the words my brain is telling it to say.

"You know . . . ," I start to say.

At the same time, Sawyer says, "About last night . . ."

And we both stop and start again.

"I shouldn't have called you," I say.

"I called you back. After."

I blink and look away. "I know."

He lifts an eyebrow. "You didn't answer."

"I thought . . ." But I can't remember anymore.

"It was nice of you," he says. "Kind of weird, but nice. I'm sorry I accused you of spying. Knee-jerk reaction. Or maybe just a jerk reaction. It was stupid."

I swallow hard, and now I picture those gorgeous lashes on his dead eyes. "Sawyer," I say, and his name sounds so weird when I say it out loud.

"I don't like this *thing*, you know," he says. "I miss . . . I mean, I wish . . ."

"I know." I look at the ground, my courage gone. He misses . . . what? He misses me? He misses the way things used to be? Did he really almost say that?

Now I can't tell him what I desperately need to say, what I told myself I'd say. Because if I do, he'll walk away from all of this thinking I'm a total mental case. And that would end everything. Every last pillow dream, every hope for that first kiss.

But he could die before any of that could ever happen. I'm so confused I don't know what's the right thing to do.

My phone buzzes in my pocket. "I have to go," I choke out.

He looks at the ground. "It's cool. I'll . . . see you?"

Dear dog, I hope so.

Fourteen

The rest of the night is a mess. Immediately every poster in every store window, every stop sign, every TV in every house I deliver to is showing me a truck crashing into Angotti's. It's like each object that is created to communicate any sort of visual message is coming alive, screaming at me to do something, to warn the victims, and they won't let up.

I can't concentrate on my orders. The Traverse Apartments fiasco put me way behind, and customers start calling to complain. Dad is overanxious and fidgety every time I drive up. Trey's trying to calm me down on the phone but I can't talk to him and drive on snow at the same time, so I just give up. I can't tell him what's wrong when he asks, even though I really wish I could. I'm getting a massive headache.

When the marquee at the Park Theatre blinks a fluorescent picture of the crash for the entire thirty seconds I'm stuck at the stoplight nearby, I think I'm going to lose it. This weird fear churns in my chest, and I can feel a flutter there, like my heart is racing, trying to urge me to go, go, go. "Stop it!" I scream from the driver's seat. I pound the steering wheel with my gloved hands. "Just stop."

But it doesn't stop. It gets worse. Every window in every house I pass has the scene plastered over it. Every poster on every telephone pole has changed its picture from whatever lost pet it was in search of to the explosion. I have to stop several times just to get a grip and figure out where the hell I'm going. I start lagging even farther behind, until it's all just so hopeless.

With one pizza to go, I can't take it anymore, because maybe all of this bombardment means the crash is happening right now, tonight. And somehow it'll be my fault.

Instead of delivering it, I turn down the street and head to Angotti's.

The building is still standing and there's plenty of parking out front. It's late, almost eleven. I call Trey and tell his voice mail that I'm fine, tell him that I have to make an extra stop and not to worry, all the while watching shadows of the Angotti's staff move from room to room through the front window. It's funny in a not-at-all-funny sort of way—this is the one window that doesn't have the explosion plastered all over it.

For a moment, watching the peaceful movement inside and for once not being bombarded with hyperexplosions at every turn, I talk myself back out of it. I think maybe I need more sleep. Maybe I just need to . . . I don't know. Talk to somebody about this vision. A professional.

The thought of telling someone what's been happening scares me to death. I imagine how they'd look at me. I imagine them pushing a panic button under their desk to summon security, or telling me they're taking me to get a Coke but really they're delivering me to doctors with white coats who will grab me and bring me to some asylum where they'll stick electrodes or whatever on my temples and armpits and do weird testing and shave my head and shit like that. And I'll have a toothless roommate who is seriously insane and who wants to kill me.

I feel my throat tighten and burn as tears run down the back of it instead of down my cheeks. I sit outside Angotti's and try to give myself a pep talk. What's the worst thing that could happen if I go inside and talk to Sawyer? In my mind, I list them.

Five bad things that could happen:
    1. I go in and tell Sawyer and he thinks I'm insane and tells everybody, and my life is over

2. Sawyer's parents shoot me dead on sight (not
   a bad option at this point, actually, now that
   I think about it)
3. The whole fucking crash happens and the
   place explodes *while I'm inside*
4. That's really all I can think of at this point
   because of all the panic and such
5. As if three bad things weren't enough

My phone rings while I'm sitting there, and it's Trey. I squeeze my eyes shut and take a breath, then turn off the phone and shove it into my pocket. I look over at the last delivery, growing cold on the seat next to me. "Sorry, Mrs. Rodriguez," I say. "I hope you don't stay up too late waiting for it." I wonder idly what my father will do when I get back home after not delivering it. It's weird how little I care about that now.

Finally I grab the handle and shove the car door open. I step out into the slush and close the door softly behind me, and then walk stoically toward Angotti's front door.

Fifteen

A little bell jingles when I open the door, and a beautiful, plump middle-aged woman looks up from behind the cash wrap.

"We're just closing down the kitchen," she says apologetically. And then she narrows her eyes and stares at the Demarco's Pizzeria logo on my hat. Her voice turns cold. "Can I help you?"

"Is Sawyer here?"

She doesn't answer at first. Maybe she's trying to think of an excuse. "I'll check," she says finally. She goes to the nearby swinging door and opens it a crack, never taking her eyes off me. "Sawyer," she calls out.

"Yeah, Ma?" I hear, and I look down at the carpet. *What the hell am I doing?*

"There's a young lady out here to see you."

He doesn't say anything. I imagine him pausing, wondering what amazing babe it could possibly be coming by to see him. Picturing how disappointed he'll be to see me.

He comes out and slides past his mother. His eyes open in alarm when he sees me, and he comes over. "What are you doing here?" he whispers. He looks over his shoulder at Mrs. Angotti, who is watching us very closely.

"I have to tell you something. It's really important," I say.

"It couldn't wait until school?" he asks, incredulous. "You had to come *here*?"

And now I start doubting myself again. But then I glance outside and see snow falling. Across the street, the Walk sign blinks an exploding truck. It's now or possibly never.

"It can't wait," I say simply, and look up at him.

The alarm in his eyes turns to concern. He keeps his voice low. "Let's step outside." He looks over his shoulder again at his mother and says gruffly, "I'll be right back."

I don't look at her. I don't want to see what she's thinking. I don't want to know the degrading thoughts she's had about me since before I was born. I reach for the handle and go outside. Sawyer follows me.

When the door closes, he keeps his back to the restaurant. "What the hell, Jules?" There's anger in his voice. "You can't just show up here. Not wearing that. Not at all."

I can understand why he's upset. I don't know exactly what sort of mess I've just put him in, but I can imagine the scenario in reverse, and it makes me cringe. I didn't even think about the hat. Maybe I should have called. But he was on deliveries tonight, so that wouldn't have helped. I don't have his cell number. It'd be the same mess. I take a deep breath. "Look, Sawyer. I'm sorry to do this to you. I know I'm probably causing a problem, but here's the thing." I pull off my cap and comb my fingers through my hair, trying to think.

When I don't continue, he folds his arms against the cold and shifts his weight. "Well?" he says after a moment. "Kinda cold out here."

I look at the Walk sign once more to gather strength, and then sigh and close my eyes, remembering the scene in my mind, frame by frame, landing on Sawyer's dead face. And I look back up at him, into his eyes. "You see," I say, and it sounds very grown-up in my ears. "I . . ."

"What?" he says, but the edge in his voice is fading.

"I'm just . . ." *Oh, shit. What was I thinking? What am I supposed to say here?* "I'm worried about your restaurant. I think . . . I mean, I have a weird . . . feeling . . . like something bad is going to happen. To it." *To you.*

In my best-case scenario, this is where he thanks me

and gathers me into his strong arms, and his face hovers near mine, and we kiss for the first time.

In my probable-case scenario, this is where he calls me a nutjob and tells me to go away.

In my worst-case scenario, this is where the restaurant explodes and I'm in one of the body bags.

None of those three things happens.

Sawyer just stares at me for a minute. And then his voice comes out cold. "Is your father going to sabotage us?"

"What?" I exclaim. "No! No, Sawyer."

He pulls out his phone. "Son of a bitch," he mutters.

"What are you doing?" I ask, grabbing his arm. "No. Listen to me."

He pauses. "Then, what? Are you delivering a warning from him, or a threat?"

"Oh my God," I say. "This is not happening. It's neither one, Sawyer. I'm saying everything all wrong."

"What is this, then? What's going on? Is he suing us? He doesn't stand a chance, you know."

"Sawyer," I say, and nothing is making sense. "Stop. Just hold on a second. This has nothing to do with my family! I—I have this vision . . . thing . . ." I trail off. It sounds absolutely ridiculous saying it out loud.

"What?" He looks at me like I've lost my marbles.

But now I'm committed. "I keep seeing a vision," I say,

trying to sound authoritative and not insane. "Over and over. You have to believe me, Sawyer, just listen. Please."

He stops fingering his phone, gently pulls his arm away from my grasp, and takes a step away from me. "A vision," he says sarcastically.

My heart sinks. I look away. In the window of the apartment across the street, I watch the scene and explain it as it happens. "Yes," I say in a quiet voice. "It's snowing pretty hard. A snowplow comes careening over the curb into your back parking lot. It hits the restaurant. There's a huge explosion." I turn back to him. "People die." I close my lips. *You, you, you, Sawyer. You die.*

He doesn't react, waiting for more.

"Obviously I'm aware that I sound crazy," I say evenly, realizing my life is now over. "I can't explain why it's happening. I don't ever have visions otherwise, and I don't think I'm insane. I just keep seeing this—on billboards and TVs and stop signs and . . ." I trail off and face him once more, trying to keep my stupid quivering lip from betraying me. "I just felt like I had to tell you, because if I didn't, and something happened to you . . . your restaurant, I mean, I wouldn't be able to forgive myself." *And by the way, I love you.*

He stands there a long moment, his eyes narrowed, snow falling and sticking to his hair and lashes. He blinks the flakes away.

"Look," I say, and I make my voice sound clinical now to keep myself from losing it. "I never expected you to believe me. I just had to say something. For me." And suddenly I know it's over, and I've done my job, and that's all I have. I nod once very quickly and add, "That's it," as if to signal an end to the insanity, and then turn away and walk to my car.

He doesn't stop me.

I get in and start it up, letting the windshield wipers take care of the snow and the defroster clear up the steamy glass caused by cooling pizza. All the while I pray for my door to magically open, for him to come after me. But I'm so afraid to look. Finally, when I start to appear either desperate or suspicious from sitting there so long, I pull out of the parking spot and dare to look back. He's still standing outside, watching me go. Gathered at the storefront window now, and peering out at me, are Sawyer's mother and two men. Next to her is a man I recognize as Sawyer's father, and next to him is an elderly mustachioed man. And as all the thoughts of what I've just done numb my brain, I realize that the old gentleman standing there must be the infamous Mr. Fortuno Angotti—the man whose caricatured face adorns the Angotti's sauce label. The man who stole our family's recipe and drove my grandfather to his grave.

Sixteen

Rowan meets me at the door. "Dad's freaking out," she says.

"Tough."

"What's that?" Rowan points at my bag.

"I messed up."

"Is that your last order?"

"Yep, sure is."

Rowan grabs it and pulls the box out. "It's . . . moist."

"Yup." I shrug. I feel like crying. I've totally messed up two orders in one night. Not cool. Not to mention that other thing.

"The kitchen is already shut down, Jules. What do you plan to do? Where have you been all this time?"

"Lost in the blizzard. Couldn't find it." I can't look at

her. I move past her and go to the sink to wash my hands and splash some water on my face.

"Dad's gonna shit a brick."

I push my fingers into my eyes, trying to stop the guilty tears from coming. But everything is so stupid. Why did I say anything? By tomorrow, everybody at school will know I'm a mental case. Sawyer must think I'm a freak.

"Are you okay?" Rowan asks, looking at me hard. Her voice softens. "Oh my gosh, are you crying? Seriously, you don't have to cry about it."

I grab blindly for a paper towel, determined not to make a single cry noise. I blow the sob out through my lips, nice and slow, and breathe in.

"Although," Rowan says, musing to herself, "I would probably cry if it were me. I hate not finishing the job, you know? Makes me feel like a total failure."

I take another deep breath and pull the towel away from my face. "You're not helping."

Trey bursts in the door with his empty bag, whistling. "Major tips, girlie," he says to Rowan, flapping his wad of money in her face.

"You have to share, you know."

"Not on Super Bowl Sunday," he says, teasing her. He notices the pizza box sitting there and looks at me. "What happened?"

"She got lost," Rowan says. "Jules, did you call the people? You had their number."

I don't want to lie anymore. "No. I just messed up, okay? Can you call them?"

Trey gives me a weird look but says nothing.

Rowan sighs deeply and grabs the phone, then looks at the ticket on the box and starts punching buttons. "Fine," she mutters. "It's, like, eleven p.m., my gosh, and—Oh, hi! This is Rowan from Demarco's Pizzeria. We are sooo sorry—"

I flee through the kitchen to the dining room. May as well face the wrath and get it over with.

Mom is rolling napkins.

"Where's Dad?" I ask.

"Upstairs. Very upset." She looks at me like she's waiting for something.

"Sorry about dropping that pizza earlier and messing everything up. I, ah . . ."

"You're fine," she says, waving it off. "But why don't you tell me what else you did?"

I stare at her. "What do you mean?"

"You know."

I hate when she does this. It's like she's trying to trick me into confessing things, which really pisses me off because I'm a good kid. I sigh. She couldn't possibly know about this most recent pizza fiasco yet, could she?

She's freaking jiggy with her ESP. "Mother, please. I'm tired."

She presses her lips together, and then says, "Your father got a call about ten minutes ago from Mario Angotti."

The implications are so heavy, so unexpected, I can't even speak. I sit down hard in a chair and put my face in my hands. "Who?"

She glares. "Mario Angotti. Son of Fortuno Angotti. Father of Sawyer Angotti, whose acquaintance I believe you've made."

"Oh, no," I whisper. "Oh, mother-fuh-lovin' crap." I can't believe they called. I didn't do anything. "No-o," I moan as it all sinks in. I can't look at my mother. "What did he say?"

"He said, 'Anthony, keep your riffraff out of my restaurant or I'll slap a restraining order on your whole family.' Or something like that."

"Wait. He said 'riffraff'?"

"It might have been another word."

"Oh." I rub my sore elbow and shake my head, staring at the ancient carpet. "How's Dad handling it?"

Mom gives me a rueful smile and reaches for another stack of napkins. "I think you can probably guess."

I stand up and start pacing around the tables. "Crap," I mutter. "What now?"

"Why on earth did you go there, Julia?"

I stop pacing and look at her. "I had to tell Sawyer something. He's the one who knocked my pizza over earlier . . ." I don't know what I'm saying anymore. All I know is that I should probably stop talking.

"He knocked your pizza over? On purpose?"

"No! Nothing like that. It was an accident."

"What kind of hooligan would do that? We should be the ones slapping a restraining order on *him*," she says.

Oh, hey, there's a way to ruin my life even more. "Please, please don't do that."

"We just might."

"Well, that's great." I get up and grab my gloves. "I'm going to bed."

I stomp into the kitchen just as Trey pulls a pizza out of the oven. "Is that the one I messed up on? They still want it, this late?"

"Yep," he says. He cuts it, grabs a box and slides it in, then maneuvers it into the bag.

I'm so frustrated I want to punch the wall. "Okay, awesome," I say. "I'll be back in twenty minutes." I reach for the bag.

"I got it," he says. "Go upstairs."

I bite my lip. He makes me want to cry. I know I should object, but I don't. "You won't believe what I did," I say.

"Probably not." He smiles and grabs his coat and keys,

then the pizza, and he's out the door. "Wait up, we'll talk. It'll be fine," he calls as it closes.

"Thanks, Trey. I will," I say, but he's gone. All I can hear now is Dad slinging crap around upstairs. I head out of the restaurant as Trey's taillights disappear, and start making my way upstairs to deal with Dad.

Seventeen

When I enter the apartment, Dad is fuming. At first, he just looks at me and shakes his head—it's the Demarco way of exuding disappointment without a word, and it works. The irony here is that he's standing in the middle of the dining room, next to where I think there might be a table and some chairs somewhere, but they've been loaded with piles and piles of his junk for the past nine years. Yet nobody ever calls him on that.

His silence is thick. Finally I speak up. "I'm sorry I went to Angotti's. I just had to tell—"

"No!" His voice thunders, and he starts in. "You do not 'just have to' anything with the Angottis. Ever. Do you hear me? Do you want to ruin our business? You want the newspaper to find out that the Angottis have put a restraining order on the Demarcos? What does that say to the community?"

"They haven't done that—"

He starts pointing at me. "Not yet. Not yet. Better be never. You stay away from that boy. Do I need to find a new school for you? Is that it?"

My jaw drops. As much as I dislike my school, at least I have Trey and Rowan there. At least I can look at Sawyer once a day. "Dad, seriously! Are you really trying to ruin my life?"

He gives me a suspicious look. "What are you doing with him?"

"Nothing! I swear."

"Then why do you have to tell him something?"

I take a breath and go with the first thing I can come up with. "School project. We're on a team. The teacher assigned us."

He narrows his eyes, but I can tell he wants to believe me. "What class?"

"Psych," I say. It's almost not a lie.

"You stay away from that place," he says once more.

"I will, Dad. I'm sorry."

When I wake up Monday morning after a terrible night's sleep, I fight off all the thoughts about what could still happen to Sawyer. I can't deal with that right now.

All I can think about is that I did what I had to do. I warned him. And just because everything's all turmoily, and my dad's a messed-up freak, and the boy I L.O.V.E. probably thinks I belong in an asylum, doesn't change the fact that I have now satisfied whatever weird business has been going on in my head, and I am now free. I yank open the curtains and look out at the windows across the street. None of them show me an explosion. I cross my fingers and hope it's over.

I also hope Sawyer won't tell the whole world what I said to him. But the chances of this? Zero.

And Dad's just going to have to get over it.

Five insanely overdramatic things I heard Dad muttering to himself last night as he paced the hallway outside my room:

1. "You have betrayed the name of Demarco!"
   (Yo, Shakespeare, live in the now)

2. "Why couldn't you just deliver the pizza to my dear friends?" (So you and Mrs. Rodriguez are hanging out now?)

3. "Now look what you've done. You've fired the first shot!" (WTF?)

4. "No more deliveries for you. We'll hire a boy." (Oh, *o*-kay)

5. "Why do you want to break my heart?" (big sigh)

And now I'm grounded for two weeks, which is no big deal because I don't go anywhere anyway. The worse punishment is that I've got to go to school and face the impending ridicule.

I brush my teeth and touch some pink gloss to my lips as Trey hangs on the other side of the bathroom door, waiting to get in, and I realize I'm the one who should be furious. After all, I bet Sawyer could have stopped his dad from calling my dad.

"He must think I'm a total nutball," I murmur as I swipe a little raisin-colored eyeliner under my lower lashes.

"I totally do," Trey says through the crack in the door. "Can you move it along? My hair needs clay before it dries like this. I practically have a 'fro."

I open the door and he stumbles in over a new pile of magazines that surfaced since last night.

"You okay?" he asks. He got home during the muttering portion of my fight with Dad, and I'd filled him in on the rest, except of course for the real reason why I had to go see Sawyer. And I get the feeling Trey thinks there's something relational going on between Sawyer and me . . . which I'm happy to go along with.

"Yeah, I'm okay," I say in a low voice. "It's just so stupid." And the bigger part of me that can't deal with the truth is crying out the thing I'm not quite ready to acknowledge. That even though I warned Sawyer, he could still die if he doesn't do anything about what I told him.

Trey sculpts his hair expertly and whispers, "What's a girl in love supposed to do? In the movies, she has to defy Daddy someday. Yesterday was your day. The first of many, I suppose." He sighs. "And we're all in for more yelling. Great."

"No, I'm done with it. No more yelling."

He washes his hands and looks at me in the mirror. "Yeah, right."

"Really," I say, putting my things in the drawer as Rowan bursts in and squeezes between us. "It's not worth this. I'll . . . just forget about him."

"Forget about who?" she asks. She slept through the fight last night.

"Nobody," Trey and I say together.

Rowan shoves my shoulder. "You guys are so mean. Move it. It's my turn in here."

Trey and I escape. He takes off to meet Carter for his ride to school, and I cautiously flip on the TV while I wait for Rowan to finish getting ready. I watch a full five-minute weather segment plus commercials, with no sign of any explosions anywhere. And a bonus—the forecast changed, like it tends to do around here. Now the weatherwoman is predicting clear skies for two days.

"Big sigh," I whisper, and I'm flooded with relief. I really think it's over. Even if I'm about to be known at my high school as the weirdest freak on the planet, at least I'm not truly insane. And at the very least, if Sawyer dies, it won't be my fault.

Jeez. What kind of sick person thinks like that?

Eighteen

On the billboard, I see Jose Cuervo for the first time in weeks. It's the most hopeful-looking thing I've ever seen in my life. "I love you, Jose," I say as we pass it. Rowan doesn't hear me. She's got her earbuds in, listening to something while she layers on more makeup in the sun visor mirror.

"Hey," I say, poking her in the shoulder when we're stopped at a light.

She pulls an earbud out. "What? Don't freaking bump me." She wipes lip gloss off her chin and starts over.

"Sorry. I just wondered how you're doing."

Rowan turns her head and frowns. "What?"

I laugh and shake my head. "Why are you suddenly so into makeup? Do you have a boyfriend?"

Her mouth opens like she's going to say something, then she closes it and says, "No," in a voice that doesn't want to be questioned further. She puts her earbud back in.

"Okay." I feel a little twinge in my heart for her. And then I picture us as spinsters living together forever, her being all sweet one minute and grouchy the next, her face perfectly made up just in case, and me leaving myself notes with sliced-vegetable lettering on the cutting board.

As usual, I ditch Rowan once we get to school—not that she minds—and keep my head down, avoiding eyes. Avoiding anyone talking with anyone else, because I'm pretty sure they're talking about me. I don't even dare take my usual glance to where Sawyer should be standing. Instead, I just stare into my locker and wait for the first whispers to reach my ears.

I grab the books I need and give myself a little pep talk, then slam the locker door and head to first hour. I keep my eyes on the floor, shoulders curved inward, and travel through the crowded hallway like a lithe bumble-bee, zigging and zagging and curving around people, one purpose in mind—getting through the morning, one period at a time. Then the dreaded lunch hour, and finally the afternoon.

And I make it through okay, only once narrowly avoiding Sawyer when I see him coming toward me after school. I duck into Mr. Polselli's psych classroom until he passes.

"Hi," Mr. Polselli says. He's grading papers at his desk.

"Oh, hi," I say.

"How's your paper coming along?"

I totally haven't started it. "Fine."

"What's your topic?"

"Um, I think, maybe, I'm not quite ready to tell you yet," I say with a guilty grin.

He laughs. "I see."

"But I do have a question. About a . . . possible topic. If a person, like, sees visions or whatever, does that mean they're, you know, insane, or crazy or anything?"

"Depends."

"Oh."

"It could mean that. But it might not."

"Oh. Well, do you know if . . . if people who see visions, do those visions ever, like, happen?"

"What do you mean?"

"Like can people see something in the future and know something's going to happen, and then it actually happens?"

He tilts his head and looks at me over his reading glasses. "Where are you headed with this? You mean like fortune-tellers? Psychics?"

I look at the floor, which has black scuff marks all over it. "I guess."

"There's a lot of debate about that. You could *probably* do some research on it and find out, you know."

I nod. "Okay. Yeah, I know. I will. Thanks."

"Anytime."

"See you tomorrow."

Mr. Polselli smiles and pushes his glasses up, resuming his grading. I check the hallway to be sure Sawyer is gone and make my way to the parking lot.

When I round the corner of the building, I run into him. Not literally, thank dog. But now that I think of it, I owe him a crash.

He's standing next to his car, his door open and his arm draped over it, talking to two of the girls—Roxie and Sarah—who were in my family's restaurant the night Angotti's was closed for the wedding reception. He's giving them that charming smile.

I stop short, then divert my path to get to my giant meatball truck, which is so inconspicuous I'm sure no one will notice me driving it out of here. I glance at him and he's looking at me, frowning, talking to the girls. They turn my way, and I barrel down a row of cars to the back of the parking lot, my face burning.

Rowan is standing—no, hopping—outside the truck, waiting for me. "Finally!" she says. Then she narrows her eyes and looks past me. "What does he want?"

I turn around, and Sawyer's jogging toward me. Alone.

My eyes pop open and I get this twisty thing in my gut. I look at Rowan. "Get in the truck," I say, unlocking her door. "Now."

"Sheesh," she says, but she gets in and closes the door, then stares at us. I turn my back to her as Sawyer slows to a walk a few feet away.

I shift my weight to one hip and lean against the door. "What."

He stops and flips his car keys around his finger a few times. His breath comes out in a cloud. "Yeah, um, sorry my dad freaked out and called your dad. I couldn't stop him."

I just look at him and hug my books to my chest. "My dad flipped out."

"I figured."

"I shouldn't have gone to your place."

He shrugs. "You're pro'ly right."

"I told my dad it was for an assignment for psych class."

He drops his gaze and gets that half grin on his face. "I'm not actually taking psych."

"Great." I'm such an idiot. I squint at the snow-covered pavement, which is brighter than white today because the sun's actually out. It's cold enough that it hasn't melted. But heat climbs up my neck to my cheeks when I think about how mad my father was.

Sawyer kicks a hunk of dirty snow from under my truck and says nothing.

"So, okay, then," I say. Every second that passes, I feel more and more stupid, and I don't like the lump that's forming in my throat. I try to clear it, but I can't control it. It's getting bigger. "I guess I don't really need the drama," I say, "of a . . . a re*strain*ing order, y'know, against my whole *fam*ily." The words are getting louder as an anger I didn't know I had builds up inside me.

He looks at me with alarm, neither one of us expecting this, but I can't stop. "So I guess after all those years of secret friendship, which you totally threw in the trash after I, like, was so scary that I *smiled* at you in public, in front of your dad, and then had the *audacity* to enter your restaurant almost four years later and throw everybody into a wild fit . . . well, I guess I'll just see you, you know, *never*. Oh, and thanks for telling everybody I'm insane." I reach blindly for the truck door and open it.

"Jesus, Jules." His arm shoots out and he pushes the door shut. "I said I'm sorry. And . . . holy shit, I don't really know what to say about all of that in the middle there . . . I—I didn't know you ever thought about that anymore." He blinks his long stupid lashes at me. "But I promise I didn't tell anybody you're insane." He steps back and straightens his jacket collar. "I figured it was, I don't know. Just weird."

Angry tears burn at the corners of my eyes, and I will them with all my might not to fall. I glance through the window at Rowan, who's sitting up, looking like she's ready to jump out of the vehicle and attack. I shake my head at her, trying to reassure her with a shaky smile. "Okay, fine," is all I can think of to say. He thinks I'm weird. "I need to go."

"And I—don't know what to say about the rest."

"Yeah. You said that." I reach for the door handle again.

"So, you know, *are* you?" He shoves his dangly keys into his coat pocket suddenly and coughs.

I look at him. "Am I . . . what?"

His face is red and he can't look at me. "Never mind. I'm an idiot. See you." He turns to go.

And then I get it. "Am I insane? Is that what you mean?"

"Forget it, Jules. It was a stupid thing to say," he says over his shoulder as he starts walking.

"Oh my God!"

He walks faster to his car. And I stand here like a total loser, watching him go.

I don't blame him. He doesn't believe me. I never expected him to believe me.

And he's obviously right in thinking that.

· · ·

From that moment, I'm bombarded with the vision once again—my peace didn't even last twenty-four hours. I drive home and every stop sign, every store window, and the billboard are covered in the scene of the crash. Rowan tries to find out what's going on, but I drive in stony silence. Eventually she's smart enough to shut up.

When we pull in the alley where we park the beast, Trey is standing there waiting where he always is so we can keep up our "all going to school in the giant truck of balls" ruse. I turn off the engine and look hard at Rowan. "Don't you ever tell Mom and Dad that I was anywhere near Sawyer Angotti, you hear me?"

Her eyes widen and she shrinks away from me. "Okay. Gosh, I never know what's happening around here."

"I mean it."

"*Okay*," she says again.

"Good." The three of us get out of the truck and walk in the back door, where Tony is whistling, Mom is adding fresh herbs to a giant pot of sauce, and Dad is nowhere to be found.

Nineteen

All afternoon and evening, the vision beats me over the head every chance they get, and it's exhausting. It's clear to me now that telling Sawyer was a good thing, but it wasn't enough. Apparently I have to get him to actually believe me too. And I'm guessing I have to get him to do something about it, which will be absolutely impossible. This is an evil game that is impossible to win.

And the thing is—that helpless, empty thing that makes me want to curl up in the corner and bawl my eyes out—it's that I know I can't make it happen. There's no way I can convince Sawyer or anybody that this crash will take place, and that nine people, including him, are going to die. And I think part of it is because I don't quite believe it myself. But if I don't believe this vision is destined to happen, then I have to believe I'm crazy.

This feels so much bigger than me, bigger than anything I can do, and I'm swallowed by it. Just thinking about facing Sawyer again, knowing he won't ever believe me, knowing if he mentions my weirdness to anyone it will ruin any reputation I have left, knowing that his family could so easily do something drastic that will make my father crack, just like my grandfather did, and knowing we could lose everything, scares the hell out of me.

I don't know what to do.

And for the first time, I think about real depression, the disease, and what that must feel like. I mean, my grandfather killed himself—he had a wife and kids and grandkids, and a business that he loved, and he just ended it all. Those good things in his life weren't enough for him. They couldn't stop his disease. To him, things seemed to crumble when Fortuno Angotti flourished. Only they didn't fall apart, they just stayed the same. And I guess that felt like failure to my grandfather. His insides, his brain, couldn't take it.

I heard my aunt Mary say once that my grandfather was a selfish person, hurting people like that, and I thought she was right. I've thought that about my dad, too. Lots of times.

But I don't know about that anymore. Everything about this, about mental illness, is so complicated. I just don't know.

The rest of the week, I am a zombie. I do what I need to do to get through the day. Talk if I have to. Get my homework done, not really caring if I do it right, seeing crash after crash after crash like I'm stuck in one minute that keeps repeating. On slow nights I send Rowan upstairs and work alone, keeping my mind occupied as best I can. Because I don't want to think about anything. I try to ignore the vision like I'd ignore a bug splat on the windshield. And I fail. It buzzes between my ears and crawls under my skin and coats the insides of my eyelids. The days blur together and soon it's another weekend. I ignore Trey's quizzical glances and Rowan's concerned looks and questions. I know I need to do something.

Maybe my grandfather knew that too. But he couldn't.

My father can't.

And I can't.

One morning I wake up to Rowan's alarm and stare at the wall. And it all becomes real. Nine real, human people, people with families and friends and jobs to do, will all die. And I am helpless, and I will never be the same again, and it doesn't matter that I actually told Sawyer what to expect, because if he doesn't believe me I'll still feel like it's my fault. The weight of this responsibility is so heavy, so crushing, I can't move.

"I'm sick," I tell Rowan when she stumbles out of bed. "Tell Trey he needs to get you to school today."

"What's wrong?"

I just close my eyes and moan. "Everything."

"You need me to get Mom?"

"No, don't wake her up. I'm okay, just sick."

I hear Rowan hesitating at the door. "I'll leave her a note to call in to school for you."

"Thanks," I say.

She closes the door.

Trey comes in a few minutes later. "Hey," he whispers.

I pretend to be asleep. There's a rattle of keys sliding off my dresser, and then he's gone.

Later, when my mom peeks her head in, I ignore her, too. Soon I hear Dad lumbering down the hallway, which means he actually got out of bed today.

I've taken his sickness from him. What a thing to pass down to the next generation.

All day, the wall is my only friend. If I don't look at the window, it's a day with few visions.

Still, the scene rolls through my brain regularly, and I

can't make it go away—the more I try, the more often the vision appears. I don't want to tell anyone—not a soul—but I admit to myself that I will need a doctor soon. And on the off chance that I'm not already insane, this vision will push me there. I think about what it'll be like to be in a hospital for people like that . . . people like me, I guess I should say. A hot tear slides from the corner of my eye into my hair. The thought of a crazy roommate scares me, like, a lot. The thought of having to take drugs that make me feel weird, of strange doctors asking me questions about the vision, of my mother with her overly cheerful face coming by to see me and pretending everything's just fine . . . I can't take it, I really can't.

Back when I was in first grade, when my father went crazy with the hoarding and the depression, he was in the hospital for a few days. I visited him—only once, though. I can still remember the smell of that place. His roommate was a scary man with white hair and a red-splotched face. His eyes bulged, and the scariest thing to me was that he didn't have any teeth. He walked up and down the hallway muttering to himself, and I was so afraid of his gummy maw coming after me that I slammed the door to my dad's room when he was coming in, and screamed when my mom tried to take me out of there, past him. Trey was with us, and Aunt Mary, too. We must have closed the restaurant . . . I don't remember. It doesn't really matter.

I wonder what goes through my father's mind every day. If it's anything like this, well, I guess I feel sorry for him.

Around two in the afternoon, I hear a soft knock on the door. I want to ignore it, but for some reason I say, "Come in."

It's my father. I turn over in bed, hoping I look as sick on the outside as I feel on the inside. "Hi," I say.

He looks scruffy and tired, but he's wearing his chef jacket. He puts a plate of toast, complete with parsley garnish, on my bedside table and sets a glass of clear carbonated liquid next to it. "I thought you might be getting hungry," he says, his normally booming voice softened. "Did I wake you up?"

I shake my head and sit up. "Thanks."

He puts the back of his hand on my forehead like Mom always does, and holds it there for a few seconds. Then he pulls it away and says nothing.

"It's more of a stomach thing," I say.

He nods, and we both know I'm lying.

"Well," he says. He fidgets with his hands, his big thumbs bumbling around each other, and I realize I hardly even know him at all. I've lived with this man for almost seventeen years and all I know about him is that he's an embarrassment to me. It kind of leaves a gigantic hole in my heart.

I wonder what he thinks about. If he ever thinks about killing himself. He turns to go, and I almost call out after him to wait. I almost whisper, "Do you ever see visions?" But I don't say anything.

The reason I don't is that even if his answer is no, I can guess that he, out of anyone in the world, will know why I'm asking—because I must be experiencing them. Which would lead to my parents putting me Someplace Else. And right now, today, a partly cloudy February day just outside of Chicago, I cannot risk leaving this bed for anything. Not for any doctor, not for any vision.

Not for any boy.

Twenty

When Trey sneaks upstairs after the dinner rush, around nine, he doesn't ask for permission to come in. He sits on the bed and looks at me.

"So. What are you sick of?"

I smirk. "You."

He rolls his eyes. "Are you going to live, or what?"

And that question, that joke, makes me hesitate. It burns through me. *Am I?* I look up at him, and my chest feels so much fear it squeezes my heart, makes it throb faster and faster.

"It's not a difficult question," he says with a smile, but I can see him searching me, trying to get inside my brain. He's been giving me a lot of looks like that lately. He knows me too well.

"Yes," I decide, thinking of body bags in the snow. "I'll live."

He rests his elbows on his knees, thumbs on his forehead, holding it up, massaging it, maybe. He closes his eyes, like he needs to think. And then he takes an audible breath and says, "I'm just gonna say this: You're not pregnant, are you?"

I almost laugh. And then my eyes get wide, because he's not laughing. "No, of course not. Is that what Dad thinks?"

"Yeah."

I let my head fall back on the pillow. "Jeez. I haven't even kissed anybody yet. I'm, like, the poster child for purity. I still have my freaking . . . my freaking . . ."

"Cherry?"

"No—"

"Hymen intact?"

I slug him. "Oh my God, shut *up*."

"Virginity?"

"Ugh! No! Well, yes, but—dammit, I can't think of the term. What's that thing girls used to wear in the olden days to keep the—just, never mind."

"Chastity belt?"

"Yeah. That. Sheesh. Joke gone horrendously wrong." I laugh, and it feels weird, like I haven't laughed in days.

Trey still holds a deadpan look. "So, to confirm:

You're not having an alien Antichrist baby from the seed of Angotti."

"Ah, no. Correct, I mean. Gross terminology threw me off."

"I will deliver the news thusly."

I stare at him. "Did he send you up here to ask me that?"

"No," Trey says, shifting his weight and relaxing on the bed. "I just read it in the worry lines on his forehead and figured I'd find out sooner rather than later, because I was wondering too."

"You?" I say, incredulous. "I am completely befuzzled by that. Don't you think I'd tell you if I managed to get close enough to Hottie Angotti to get pregnant?"

He shrugs and picks my cell phone up off the dresser. "You don't seem to tell me much at all lately," he says. He starts playing with it, pushing things on the screen.

I narrow my eyes and he turns so I can't see. "What are you doing? Searching my contacts or something?" I reach for the phone and he pulls it away. "Hey!"

"Calm it down, Demarco. I'm just playing Angry Bunnies."

"Oh." I struggle to sit up. I can feel my hair is all matted on one side. "Really? Or are you just saying that?"

"Yes, really. So what's going on with you?" he says, his eyes on the game, but I don't think he's actually playing it. "You're acting extremely weird these days."

At his words, memories of the vision pop into my mind again. I let my head bump against the wall, and I close my eyes. Like a rain cloud, all the dread, the helplessness, the fear, rush over me again, a waterfall of hurt, and I start to drown in it. A sigh escapes me, and then another, and another, until the sighs admit they are sobs and the bed starts to quiver.

"Aw, dang it, Jules," Trey says. "Come 'ere, then." Trey tugs on my arm; I bury my face in his shoulder and the tears come pouring out, a flood of them, and I can't stop it.

This is what I tell him through the sobs:

I am afraid of my life.

I am afraid of turning into Dad.

And, sometimes, I see things that aren't there.

He doesn't freak out, thankfully. But he's seriously concerned.

"What kind of things?"

"I don't know. . . ."

"Well, like giant spiders, or clowns, or imaginary friends, or ghosts, or what?"

I suck in a breath and let it out, beginning to regret the last five minutes with all my heart. I shouldn't have told him. "Like . . . a crash."

"You see car crashes that don't actually happen?" He

sits up straight, forehead wrinkled in alarm. "What, so you're crossing the street, and boom, there's a crash, metal crunching, people getting mangled and all of that, right in front of you?"

"No, not an actual crash. Just, like, a movie version of it. It's not physically happening in the street, I just see . . . pictures. Like a film. Like, everywhere."

"And you're aware . . . I mean—" He stares hard at my phone now, and I know what he's asking.

"Yes," I say, my voice turning clinical. "I'm cognizant of the fact that this is not normal, yet I can't stop it."

He blinks. "I don't get it."

"Me neither."

Trey stares at me for a long moment and puts my phone on my bedside table. "Kiddo, I know you don't want to hear this, but I really—"

"No."

"Jules, I mean it—"

"No, Trey," I say again, firmer this time.

"I think," he says even more firmly, "we should tell Mom."

"No!" I say. "No! Please—I trusted you. And we can't tell her. No way. She'll . . ." I imagine all the things she'll do, unable to decide which is the worst. Freak out. Pretend everything is fanfreakingtastic. Or worst of all, tell Dad. "Ugh," I say, sliding down in the bed, turning to face the wall, and pulling the covers over my head. And then I say softly, "She'll put me in the hospital, Trey. Like Dad."

At first, I can't tell if he hears me. He doesn't deny it. He doesn't answer at all. And then, once time begins again, he sighs deeply, and I feel his hand squeeze my shoulder. "Okay," he says. "We'll think about it. Talk it through, figure out what to do. All right? Let me know if it gets worse."

I close my eyes and let out a breath of relief. "Yeah."

Twenty-One

All night I dream about it—the crash, the explosion, the nine body bags in the snow, the fire. Sawyer's dead face. But in my dreams the events happen in random order. At the end, the body bags stand up and dance around in the snowy, fiery night, as if they are ghosts trying to get out of their containments. Sawyer's eyes fly open and he cries out to me for help, but I just walk away, going into a hospital that magically appears next door. Doctors take me by the hands and I begin to shrink. As I get smaller they swing me like a little kid down the hallway, and then they let go and I soar into a jail-like cell with bars on the doors. The doors clank shut. I hear someone muttering and cackling, and when I look up, a toothless, red-faced scary guy is locked in my cell with me.

I wake up kicking and sweating. Rowan is standing next to my bed saying my name.

I stare at her. It takes me a second to remember where I am. "Oh," I say, breathing hard. "Hey."

"Are you okay?"

I swallow, my throat totally dry, and then nod. "Yeah. Bad dream."

"Oh," she says. "Well, you were kind of moaning, or crying or something." She goes back to her bed and sits on the edge of it, facing me.

"I was?" My brain is a cotton ball.

She nods in the dark. "You kept saying, '*Listen* to me!'"

I unwind my leg from the bedsheet. "Huh." The nightmare is already starting to fade and the jagged pieces of it aren't fitting together anymore. "Did I say anything else?"

"Nothing that I could figure out. Are you still sick?"

I continue to untangle myself from my blankets and ponder the question. When I think about going to school, about seeing Sawyer, about the vision everywhere, my stomach churns and I feel like throwing up. "Yeah," I decide. "I'm still sick."

It's light in the room when I wake again, and I feel refreshed, like I've slept a hundred years. Rowan is gone, the house is quiet, and the first doughy smells of the day are wafting up from below. I sit up and check the clock. It's almost eleven, and I'm starving. My head feels . . . I don't know. Less heavy or something. I can't really identify the feeling, but it's a kind of restlessness. Like my feet are tired of being in this bed. My legs won't stay still.

I get up and stretch, testing my muscles, and tentatively think about the vision, bracing myself for that overwhelming fear to take over, but it doesn't. The fear is still there, all right, but it's . . . I don't know. More manageable. Softer, maybe. The vision appears on the window, as it has been doing lately, but today it is less in-your-face. It stays in the background, and I can actually think around it. I don't even know if that makes sense, but that's how it feels.

I pad softly to the kitchen and toast a bagel in the quiet. It's so strange to be the only one up here. So nice. I take my breakfast to the chair in the living room and tuck my toes up under my nightgown. I sit there and soak in the sounds of the street below—a garbage truck, an occasional honk of a horn, an exuberant Italian greeting a friend now and then.

I think about the snowplow again and close my eyes to ward off the panic, but the panic doesn't come, only a controllable fear, one that I can handle. I marvel at myself, wondering where the calm came from. Maybe it was the twelve hours of sleep, or crying it out with Trey last night, or the nightmare working something out for me in my subconscious, like Mr. Polselli talked about once in a section on dreams. But as I sit here, I think maybe it's something else. Maybe it's coming from the same source that brought me this vision in the first place. Maybe it's telling me that it's not quite as futile as it seems, and it's trying to give me directions now and then if I would only listen.

I think about that for a long time.

Later, I take a rare long shower. With one bathroom for five people, there's hardly ever enough time or hot water for something so luxurious. But today I stand here, eyes closed, letting the water beat down and the steam float over my skin and into my lungs. I wash my body, scrub the grease out of my hair, and smooth conditioner through it. At one point, thinking about the conversation yesterday with Trey, about how he and Dad thought I was pregnant, I just shake my head and almost laugh.

But then my mind wanders to Sawyer. To sixth grade, and to my Sawyer pillow, and my dreams of kissing him. The water burrows down on my lips, my neck. My collarbone. I turn my hips slowly side to side, and suddenly I can feel every thread of water moving over my skin, making it come alive.

I don't really understand why a shower feels so good sometimes, and other times it's just a shower, but I guess I needed it to feel good today, and it does. I let out a heavy sigh, and my fingers, down at my sides, travel lightly against the current, up my thighs and over my hips, my stomach, to my breasts, and back down. When the water starts to turn cool, urgent heat keeps me warm from the inside. My head bows, streams of water pouring off my hair. I squeeze my knees shut, hands clenched between my thighs, and I just crouch there, feeling so much life and love and risk and terror pulsing around me, inside me, that I don't know what to do with the overwhelming all-ness of it.

A painful longing takes over my skin and bones, and I move to let the water splash on my face and chest once again. It exhilarates me more and more the colder it grows, until it's shocking enough to halt and restart my breath a dozen times, and I'm almost too cold to turn it off.

I think it shocked me into reality or something. I stand in the tub for a minute, dripping, not shivering, my cold skin glowing from the adrenaline and utter grief inside. I think about how weird it is that loving someone just makes everything hurt so much more. But I guess it's that pain that means you're alive, and love and pain are so . . . so twisty. I wonder if love would feel as good if there wasn't any pain. I don't think it could. So I guess that's kind of what makes life worth living.

It's so bizarre, but I feel like I grew up in this one moment.

118

Before my heart rate slows and my skin is dry, everything becomes so clear to me. And despite the grimness of my task, I can't believe I've let so much stand in the way of this thing I have been mysteriously tasked to do.

Twenty-Two

With Mom and Dad downstairs in the restaurant and Trey and Rowan at school, I have the whole apartment to myself. I flip on the ancient computer and then rummage around for a sandwich, waiting impatiently for the weather forecast to load. Out the window, the sun shines, unless you look a little farther down the road, where in a storefront window, a crash and an explosion in a snowstorm is happening right . . . now.

The page loads and, surprise, in place of each little weather icon is a picture of an explosion. Nice touch, weird brain. At least the forecast description is still there. As of this moment, there's only a 10 percent chance of snow showers tonight. A 20 percent chance tomorrow, and a 40 percent chance Friday, and then it looks like there might be a storm coming on the weekend. I study it, and it's a bit of a relief that the next couple days look reasonably clear.

"Okay," I mutter, feeling hopeful. "Okay. We most likely have some time to work with here." But it would be really freaking nice if I could narrow down the date of this crash. That one thing would make this huge uncertainty more manageable, and it would make it easier to convince Sawyer . . .

"Oh, hell," I say. "What am I thinking?" Convincing Sawyer will be one of the hardest things I've ever done in my life. None of this will be easy. Not one thing about this will be easy at all. And I'm almost certain I'll fail.

Nine body bags in the snow.

Before I can send myself back to the overwhelming abyss of hopelessness, I grip the desk and grit my teeth and take a deep breath, letting it out slowly. "Hang on, Demarco. Just calm it down and hang on."

First things first. I have two hours with the TV to myself, and by the time it's over, I will know every detail of that scene backward and forward and inside out.

I flip on the TV and I don't even have to search for it. It plays on a loop. I watch it like that for several minutes just to get back into the timing of the events. Obviously the scenes are not one continuous shot, but where exactly are the breaks? I grab my notebook and take notes about my observations:

Scene 1: The snowplow is coming down Cottonwood Street behind Angotti's. My view is approximately from the parking lot near the Angotti's building. While it's dark, it's only a little hard to see the truck, because the streetlights are on. It seems to me that the truck is going way too fast for a mostly residential neighborhood. It's not going very straight. It crosses to the wrong side of the road and angles toward the back parking lot of Angotti's. It hits the curb, goes over a pile of snow, and bounces roughly. That's where the scene breaks.

As I watch, I realize a couple of things. First, how can the snowplow hop the curb like that if the plow is down? I rewind and watch again in the earliest second of the scene, and I can see in the dark that the plow is not actually down. Yet the street is pretty freshly cleared.

Scene 2: It appears that this scene immediately follows scene 1, but the viewpoint is different. I see the snowplow from the back this time, as if I'm standing in the rear of the parking lot, and the plow is still rocking after jumping the curb and snow pile. It has a clear path to the restaurant, which is now in sight, and I can see people in the window. The snowplow doesn't slow down at all. It hits the building, and the people inside never even appear to see it coming until that last second. Some glass flies before I see fire and the rest of the place exploding. Then smoke and pieces of brick and glass falling all around. That's the end of scene 2.

As I watch this scene over and over, I take note of the height of the snow piles in the parking lot—there's been a decent amount of snow plowed along the parking lot edges, and it's almost all white, not too dirty, which makes me think it's quite fresh. I stare at the pile height and try to find something physical I can compare it to. I crawl up close to the TV and look hard. There's a No Parking sign on that side of the road. The snow comes about a third of the way up, I guess, but it's hard to tell. On the opposite side of the street I see the top of a fire hydrant sticking out. I draw a picture of it in my notebook, showing where the snow line is. I bite my lip in anticipation, feeling the tiniest bit of hope that I'll be able to narrow down the day this happens by taking a daily drive up that street and seeing where the snow level is.

Scene 3: It's a simple scene. My viewpoint this time is from the rubble, it seems. There are nine body bags in the snow. They are laid out on the far edge of the parking lot, along the avenue parallel to Cottonwood Street. There's a band of yellow police tape attached to the maple trees that line the road on that side. There are people in stride and standing about, but their heads and shoulders are all cut from the scene, which centers on the bags. There is a wisp of smoke, and while I don't see any emergency vehicles in this shot, the snow has a red glow to it in one spot, and blue in another, which makes me think lights are probably on.

Vehicles are still there. Then the final frame—a close-up of the three bags on the right. The one on the end is open, and Sawyer's dead face is visible.

It stops me cold, even though I've seen it at least a thousand times by now. There's something about today, about the good night's sleep and the shower and the personal pep talk and the notebook, writing down details, that finally makes this seem very real. "This is happening," I say, staring at the screen, and for the first time I'm deeply convinced. It's not a joke. It's not a mind game. And what's more, I'm starting to think I'm not insane—or I'm caring less about my own personal crap and how this crash will affect *me*. "This is really going to happen, Demarco. You're going to have to do something."

Of course, if you ask any psych student, they'll say that's the first sign you're insane—that you think you aren't. There's no real win in the insanity department. And I realize, as I sit here staring at Sawyer's closed eyes, that even on the totally off chance I can get Sawyer out of that building at exactly the right time to save him, it won't matter much, because he'll be so traumatized about losing everything else.

And everyone else.

Who else is in those body bags?

The enormity of the task overwhelms me again, and I can feel my gut begin to twist. It makes me want to crawl back into bed and hide, pretend this isn't happening. Instead, I crouch down on the living room floor, among the hoarded junk, and wrap my arms around my knees, rocking back and forth a little, thinking. Thinking it all through.

Wondering if there's a way I could shut the whole restaurant down for one night so the plow crashes into a vacant building. Maybe I could somehow break the big window or cut the electricity. But I know that wouldn't keep the family from being in the restaurant—that's exactly where they'd all flock to so they could figure out how to fix things. So there goes that idea.

But then a brand-new wonder hits me.

Do the body bags in the snow mean it's inevitable? Will those nine people die no matter what I do or don't do? Is it really their time to go, or can death be prevented? I don't know.

I just don't know.

Twenty-Three

I'm staring at Sawyer's dead face for the zillionth time when I hear people coming up the steps. Rowan and Trey jostle each other in the tight entrance, taking winter gear off. I push play and wonder what TV show I'm actually watching—what they'll see and hear. To me, the crash scenes loop as usual with no sound. I guess this means I won't get to watch anything again until this is all over.

Rowan and Trey come in and see me. Rowan glances at the TV and frowns. "You must be very sick to watch that crap," she says. "Sheesh. Turn it down. The customers will hear."

I shrug. Curious, but too lazy to try and figure it out, I turn the TV off. "I'm feeling a little better."

"Good," Trey says. He has a new, concerned look in his eyes, and he's trying not to be obvious about monitoring me. I wonder what he's thinking. I smile at him like we share a secret, and I think that reassures him.

"So, school tomorrow, maybe?" he asks.

"Maybe."

"Hey, are you, like, pregnant or something?" Rowan says out of the blue.

"Oh my gosh," I say, giving Trey a look. "Where would you possibly get that idea?"

"I heard Mom and Dad whispering last night."

"Great. Can one of you please hurry up and assure them that I am not pregnant? I have never even kissed a boy." I hesitate. "No, don't tell them that. Mom'll tell everybody who walks in the door."

"You don't have to be kissed to get pregnant," Rowan says. She pulls a piece of gum out of her backpack and shoves it in her mouth.

"I'm aware of the process, thank you," I say.

Trey laughs. "Apparently, so is Rowan."

Rowan blushes furiously. "Shut up."

Trey pushes her shoulder and she pretends to fall over. "I'm heading down in a minute," he says to me. "I'll make sure everybody in the restaurant knows you are not pregnant."

"This is all really embarrassing, you know," I say. Trey

leaves and I call out after him, "How is it that everyone in my family thinks I'm out having sex? I don't ever leave this place. There's no time to get pregnant around here!" I look at Rowan.

She's watching me, grinning.

"Go," I say. I point to the door. "Don't you have to work or something?"

"Somebody around here has to. Lazy butt."

"Go!"

She leaves to change clothes, and I sit here again to stew over what to do. I look outside in the waning afternoon light on a cold, snowless day and again feel relieved that I've got a bit of time on my hands to work with.

I'm just not sure how to tackle the next thing on my list—convincing Sawyer that something bad is going to happen, and watching him look at me like I'm nuts, all while avoiding threats from his father that could make my father kill himself.

This is where the whole love-and-pain thing comes in, right here. But I'm newly determined, and I can't let my heart stop me from totally alienating the boy I love . . . or soon all I'll be loving will be the memory of him.

Before Rowan goes down to the restaurant, she peeks into the living room again, and hesitates. "Hey, Jules?" she says in an earnest voice.

"What's up?" I say. I pat the arm of my chair, which

is the only place she can sit. She comes over and perches next to me, and I put my arm around her waist like when we were younger. "You okay?"

She nods. "I guess. I just . . ." She looks at me. "What do you think about long-distance relationships?"

I stare at her and skip over the formalities. "What? Why? With who?"

"I don't know, just in general—"

"Who?" I demand.

"A guy."

"How did you meet this guy who doesn't live near us?" I know my voice is getting loud, but I have a weird feeling. "Not on the Internet or anything, right?"

She scowls at me. "Yeah, his online username is ChildPredator77. I sent him pictures of my naked budding bazooms and he wants to meet me behind the Dumpster at Pete's Liquor to give me candy. Jeez, Jules! Of course not. I'm not stupid."

I sigh in relief. "Okay. Wow. Sorry. Of course you're not stupid. So how . . . ?"

"Soccer camp during fall break."

"Oh." I search my memory, trying to recall if she ever talked about a boy. "Have you been in contact with . . . wait, what's his name?"

"Charlie. Yeah. We video chat during second hour almost every day."

I blink.

"I have study hall in the library. He's sort of home-schooled. I met his parents when they picked him up."

My lips part but I can't think of anything to say.

She turns to look at me. "They've invited me to come for spring break."

Silence.

"They offered to pay for my ticket, but that felt weird so I'm saving up my tips to go. They live in New York." She snaps her fingers in my face. "Hello? Any reaction at all would be appreciated."

I shake my head, dumbfounded. "But . . . a week or two ago you said you didn't have a boyfriend."

"It wasn't official yet then. We've been taking it slow."

"New York? Really?"

She nods. "So? What do you think?"

I say the first thing that comes to mind. "You're fifteen. There's no way Mom and Dad will let you."

Rowan rolls her eyes to the ceiling. "Besides that."

"Have you two . . . did you . . . ," I stammer. "Um . . ."

"We held hands and kissed once. That's all."

"That's all," I echo, lost in melancholy thoughts. And then I catch myself and shoot her the best smile I can fake. "I'm really happy for you, Ro."

"And the long-distance thing?"

I shrug. "I think if anybody can make it work, it's you."

She grins and hops off the chair arm. "Thanks, Jules. I was hoping you'd say that. I really like him." She reaches down and hugs me, then hurries to the restaurant, leaving me alone to dwell in the chair as dusk settles over the hoards.

But there's no time to feel sorry for myself. I mean, big whoop—my younger sister likes a boy and she's making it work. Do I care that she kissed somebody before me? Hell no. Hell no I don't. It's not a contest. Besides, I have a lot of other, more important crap to think about right now.

Around seven, when I know everyone will be busy, I grab the meatball truck keys from Trey's room and sneak out.

It takes me a little less than five minutes to get to Angotti's. I park on the next block so they can't see my truck. As I walk I pull my collar up and my hat down to my eyebrows and wrap my scarf around my face.

When I reach their enormous back parking lot, I do a snow-level check. There's definitely a little snow piled up along the road, but it's nowhere near a third of the way up the No Parking sign or the top of the hydrant across the street. One good snow could change all that, but it'd have to be a decent storm, I'd say.

I walk slowly up the sidewalk, studying Angotti's from the back, trying to pretend that I'm just taking a walk on this cold evening in case any of the family or employees pop out the back door to take out trash. I get a decent look into the dining room window. People sit in the booths there now, enjoying pizza and beer. I look for Sawyer but he's not in the dining room, as far as I can tell.

As I get closer, I try to remember all the things I wrote in my notebook and curse myself for forgetting to bring it with me. I stop for a moment, push my hat back, and give myself more room to breathe around the scarf, and look inside as much as I can, trying to figure out the exact layout. I should have looked a few days ago when I was inside, but I'd had other things on my mind and didn't think of it then. And something seems off. I can't place it, but it doesn't look exactly the same as the scene. I can't tell what it is. I take a few steps closer, trying to stay in the shadows so that people inside won't notice me. I look all around the dining room, from the service station to the giant forks and knives on the walls to the antique clock with ivy all around to the arrangement of the tables. Maybe that's what's off—the tables aren't quite in the same spots as in the scene I keep seeing. I narrow my eyes. But I still can't place it.

My teeth start chattering, but I weave my way between a few cars in the lot, trying to get a closer look at the building itself. The back door flies open and I spin around, pretending to walk toward a car. I glance over my shoulder, and it's a short-haired blond girl with heavy eye makeup carrying a trash bag. She props the door open with her foot and picks up a second bag, maneuvering them through the opening.

"The fifteenth," she's saying to someone in the kitchen. "No, I can totally work Saturday. Not going to the dance. I need the *fifteenth* off." She lets the door close and walks over to the Dumpster, hoists the bags inside, then wipes her hands on her pants and pulls a pack of cigarettes out of her coat pocket. She flips one out and lights it, taking a deep drag.

I crouch behind a car, stuck here until she goes back in, unless I want to risk her seeing me appearing out of nowhere and walking away. A car pulls into the parking lot and I turn to look at it, its lights bouncing on me for a few seconds.

It would have been better if I hadn't done that.

It's Sawyer's mother. She takes one alarmed look at me, then hits the gas and pulls up to the back door of the restaurant.

I bite my lip, not sure what to do. In a panic, I make a run for it, down the sidewalk into the neighborhood. "Shit!" I say when I'm far enough away. I keep running, turning the corner, around the block to my meatball truck. "Shit, shit, shit." And then I'm speeding home as fast as I can so I can get back upstairs, get into my pajamas, and establish my alibi.

Thoughts fly through my head. Did I leave any finger-prints anywhere? No, I was wearing gloves the whole time. But the meatball truck's engine will be warm. The restraining order police will check that when they come after me, and they'll know I'm lying. Should I just tell the truth? What's my dad going to do? I park the truck and throw snow on the hood to make it look like it's been sitting there all day, which I know is stupid, but I'm not thinking straight, and then I fly up the stairs, hoping, pleading, that there's no one up there waiting to catch me.

The apartment is empty.

Just as I left it.

I breathe a sigh of relief and hang up my winter things.

Five minutes later, the phone rings.

Twenty-Four

I stare at the phone, and then make a mad dash to check the caller ID. It's a cell number, no name. The area code is local. And I don't know what to do. If it's Mr. Angotti, I'll die. But it's probably a telemarketer. But what if it's not? If it's Mr. Angotti, I don't want him to leave a message . . . or worse, try the restaurant line and get my dad.

That decides it. I lunge for the phone and pick it up, forcing myself to control my voice.

"Hello?" I say, like my mother would say.

There is a momentary silence on the other end, and I think it must be a telemarketer after all.

And then, in a puzzled voice, "Jules?"

I die inside. "Yes?" I say, my voice filled with air,

not just because of the exertion of lunging halfway across a room.

"It's Sawyer. Look, what the heck are you doing?"

Now I'm silent. And guilty. But I'm going to fake it. "What are you talking about?"

"My mother saw you."

"Saw me where?"

"In the parking lot. Tonight. Come on."

I hesitate. "Dude, I've been home sick for two days."

"I know that. Doesn't mean you weren't out in our parking lot twenty minutes ago."

He knows that, he said. He noticed I was sick. I feel a surge of confidence bordering on recklessness. "You're sounding a little paranoid, Sawyer. Why, exactly, would I be in your parking lot in the freezing cold when I'm sick?"

"You tell me."

"This is an extremely weird conversation."

He pauses, and I think I hear a soft laugh. "Yeah. Pretty weird." His voice goes back to normal. "So you really weren't there?"

I sigh. "Oh, Sawyer," I say, and my voice sounds all throaty—almost sexy, which is, um, new for me. I blink at my reflection in the computer screen.

Now he laughs sheepishly. "Okay, so my mom's the paranoid one. Sorry about that."

"Where are you?"

"Ahh," he says, and I wonder if he's not sure, or if he's afraid to tell me. "I'm . . . out. For the moment."

"Don't worry, I'm not going to stalk you. Look, since I've got you on the phone," I say carefully, "I wonder if you've given any more thought to the little thing I told you last Sunday. You know, the thing where there's going to be a crash, and I'm kind of trying to save your life, and you think I'm insane. Because, to be honest, I could really use your help."

"Jules, no," he says, and I can hear a hint of annoyance in his voice. "I mean, yes, I thought about it, and no, I'm no longer thinking about it, and it's really weird and creepy, and I was hoping you'd have moved past it too. And maybe we could pretend it didn't happen."

I nod, phone plastered to my ear. "Yeah, that's what I figured. Okay. Well." Suddenly I get all choked up, because it's all so newly real to me, and it's so weirdly fake to him, and I can't stop the emotion, because I'm just . . . mired in this. This thing is running my entire life, but it's just a tiny blip in his. Until one day, *bam!* And then it's over for him. None of this is fair in any way.

But I'm determined not to let him die without me making a complete fool of myself in an effort to stop it. I close my eyes. "Well," I say again, my voice quavering, "I just want you to know that whether you help me or not, that's okay. I understand. And I'm still going to, ah"—my voice turns to gravel—"do whatever I can to . . ." I can't say it.

He's silent, and I wonder if he hung up.

I take a breath. "Are you still there?" I ask.

"Yeah," he says.

"Oh."

There's a pause.

"Whatever you can to . . . what?" he says.

"Um . . ." I close my eyes. And I figure he's going to die, so why not? "Save you. Yeah."

"Jules," he says again. "You're nuts."

"Sawyer," I reply, and now I'm pissed because he actually said it to my face, or to my ear or whatever. "I'm not nuts. I don't know what I am, but I'm not nuts. I'm not normally weird, even though this particular episode in our lifelong soap opera seems that way. But I do—I—I do—I care about you. And I'm going to save your life, and you probably won't even know it, or believe me afterward, either." I take a breath. "But I can't *not* do it. So I don't care if your father puts out a restraining order on me, or your grandfather breaks my father's heart after he already did my grandfather in, or whatever. You just do whatever you Angottis have to do to feel superior to the Demarcos until the end of time—that's just, you know, fine with me, and that's, like, capitalism and shit. But goddammit, Sawyer, despite all that, I'm going to save your fucking life anyway, because I love you, and one day you'd better fucking appreciate it."

I wait, shocked at myself.

After a long pause, he says, "Wow."

"Yeah? So?"

"So basically, what you're saying is, my mother actually did see you in the parking lot tonight."

My eyes spring open, and before I can think, I yell, "Ugh! My God! You are such a jerk!" And I slam down the phone in disgust.

Then I realize that slamming it didn't actually hang it up, so I pick it up again and jab the off button really, really stinking hard, and bang the phone down into its cradle again.

I stare at the desk, and all I can do is shake my head at myself. "You? Are bumblefucking nuts, Demarco."

Five reasons why I, Jules Demarco, am nuts:
1. I just screamed at the boy I love
2. I just told the boy I love that I love him.
   Ugh.
3. I pretty much admitted that I was lurking in his parking lot
4. And tried to make his mother look paranoid
5. Then there's that vision thing

You know, though, there's something really energizing, or, no, that's not even the right word—empowering, I suppose one of those Dr. Phil speaker types would say—about screaming at someone, and almost not caring what they think anymore. Because what's happening here is so much bigger than all of that. After nine years of loving Sawyer Angotti, and worrying about everything I say and do in or near his presence or in the presence of anyone who knows him, and being mad and embarrassed at myself repeatedly for laughing too loud, or saying something that wasn't *good* enough for his ears to hear, I feel pretty freaking awesome.

Awesome enough to think about putting a big sign on my head that says, "Yeah, I love you. So the hell what?"

Before I head to bed, I go back to the phone and grab Sawyer's cell number from the caller ID, enter it into my cell phone contacts, and erase the number from caller ID memory.

Because I just might need it one day.

Twenty-Five

I catch the scenes on TV while waiting for Rowan to finish up in the bathroom. And they're everywhere I go. I have to be careful driving now—all the road signs are stills of the explosion or of Sawyer's face, so I either have to recognize the sign by shape or go by memory of where stop signs are, and remember what the speed limit is through residential areas. The trip from home to school is an easy one, but this could be a problem the next time I do deliveries.

However, I don't spend a lot of time thinking about road signs. I don't even bother to look at Sawyer once I get to school, as much as it pains me. I don't think all that much about what people might be saying about me behind my back, and to my own amazement, I care even less. All day at school my mind is occupied with details. What am I missing? How can I figure it out? Even brief thoughts of Rowan vid chatting with her boyfriend during second hour don't sway my focus.

And then, in the middle of fifth period, when I'm going over the details of last night's visit to the parking lot, what I need to do hits me like a freight train.

Between classes I text to Trey and Rowan: "Rowan, go home with Trey. Have to stop at library for stupid research paper." I almost run over my former friend Roxie and her BFF Sarah, who are standing in the middle of the hallway as I type. My shoulder brushes Roxie's armload of pink and red construction paper and sends it sliding across the floor in all directions.

"Watch it, freak!" she says.

I almost apologize. I almost help her pick it all up and let her call me a freak and just take it, take it, take it—that's the Demarco way. But instead I look at her, and at Sarah, and back at Roxie again. "That's *insane* freak," I say. "Get it right." And I keep walking.

After school I high-five Trey and head out the door, right past Sawyer and his group of friends, including Roxie. He raises an eyebrow at me, and I shrug. Yeah, I love you. Yeah, I was in your stupid parking lot. So the hell what?

That stomach flip is still there, big-time. But my sudden decision to be the insane freak at school makes me feel like a totally different person—like nobody can touch me, because I'm on my own.

Oh yeah, baby. I'm on my own.

At the library I make a little wish as I head to the computers. I don't know if this is going to work, but I'm going to try. I find a vacant station in the corner, away from others, and sit down. I pull up an entertainment website and click on the first TV video I see—some reality show called *Skinny Wallets, Fat Love*. It doesn't matter what it is. The video loads a hundred times faster than it would at home, and I push play.

"Nice," I mutter as the all-too-familiar scenes play out. I maximize it and expertly hit pause at just the right place, the frame where we're looking into Angotti's dining room. I squint, trying to see past the snowflakes, past the people in the window, to the interior wall, where the giant antique clock hangs.

I take a screenshot and zoom in, hoping I can still make out the whole pixilated mess.

And there it is—the clue I've been searching for.

It's the giant clock on the wall, and its hands rest on four minutes past seven. And since Angotti's isn't open for breakfast, it's definitely got to be in the evening.

"7:04 p.m.," I whisper. I stare harder, trying to make out the second hand, but it's no use. The exact second won't be known, but getting it down to the minute is pretty awesome.

"Jules, you are a genius," I whisper. "Now you just need to synchronize."

A voice startles me back to the present. "Yo, insane freak. Talking to yourself?" It's BFF Sarah, trying to sound tough, sitting down at the computer two seats away. She takes out a notebook.

I frown. "What do you want?"

"You messed up our V-Day Dance decorations."

"Maybe you shouldn't be standing in the middle of a crowded hallway with them, then." Where I'd normally be scared, I am now bold. I look at her and wait for her response.

She wavers just slightly. "You're pissed because nobody ever invites you. That's why you did it."

I glance back at my screen and minimize it, then look back to her. "Invites me to what?"

"Anything. Homecoming. Winter Ball. Valentine's Dance."

I sigh and wonder if she's feeling *empowered* today too. If she is, it's not working. I lean toward her. "Did you come here to harass me?"

She doesn't respond, probably because she's so dumb she doesn't have an answer. She pulls out some papers and ignores me.

I go back to studying my screenshot.

But she's not done. A minute later, she says, "Is that what made you insane, freak? You're in love with Sawyer Angotti, but he never asks you to anything, and now you've lost your marbles. It is, isn't it." It's not a question.

My neck grows warm. There's only one way she could have found out I told Sawyer I love him. Unless she's just digging at me. That's probably more likely. I stare at my computer screen and say nothing, heeding the inner instinct to brace myself for more.

"But you can't help being insane, can you," Sarah says in a pitying voice. "Your family and all."

I close my eyes and grip my chair arms. In my mind, I decimate her. I scream, I kick, I hurt her on the outside for what she just did to my insides. I take a measured breath, and then I open my eyes and turn slowly toward her, covering my teeth with my lips and imitating that scary, gummy man from the hospital when Dad was there. In a harsh voice, I whisper, "Do you want to find out how crazy I really am?"

Twenty-Six

It was pretty awesome seeing Sarah react to that, I have to admit. She pushed her chair back with a loud scrape and her eyes went wide, her mouth open, her wad of gum just sitting there, tempted to roll out. And then she pulled her stuff together, called me a lunatic, and took off. I wonder if she got her assignment done. Tsk.

I spend an hour studying close-ups of each scene, landing again on the one quick shot of the dining room window. There's still something odd, but I can't figure it out. I spend a couple bucks to print out all the screenshots, but when I go to pick them up off the printer, they're not there. There's just a stack of color shots of

Skinny Wallets, Fat Love. Now I really do look insane.

"Big sigh, Demarco," I mutter under my breath. "Maybe next time print just one and check it, hey?"

Once I get home, everybody's down in the restaurant already. So I start digging for a disguise.

I sort through the hoards and piles and boxes. Because I know that somewhere in here, there's a whole crap ton of Halloween costumes. And I definitely can't be recognized again—at least not right now.

After an hour, and just when I'm about to give up and get my butt to work, I find the mother lode in the far corner of the dining room, under a musty box of canning jars, which we keep in case we ever decide to fix the seventeen broken pressure cookers in the living room, which we'll do if we ever learn how to can things. It all makes sense, doesn't it? Especially since we have all this spare time to take up hobbies.

Anyway, right on top of the pile are some retro glasses and three wigs: Elvira, Marilyn Monroe, and a generic one with brown dreadlocks, or maybe it's Bob Marley, I'm not sure. I shake them, and only dust falls out—a good sign that even the mice are repulsed. A careful sniff of each doesn't kill me or even knock me flat, so I confiscate them, putting them into a plastic bag and shoving them under my bed.

●   ●   ●

Five useful things about living with a fairly clean hoarder:
1. If you look around long enough, you're bound
   to find something for a science project
2. There are endless opportunities for organizing
   if you have OCD
3. The potential for canning is good to great
4. It's easy to hide things in plain sight, like
   gnomes and bird cages an' shit
5. Survival rate is over one full year when zombies
   attack

When I walk downstairs and into the restaurant, Rowan and Trey are standing on chairs at the entryway to the dining room, both with rolls of masking tape on their wrists and strings of shiny heart cutouts around their necks.

I tie my apron around my waist and squint up at them. "Seriously? Do we really have to encourage it?"

"Sing it," Trey mutters. He slaps a circle of tape on the back of a red heart and sticks it to the trim work.

"Oh, come on," Rowan says. "It's a beautiful tradition. Mom found those heart-shaped pizza pans."

"Wasn't too beautiful for the martyred dude," Trey says.

"Heart-shaped pans. Like we need more crap," I mutter as the front door jingles and Dad walks in with two magazines and a newspaper. Trey snorts and Rowan's eyes bug out.

"Feeling better?" Dad asks me. He doesn't look quite so freaked out as he did the other day. I glance at Trey, who has a ribbon in his mouth. He nods once from his perch.

"Yeah, I guess it was just the flu or meningitis or black hairy tongue disease or something other than pregnancy."

Dad blushes and pretends he doesn't get it. "Take it easy tonight. You need to be ready for Saturday."

"I know." Mentally I calculate the date and day of the week—being sick always throws me off. I've been thinking it's Monday all day, but it's Thursday. No wonder everybody's hanging pink and red stuff everywhere. When Valentine's Day falls on the weekend, it's always out of control.

I get into the dining room to give Aunt Mary a hand as five o'clock rolls around and the early bird diners arrive, right on cue. The decorations are all up in here already. Trey and Rowan must have started right after school. They have them draped in a lovely, nontacky way across the picture windows. Both Rowan and Trey are pretty artistic, which is why they're hanging decorations and I'm serving. I get the drink orders for the first two tables by the windows while regretting being unable to print the pictures I wanted at the library.

When I'm setting down their drinks, a shiny, dangling heart turns on its twine and catches the light, sparkling. I fight off the twinge of longing inside. Maybe BFF Sarah is right, and I'm sad and pissed that nobody ever asks me to go to any dances. And that I'm almost seventeen and I still haven't had my first kiss. I stare at the heart for a second and then turn away before the patrons think I'm weird.

And then, halfway to the kitchen, it hits me. I stop, stand, and pivot to look at it once more as it catches the light. "Shit," I whisper. "Really?" I drop off my tray and run through the kitchen, past Tony and Dad, and out the back door, almost wiping out in my haste to get into the door to the apartment, and race up the stairs.

I flip on the TV and watch the scenes unfold, pause on the dining room window, and stare at it. Crawl up to the screen and stare harder. "Oh my dogs," I say. I turn the TV off, grab the spare delivery-car key, my coat, and the Marilyn wig, and fly back downstairs, outside, to the car, and take off, not even caring if anybody's watching me, or if anybody needs a pizza delivered. Because this can't wait.

Twenty-Seven

I pull into the parking lot of Angotti's as dusk turns to dark. On my head is the platinum-blond wig, and I'm trying hard not to think about there being any bugs in it. I have one directive—I need to get to approximately where I'd be standing if I had been recording the scene, about twenty or thirty feet from the building and slightly off to the side closer to the back door. I need to have that perspective. I turn the engine off and hop out, holding my wig on my head and using the car as cover.

In my vision, there are light fixtures in the window, hanging from the ceiling—I could see them through the window. I remember noticing they weren't there the first time I came here to look at everything, but that was because it was the night of the wedding, and I assumed the tables were all rearranged.

But they're still not there. Nothing's hanging in the window. People sit there eating, but the lights are either recessed or too high to be seen.

Or maybe they weren't lights at all.

Maybe they were decorations.

"Valentine's Day," I murmur, and the missing piece falls into place. "Snowstorm forecasted for this weekend. Those were decorations hanging down, not lights. Jeez." I shake my head. "This whole thing happens on Valentine's Day?" A surge of fear pulses through me. "Could the timing be any worse?"

As I stand there in the shadows, the back door to the kitchen swings open hard, slamming against the block wall and ringing out into the quiet night. It's Sawyer. "Let it go," he's saying to the bright beam of light that follows him. His voice is angry. "I'm telling you, don't engage with that son of a bitch. You're just enabling him."

The blond girl I saw the other night follows Sawyer out and slams the door shut. She stands on the step lighting a cigarette while Sawyer tosses broken-down cardboard boxes into the recycling bin. "I can't help it," she says. "He drives me insane."

Sawyer closes the recycling bin and joins the girl on the step. He shoves his hands in his pockets and bounces on the balls of his feet. I shrink back into the shadow of the car. I don't think they can see me out here, though in retrospect, I should have chosen Elvira rather than Marilyn.

"If you try to argue with him, he'll engage. He'll bring out his whole *tradition* and *honor* bullshit and use that as an excuse to be a bastard. And everybody else just looks the other way."

She takes a long, angry drag on the cigarette and, as smoke trickles out the corners of her lips, says, "What do you mean, engage?"

Sawyer stops bouncing and turns to face her. I strain to hear. "I mean he'll probably fucking hit you, Kate, okay? So just . . . don't."

I lean forward, as if that'll help me hear them, but a car pulls into the parking lot and their words are muffled by the noise of the tires. It sounds like she says "You marry me, one chicken?"

And while the driver parks, Sawyer says something like "I make you table, butterface."

"Shut up!" I hiss under my breath at the offending car. The driver turns off the engine and gets out.

The girl takes another drag. She and Sawyer just stand there and nod at the guy as he approaches the customer entrance and goes inside.

Kate blows out smoke and drops her cigarette butt to

the ground. She stomps on it and twists it out slowly. "He hit you, then."

"You could say that."

"A lot?"

He shrugs.

"Still?"

"No."

"Because . . . ?"

Sawyer is quiet for a minute. "Because I gave up."

Kate stares at him. "Gave up on what?"

He hesitates, like he's thinking about the answer. "It doesn't matter anymore."

"Come on, tell me."

Sawyer shakes his head. "No. You done? We need to get back in there." He takes the girl gently by the shoulders, turns her around to face the door, opens it, and ushers her in. The door closes hard behind them.

And I stand in the parking lot, dumbfounded. Somebody hit the guy I love. I want to kill whoever it is. But first I have to save my boy. On Valentine's Day.

Fuck.

My phone rings, jolting me back to reality. It's not Trey calling, like I expect. It's Demarco's Pizzeria. Which means it's a parental unit on the other end.

"Crap," I mutter. Customer guy walks back out of

Angotti's with a takeout package as I answer. "Hey," I say, trying to sound breathless. "I left something at the library—my purse. Really important—on the way home now."

There is ominous silence on the other end. I squinch my eyes shut. "Hello?" I say finally.

The normally booming voice is eerily quiet. "Get back here. Now."

"I'm coming!" I start to say, but he hangs up.

I was grounded before. Now it's like I'm the haboob of groundedness. Back at the restaurant, in between tables, Trey gives me concerned looks. My mother is worried that I'm getting addicted to something—it doesn't matter what, she just keeps saying, "Are you addicted?" every twenty minutes. My father goes upstairs as soon as he supergrounds me, apparently overwhelmed by my disobedience, and Rowan looks like she's going to cry because her big sister never used to get into trouble and it's apparently scary as hell for her to see me "like this." Whatever *this* is.

And I'm floored. "All I did was leave for, like, a half hour," I keep explaining. "I came right back. I'm not doing drugs, I'm not *addicted* to anything, I'm not pregnant, people. Jeez." I feel like a broken record. "I'm sixteen, Mom," I say to her. "Do I really have to tell you everything? I think you need to let me grow up a little, and stop . . . hovering."

"Hovering!" she says. "Hovering? As long as you live in this house, I'll hover all I want, thank you very much. We feed you, we give you a warm place to sleep, you have a nice job in the family business, and what do you give back? You go off without telling anybody, you leave your customers, you cavort with that Angotti boy, and you don't appreciate anything we do for you. And then you say 'Stop hovering'?"

I sigh. "Mom, please don't yell. The customers can hear you. I'm sorry. I appreciate you. I should have told somebody I was leaving—I get that. I get that an ordinary worker would be fired for taking off like I did. I just . . . I panicked when I realized I forgot . . . something." I take her hand. "I'm sorry, okay?"

She shakes her head, all worked up. "You are going to be the death of me," she says. "And your father. And your little sister. What kind of example are you?"

Oh, that's so, so nice. "Well, maybe you'd better ask my *little sister*—" I start to say, but then I soften when I see Rowan's face, her wide eyes begging me not to tell her secret.

"Ask her what?" my mother says. "She's not the one in trouble here."

"Ask her . . . why . . ." I falter, unable to think.

Rowan steps up. "Ask me why I didn't tell you she was leaving," she says. "Jules told me she was leaving to look for her . . . thing. And I didn't think to tell you. And she was just . . . being . . . noble by not ratting me out. Or whatever."

I hold Rowan's gaze for a minute, both of us knowing our story sounds ridiculously contrived.

Mom's not buying it. She shakes her head. "You're in cahoots. I don't believe either of you anymore." She turns away and takes her next order from Tony, leaving Rowan and me standing there, afraid to even look at each other. We both disperse and get busy, working like our lives depend on it.

When the rush is over, Trey pulls me aside. "What are you doing?"

I'm tempted to say I'm waiting tables, but the look on his face tells me not to screw around. "Nothing. I don't know. I had to check something so I left. Mom's pissed."

He frowns. "Are you still seeing those . . . crashes?"

"Yes," I say. "And it's just one crash. I see one crash, the same one, over and over. Snowplow hits the back of Angotti's, and the place explodes. Dead bodies. Happy?"

He shoves his hands in his pockets and bites his lip. He can't look at me. "Jules, I think it's time . . ."

"Look, I know what you're thinking. Just give me

through Saturday, okay? If it's still happening on Sunday, I'll do whatever you want. We can tell Mom, I can go see a shrink—whatever you want, okay? Promise. I just need to get through Valentine's Day."

Trey looks into my eyes, and I can tell he's trying to see if I'm lying.

"I mean it," I say. "Please. Just, like, three more days."

"Are you going to follow the house rules and stop doing weird shit?"

I hesitate. "I can't say for sure," I say quietly. "And I also don't think I'm crazy, Trey. Not anymore."

His forehead wrinkles in alarm. "Oh, that's just great."

"No, I know what you're thinking, but I feel perfectly normal otherwise. I think . . . okay, this is going to sound really weird, I know, but I think I'm seeing something that hasn't happened yet. Something that's going to happen. Like a psychic thing." I pause, trying to gauge his reaction. "So when this event does happen . . . it should hopefully all be over for good." *Unless there's another crash after this.* . . . But I don't say that. I can't stand the thought of that. Besides, I need to get through this one first.

Trey looks dubious. Finally he says, "How do you know it's happening on Valentine's?"

I bite my lip and look down at the carpet. Shake my

head. "I'm still figuring it out. But I promise I'll tell you once I do know. Deal?" *Please.*

He sighs heavily and throws his hands in the air. "Sure, whatever. Okay. So Sunday, we're telling Mom."

I grip his forearms and grin wide. "Yes. Thank you."

"Just . . . be safe, okay? I'm watching you. Don't go anywhere without telling me. Or, I know—why don't you just stay home like you're supposed to."

I nod to appease him, and for the first time in my life, I look my dear brother, my best friend, in the eye, and I lie my face off. "I will."

Twenty-Eight

When I finally get a free minute, I step outside to take out the trash and call Angotti's using star 67 to hide my number, knowing it's a lost cause but feeling like I have to try. Luckily, a woman answers.

"Angotti's!"

"Good evening. I need a reservation for eight people this Saturday night at seven," I say, trying to sound rich and important.

She nearly laughs. "For Valentine's Day? We've been booked solid for weeks. The only time I have open is at eleven in the morning. I'm very sorry."

I squinch my eyes shut. "I can assure you we'll make it worth your while. I need the two window tables, please. Seven p.m. Six forty-five would also work if seven isn't available."

She hesitates. "I'm very sorry, ma'am, but it's really not possible. We're booked."

"I'm a big customer," I say. "May I please speak to the owner? Perhaps we can work something out so I don't have to take my business elsewhere."

She clears her throat impatiently, and I know now it's Sawyer's mother and I'm toast. "I *am* one of the owners," she says, and I hear the authority rising in her voice, yet she remains calm. "And I'm sorry, but as I said, and as I continue to say, we are booked solid. I am unable to fulfill your needs at that particular time. Perhaps you'd like to come in Friday or Sunday evening instead?"

Trey peeks his head out the door and I wave him off. "I'm afraid that won't work. Thanks anyway." I hang up before she can respond, and then I go back inside. My mind won't stop.

At one thirty in the morning I'm still lying awake, thinking, trying to figure out all the pieces of the puzzle. And all I know is that I just have to try one more time to convince Sawyer to believe me. And there's only one way I can think of to do that right now.

By two I've managed to sneak out without waking anybody up, and I'm standing behind Angotti's Trattoria, hoping the beat cop doesn't decide to come by right now. I whip my head around when an icicle crashes off the building, and my stomach buzzes. It's warming up to the low thirties or so, according to the forecast, and the weekend snow is about to start. Out here, before the snow falls, it's so quiet that you'd never know we're in a suburb of the third-largest city in the United States.

I'm standing three feet from the window that will shatter. Four from the tables where the people will be sitting. I can see the clock inside thanks to the emergency lighting, and I synchronize my old Mickey Mouse watch.

Out here, a few feet to the left of the window, there's an old gas meter and line that goes into the building—something I hadn't been able to get close enough to see before now—and I guess that the kitchen is on the other side of it. It's where the truck hits. That explains the explosion. I wonder what ignites everything once the gas flows freely. Or does it happen inside, maybe? I don't really know. I don't understand gas lines.

I stare at the back of the building, mesmerized, picturing everything and how it will happen.

In my hand is my cell phone. I've been holding it for practically an hour, debating, not daring to intrude again and risk rejection once more. But finally I do it. I have to. I call him, hoping he keeps his phone on all night like I keep mine. Hoping I don't wake the whole family. Hoping.

It rings five times in my ear, and then it clicks. He says in a deep, sleepy voice, "Yeah?"

"Hi," I say softly, and I realize I didn't plan this out. "It's . . . it's me. Can you, um, come down? Out back?" I'm an idiot.

I hear a whoosh of breath, and feedback like his phone jostles, like he's sitting up in bed, like he's confused and thinking, and I expect a multitude of exasperated questions like "Who is this?" and "Are you insane?" But those don't come.

A light in a window above me turns on, and I suck in a breath and crouch down against the block wall as if being smaller will hide me from the light.

A moment later he's back. "Yeah," he says. "Be there in a minute."

And it's like we're in sixth grade again, and no time has passed, and we're standing by our lockers planning what time we're going to meet under the slide on the elementary school playground.

The phone goes dead. I keep it to my ear for a few seconds, and then lower it and put it in my pocket. Tiny bits of snow begin to float down, or maybe they were there for a while and I just noticed them. I shiver and do a mental count. Forty-one hours to go.

A few minutes later, carefully and almost silently, a figure emerges from the building, and Sawyer Angotti, the guy I've loved since first grade, comes over to me.

I stand up. Look up at him, at his sleepy eyes. He holds

a finger to his lips, tugs my coat sleeve, and gestures to the far street, whose name I don't know. We walk together without speaking. When we get to the sidewalk along the road, he just puts his hands on my shoulders and looks into my eyes. "Oh, Jules," he says, shaking his head. "What are you doing?" He gives me the half grin that almost kills me.

I swallow hard. Glad he's not mad. "I had to come one last time to talk to you."

He nods, resigned to listen. "All right, then. Go."

I look down at the sidewalk. "Something bad is going to happen here," I say, as painfully aware of his hands on my shoulders as I am of the fact that he's not believing me, and for the millionth time I doubt myself and my own sanity. "I know when it's going to happen now. Valentine's night, 7:04 p.m." I continue talking, staring blindly at his slipper shoes. "I know you don't believe me, and it's okay with me if the whole school thinks I'm insane. I just need to ask you to please be careful, and if there's any way you can *not* be in the building or in this back parking lot at 7:04 p.m. on Saturday night, just even, you know, step outside the front door for a few minutes . . . please . . ." I bite my lip to stop my voice from pitching higher, into frantic mode. I can't look him in the eye.

I hear him sigh, feel its weight in his hands on my shoulders. He rests his chin on my bowed head for a moment and pulls me closer, into him. And then he moves his face next to mine. He smells like a man now. I wonder how long it's been since he smelled like a boy.

My eyes close, but all I can do is stand there numbly. I wasn't expecting this response, and I don't know what to do with my hands—they hang stiffly at my sides. I want to wrap my arms around him, hold him, but I don't. I can't.

As we stand there together, bodies nearer than they've ever been before, I wonder how many times I will regret not holding him.

Twenty-Nine

The saddest part, the part that makes the tears rush out of the corners of my eyes as I lie in bed an hour later, staring at the ceiling, is that he thinks listening to me is enough, and believing me is too much.

In school Friday I can't help but look for him, and I find him looking for me, his melancholy eyes sending me a weird, pitying glance, like he's trying to empathize, and it only frustrates me.

I get it now. He's being Sawyer, the guy who is nice to the outcasts—one of my favorite things about him. That's the kid, the guy, I've always loved. But I never, ever wanted to be the target. I wanted to be the partner. He believes he's protecting me in a way, but it feels like he's leading me on with his listening ear, trying to be there for an old friend who's losing her marbles. He even sends me a text message. "You doing okay? We should talk at lunch. Under the slide? ☺"

And that about does me in. I can't even answer it, because when he's dead, I want this to be the only text in the thread on my phone.

Dear dog, I'm such a mess.

He finds me at the drinking fountain.

"Hey!" he says in a strangely cheerful voice. His smile isn't the one from last night. It's the volunteer smile, the good-student smile. The fake smile.

"Hi," I say with as much enthusiasm as I can. I bite my lip, wondering when, between two in the morning and now, things actually changed for him. When he became distant, nice-guy Sawyer, and if he regrets going down to meet me in the middle of the night when he might not have been thinking straight.

"You doing okay?"

I smile and nod. "Mm-hmm. You?"

"A little tired." He laughs.

My heart is breaking. I don't want to be in this conversation. I don't want to be his animal shelter favorite. I'd rather be ignored than that. "Yeah," I say. My laugh is hollow, and I wonder if he notices.

"Hey, about last night," he says, lowering his voice

considerably. "I probably can't ever do that again, okay? So maybe don't . . . come over. Anymore. It's just a bad idea, you know? The family thing and all." His face is strained, about to crack from the perma-smile. "I'd get in a lot of trouble if I got caught."

"Sure, yeah," I say. "Yeah, no, I won't do that ever again. It was definitely a one time thing." I turn my head, looking for a distraction so I can get out of here. "Just did it for old times' sake, I guess. I don't know. It was dumb."

He relaxes a little, and the awkwardness, still there, has a veil over it now. "Okay, cool." He shuffles his feet, suddenly at a loss for words. He points with his thumb down the hallway. "I'm supposed to be meeting . . . someone . . ."

"Of course, yeah. Go. Good to see you." I wave him away and turn back to the drinking fountain.

"And—" he says in a smiley, awkward voice. "And, um, I'm not actually going to be working Valentine's Day anyway. I'll be at the dance. So, you know, whatever that thing is you're worried about, well, you don't need to worry anymore, 'cause it's cool."

I stare at the stream of water in front of me, not thinking about anything except the fact that this is my last good-bye with him, and it sucks. I don't look at him. "Okay, great."

He hesitates and then starts walking away, and I'm cursing myself because this isn't how I want it to end. Not like this at all. These words of sheer idiocy cannot be our last words.

I let go of the spigot and stand up. "Hey, Sawyer?"

He stops and turns back, and the fake shit is gone from his face. "Yeah?"

I press my lips together and thread my fingers, bringing my hands up to my chest nervously, and then I smile while everything breaks inside. "It's okay," I say, nodding, and I can feel my bottom lip quivering anyway. "It's okay that you don't believe me. I'll leave you alone now. I really do love you, like I said the other . . . that one time. The other day. I just want you to know that."

He stands there, his face stricken and real, and falling. He opens his mouth as if to speak, and then closes it again, and pain I've never seen before washes across it. He nods once, says, "Okay, thanks," and then he turns away and walks slowly toward the cafeteria, ripping his fingers through his hair as he goes.

Thirty

When he's out of sight, I go the other way on numb, stupid feet, all the way to my locker, and I stand there not knowing what to do with myself now. I open a book and there are no words, only scenes screaming at me. There's nothing I can do today anymore. I have to get out of here. I have to go away. I can't see him again.

There are two periods left in my day, and I will spend them in the meatball truck, waiting for Rowan to come. That's the only thing I can think of doing right now.

I grab my books like I always do on Fridays, as if I'm going to get any studying done this weekend, and head out to the truck. There's a teacher on rat patrol at the entrance, and I walk right by him. "Orthodontist appointment," I say, even though I got my braces off two years ago. Worked like a charm then, and it does now, too. He doesn't even try to stop me.

When I push through the door, it's snowing.

I walk to the truck, the cold flakes kissing my cheeks and making my eyelashes heavy. This is the beginning of the snow that I see in the vision, I think. The beginning of the end. Thirty hours to go. I get into the truck and start it up, letting it run for a few minutes to get some heat going, sit back to wait for the weather report on the radio, and close my eyes to figure out how the hell I'm going to shut that restaurant down and save nine people's lives.

And then my eyes spring open, and it finally hits me, what Sawyer said. He said he's not going to be there. He's going to the dance.

He's going to the fucking dance, and he's not going to be at Angotti's.

So how the heck is he ending up in a body bag? Does he come home for some reason that he doesn't expect? Does he get a frantic call and return to the restaurant, and something happens after? Does he go in to save someone and die that way?

"Oh. My. Fucking. Dogs!" I yell, and pound the steering wheel. "What the hell is going on? Why can't you just tell me what's happening? Tell me what to do, whoever, whatever, you are! Ugh!" I slam my body back into the seat and scream at the top of my lungs, way back here in the last row of the parking lot, where no one can hear me.

Maybe I am insane.

Maybe I really am.

Maybe this vision means nothing at all, except that I am losing it.

Around and around we go again. Again. Again.

I don't have time for this.

As the snow builds up on my windshield faster than it can melt, things grow cold and dusky inside my truck, and the vision plays out more clearly on the glass. Teeth chattering, I start up the truck again, flip the wipers on, and whisk the snow away, realizing it's coming down majorly hard right now. So hard that I wonder aloud, "If this doesn't stop, is it going to be too much?" A few minutes later the weather report is in—a blizzard watch, and it calls for twelve to eighteen inches in the greater Chicago area over the next twelve hours.

"Jeez," I mutter. I've seen my share of snowstorms, and one foot of snow is actually way more than a foot of snow when it has to be removed from half the city and put into the other half. If this pace keeps up, the fire hydrant will be covered in the first plowing.

The facts race through my head. Too much snow. Sawyer not working. Nothing's adding up right to fit the vision. *Maybe I do need to be committed to a hospital*, I think for the millionth time. I give up on it as Rowan trudges through the snow and gets into the truck.

"You're here early," she says.

I put the truck in drive and hit the gas, trying to beat the rush of students. "Yep."

Rowan just looks at me, and then she says earnestly, "What's wrong with you, Jules? What have you really been doing?"

I glance over at her, and she looks scared for me.

"Nothing. I'm fine." I turn the corner and then peek at her again. "Really." She doesn't say anything, so I reach over and pinch her kneecap, which she hates. And then I grin at her. "Seriously, kid. I'm fine. Things are really kind of bizarro world right now. Mom and Dad are cracking down on me for dumb stuff, but I messed up, too, by leaving customers without telling anybody, and that was dumb of me. And nice of you to try to cover, even though it didn't work. But other than that, we're all fine. 'Kay?"

"Okay," she says dubiously, and leans her head against the side window. "I just hate it when everybody's too quiet or too loud."

"Yeah, me too." I turn the wipers on high as we truck along, and turn the radio up so we can hear it against the beat and squeak of the wipers and the roar of the defroster.

I peer out through the windshield, trying to ignore the vision. "Dang, it's nasty out here."

"Maybe we'll get a snow day tomorrow," Rowan says, excitement in her voice. "Oh, wait."

"Yeah," I say. "Saturday. That's the breaks."

"Work is going to suck."

"It always does on Valentine's Day," I say. And I have to angle my head away from her because tears pop to my eyes. "It's really going to suck this year."

"Because of Sawyer? You like him, don't you? That's what everybody's mad about. Right?"

I think about that as I turn into the alley and park the truck, and we sit and wait for Trey to get here so we can enter as a force as usual. "I guess you could say that. But he doesn't like me, so it's not a problem."

"I think he does."

"What do you know?"

"He follows you around, he watches you. I see him."

I turn to look at her. "He does not."

She shrugs. "Hey, I'm not blind. But like you said, it's better if he doesn't like you."

I frown. Rowan is sneakier than she looks. But this news just makes everything worse. The aching crevasse in my chest opens up a little more. "Hurry up, Trey," I mutter.

Finally he comes and we all go inside. It's 4:04. I

have exactly twenty-seven hours to figure out what I'm supposed to do.

"I wonder what kind of crowd we'll get tonight," Mom says cheerily. "Look at it coming down."

Mom and the three of us kids stand at the front entrance as it nears five o'clock, ready and waiting for the early birds, but not sure if they'll come out tonight or if they're all at the grocery store stocking up on toilet paper. I feel like we could make a public service announcement letting Chicagoland know that if they need anything, anything at all, we probably have it upstairs.

"We're going to be slammed with deliveries, I bet," Rowan says. She's the queen of gauging delivery orders.

We all agree, mesmerized by the heavy flakes. I shake my head and turn away, going into the dining room to make sure everything's ready for the brave souls who venture out, and it is, of course. I plop down in a booth and stare out the window, wondering what Sawyer's doing right now. If he's remembering our awkward conversation, or trying to forget it. Wondering what'll happen, and how. My stomach churns as now, in all of our windows, the vision plays out over and over, and I can't get away from it. It plays out on the front of the menus, too, and the paper place mats on the tables, and the computer screen up at the cash wrap. The urgency of the vision is coming through loud and clear. "Okay, okay," I mutter. "I know already."

I twist the heels of my hands into my eyes, trying to rid them of the vision, feeling myself slipping back into that place of hopelessness. Nothing's right. Nothing is what I expected. Nothing is as it seems. I think that if I were a comic book character, I'd have the most desolate story of a wasted life—a wannabe hero who doesn't come through for the victims. The end.

When I feel a hand on my shoulder, I look up. My mom squeezes my arm and then slides into the booth across from me. She's always been pretty, but she looks older than she is. She has dark circles under her eyes, like me.

She puts her elbows on the table and rests her chin in her hands, gazing at me. "Where'd you go last night?" she asks.

I hesitate, suspicious. "To the library. I told Dad—"

"No, I mean in the middle of the night."

I lean back in the booth, trying to keep a poker face, but I wasn't expecting this. "Oh."

She nods, waiting.

And really, what does it matter now? On Monday we're going to have another talk. And I'm going to end up in the hospital with scary people. So I tell her the truth. Sort of. "I went to see Sawyer Angotti, to say good-bye."

She is silent. And then she takes my hands and holds them and says, "I'm very sorry about that, Julia."

I tilt my head, perplexed, and really look at her. She *is* sorry. I can see it. Wow. "Thanks," I say. "That was . . . unexpected."

She smiles grimly, collapsing her arms onto the table, and sits back in the booth. "You're not the first person who's had to say good-bye to an Angotti. I imagine it's hard. Some of them are actually decent people, even if they make mistakes."

I stare. "What . . . you?"

The bell over the door tinkles with the first dinner customer, and she gets up to take the hostess stand tonight. "No, not me."

"You mean Dad?"

But she doesn't answer me. Instead, she says, "Why don't you take tonight off? You could use a break."

Thirty-One

Upstairs, I can't do anything. The windows are plastered with the scenes. So are the mirrors. The scenes dance around the pile of Christmas tins, play out on every board game cover, every magazine, every newspaper. Every schoolbook I open screams explosions at me. There are no words, only the crash. The crash is my life.

Sitting in the chair as it gets dark, I think about checking myself into the hospital. I don't even know if I can drive when all the windows are playing the scenes. I can't concentrate on anything, it's getting so bad. I can't imagine it being any worse. And finally, I wonder if maybe it's trying to tell me something *else*.

Maybe it's trying to scream at me that I've got the facts right . . . and the date wrong.

And that I'm an idiot.

And that this. *Crash*. Event. *Crash*. Is imminent. *EXPLOSION.*

I lean forward in the chair with a gasp, pressing my fingers into my temples and squeezing my eyes shut. All this crap circulating in my brain is making everything harder to comprehend, and it's a stupid shame that I haven't figured it out before now. But with this snow, it's got to be. "Maybe," I muse. "Maybe they put the decorations up *this morning*. And maybe Sawyer is working *tonight*. No doubt he is, he's got tomorrow off . . . and the snow . . ." I slam my body back into the living room chair with a groan, knocking a box of recipes off the table next to me, and then scramble to my feet to check the time. "Holy shit."

Because with these facts—the snow forecast, Sawyer not working—this crash cannot happen tomorrow night. It's happening tonight.

It's 5:42 when I realize that I do not have twenty-five hours and twenty-two minutes to save the world. I have one hour and twenty-two minutes.

ONE HOUR. TWENTY-TWO MINUTES.

My hands start to shake and my throat goes dry. The scenes from the vision are no longer attached to windows and walls and screens and books, but they swirl around me, giving me vertigo. I grab the wall to steady myself, and then I go to the phone, because the only thing that screams in my ears right now is the conversation I had with Sawyer's mother yesterday when I was trying to get a reservation. *How about Friday or Sunday? Friday or Sunday? Friday or Sunday?*

I have the wherewithal to dial star 67, and then yank the restaurant's phone number from somewhere in my memory, because I certainly can't look it up right now. When a young woman answers, I say in the same voice as the one I used yesterday, "Hello, there. Any chance I can make a reservation for tonight? Party of eight, seven p.m.?"

"Sure, one moment. I think we had a cancellation."

I keep my eyes closed to stop the spinning, and count every second that goes by.

She comes back. "All right, no problem. Last name?"

My eyes spring open and I have to hold myself back from blurting out my real name. "Uh . . . Kravitz."

"Kravitz? Seven o'clock. You're all set."

I almost shout, "Can we have the window tables?"

She hesitates. "Um, sure," she says, and I think I may have scared her.

I force myself to speak calmly. "Thank you. Thank you so very much. You'll have the tables ready right on time, right? We won't be able to wait." My head is aching.

"Of course, Ms. Kravitz. We'll take good care of you."

"Thank you."

We hang up, and I feel like the band around my chest

has loosened slightly. When I open my eyes, things have slowed down. In fact, something's quite different. I lunge for the TV remote and turn it on, hitting slow motion immediately. And there it is. The difference. I pause it, hands shaking.

On the window scene, the tables are empty, and on the last scene, something else is different. Now in the body bag scene there are only four bags.

Only four! One phone call saved five people's lives. "Holy mother of crap," I whisper as I stare at the new frame.

But Sawyer's dead face remains.

Thirty-Two

Despite staring at Sawyer's dead face, I feel a surge of hope. The swirling scenes around me have calmed down, as if I'm being rewarded for figuring something out, for getting something right. I glance at my watch and try not to freak out. My next move is figuring out how to get my grounded ass out of here without being noticed. But first . . .

"I need you," I text to Trey, and then I turn on the computer. Everything I see is the new crash vision.

In less than two minutes, I hear the pounding—Trey taking the steps two at a time. He bursts into the apartment. "You okay?"

"So far. Can you do something for me?"

"What is it?"

"Search 'exterior gas valve shutoff.' Hurry."

He only hesitates a split second, and then he does it, but the computer takes agonizingly long to load anything. "Why am I doing this?"

"Because I can't see the web pages. I only see the crash."

"Oh, God, that's so weird."

"Please hurry."

"I'm trying," he mutters, shaking the mouse side to side. "You'd think Dad could start collecting newer models of computers, but no, that's too logical." The minutes tick away, and he types and taps his fingers on the desk. "Here it comes, finally," he says, and then reads everything he finds about shutoff valves.

I jiggle, nervous energy pulsing through me. He can't read fast enough. "Okay, thank you. Trey?"

"Yes?"

"I love you."

He looks at me. "Jesus, Jules. What are you doing?"

I bite my lip. "I have to go out for a bit. The crash—I think it's happening tonight." I want to say more, but I can't. I need him to say something. Something big, so I know he's on my side.

He doesn't move. Only his eyes flit back and forth on mine. "Tell me everything," he says finally.

I glance at the clock and jump to my feet. It's after six. "I don't have time. It's happening at 7:04 p.m." I glide through the piles of junk to my room and grab the Elvira wig. "I gotta go." I slip my arms around his waist and hug him.

He hugs back. "But, Jules, this is cra—I mean, this is, ah . . ."

"It's okay if you don't believe me," I find myself saying for the second time today. "I just have to do this, and I'll—I'll see you later. I'll be at Angotti's. Don't tell them—Mom and Dad—unless . . . unless it's absolutely necessary."

"Jules, you're talking scary. Just sit tight, okay? Stay here. I'm going to get Mom."

"Trey," I say, and I've never been more calm. "If you stop me from saving Sawyer Angotti, I will never, ever forgive you. If I'm actually crazy right now, nothing will happen to Angotti's or to me, and I'll be fine, and you can tell Mom everything then. But if I'm not crazy, and this crash is really about to happen, I have to do something. I have to. I can't *not* do it. I have a feeling this vision thing won't totally leave me until it's all over, but it calms down when I do the right thing. And right now, I'm doing the right thing—that's all I'm sure of." I look at him. "I need you to keep Mom and Dad from noticing that I'm gone, or I'm totally screwed. Okay?"

He shakes his head at me, a perplexed look on his face. "Jesus, Jules." He leans over and grips the back of the desk chair and gives it a little shake.

"You said that already." I grab his arm. "Trey, come on. Don't doubt me. You know me. I'm not insane." *Is it a lie? I guess we'll find out.*

"We should call the police, then," he says, turning back to face me.

"And tell them what? That a crash is about to happen? Yeah, that'll work." Worry grips his face, and I totally understand why, but I'm running out of time. All the muscles in my body are twitching, urging me to go out the door, but my brain tells me I have to get at least one person to sort of believe me or everything else will be messed up.

He just shakes his head, and I can hear his phone vibrating in his pocket. He checks it. "Mom," he says. He gives me an urgent look. "Okay," he says finally. "I'll cover for you. Just don't do anything stupid, don't be Superman, and call me immediately when it's . . . over. Or whatever. Right?"

Electricity surges through me, like I've won a battle. "Thanks. I'll call you. I promise!" I grab my wig, coat, and keys and fly to the door.

"Wait," he says. He looks around the dining room frantically. "Hold up a sec. You need . . ." He spies something and goes to it, wrestling a red box from the middle of a pile of junk. He pulls it out, causing an avalanche, and opens it—it's a toolbox. "You need this," he says, handing me a wrench. "For the gas valve. A quarter turn will shut it off. Do it and get the hell out of there. Promise me."

I take the wrench. "Promise." I reach up and grab him around the neck, giving him a quick kiss on the cheek, which he doesn't even wipe off. "See you in a bit." And then I turn and go down the steps as quietly as I can and escape out the door to the alley and hop into my giant meatball truck.

On my wristwatch: Both white-gloved Mickey Mouse hands point at the six. Thirty-four minutes to explosion. Way too much time wasted. I wind the giant meatballs around town, and the route that normally takes me just under five minutes takes twice as long because of the snow and the cars. I want to barrel right over them. "Hurry up!" I scream, shaking the steering wheel. Finally I drive past Angotti's, and my suspicion is confirmed. The decorations are up now—giant puffy crepe-paper pendant-like hearts that look like . . . well, apparently they look like light fixtures from far away. The Angottis must have hung them this morning.

But I don't have time to ponder trivial things. I drive to the street where the snowplow will come from. At 6:41, I park a couple blocks away so nobody sees my truck.

I take out my cell phone and text Sawyer, not caring what he'll think of me when he gets the message. "I was wrong. The explosion is TONIGHT at 7:04. Please,

Sawyer . . . I won't bother you again, I just had to tell you. Get out of there."

I don't have time to wait for a reply. I grab the wrench, shove the wig on my head, and fly out of the truck and down the street in the snow. I pass the sign and glance at the fire hydrant across the street. The snow level isn't right—it's too low—and I almost stop, but the vision's frequency ramps up when I start to slow down, so I keep going. I reach the back of the building and sneak along it, edging under the window, praying that nobody comes out the back door right now.

When I get to the gas meter, it's covered in snow. I wipe it clean and look for the lever that Trey described to me. Finally I find it, but it's encased in ice. I try to break the ice around it with my hands, but it doesn't budge. I chip away at the ice with the Crescent wrench, cringing at every noise it makes. Sweat pours from under my wig as I whip my gloves off to get a better grasp on the joints around the lever, and I can't even think about how much time is passing because it just makes my fingers fumble. At one point the wrench slips and splits open my knuckle. "Faaaaahck," I mutter. But I keep going, blood and all.

Finally the lever is free. I glance at my watch and frantically figure out the timing. If I turn the gas off too soon, their stoves will go out and they'll come out and check on it at just the wrong time. *So many ways for people to die here,* I think.

My watch says 6:53. I close my eyes, my thighs quaking from sitting on my haunches for so long, my finger still bleeding and starting to throb. Gingerly I put my gloves back on, watching a stain form in the cloth, but there's no time to worry about something so trivial now. I still haven't figured out how to save Sawyer and the other three.

I glance at a window of a nearby house and watch the scene. If Sawyer believes me and plans to get out of there, my bet is that his body bag will disappear. But it only takes a few seconds to find out that there are still four dead from this event. "Come on, Sawyer," I whisper. "Believe me."

It's 6:56, and I'm still sitting here. My phone buzzes in my pocket but I can't look at it. When I hear a rumbling, I look up and almost wet my pants. A snowplow is barreling up the road in my direction, eight minutes early. I shake my watch in case it stopped, but the second hand keeps ticking away.

A second later I realize the truck is going slower than the one in the vision, and its plow is engaged. It hits me now—in the vision, the road is freshly plowed, and the out-of-control truck has its plow up. This is not the same truck. I breathe a sigh of relief and mop my sweaty forehead.

The plow reaches the end of the road, sweeps around, and does the other side. The snow pummels the sides of the road, reaching the top of the fire hydrant and a third of the way up the signpost. If I weren't so freaked out, I'd be amazed at the way everything is coming together.

As soon as 6:59 hits, I take the wrench, engage it with the lever, and pull until it's crosswise from the pipe, a quarter turn. And then I get to my feet and run like hell, hoping it'll take at least five minutes for the kitchen to figure out the ovens aren't firing.

It takes me less than a minute to run the two blocks back to the truck, and I'm using some strange superpower energy that I don't normally have. Chest heaving, I climb in, start it up, and hit the gas. I barrel over the pile of snow left by the recent plowing and drive to Angotti's and into their parking lot. It feels eerily like what the snowplow will be doing in about three minutes.

Then I stop the truck and just look at this crazy scene, so familiar, so freaking spooky. All the cars are in exactly the right places, the lighting and snow are right, the tables I reserved are empty. I stare for a second, amazed at how everything is exactly as it is in the vision. It's like being in some weird *Twilight Zone* episode. But I have no more than a second to ponder it, because I'm still not sure exactly what I'm going to do with this truck.

What I'd like to do is park it in the path of the snowplow and make a run for it, but then it'll plow my truck into the restaurant too, so I know I'll have to gun it as it hits me to try to spin the plow. I pull up into that area just to see what happens, and now there are five body bags in the vision. That's obviously not the way to go. I back up and the bags number four again. "Jeez," I mutter, checking my watch: 7:02. "A little help here, please."

I grip the steering wheel and get no inkling, no clue from the vision god. "Ugh!" I yell. "Don't do this to me!" But the vision just plays in my side mirror, not giving me any help at all. I peer down the road and suck in a few breaths, trying to keep my hands from shaking, and back up a little farther.

Before I can check the vision again to see if my move changed anything, I see a dark figure running toward me. For a second I'm paralyzed, unsure of whom this could be, because there is no scene like this in the vision. Then my passenger door opens and Trey hops into the truck. "Nice hair," he says, breathing hard. He slams the door shut.

"What are you doing?" I scream at him. "You have to get out!"

"I can't let you do this," he says. "Do you know what you're doing?"

The vision plays brightly on the windshield like a warning, and suddenly there are five body bags again. "Shit," I say. "Shit! Trey, get *out*. You're going to die if you don't get out of here!"

He stares at me and puts his seat belt on. My watch says 7:03.

"Fuck, Trey, I'm serious. Get out! The snowplow will be coming from there in one minute," I scream, pointing, "and you'll get crushed!" I can't scream any louder.

"Just calm it down, Demarco!" he yells back, and then he softens. "I can't let you do this alone. What if you're one of the people who ends up dead? How would I live with that, huh, Jules? Did you think of that? Just don't get T-boned."

I stare at him hard. "Don't get T-boned," I whisper. And then I see it in my head—I'm doing it wrong. I need to sideswipe the plow, not let it hit me full-on. I whip the truck into reverse. "You're brilliant, you stupid jerk."

"I know," he says.

I barrel around to the back of the lot and turn my truck to face the restaurant, parallel to the road. I'll be able to get a moving start alongside the plow, then angle into it where it jumps the curb to steer it back to the street, where it belongs. "Okay," I say. "Get into the middle seat and strap in, you stubborn fuck. I got this. Shit, damn, hell! It's 7:04."

There's no time to focus on the mirror, and I can't afford to lose my concentration now. No time to know if this is a winning plan or not, I just have to do it. I suck in a deep breath and grip the wheel tighter, watching for it, rolling forward slightly to get traction.

"Oh my God, look . . . ," Trey says, the words trailing off. His head is turned and he's looking behind us out the window. He points and his voice turns to wonder. "Holy crap, Jules. You were right. Here it comes." He turns and gives me a look of utter terror. "You're going to have to gun it!"

Thirty-Three

I glance at the restaurant one last time and see Kate, the smoking girl, coming outside. "No," I shout, though there's no way she can hear me. "Get back!" She must be one of the people in the body bags, I realize with a pang. I ease onto the gas so we gain speed without spinning out, just before the snowplow jounces over the curb and the snow. By the time it comes up alongside me, we are moving well, and I edge my nose in front of it, hanging on for the initial jolt. The snowplow's not slowing, and I have to floor it to stay in front. I tap it twice more. "It's not moving over!" I scream, and then I swerve hard into it, breaking Trey's window. It's bumper cars for the big leagues.

"Shit!" Everything goes in slow motion. My insides

quake and slam against each other. My head bangs against my window and then cracks into Trey's head, but I feel no pain. The hood of our meatball truck flies open as I find the gas pedal again and gun it once more, blinded but trying with all my might to push the plow away from the building. "Help me!" I scream. "I can't hold it! I can't see!"

Trey grabs the wheel and together we crank it, and I catch a glimpse of the snowplow driver's head smashing against his window and flopping forward, his body held up only by his seat belt.

"Hang on!" Trey yells.

The grinding sound of metal on metal makes my head want to explode. I lean left to try to look around the hood, seeing the restaurant window and the blond girl safely off to my left. "We're doing it!" I yell.

A split second later all I can see from my side window is a brick wall coming at me. I try to get away from it, leaning my head toward Trey, but momentum is against me and the rest of me won't follow. I feel my body pressing hard against my door, against my will.

When the plow slams us into the corner of the restaurant, there is an enormous crunching sound, and pressure, pressure. Pressure.

All goes black.

• • •

Sirens. All I hear are emergency sirens trying to play a song, but nobody gets the tune right. I want them to play a song I know, but they don't listen to me. They can't hear me.

In the background of the horrible siren song is the vision, playing slow, and I can see through everything like they are ghosts. It's a different story now. The snowplow speeds toward the restaurant, swerving to the wrong side of the road, jumping the curb, where a food truck in the back of a mostly empty parking lot speeds to meet it. The truck noses in front of the plow, trying to guide it away from the restaurant, but the plow doesn't help it. The food truck turns sharply, smashes its passenger side into the side of the snowplow. A smoking girl watches dumbfounded from the back step of the restaurant, about to be smashed to bits, yet frozen, unable to move. A young man in the window stares wide-eyed. He checks his watch, drops settings on an empty table, and runs.

The food truck makes a last grand effort to push the plow away from the building, and finally it succeeds, just barely. But there's not enough room for both vehicles to clear it. The food truck slams into the corner of the building as the snowplow is forced to turn toward the road. It ramps up the hood of a parked car, tips over it, and lands with a shudder on its side, sliding and coming to rest in a quiet intersection. The food truck, wrapped around the corner of the building, is bent like an elbow and hissing. Two giant meatballs have snapped off and soar through the air, coming to an abrupt rest in a snowbank.

No one moves.

The smoking girl comes to life. She makes a phone call with shaky hands and opens the door from which she came, screaming for help.

When red and blue lights make the evening glow, two body bags lie in the snow.

A moment later, one of them disappears.

The vision ends before the wheels of the snowplow stop spinning.

Thirty-Four

I hear things. People talking, shouting. I hear a familiar voice, but I can't place it. For a second I open my eyes, looking for the vision in the shattered, blood-spattered windshield and not seeing it. A voice shouts my name. But it's very noisy there. I have to close my eyes and go back to where it's quiet again.

Every time I open my eyes, I hear the shouting and the screeching and the buzzing, and I can't stand it. I need to get away from it. My stomach hurts and I feel like I am in a lot of trouble. I snuck out again. My father is going to be so mad. But I can't think for long because I have to get away.

• • • •

When I wake up, an animal is attacking my face. I try to reach for it but only one of my arms moves. I grab the animal and pull its skinny legs out of my nose, but that only hurts more. I have to get out of there. I have to get it off me. I hear noises again, but it's all muffled—everything is muffled, and I wonder if my wig has slipped down over my ears.

Somebody holds my arm and I go back to sleep.

The next time I wake up, I just open my eyes and stare at the weird ceiling above me. For a moment I wonder if Dad did something to our bedroom. I frown at it, puzzled. I try to swallow and my throat hurts. I blink a few times, not quite sure if I'm going to get out of bed today, but I know I probably have a test or something . . . or wait, no—it's a food holiday so it'll be busy. I have to work. I brace my right hand on the bed to try and scoot myself up to sitting, but I'm just too tired. I'll try again later.

"Julia?"

I turn my head slowly and see my mother. She looks terrible. "What's happening?" My voice comes out all raspy.

She nods and smiles, tears in her eyes, dark circles even darker below them. "You were in an accident. You're in the hospital. How do you feel?" There's a noise from another part of the room and I turn my head in slow motion. Nothing wants to move today. It's my father, and

I'm too tired to be scared. Rowan is back there too, I see.

"I'm okay," I say. And before I can say "What happened?" bits of things rush back to my memory. I struggle to sit up, alarmed, but it hurts so much to move. "Where's Trey?"

"He's at home," Mom hurries to explain, reaching out and gently pushing my shoulders back down. "He's fine. He just got banged up, some cuts and bruises. He's sleeping. He's . . . he's fine."

I fall back in relief, and then vaguely I remember the last vision. "So . . . who's dead? Is it Sawyer?" I close my eyes, and in spite of the fuzziness in my brain, pain sears through my chest. "Oh, God. Not Sawyer." I don't care if my father's listening.

"Honey," my mother says, "you just need to rest now, okay? Don't get all worked up."

"You have to tell me. I know someone's dead. Who is it?"

Rowan comes over to the other side of the bed and touches my shoulder. "It's not Sawyer," she says. "He's fine." She gives me a look like she wants to say more but can't.

I sigh as much as my body lets me, which isn't very much, and I'm exhausted again. "Thank you," I whisper. Good old Rowan.

Mom holds a glass of water for me and I drink some from a straw. Everything takes so long to do.

My father just stands there, looking like a big oaf.

I gaze at him under half-closed lids. "I'm sorry about the truck," I say, and tears start spilling, not just from my eyes, but his, too. I haven't seen him cry in a long time.

He comes closer and takes my hand. "The truck doesn't matter," he says. "You matter. I'm glad you're going to be okay." He swallows hard and then says in a gruff voice, "You saved a lot of people. I don't know if you know what you did."

I almost laugh. "I have an idea," I whisper. I want to know more, but my eyes won't stay open, and once again everything is dark and quiet.

When I wake up again, I am alone. I open my eyes cautiously, expecting to see scene after scene reflected in the monitors and windows, but there are none. Instead, there are heart balloons and flowers by the bed. "Big sigh, Demarco," I whisper.

My body aches, especially when I breathe. If I yawn or cough, it feels like a knife is slicing through me. I reach for the nurse's button and push it.

A minute later, a petite black-haired nurse comes in, all smiles. "Well, there you are," she says. "I'm Felicia. How are you doing? Ready for some pain meds? Let's make your Valentine's night a little happier, shall we?"

"Yes, please." It hurts so much I feel like crying.

She pushes a button that raises the head of my bed.

"Sorry I can't just set up a morphine drip. Your parents said they didn't want you to get addicted." She smiles when I groan in embarrassment. "The pills take a little longer to kick in, but you'll feel better soon."

"What's wrong with me?" I swallow the pills she hands me.

"Oh, let's see here." She checks the chart. "Your left arm is fractured, you have two cracked ribs, and we had to do some surgery for internal injuries. Looks like you are now without a spleen, and everything else got stitched up inside." She smiles. "You have a killer black eye, and some other bruises and cuts."

"I cut my finger," I say, remembering. I bring my casted arm up so I can look at it. There are three little blue Xs across my knuckle.

The nurse grins. "Yes, that too. You're definitely going to be sore for a while."

I put my arm back down, exhausted. "Please tell me who died. Do you know?"

She smiles ruefully. "Everyone knows. It was pretty big news. The man who died was Sam Rutherford. He was the driver of the snowplow."

My eyes flutter closed, but I'm not asleep. "Shit," I whisper. "I never thought about him."

"He didn't die in the crash, though. They're saying he had a massive heart attack before he hit you. The witnesses who saw the whole thing talked to the cops. They told them what you did. You're kind of a hero, Miss Julia." Felicia smiles. "The police will be by tomorrow to talk to you if you're feeling up to it."

I'm glad I didn't cause the driver's death, but I still feel terrible about it. I nod. "I guess that's fine."

"And meanwhile, there's been a sweet, very worried young man in the waiting room since last night hoping to visit you. One of the witnesses. His name is Sawyer. Do you want to see him?"

My good eye opens wide. "He's here?"

"Yes."

Ohh, dogs. My good hand flutters to my hair, which is all matted and gross. "What do I look like?"

Felicia smiles warmly and says, "You look like a girl who just saved that guy's life."

I press my lips together and nod. "That'll do. Yeah. Send him in."

Thirty-Five

He peeks his head in the door, and it's so weird to see him in this situation, with me lying here all vulnerable like this. His dark hair is disheveled and he's wearing an Angotti's shirt, as if he came straight from work.

There's a look on his face that is so pained, I almost feel like I should offer him some meds—they're starting to kick in, numbing some of my aches.

He sees my eyes are open and he stops and just stands there, six or eight feet away, like he's feeling bad for intruding. "Hey," he says, and his voice cracks on that one syllable, and then he's bringing his hand to his eyes, and his shoulders start to shake. I watch him react, and a lump rises to my throat. I am overcome.

"Oh, hell, Jules," he says after a minute. "Oh my God." It's all he can say.

"I must look really terrible to get that reaction," I say, slurring my words. I'm starting to feel a little loopy from the drugs. "Come and sit. Aren't you supposed to be at the dance or something?"

He comes over and eases into the chair by the bed and just looks at me, all this pain in his face that won't go away.

"Hey." I reach out my right hand toward him. "Why so serious?" I tease.

He takes my hand in his, holds it to his warm cheek, and leans in and hesitates, then gently strokes the hair off my forehead.

"I just—" he says, and the words are so hard for him that I want to find my Crescent wrench and yank them out. But I stay quiet. Because the truth is, he thinks he owes me this. I understand that. And he does owe me, but not for saving his life. He owes me something else.

"I—" he starts again, and this time he continues. "I'm so sorry. Jules, I'm . . . God, I was so wrong, and I didn't believe you and I should have, and I feel so . . . so guilty about it, I feel terrible about everything. About not believing you, and about the last few years, which . . ." He sighs and shakes his head. "I'm just ashamed of the way things have been, and . . . the way I treated you."

I touch my thumb to his lips and he closes his eyes.

And then he goes on. "When they couldn't get you out at first, you almost died, and they had to use the Jaws of Life . . . and Trey was begging the paramedics not to take him away because he couldn't leave you . . . I mean, I just wanted to die too. And I can't believe I let this happen because of our stupid families."

I blink hard. Jaws of Life? I almost died? "So that was me in the second bag," I murmur.

"What?"

I try to focus on him, but I'm starting to get sleepy again. "In the final vision, there were still two body bags in the snow, but one of them went away." I close my eyes and can't open them again. "That must have been me."

Sawyer squeezes my hand and presses his lips against my fingers. "I'm sorry."

"Hey," I say. The thoughts and words I mean to say are jumbled up in my head, and none of them come out at all, and then I'm slipping away again.

The third time I wake up, I see the face I've needed to see this entire time.

"Hey, good morning, Baby Bop. All purple and green."

"That's not nice," I say, grinning sleepily. "That's a great, um . . ." I point to his neck. "What's the word?"

"Scarf?"

"No."

"Noose?"

I laugh. "Ow. No, like Fred What's-His-Name wears."

"Who?"

"You know. From *Scooby-Doo*."

He raises an eyebrow. "Oh, an *ascot*."

"That's it. Is it new? Oh, hell, this joke isn't even funny anymore."

He adjusts the white brace around his neck. "You like it? It came free with the whiplash and approximately two trillion dollars in hospital costs. My sister's a crazy driver."

"It's lovely."

Trey smiles and reaches toward me, fixes my pillows. "You okay, kiddo?"

I nod. "They call me the girl who lived."

He smiles, and then grows serious. "I'm sorry I doubted you."

I take his hand. "You didn't doubt me. You believed me. Or else you wouldn't have come."

"Actually," he says, cocking his head, "I was just delivering a pizza down the street and saw the truck, thought I'd say hi."

I roll my eyes. "So, what's everybody saying? Where's Mom and Dad?"

"Mom and Dad were here overnight. You slept the whole time, they said. They just left when I came. Rowan's home getting ready for the big day-after-Valentine's rush."

I laugh and pain sears through my side again. "Stop hurting me."

"And the news story was interesting but fleeting. You had your fifteen minutes while under the knife, sad to say. But we were superheroes there for a minute or two." He leans toward me conspiratorially. "*You* were, actually. But I was happy to take credit during your incapacitation."

"Oh, good job, vice president of awesome. So . . . what do Mom and Dad think about me stealing the food truck?"

"It was a bit of a shock. They didn't know you'd ever driven it before, so obviously they think you're going to become a crazed food truck thief. And probably a mobster, too. An addicted one." He gives me a sad, sideways grin. "Truth is, they think this is all Sawyer's fault, and he's turning you into some lovesick emo rule-breaker. I'm not sure this whole thing did your relationship any favors."

I let that sink in. "Oh. That's bad." I don't yet know how I'm going to explain the truck. Or the relationship. I ponder it for a moment, and then put it aside for when I can think more clearly. "Did you talk to the police?"

"Yeah. They wanted to know if the gas line shutoff was related to our adventure, because Grand Poohbah Angotti was apparently grumbling about it. I said I knew nothing of it."

"Are you serious?" I shake my head. "He was grumbling about it? We saved his fucking restaurant and his family, and he's mad because he probably had to throw out a few pizzas? Besides, I don't remember any gas meter being turned off."

Trey regards me. "You don't?"

I grin so he knows I'm teasing. "All I know is that we saw a snowplow driving crazily, and we acted on instinct when we saw it was aiming toward our rival's restaurant. We headed it off so it wouldn't hit people, because we are human beings like that. That's it, that's all. End of story."

"So you're not going to mention the vision thing?"

"What vision thing?" I smile sweetly.

Trey laughs. "You don't know how relieved that makes me. It's gone, then?"

I nod. "It's gone."

"Phew."

"Right? Totally gone. But back to the reporters. They said what about me, exactly?" I bat my eyelashes. My lids feel all puffy and weird.

"They said a sixteen-year-old girl driving illegally with her stunningly handsome brother—who is eighteen and available, by the way—saved the world with their giant balls. Ah-ha-ha-ha."

I roll my eyes.

"They interviewed Sawyer's parents, who actually sounded grateful, and his cousin, Kate, I think her name was, who saw the whole thing from the time we were rolling. She said if we hadn't been there, the snowplow would have hit right where the dining room window is, right next to the kitchen. The cops said that with the gas meter and kitchen ovens going full blast, there could have been a tremendous explosion. But PawPaw Angotti said the gas had been manually shut off just minutes before, ruining some food—yes, he really did mention that on TV, making him look like a total douche."

"Hmm. Must have been an angel or something who turned off that gas."

"One of the world's unexplained mysteries, right alongside the Loch Ness Monster and the purpose of 'being all gangsta.'" He leans back in his chair. "Oh, and then a honey of a boy came on the interview, almost forgot. The heir to the emporium, as it were."

"Sawyer?"

"Indubitably. After his little statement, I think I'm sort of back in love with him again."

"You jerk. Tell me what he said!"

He pauses. "Okay. In all seriousness, he said something like Julia Demarco was a real hero, putting herself in harm's way to save the lives of diners and employees of a rival business, and that the Angottis were indebted to her and the entire Demarco family. And then he choked up on camera, which was superhot, and all of Chicagoland melted just a little bit that day."

"Shut up."

"True story. I'm not kidding. I watched it ad nauseam from the chair in the living room Friday night and all day yesterday."

"Did you record it?"

"Rowan recorded it just for you."

I grin. "Aww. She's so awesome."

"Ahem."

"I mean, you guys are so awesome. Thank you for coming out to find me, Trey. I'm not sure we would have made it if it hadn't been for you."

"Of course."

It's quiet for a moment. And then I tell him, "Sawyer came by. I guess it was last night. I'm kind of groggy on what day it is."

"Don't tell Mom and Dad I told you, but he's been here the entire time, almost. He's in the waiting room. He sleeps there, leaves for an hour now and then to eat or shower or whatever. Then he comes back."

My stomach flips. "Are you serious?"

"And please don't mention to Mom and Dad that you let him in here. They don't want you to have anything to do with him—they're being really cold assholes to him, actually. Dad, mostly. I mean, obviously they're upset about all of this, but I think it's also the family rivalry thing."

I close my eyes and sigh. "So this didn't cure anything."

"I don't know. Maybe it will eventually."

"Why does he come here?"

Trey snorts. "Duh. He's into you. I talked to him. He feels guilty, definitely, but he's always had a thing for you, I think. He told me he was sorry about fifty times. I asked him to make it up to me, but he rejected every one of my suggestions."

My eyes fly open. "Stay away from him, he's mine." I narrow my gaze and frown. "You really think he's into me?"

"Sister, trust me. He's into you."

"Well, why the hell has he been blowing me off since seventh grade, then?"

Trey wrinkles up his nose. "You should probably ask him yourself, but I think something strange is going on over at the Angottis that nobody knows about."

"You mean like maybe his dad is a hoarder with depression issues?"

He laughs. "Maybe. Though that would be a really weird coincidence."

I think for a moment of the conversation I had with my mother before the crash. "Mom said I wasn't the first person who had to say good-bye to an Angotti."

Trey sits up. "Say whaaa?"

"She said that. Really! And I said, 'You mean you?' And she said it wasn't her. So who does that leave, besides Dad?"

Trey sinks back down. "Well, there's me."

"You?"

"No, it wasn't me, but I don't like to be ruled out without a scandalous discussion first."

I laugh again and grab my side. "Oh, my aching—stop that!"

"I guess we have a mystery to figure out."

I nod and lie back, exhausted from the conversation, but not sleepy for once. "Two mysteries, even."

He nods and squeezes my hand. "Mom and Dad and Rowan will be back later. They're closing up early tonight to see you. Eight o'clock. So it's just you and me, and whoever might be out there, and I have homework I can do . . . just so you know."

I nod, and we share a look that says, *Bring the hot boy to Jules.*

———

Thirty-Six

"We need to talk about some things," I say to Sawyer as he sits down.

He nods. "We do." His dark hair hangs in little ringlets on his forehead, and he appears freshly washed today, which is better than what I can say for me. He's not wearing an Angotti's shirt anymore, either.

"First, I don't want you to mope around feeling guilty anymore, okay?"

"Okay."

"Second, what the hell happened in seventh grade that made you hate me?"

He holds my gaze, unwavering, his green eyes sending lasers into mine. "Fair question," he says finally. He drops his gaze to my bedside table and picks up a pen, weaving it through his fingers.

"You don't want to answer it?"

"No. But I need to. I'm thinking."

I take in a quick breath, moved by his honesty, ignoring the searing pain that the motion leaves behind. And I stay quiet.

"Where to start," he says, lost in thought. "My grandfather," he says eventually, "is a very controlling man."

I nod.

"He used to hit me."

My eyes spring open wide. "Your *grand*father? Didn't your parents stop him?"

He hesitates. "No. They didn't. My mother couldn't, and my father was angry enough that he wouldn't."

"I don't get it. Why couldn't your mother stop him? What kind of a—"

He sets the pen down and clasps his hands together, staring down at them. I look at his hands too and remember the feel of his touch on my cheek. And then he looks up at me again, his eyes unwavering for an almost frightening amount of time.

"Your father and my mother had an affair, Jules."

The words take a moment to register. "What?" I say, incredulous.

"My mother just told me everything yesterday, after all

of this—" He waves his hand at me, at the hospital. "When I was so angry and upset, and I didn't understand why things had to be the way they are between us. She made me promise not to tell you, but I can't help it. I think you need to know."

I bring my hand to my hair and try to work my fingers through it. It's weird. I don't feel anything about this. No emotion, nothing. And then I think about my poor mother, and my heart cracks. "When?" I say.

"A long time ago, when we were really young."

"Wow." I stare up at the ceiling, trying to process it.

"It was short, and Mom said both of them eventually realized it was a mistake, but it happened," Sawyer says. "I can't believe she told me all of this, but she'd been drinking. It was late." He glances at the door and then says quietly, "She said they planned to leave their spouses, combine restaurant assets, and become an enterprise. Take over business from the chains, sell products commercially and all that."

My mouth drops open. "Products? Made from secret family recipes?"

"Yes." Sawyer takes a deep breath and can't look at me. "From what I know, your father gave my mother his family's special sauce recipe, which my grandfather had been after for years. When your dad and my mom broke it off, and my father and grandfather found out, they were seriously pissed off. To try to redeem herself, my mother gave them the recipe. Kind of a last-ditch effort to try to diffuse things and keep the family together." He stares at the ground. "And my grandfather took it. And he patented it."

"You are not serious." I look at him in wonder. "That's probably what put my grandfather into his big downward spiral. Betrayed by his son and his biggest rival." A new realization hits me. "Maybe that's my dad's problem. It's the guilt. Not just losing the recipe, but driving his father to kill himself. Holy shit."

Sawyer nods. "It all sounds extremely dramatic, but that's because it was, according to my mom."

"Yes."

Sawyer looks up at me, remorseful. "When you and I were in first grade, our stolen sauce line went to market, and it was a hit. Your father tried to sue us, but he didn't have the proof he needed to win. It was a verbal recipe, handed down for generations, my mom said. He'd known it by heart. Never wrote it down."

"Oh my God," I say. "That's when the hoarding started." All the recipes and cookbooks piled up in our apartment. None of them holding a candle to the one that remained unwritten.

Sawyer doesn't say anything for a minute, and I stare at the ceiling, letting everything sink in.

"My grandfather was furious that your dad would dare

to sue him. My father was hurt and angry over my mother messing around. And your parents had plenty of reason to hate us as well. So when you and I ended up becoming friends, it practically started a war all over again."

"Wow," is all I can say. I struggle to sit up, and Sawyer rises to help me. He lifts me gently, and his fingers linger on my shoulders before he sits back down.

"We hid our friendship really well, for a while, at least," he says ruefully. "Didn't we?"

"Until I saw you—" I say as he says, "Until the day before—"

"Seventh grade," we say together.

"My father saw you with your dad, saw your smile, and he watched my face light up to see you. He knew it wasn't just an acquaintance kind of smile. Back at home we 'had a talk,' which consisted of him and my grandfather telling me I was not to speak to you again, ever. When I protested, my grandfather got so enraged, he grabbed me by the collar and dragged me to my room. And then he started hitting me."

"Oh, Sawyer," I whisper.

He shoves his chair back and starts working his hands together. "He beat me pretty hard, but not anywhere you could see bruises. He was very careful about that. My mother couldn't do anything—he threatened her, too, threatened to force my dad to divorce her after what she'd done, take us kids away from her, and leave her with no money."

"That's insane."

"It's different when a man like that lives with you. Holds so much power over you—there's no way you could understand." He taps his fingers on the chair arms, distraught. "So I agreed to stop talking to you just to get him to lay off me. And that time," he says, standing up and starting to pace around the bed, "that one time you and I had to do a project together, he found out somehow. And he beat me up, even though I cried and told him that I didn't have any control over who got paired up. It didn't matter. He wanted to make sure we never spent time together, ever again."

I don't know what to say.

Sawyer paces, agitated. "But the worst thing is that I let him hold that over me so long, even up until last week, even though I could probably take him in a fight now if I had to. He just kept that fear and control over me like he has over my parents, and I was just dead inside. All that time I didn't talk to you, Jules, I wanted to. I watched you. I saw your hurt face and I made a choice against you. I didn't do the right thing." He rips his fingers through his hair and I can tell he's upset at himself. "I'm so beyond sorry. And I'm not letting that happen ever again, even if it means I have to walk out on all of them."

He comes over to the bed and grips the side rail. "I can't believe I kept walking away from you instead of them, over and over. Even after you said . . . what you said . . . in the middle of the night. And the other day at school. It killed me, walking away from you at lunch, but . . ." He shakes his head. "It's no excuse. But then you almost died because you wanted to save me. And it finally sank in. I'm the biggest idiot on the planet. And I'm done making bad choices out of fear."

I don't have any words to say. All I can do is watch him pull his heart out and set it in front of me. Watch him tell me he cared about me too, all that time. Watch him say how sorry he is, how much he wants to be the opposite of the kind of guy that his grandfather and father are. Watch him stand there, asking me to give him another chance.

And what am I supposed to do?

Thirty-Seven

But before I can say anything to Sawyer, strangers wearing scrubs come in to announce the removal of my catheter. Awesome. Thanks, guys.

Sawyer makes a hasty retreat, and before you know it, I have my faculties back, and they have me easing out of bed and standing, and then walking a few steps, and every muscle in my entire body screams at me. By the time I get back in bed and have some dinner, I'm done for. Trey comes back to say good night, and he looks tired too.

And as much as I want to continue the conversation with Sawyer, I definitely need to rest. I tell Trey to send Sawyer home. With Mom and Dad coming, there's no reason for him to stay and make the situation worse.

I'm not really sure what to think about what Sawyer

told me, and it's a little hard to process. Maybe because it's so weird to imagine my dad having an affair, and maybe because of the painkillers—everything is taking just a little longer to comprehend these days. But what I have comprehended is that my dad is a big rotten cheater, and my mom just keeps smiling that agonized smile all the time, and now I think I know why. Just who the hell does he think he is?

I don't want to see Dad, that's for sure. Before Sawyer left, I promised him I wouldn't say anything. I don't want to cause more problems between our families, especially now.

When my parents come they wake me up, and I remember all over again.

It's like I'm looking at two strangers. I wonder why my mom stayed with him. I wonder why Mr. Angotti stayed with Sawyer's mom. Maybe it was for our sakes.

I can't actually stand the thought of talking to my father right now, so I just focus on Mom and Rowan. They made it through Valentine's Day without Trey or me, and customers were sympathetic. Today, too, the place was packed with supporters, they said. Seems we got an unexpected sympathy rush out of the ordeal, which is awesome. I guess. Dad hired Aunt Mary's deadbeat son, our cousin Nick, to help out for a while until Trey is feeling up to coming back.

And then there's Rowan. Poor girl. She never gets a break. I think of all the times she's covered for me lately, and she doesn't complain. I try to make her feel awesome. I wish Mom and Dad would go away for a while so I can just talk to her. Find out how her boyfriend is. See how she's doing with everything.

Before they go home, my father, who's been agitating over in the corner all alone, apparently feels like he just has to say something.

"Now that you're feeling a little better," he says, "I want to make sure you only let family in to see you. Nobody else. Okay? And soon you'll be home."

I see my mother flash him an annoyed look, and Rowan's eyes go wide. I think about fighting him on it because it's stupid, but I'm also really tired and ready to sleep. "Who else is there besides family?" I say. "Of course, Dad. I don't want anybody else seeing me like this."

"And then we'll talk about why you would steal the food truck just to go see that hooligan."

I nod. "Fine."

He hesitates, then seems satisfied. I yawn, trying not to split my chest in half. "I'm really tired, guys," I say. "They're talking about sending me home Tuesday. I just want to get there. So I'm going to sleep now, okay? Please don't stay. You need your rest too. I'll sleep like a baby with these meds. I'm fine, okay?"

"Of course," Mom says, and she stands up. I'm a little surprised she doesn't argue, but she seems preoccupied. "Come on, Antonio," she says to Dad. "We'll see you tomorrow, sweetheart." Her effervescent smile is as fake as they come.

In the morning, my task is to take a shower, and I actually see for the first time all the places I have cuts and contusions. My entire outer left thigh and butt cheek are so purple they're almost black from the door smashing in on me. They said it was amazing I didn't break my hip or leg. I've got stitches in my scalp, my chin, and one knee in addition to my stomach from surgery and my knuckle from the Crescent wrench. My black eye is less puffy but still purple with a hint of yellow.

After the shower a volunteer comes in and does my hair and makeup, which almost makes me cry because it's so sweet. It feels good to not look like a total train wreck again. When I think of how I looked in the hospital bed, I know that Sawyer could have run away screaming, but he must really like me if he could stand to look at me that way. I feel a little extra energy today coming from inside—relief, or happiness, I guess.

Once I'm all fresh and clean, my next required task is to take a walk down the hallway. The day is full of challenges, isn't it? Mom stops by before the restaurant opens to bring me one of her homemade bran muffins, which are amazingly delicious. She must have gotten up early to make them, and once again I feel a pain in my chest for her. She sits for a bit, and we just talk about our days, and avoid talking about anything that could get weird.

But ever since Mom told me that I wasn't the first to have to say good-bye to an Angotti, I sense she wants to talk about something more. And for the first time, I actually think that's a good idea. Maybe it's because of what Sawyer told me about my father, so I feel sorry for her now or something. But maybe because I think she knows that I'm really in love with Sawyer, and she's okay with it. It wouldn't be a bad thing to have her on my side.

But that talk doesn't happen.

When she leaves, I have lunch and a nap, just killing time waiting and hoping for visitors after school. Hoping Sawyer comes back.

I wonder idly what happened to my cell phone in this whole ordeal. All I know is that I don't have it. It's probably smashed to bits.

Trey and Rowan come straight from school. "Trey's a freaking hero," Rowan says as they burst into the room. "Everybody loves him. He won't stop talking about his own awesomeness." She flops into the chair next to my bed, and I can hardly contain my delight. I missed my sibs.

No matter how crowded the house can be, it's still fun to be crowded with them.

"I'm not surprised," I say. "He can't ever get enough attention."

"Hi. I'm right here," he says.

"See?" says Rowan. "As if seeing him isn't enough, he has to announce his presence."

"It's disgusting," I say.

Trey's jaw drops. "Fine," he says. "I'll just go hang out with my new BFF, Sawyer Angotti."

"What??" both Rowan and I exclaim.

"We had lunch today in the caf," Trey says.

"I hate you."

"Me too!" Rowan says, and then turns to me. "Wait, why do we hate him?"

"Because we're jealous, dumbhead."

"I'm not jealous. I don't get what you two see in him. He's so . . . broody and dark and Italian."

Trey thinks for a moment and says, "You know, Rowan's right. I could go for a nice Scandinavian."

Rowan agrees with a hearty nod and a secret smile at me. "Blonds are hot."

"You know who's hot?" Trey asks. "Jules Demarco. Amazing what a shower does for that girl."

I sink back into my pillows with a grin, feeling like all is well in the world.

. . .

When they leave to get to the restaurant before the rush, there's a knock at the door, and I know it's him. I can feel it. "Come in," I say.

He pushes open the door and ducks his head in a shy sort of way, which makes my thighs ache, and not because of the bruises. He's holding a bunch of grocery store flowers with the price sticker still on them. He hands them to me awkwardly. "I'm sort of new at this," he says. "The clerk at Jewel said you'd definitely like these."

I squelch a grin. "You asked for help?"

"Sure," he said. "My cousin Kate said I should bring you flowers, which—I know, I know—I didn't need her to tell me that, thank you very much. But I didn't really know, like, what kind."

"I love them," I say, and I can't stop grinning.

And then, from his shirt pocket, he pulls something else out and hands it to me. "Do you still like these?" It's a butterscotch sucker from their candy jar.

I stare at it, take it in my hand. "Yeah," I say. "I do." Okay . . . that almost made me cry. And I know that there's no question that I will give him a chance to do things differently, to stand up for the things he really wants.

I love you, I want to say. But it feels very weird today to say something like that. Now that the danger is over, that is, and it appears we'll both live. At least until our parents find out we're hanging out again, anyway.

I slip my hand in his like it's the most natural thing in the world, and we're talking like we're sixth graders again, sitting under the slide with our suckers and doing that innocent, flirty thing. Every time he says something funny, I laugh even though it hurts, and when he blinks those long lashes and looks at me with that shy grin, my stomach flips. He stays for hours, and I want the night to go on forever.

Sadly, we lose track of time.

Thirty-Eight

When my parents come in and see that Angotti boy holding my hand, and they see the flowers in the crook of my broken arm, I think my father is going to have an aneurysm. Sawyer stands up faster than the speed of light and his chair topples to the floor behind him.

I struggle to sit up.

"Get out," my father says to Sawyer.

Sawyer looks fleetingly to me, then back to my father. "Sir," he says, and I feel a rush of warmth when he doesn't just go. "Can we talk about this?"

"No. Out." My father points to the door. He's being calm. Too calm. "You are not to see my daughter again."

"Mr. Demarco," he says, "Trey and Jules saved our restaurant and our lives, and I'm just—"

"Well, maybe they shouldn't have done that. Did you look at her? She almost *died* because of you!"

"I know, sir, and we are very grate—"

"If you don't get out of this room right now, I will call security."

I can hardly breathe. "Dad, stop!" I say. "Don't be crazy." I cringe after I say it. "He's on his way out anyway, and I'm glad he stopped by, and I hope our families—"

"Pipe dreams!" my father says bitterly. "Our families will never be friendly as long as I'm alive, and you, young lady, had better get that figured out right now. This is over. Do you both hear me?"

Sawyer stands his ground and stays cool, and in that moment, I see him acting on his own desire to be different from the father and grandfather he described yesterday. "I'm sorry you feel that way, sir," he says in a calm voice, yet he commands the room. "I'll leave now out of respect for you. But I'll never leave Jules again because of something personal that happened between other people, so you might want to get used to seeing me around." He gives me a look that makes my heart quake, and then he smiles politely at my mother. "Thank you for what your family did for my family, Mrs. Demarco," he says. And then he slips out.

My father slams the door behind him.

"Antonio!" my mother says, her voice raised, which is exceedingly rare.

He startles and looks at her. "What?"

She shakes her head. "Act your age once, will you? Honestly. We're in a hospital, for Christ's sake." I've never heard her talk like that before. Ever. "Maybe you should go cool off so I don't call security on *you*."

"Why, what did I do?"

"That boy did nothing to you. Leave him alone."

"He is just as his family is," Dad says.

"Oh my dogs," I say, disgusted. "You don't know anything about him! And if he is as his family is, then what does that make me? Am I just as my family is too? A bitter, psychopathic hoarder?"

I don't know if it was the drugs. I think it probably was—I'm pretty good at hiding my thoughts otherwise. At least I didn't call him a cheater. I don't think I did, anyway. Everything got a little fuzzy right around then.

Mom says a hasty good-bye before he can explode, and she drags him out of the room.

By the time I get discharged on Tuesday, my father and I haven't spoken one word to each other, and it looks like we won't be speaking anytime soon. And frankly, I'm really fine with that, because he's acting like the biggest asshole on the planet.

I spend the next week and a half at home and I can't stand it. No cell phone, no communication with Sawyer other than a few e-mails. My father has the home phone forwarded to the restaurant so that I can't receive any calls, and he threatens to watch the phone bill like a hawk to see if I'm calling anybody. I argue and fight, and it only makes things worse—he takes the Internet cable with him to the restaurant whenever I'm home alone. Stupidly, I talked him right out of getting me a replacement cell phone . . . at least until I'm out of this prison and I need one for deliveries again.

In the evenings up in our room Rowan entertains me with a few tidbits about her video chats with Charlie, whose full name is Charles Broderick Banks, and who isn't really homeschooled—he has a tutor and a house in the Hamptons and has never made a pizza in his life. Rowan's going to keep her secret from Mom and Dad for a while longer. Hopefully they'll calm down enough to be reasonable about it, but I have a feeling Rowan won't be going to New York anytime soon. And that's really sad, because Charlie seems like a good guy.

And thank dog for Trey, who is acting as a secret liaison between Sawyer and me. I honestly don't know what I'd do without him right now. On the last Friday of my confinement, Trey comes home with a note for me in a sealed envelope. When I am alone, I open it, and in Sawyer's old familiar handwriting, I read:

I don't want to risk you getting caught,
but I really have to see you as soon
as possible. I'll be by your back door
tonight at 2 a.m. If you can't come
down, I understand.

Miss you so much. Want to hold you . . .

SA

I die a little.
No, a lot.

I take a nap in the late afternoon to prepare, and wait impatiently for everyone to come back up to the apartment and go to bed. I fake sleeping, and finally everyone else is sleeping too. I hope.

At 1:45 a.m. I slip out of bed and put my clothes on. I'm starting to get the hang of dressing with my cast on my arm, but it still takes me a while. I peek out my bedroom window, and there's a car out there with no fresh snow on it. I think it's his car. I ease my way out of the bedroom, careful not to make any noise with doors, grab my coat, and sneak down the stairs, taking each step gingerly. All I know is that if I get caught, I sure as hell can't run very fast right now.

When I open the door, a figure gets out of the car and closes the door softly, and then he lopes over a snowdrift and comes to me. I bite my lip and close the door behind me.

The grin I expect isn't there, only an anxious, hungry look. He reaches for me, slips his fingers gently into my hair, and looks at me like I'm water and he's the desert. Gently he pushes me back a step so I can lean against the wall, and then, without a word, he traces his finger over my lips and I'm mesmerized. He leans in and his lips brush mine, and I'm surprised and thrilled and trying to make sure I'll never forget my first kiss, but soon he's pressing harder and I'm reaching for him and I can't be bothered to think or remember anything at all. I just need to be in it and try to breathe without hurting anything.

I slide my arm inside his jacket and run my hand around his waist, feeling the warmth of his back and holding him like he's the first human I've ever touched before. As we learn how to kiss, I feel him touching me, caressing my hair, being careful around my sore spots, and I never want him to let go.

When our lips part and his tongue finds mine, we are warm and breathing hard into the cold February night. And when we stop for air, I think about all we've been through with the vision and the crash, and nine years of family rivalry. I feel like if I can overcome that, I can overcome anything. And while it won't be fun to fight my dad, I will do what is necessary to allow myself to have this moment again, and soon. I won't let him take this from me. Not now. Not ever again. As long as Sawyer is with me, we can do this.

I look up at him, touch his cheek. "Hey," I say softly, my voice stuck somewhere south of my throat. "That was totally worth a trip down the stairs."

But he doesn't smile. He just looks at me with this fear in his eyes, and my heart drops into my gut. "What's wrong?" I whisper.

He opens his mouth to say something, and then closes it again. "Jules," he says, like it's agony to say it. It's all he can say.

I stand up straight, grip his jacket. "What's going on?" And then I suck in a breath. "Is this a good-bye? Sawyer, say something. Don't scare me."

He shifts his glance away to the side, biting his lip, and then he takes a step back and his hand finds mine. He turns, and with his other hand he points toward Chicago, far off in the distance. "You know that billboard?" he says, his voice a shaky mess.

I grip his hand and fall back against the wall as the question bounces around in my head. Pain sears through me. I can't breathe. "What? What did you say?"

He swallows hard. I can see his Adam's apple bob in

the light of the neon Demarco's sign. "That billboard. Jose Cuervo," he says, his voice dull.

I can't breathe. "Yes."

He turns to look at me. "There's something else on it now."

"Oh, God. No." I grip his arm and murmur what I know has to be true. "And only you can see it."

He nods slowly and, in a whisper, echoes my words. "Only I can see it."

We hold each other, staring off toward a billboard that displays a hint of the future only Sawyer can see. And as we stand there, thinking about the incredible heartache of the visions and the burden of it all, I hear the heavy footfalls of a bitter, pissed-off man coming down the stairwell of my home. I grip Sawyer's arm tighter in front of me, ready to stand my ground or run if I have to, and all I can think about is that this crazy drama in our messed-up lives isn't even close to being over. And before it ends, one or both of us could wind up in a body bag.

Again.

bang

To awesome green-eyed boys everywhere

One

It's been over a week since Sawyer kissed me
and told me *he* was seeing a vision now, and it's all I can
think about. I can't wait to get out of this apartment, which
I am tethered to until Monday—that's when the doc said
my internal injuries will be healed enough so I can go to
school again. My older brother and best friend, Trey, has
been great, of course, slipping notes to Sawyer for me and
delivering replies back to me. But for some reason Sawyer
won't explain his vision on paper. "It's too . . . frightening.
Too gruesome. Too . . . everything," he wrote.

And me? I'm sick about it.

Absolutely sick.

Because it's my fault. I was so relieved when my vision
ended—no more snowplow crashing and exploding into

Angotti's restaurant, no more body bags in the snow, no more Sawyer's dead face. After weeks of that stupid vision taunting me, and after nearly getting killed because of it, I was naive enough to think it was all over and I'd get to live a happy life. Relatively, anyway. Under the current parental circumstances, that is.

But then, once I got home from the hospital, Sawyer sent me that note. He had to see me, he said. That night, 2:00 a.m. And I wanted to see him, too. I eased my broken body down the stairs and we stood in the snowdrift surrounded by breathy clouds and he kissed me, and I kissed him back, and it was the most weirdly amazing feeling. . . .

And then the amazingness of my first kiss was over. He pulled away and looked at me, his gorgeous green eyes filled with fear, and his voice shook. *You know that billboard?*

Those words haunt me.

Obviously I was not only psychotic enough to *have* a vision, but I managed to give the stupid vision disease to the one person I was trying to save.

It's beyond horrifying, sitting here knowing he must be experiencing the worst kind of frustration and pressure to act on the vision and—Did he say "gruesome"?

Let me say it one more time. Sick. That is what I am. And so very sorry.

I rack my brain trying to figure out how this could have happened. Was it because he hugged me on the street the night before? Because he held my hand afterward in the hospital? Maybe there's some kind of physical transference going on. I have no idea.

I have done something horrible to the boy I love, and I don't know how to stop it.

All I know is that I need to get out of this hoardhole before I *lose my mind*.

Oh, wait.

Two

Finally. School.

I get up a little earlier than Trey and my younger sister, Rowan, partly because my eyes fly open at five thirty in anticipation of seeing Sawyer, and partly because it takes me a little longer to get my makeup on with the half-arm cast wrapping around the base of my thumb.

I sneak out of the bedroom I share with Rowan, plastic-wrap my cast, and grab a shower, then try to do something with my hair—the bedhead look was fun for a while but, well, you know.

At six, like clockwork, I hear two doors open almost simultaneously, and then the precarious race to the bathroom as Trey and Rowan dodge my father's hoards of junk that line the hallway. I open the door a crack and Trey bursts in.

"Dang it," Rowan mutters from somewhere behind him.

"Look at you, hot girl," Trey says, keeping his frame in the doorway so Rowan can't sneak past.

"Yeah?" I say, biting my lip. I freaking love my brother. Love him to death.

"You know you're going to get mobbed, you big hero."

Rowan pokes Trey in the back. "Come *on*," she whispers, not wanting to wake our parents. "Either let me in or get your own butt in there."

"Whatever happened to sweet morning Rowan?" I ask Trey like she's not there.

He shrugs.

"Sweet morning Rowan died looking at your face," Rowan mutters. She gives up and goes to the kitchen.

I snicker and do a final inspection. My black eye has healed, my various stitches have been removed, and my hair actually does look kind of awesome. My arm doesn't hurt anymore. My insides are feeling pretty good too, though I'm not allowed to drive quite yet after the surgery. Only my stubborn left thigh remains a beastly mottled yellow-green, having abandoned black, blue, and purple as the weeks passed. It still hurts to press on it, but at least no one can see the bruise under my clothes. And hopefully I'll have this arm cast off in a few weeks.

As I slip out of Trey's way, I stop. "Any chance we can leave a few minutes early?"

"If you get out of here already," Trey says.

"I'm gone." I step into the hallway with a grin and he closes the door in my face.

In the kitchen, Rowan has her head in the sink and the faucet extended. She's washing her hair like it's frisée lettuce.

"Gross," I say. "Getting your hair germs all over Mom's nice clean sink."

"Listen, you wanna know what goes in here?" comes her muffled reply as she turns the water off and replaces the faucet. "The juice of meat. I'm telling you right now this sink is freaking overjoyed to see my awesome hair in it."

Did I mention I adore my sister, too?

I grab breakfast while she wraps her head in a towel and starts doing her makeup in the reflection of the kitchen window. "We're leaving a little early today," I tell her.

"I figured," she says, the cap of her eyeliner pencil in her mouth. Her head towel falls to the floor and her long auburn hair unfurls.

"You going to talk to Charlie today?" I bite a hunk off some cardboard-tasting health bar rip-off and wrinkle my nose. Chew it anyway. I'm too nervous to eat but I know I need something.

"Yep." She starts working a wide-toothed comb

through her hair, and when it sticks, she looks around the kitchen with a scowl until her eyes land on the carafe of olive oil. "Aha," she says, and puts a few drops into the palm of her hand and works it into the knot.

"Resourceful," I say.

Charlie is Rowan's boyfriend. He lives in New York. They met at soccer camp, and now they video chat every day from school during Rowan's study hall. "So everything is good with you two?" I look around, unsettled. Anxious. I got up way too early.

"Yep," she says again, and then gets a hair dryer, plugs it in, and turns it on.

I drum my fingers on a stack of crap on the table and glance at the clock. "Okay, then."

My stomach flips as I think about school. I don't want to be a hero. I don't want to be noticed by anybody. It's embarrassing. And I'm so beyond what happened when Trey and I barreled into that snowplow to keep it from hitting Angotti's Trattoria. Ever since Sawyer told me he's been having a vision now too, I haven't been able to stop worrying about him, and about what horrible thing he's going to be forced to go through.

My chest aches thinking about it. It was the worst time of my life. I felt so alone. "Poor Sawyer," I murmur.

"Yeah, poor guy. He's really dreading seeing you," Trey says sarcastically from behind me.

Rowan catches sight of her bathroom opportunity, yanks the hair dryer cord from the outlet, and runs for it.

I smirk at Trey. He is so awesome that he actually believed me when I told him what was happening to me—after a while, anyway. Like, thirty very important seconds before the crash happened.

But he doesn't know about Sawyer.

Three

We all climb into the pizza delivery car since there's no longer a giant truck o' balls—I totaled the sucker.

Luckily, har har, the insurance money is going to provide us with a new one. Dad's having the old balls fixed and mounted. Apparently they snapped off pretty cleanly in the crash and didn't get banged too hard (dot-com), thanks to the snow.

Trey drives, Rowan's in the back, and I'm riding shotgun, peering out the windshield as a flurry of snow buzzes around the car. I can't concentrate on anything, but I stare at a vocab worksheet for a test I've been told we're having today.

I glance up as we pass the infamous billboard, and

there's Jose Cuervo, thank the dogs. I wonder for the millionth time what Sawyer sees.

As we near school, my right leg starts jiggling and I put my vocab paper away. It's useless to do anything. Out of habit, I reach for my phone, but of course it's not there—it was pulverized in the crash and so far my parents haven't been too keen on replacing it. Trey glances at me as we pull into the parking lot. "You okay?" he asks.

I let out a little huff of breath. "I think so. It's weird."

"Nervous?"

"I—I guess. I've been gone a long time." The truth is, I'm nervous because Sawyer and I never talked about what would happen at school. Like, are we a couple? Or are we being secretive so nobody tells our parents? Or . . . am I not cool enough for his friends?

I hate that I just had that last thought. What the crap happened to turn me into an insecure loser? I was doing so well there for a while, back when I accepted the fact that I was a total psycho. Amazing how freeing that was. I take a few deep breaths and find that old crazy confidence as Trey parks and turns off the car, and then I ease out, making sure I move carefully. I don't want to overdo it or anything, or I'll get stuck back home again.

"Don't worry, Jules," Rowan says, surprising me because I thought she was listening to her music all this time. "We got your back."

Trey takes my backpack since I'm not allowed to lift more than, like, twenty pounds for another week or so, and the backpack, with a few weeks' worth of work in it, officially weighs forty-seven tons. And then we walk into school. The three of us together in a line, like we're the friggin' Avengers, gonna take somebody down.

I stare straight ahead, Trey on my left, Rowan on my right, feeling totally badass despite my nerves. We get a few glances, a few people shrugging in our direction or outright pointing at us. At me. We even get a smattering of applause from some of Rowan's ninth-grade friends at their lockers, and everybody's saying hi to Trey and me like it's opposite day here in Chicagoland. I ease my way up the half-dozen steps to the sophomore hallway, not able to take stairs at full stride quite yet, using the handrail to help. And then we're nearing my locker and I have to work hard not to strain to look for Sawyer. I want *him* to look for *me*. That's how this is going to go. I just decided.

"That's good, you guys," I say, and I hate that I'm a little winded. I think that's the longest distance I've gone in one stretch in a while. "I got this."

Trey sets my overladen backpack inside my locker and gives me a quick grin as he leaves. "See you at lunch."

Rowan hangs around for a second like she doesn't want to leave. "You sure you're good?"

I nod. "Sure. Say hey to Charlie for me and I'll see you

after at the balls. Dot-com." I pause, realizing what I just said, and then we both make faces. "At the car, I mean."

"Okay. See ya." She heads back toward her hallway.

I turn to my locker to pull out a few books as the guy whose locker is next to mine says, "Hey, Jules. Welcome back."

We've barely spoken before. This is weird.

"Thanks," I say, suddenly shy. I take my coat off and go to hang it up, when I hear the voice that makes my thighs quake.

"Catch you later, guys. Hey, Jules."

Before I can turn around, he's turning me around, and then his gentle arms are hugging me, lifting my feet off the ground. Holding me. Right here in public. I let my coat fall from my fingers and I wrap my arms—cast and all—around his neck like it's the most natural thing for me to do in the middle of a crowded high school hallway.

"I missed you so much," he whispers into my hair, and the world goes quiet around us. My body pulses with energy and I can feel his warmth seeping into me.

I close my eyes and breathe, wishing everybody would just disappear.

He sets me back down and I look at his face for the first time in what seems like forever. He smooths my static hair and keeps a hand on my shoulder. The corner of his mouth turns up on one side, just the way I like it. But his eyes are tired.

"I missed you too," I say in a quiet voice, suddenly hyperaware of people staring at us, my former friend Roxie and her BFF Sarah among them. Which makes me feel really awkward, so I try to pretend they're not there.

He observes the cast on my arm and smooths a thumb under the eye that used to be black. "Nice," he says. He glances over one shoulder, then the other, gets a goofy smile on his face, and moistens his lips. "I really want to kiss you," he says quietly near my ear. But I think we're being cautious, or else he spotted a teacher, because instead of kissing me he just runs his thumb across my lips and looks at me so longingly it hurts.

"Dang," I say, a little breathless. "Where's a stupid playground when you need one? This, uh, environment feels . . . awkward."

"I wanna be your playground," he says in my ear, and I feel the heat rushing to my face. I can see he's just messing around, flirting, but he stays close, like he can't stand to have much space between us, and I like him there.

"Rowr." I grin, but I'm preoccupied, searching his eyes, and the grin falls away. As he watches me watch him, his face changes, like he can read the question in my mind.

"About that," he says, as if we started the conversation already. "I desperately, *desperately* need to see you alone." And even though his eyes are hungry, this is different.

"I know." I've been thinking about this already. "Mr. Polselli is on parking-lot duty during lunch on Mondays. He'll let me eat in his room. I'll claim I need your help because of the cast."

"You're brilliant," he says with a breath that trickles down my neck. "I'm sorry I haven't told you—I'll explain everything, it's just—"

I press a finger to his lips and watch his eyelids droop halfway in response. "I get it," I tell him, and reluctantly pull my finger away when the bell rings.

His gaze lingers and burns. "See you at lunch," he says. "I'll bring two trays and meet you there."

When he disappears in the crowd, I turn back toward my open locker and stare into it, dazed. *Holy big sizzle, Demarco.* Is it hot in here or is it just my gorgeous boyfriend? At this rate, we'll have, like, nine babies by the end of our senior year.

Four

Before lunch I dodge strangers and classmates trying to talk to me, which is absolutely the weirdest experience of my school life, and find Trey to let him know I'm going to have a private lunch with Sawyer, so I'll see him in art class.

He smirks. "Tell the two-timing lunch whore I said hey."

"I will kiss him for you," I say, and then I add, "I hope, anyway." But Trey has moved on with the hallway traffic.

I slip into Mr. Polselli's empty room, sit at a desk, and wait, forcing myself to work on a math assignment. When the door opens, I look up and my smile freezes on my face. Not only is it Sawyer with two lunch trays, but Roxie and BFF Sarah are with him, apparently there to open the door.

Sawyer and Roxie are laughing at BFF Sarah, who rants about something, and all I can think about is how I want them gone.

"Oh. Hi, Julia," Roxie says to me, like she didn't expect to see me. "Thanks for saving our favorite restaurant."

I stare at her, wondering if she's really that rude that she values the restaurant over the human lives—Sawyer's life—or if she's just stupid. But new Jules isn't going to smile and walk away. "Wow. Did you really just say that?" I say. I glance at Sawyer, who looks almost as offended as I feel.

Roxie looks confused. "Yeah, did you not just hear me?"

BFF Sarah's lack of greeting brings frostiness to the air. She's probably still peeved about the V-Day decorations I knocked out of her hands.

"Okay, well, thanks for the help," Sawyer says pointedly to them. He sets a tray on my desk and then sits down at the one next to me. "Can you close the door on the way out?"

Roxie's hands go to her hips, and her lips part as if to protest, but Sawyer ignores them both. He reaches out and strokes my shoulder. "How's it going so far? You taking it easy?"

BFF Sarah rolls her eyes, mutters, "Whatever," and walks out the door, then stands in the hallway waiting for Roxie.

"It's good," I say. My mouth has gone completely dry from the tension.

Finally Roxie turns and leaves, letting the door close hard behind her.

I press my lips together and form a smile. "That went well."

"I don't want to talk about them," Sawyer says. He leans toward me and slides a warm hand along my cheek, sinking his fingers into my hair and pulling me close. I close my eyes and our mouths meet. Blood pounds through his fingers and lips, echoing in my ears. My head spins with all kinds of surprising thoughts as my fingers explore his shoulders through his shirt. Thoughts like how I saw his bare, bony torso once when the boys played shirts and skins in fifth grade, and now, even though he's still lean, his sinewy arms and back are roped with muscle, and I really want to see that chest once more.

When I come to my senses and realize the trouble we'll be in if Mr. Polselli walks in right now, I reluctantly pull back, a little breathless.

Sawyer opens his eyes. "I've been waiting a long time for that." He pulls his fingers from my hair and smooths it back into place.

"Tell me about it," I say, and then I get a little shy, because here we are, in school, having hardly spoken to each other for years, and now we're making out. In a way everything with Sawyer is so new and raw, but in another way, it feels like the most natural progression. We were so close before, and I still feel like I *know* him, you know?

"So . . . ," I say, still tasting him on my lips. "Are we, like, going public with this? And if so, is that a good idea?"

He grins. "I've been thinking about that, and you know, Jules, I don't want to hide it. But it's up to you. If you feel like we need to because of your parents, I totally understand. Obviously."

"What about your parents and your grandfather?"

Sawyer's face sets. "Like I said in the hospital, I'm done playing along with their stupid game."

"But—" Impulsively I reach out and brush my fingers across his cheekbone, imagining his grandfather beating him, and let my hand rest on his arm.

"He can't hurt me anymore," he says in a quiet voice, and I feel his biceps twitch through his sleeve. "Besides, I've got other shit to worry about."

"Aaand there's that," I murmur, and turn to our lunch trays. I grab a few carrot sticks and blush when I bite down and they explode like firecrackers in the quiet room. "Ready to tell me?"

Sawyer's eyes close and he lets out a resigned breath. He shakes his head the slightest bit, and then he opens his eyes and stares at the whiteboard in front of us. "I'm not exactly sure how to explain this," he says. "I mean, I'm not sure what happened with you or how you saw your . . . your clues, or whatever. . . ." He looks at me for help, and I realize I've never actually had a chance to describe to him what happened to me—I'd only told him that I saw a vision of a truck hitting his restaurant and exploding.

"The first time was at the movies," I say. "Before the previews, when they have that 'Turn off your cell phones' ad. I saw a few seconds of the snowplow careening over the curb, smashing into your restaurant, and exploding. There was never any sound, just the picture. And then the Jose Cuervo billboard—it had a still shot of the truck explosion." I hesitate as I relive it, having tried so hard to block it out. "Then I saw it on TV—and there was a new part added. Nine body bags in the snow. One of them was open, showing a face."

I drop my head into my hand, not wanting to say the next part.

"A face?" he asks.

I nod and whisper, "Your face."

He is quiet for a long minute. Then he stands up and shoves his desk right up to mine, moving our uneaten food to a different desk. He sits back down and we drape our arms around each other as I tell him the rest of it. I tell him about the gripping fear when I found out Angotti's was closed that one Saturday night. All the times I drove past his restaurant to check if it was still there. The way

I studied the scenes and tried to figure things out by the snow levels on the street. The vision's growing frequency, intensity, and urgency until almost every place I looked was covered in the scene being played out. And my weird phone calls and visits to him, knowing there was no way he'd believe me, but having to do something about it.

When I finish, he nods slowly. And then he says, "Mine has sound. But not voices or street sounds or background noises. Eleven sounds, to be exact. All the same." He makes a gun with his finger and thumb and points it at Mr. Polselli's papier-mâché bust of Ivan Pavlov. "Bang."

Five

My hand goes to my mouth. "A shooting?" I whisper.

His mouth twitches. "A school shooting."

"Oh my God." I look around the room as the shock of it hits home. "What, here? Our school?"

His Adam's apple bobs and his eyes turn desperate. "I don't know, Jules. I can't tell where it is."

"Tell me everything you can think of."

"At first it was so quick I missed it. I remember thinking, 'Wait, what just happened?' and then brushing it off as me being tired. But then I started catching a glimpse of something out of the corner of my eye in the restaurant window, like there was a person standing there on the other side with his arms raised straight out, but whenever I'd look full on, he was gone."

I rest my head against his shoulder and stay quiet, not wanting to interrupt.

"The next thing was the billboard. A still picture of a figure, arms raised and pointing straight ahead, firing a gun—muzzle flash and everything."

I frown. "Muzzle flash?"

"When you pull the trigger of a gun, it ignites gunpowder, which explodes, pushing the bullet out. There's a little flash of fire that comes out the barrel, but you can't usually see it."

"Why not?"

He shrugs and thinks about that for a minute. "Partly because it happens really fast. But also because there's usually too much natural light, I guess."

"Ah. So this vision of yours—it happens at night?"

He frowns. "Huh," he says, and then he looks at me. "Maybe. You're good at this."

I give a sordid laugh. "Forced on-the-job training makes you an expert in a hurry. You'll learn, kid. Stick with me."

"No worries there," he says, looking slightly relieved.

"So you're only seeing stills? And you hear gunfire from them?"

"No, no sound from the stills. We have TVs in the restaurant bar, and not long after the billboard incident, when I was busing a table, I glanced at it and saw the same figure—person with a gun, arms outstretched, and he was stepping backward and swinging the gun wide, like he was feeling threatened. I stopped working and stared at it, and then the gunshots exploded in my head and I dropped my tray."

I wince. "Was it dark?"

He hesitates. "Well, I could see the guy. Not his face—he was turned away. And I could see, um, bodies. But it wasn't sunny or bright in there or anything."

I knit my brows, thinking. "How do you know this guy is at a school?"

"I don't know—it just looked like a school. It was all really fast—it felt . . . schoolish."

"Yeah, okay," I say, trying not to sound impatient. I remember how many hundreds of times I had to see mine before I caught everything. "You'll get more information eventually."

Just then somebody opens the door, sees us, and says, "Oops!" really loudly. I can hear people swarming the hallways. The dude closes the door again, and I glance at the clock. Four minutes until lunch is over.

Sawyer follows my gaze. "That went way too fast," he says, getting up. He picks up the food trays and stacks one on top of the other like the server pro that he is, balancing them with one hand. "I guess I should get these back to the kitchen."

I stand up too, grabbing a roll from the top tray and pulling a hunk off. "You should try to eat something," I say. "You're going to need the energy."

He gives me a weary smile. "Does that mean it only gets worse from here?"

I nod, taking a bite of the roll.

"And it doesn't end until . . . ?"

I swallow. "Until it's over."

We walk to the door and he pauses. "Wait a sec." With his free hand he reaches into his pocket. "I hope this isn't weird," he says, "and you can say no and I won't be offended or anything, but I can't stand not being able to talk to you, especially with . . . *this* thing going on." He pulls out a cell phone and hands it to me. "It's just one of those cheap prepaid ones. No frills. Phone only."

I take it, and it feels like I just got out of jail. "You are brilliant," I say, turning it over in my hand, and then I look up at him and my heart swishes. "Thank you."

"Don't get caught."

"I won't." I shove the phone into my pocket and reach up, thumbing the corner of his mouth until he gives me the smile I love. "I'll call you tonight." It's amazing how nice it feels to be able to say that.

He hesitates, his hand on the doorknob. "Jules?"

I look at him.

"In the vision, I don't see any faces I know."

"Oh." I'm not sure what he's trying to say. "Okay, well, that's good, right?"

But that's not what he means. He hesitates, and then he squeezes his eyes shut like he's making the hardest decision of his life and says, "I was kind of wondering what happens if I don't want to do this."

Six

The bell rings before I can answer, and besides, the question is too much to absorb in ten seconds, so we say a hasty good-bye. All afternoon I think about what he said. And I wonder. If he doesn't know or care about any of the people in the vision, does he have to do something? Is he legally obligated to do something? What about, like, morally?

My guess is that my vision probably would have gone away whether I saved people or not, but I didn't know that back then. Does that change anything? I go back in time in my mind. If I knew that the vision would stop pounding me at every turn if I only waited long enough, would I have done what I did?

That one's not hard. Sure I would have, because of

Sawyer's dead face in the body bag. But then I wonder how I would have looked at it had it been a stranger's face. If every part of the vision stayed the same except Sawyer wasn't going to be hurt or killed, would I have done what I did?

Not quite as simple, but the answer is still yes, because it was Sawyer's family business, and chances were good that some family members filled the other body bags. And as much as we both are disgusted by our parents' behavior—and I'm not talking just my dad's affair with Sawyer's mom, but also the ridiculous rivalry over a stupid sauce recipe—that doesn't mean we want them to die, and I wouldn't want Sawyer to go through that pain.

But what if I knew back then what I know now, and it *wasn't* Angotti's restaurant but some other restaurant somewhere else? If I knew that the visions would get worse and become insane, but I knew that it would end as soon as the crash was over, would I still risk my life to save those people?

I don't think I know the answer.

In the evening, while everybody's still down in the restaurant and I'm stuck doing mountains of worksheets and make-up quizzes that didn't come home with one of the sibs, my mind wanders to it again. I pull out the cell phone, wondering if Sawyer is working, wondering if he's slammed or if he maybe has time to talk.

I start pressing the numbers I know by heart but hardly ever get to use thanks to my father, and the phone's address book recognizes them and brings up Sawyer's name with a <3 next to it. I smile and look at it for a minute, and then I press the call button. It rings a few times, and I cringe. He's probably busy.

"Hey," comes his breathless voice.

Why is it that every time I talk to him I feel like my brain won't work? It takes me a full second to form the word "Hi" in response. "Are you slammed?"

"Nope," he says. "I just got back to the car. Delivered my last pizza for the night. How's your new phone?"

"Love it," I say. Love *you*. "Everybody else is still downstairs, but if I hang up quickly, you'll know why."

"I will always assume a quick click means the proprietors are coming, and not that you're mad or something," he teases.

"Oh, I'll let you know if I'm mad."

There's a smile in his voice. "I do not doubt that. As long as every now and then you still drag me out of bed in the middle of the night to tell me you're sorry I'm going to die, and tell me that you . . ."

He doesn't say it.

I don't know what to say.

When you tell a guy you love him before you're in a relationship with him, does it mean love love? Or just love? And what words do you use *after* you start the relationship? You can't say "I love you" after a first kiss, I don't care who it's with. That screams of one of those crash-and-burn relationships half the school is in. I think I have to go back to saying "like." For a while, at least.

"Anyway," he says in the awkward pause.

"Anyway," I agree. "So, um, I thought about your question."

"Me too."

"I guess all I can say is that I don't think you have to risk your life for strangers." And I stop there, even though there's so much more I have to say. And want to say.

He's quiet for a long moment. "What do you think will happen if I don't try to save them?"

"The vision will get stronger and more frequent, and you'll see it everywhere. You might not be able to drive—I was really struggling there at the end."

"I'm so sorry—"

"Don't. It's really okay. I never expected you to believe me." I pause, listening for footsteps on the stairs, but all is quiet. "The main thing you need to get you through it is to remember it'll end eventually."

"How do you know that for sure—that it'll end?"

His question stops me. "Um . . . because it ended for me?" I say weakly.

"Yeah, but you did what it wanted you to do," he says.

"Will my vision still end if I don't do what it wants?"

"I—I guess I don't actually know." I think about it, wondering if I'd still be tormented by the vision today if I hadn't stopped the crash. If I'd have to look at Sawyer's dead face in the body bag until the end of time. And for whatever reason, I think about my dad, and his own apparently tormented life. But Sawyer interrupts my thoughts.

"It's getting worse," he says. "As I'm driving around doing deliveries, it's showing up on street signs."

I frown. "Any new scenes?"

"Not so far. I'm going to try to watch some TV tonight to see if the vision shows up there. Try the rewind/slow motion thing like you said."

I feel helpless. I sigh heavily and say, "I'm just so sorry about this."

"Yeah, well, I blame you, of course."

I afford a small smile, but I can't help it. I feel responsible. This is happening because of me, and it's, like, bodies and bodies—eleven gunshots? Holy shit. "So . . . you aren't going to try to stop the shooting, then?" The words come out strained, because I've already made my decision on what has to happen if he decides not to save anyone. I'm going to have to save them myself.

He's quiet. "Jules," he says finally, sounding a little hurt. "Do you really think I could do that? I volunteer at the freaking Humane Society, you know. How could

I possibly not try to save eleven people from some crazy gunman?"

My heart floods with relief. "I didn't think you would—or could. I just didn't want you to think I'd blame you for hoping to try and make it go away."

"Well," he says, "whatever controls this vision thing sure knows how to pick the right people to get the job done."

I hear a door shut at the bottom of the stairs and my heart races. "Gotta go," I say in a hushed whisper. "But I'm with you on this."

"Thank dog for that," he says, and we hang up.

Eleven fucking gunshots. And his vision is getting worse. I feel like I'm going to puke. All I know is that we gotta get moving on this thing. Now.

Seven

Mr. Polselli is back in his room at lunch, so Sawyer and I eat in the caf the rest of the week with Trey, but we don't talk about the visions. Too many people around. There are a few fleeting moments at my locker and a few short phone conversations, but as the week progresses I get more and more stressed out by the fact that I barely get a chance to see Sawyer, much less talk about what he's going through.

Add to that, I'm feeling guilty about still not going back to work. Plus I'm broke. And the sooner I get working, the sooner I'll be able to do deliveries again now that I'm allowed to drive, which means I'll be ungrounded and I'll get a real cell phone that can do more than just make phone calls, and maybe Sawyer and I can arrange a few clandestine meetings. Not to mention Rowan's been working her face off covering for me. So I ease back into the work scene.

"It's just like old times," Trey says as we three head downstairs to the restaurant together Friday after school. Rowan is in a good mood too—she only has to get us through the dinner rush and make sure I'm cool with everything before she gets the night off to do who knows what.

And it's pretty easy rolling back into it. My body gets tired a little sooner than it used to, and I'm not quite as fast as I'd like to be, but the cast doesn't really get in the way too much and it's actually getting me some pretty nice pity tips.

Trey is out most of the night with deliveries while Mom and I cover the tables and Aunt Mary works front of house. Dad's having one of his depression days and hasn't shown his face, which is actually kind of nice since we really aren't talking right now.

In a lull, Mom joins me in prep and we roll silverware.

"Keeping up all right?" she asks.

"Yep," I say.

"Good."

It's awkward between us, too. Ever since before the crash, I've thought Mom wanted to sort of confide in me—she did already, a little, when she told me she knew it wasn't easy saying good-bye to an Angotti, and she wasn't talking about herself. But she doesn't know I know about Dad's affair.

And the weird thing is, I don't know what to do. Like now, we could talk if she wants to, I guess. "How's everything going for you?" I ask. And I realize I never ask her this.

She tilts her head and smiles, seemingly pleased that I have put aside my selfish ways for the first time ever. "Not bad," she says. "Old Mr. Moretti pinched my butt again. I think he's going senile."

"Maybe you're just a hottie," I say, grinning. "He never does that to me."

"He'd better not or he won't know what hit him. I don't want you girls waiting on him." She pauses and lightens up again. "If he weren't senile I'd kick him out. But I haven't been pinched in public since the nineties on the L." She says it wistfully.

"*Mom*," I say. I don't want to know about her glory days or whatever. Then I think about it. "You know, that's really kind of sad. You should get pinched at least once a week."

"You'd think," she mutters, and then she laughs and tosses her hair a little.

I set down a roll of silverware and glance at her. "How's Dad these days?" I ask, tentative. "Any chance he's ready to unground me yet?"

She laughs again.

"I'm seriously asking you."

She pulls in a breath and sighs, and then she shakes her head a little, grabbing a new package of napkins and slicing the wrapper open with a little retractable utility blade she keeps in her apron. "Julia," she says, turning to me, "it's complicated. And no, I don't see you getting ungrounded anytime soon."

I scowl and glance at my lingering guests. "What's so complicated? You guys are—" I clamp my mouth shut, knowing pointing fingers isn't going to get me anywhere, especially when I think Mom might be on my side. "Sorry. It's just frustrating. I don't feel like I'm doing anything wrong."

"Whoa. Seriously? Leaving work, stealing the meatball truck and wrecking it, not to mention yourself, seeing a guy you are forbidden to see, and sneaking around with him at two in the morning?"

I try to breathe. "I wouldn't have to sneak if you guys weren't so—" *Ugh.* I catch myself again. "Look," I say as a customer catches my eye, "I just think the Angotti-Demarco rivalry is so . . . Middle Ages. Or whatever. Shakespearean. Overdramatic. It's ridiculous that Dad can't get over it."

"It would have been a lot of money," Mom says.

"Only if Dad had the drive to actually manufacture

and sell the stinking sauce, like Fortuno did." I pause. "Or do you mean the money you would have gotten from suing the Angottis over it?" I set down my last roll of silverware hard. "Customer," I say as I walk off, so she doesn't think I'm stomping away mad.

"Who knows? Ask your father," she mutters under her breath. I don't think she expected me to hear that.

Eight

The weekend is endless. I'm working when Sawyer's off, he's working or volunteering when I'm off, and we don't even manage to connect for a quick phone call. I hate this. Hate not knowing what's going on, hate that hours and days are ticking away and we're not doing anything. I'm worried as hell.

The phone vibrating in my hand wakes me at two in the morning. It takes me a second to pull out of my dream and figure out what's happening. I sit up on one elbow and answer it.

"Hey, are you okay?" I whisper, my voice full of sleep and air.

He doesn't answer for a second, and I think maybe it's an accidental rolled-over-on-his-phone-in-the-night call.

But then he says in a quiet voice, "Jules, I'm—I'm just—I'm freaking out a little."

I glance at Rowan and she hasn't even moved. "What's happening?" I turn my face away from the door, as if that'll keep my whispers from slipping under it.

"It's, well, I had a chance to watch the vision on TV a few times. Like fifty, I mean, and it's—" I can hear the whir of anxiety in his voice notching up. He takes a breath. "It's really horrible. It almost made me puke. I swear."

I press my lids shut with my fingertips. "Oh, God," I say. There are no other words. "Are you taking notes? Writing it all down?"

"Yeah. Some."

I think I hear a creak of the hallway floor, but it's nothing. I pull the blankets over my head. "What can I do? How can I help you?"

I hear the tightness in his throat as he swallows hard, hear the air rush from his nostrils into the phone, a tiny blast of emotion. And then it comes again, and he doesn't speak, and I know he's trying to hold it together.

"Shit, I remember this," I say. My gut twists. "I know how tough it is." I cringe, thinking I sound like a condescending jerk when what I really mean to say is, *It's okay to cry with me.*

It turns out he doesn't need my permission. After a few minutes of him in not-quite-silent sobs and me staring into the caverns of my blankets, wishing I could be with him, remembering and remembering, he blows out a breath and says, "I don't think I can do this alone."

"You're not alone, Sawyer."

His silence tells me he feels otherwise, and suddenly I'm furious. Not at him. At my parents, and at his parents. And at the ridiculousness of this. I can't see or help my friend, my boyfriend, because of something gross my father did.

"This is nuts," I mutter, throwing my blankets off and sitting up on the side of the bed. I can hardly contain the surprise tsunami of anger that floods me. "Where are you?"

"In my room."

"Do you want me to come over?" I cringe again, imagining the trouble I could get into, but the anger is bigger than that fear, and the boy across town is more important than the man in the next room.

"No. I mean yes, of course, obviously. But no. I'm okay now, and we don't need any more trouble with the proprietors. I'm just glad . . ." He trails off for a moment, and his voice goes soft. "I'm just glad you answered. And that you're there."

I can hardly stand it. "I'm here. We'll figure out something. I can't take this either. I need more than a few minutes at my locker with you." I don't think I would have said that if it weren't for the cover of darkness.

"Oh, God, Jules," he says, and it sounds like he's about to break down again. "I miss you like you have no idea. I know I sound like a basket case, and I'm sorry for—jeez, for slobbering all over—but this has been the longest week, and everything's so . . . fucked up. . . ."

"Yeah."

"I need to tell you about it. There's stuff I haven't told you."

I nod. "I want to hear it all. I want to help you. I will be there, helping you. Okay? I mean, do you know when it's going to happen? Probably not . . ."

"No idea."

I close my eyes, feeling defeat. "We'll get it. I just need to figure out how to get out of here. I'm suffocating."

"We both are."

We're quiet for a minute.

"Stay on the phone with me," he says. "Please?"

"I will." I climb back into bed and pull the blankets over me, keeping the phone to my ear. "I've never slept with a boy before," I say.

He laughs a little and it makes me feel better for him. We whisper a little bit, and soon we're quiet. My eyelids droop.

In an instant, it's morning.

Nine

"What happened to your face?" Rowan asks as we stand in the bathroom together, putting finishing touches on our makeup.

I glare. "Nothing." The imprint of the cell phone remains on my cheek, though it's not nearly as pronounced as when I first got up.

She narrows her eyes at me, suspicious. "You know," she says, "I don't mind picking up shifts for you in case you're, like, feeling a little *overtired*. Or if you need to go to the *library* for a *project* or something. I like money."

I pause and look at her in the mirror.

"Or maybe you want to, I don't know, *volunteer* somewhere on Saturday mornings."

I set my can of hair spray down. "Hmm."

"You need to get a little creative is all I'm saying. Don't you want to join a club after school? Try out for a sport?" She blinks her lashes rapidly and smiles.

I snort. "Yeah," I say, waving my cast. "Sports."

"Well, I'm just trying to help." She puts away her makeup and glances at one of the seventeen clocks—the top one, which actually works—that the hoarder decided would look great piled on the towel rack above the toilet. "Let's go."

I nod. "Thanks."

As we grab our coats and backpacks, I ask her, "What do you do with all your money, anyway?"

"Save it."

"For what?"

"My trip to New York. Spring break. I'm going to see Charlie." She patters down the stairs.

My jaw drops, and I follow her. "You're what?"

She shrugs. "I already have my plane ticket."

"You—you—" I sputter. We climb into the running car, where Trey is waiting, tapping the steering wheel with an annoyed look on his face. "Mom and Dad are letting you go? I can't believe it."

"Letting her go where?" Trey asks. He takes off quickly down the alley and turns onto the street.

Rowan is quiet from the backseat. I turn and look at her, and she's pressing her lips together.

"Oh my dog," I say. "You haven't told them?"

"Told them what?" Trey asks.

"Well," Rowan says, "since I have you both here, I'm going to need some help covering my shifts. You both owe me plenty."

"What's going on?" Trey says in an outdoor voice.

I stare at Rowan. "Do you have any scope of realization of what you are about to unleash upon us all? They'll call the freaking cops! Report you as a missing person!"

Trey pulls the car over on the side of the road. "What. Is. Happening!" he shouts, eyes ablaze.

I turn my attention to Trey. "Rowan has a boyfriend in New York and she's going to see him over spring break."

Trey whirls around, eyes bulging. "What?"

Rowan's gaze settles somewhere to the left of and below Trey's jaw. She starts biting her lip. "I'm going," she says weakly.

"You're fifteen!" he says. "Mom is going to blow a freaking gasket. Who is this loser?"

Rowan gets her courage back. "He's not a loser! He's—his name is Charlie."

"Charles something something Banks," I interject.

"The third," Rowan adds, which is news to me. "His parents invited me. They paid for my ticket, but I already told them I'll pay them back when I get there." She adjusts her collar. "We met at soccer camp."

"He has a live-in tutor," I offer.

"Not live-in," Rowan says.

"She's met his parents."

Trey blinks. And then he shakes his head. "You little creep," he mutters, checking his mirrors and pulling back onto the road. "Why can't I ever find a Charles something something the third?"

I face forward. "So you're okay with this?" I ask him.

He gives a bitter laugh. "Fuck," he says. "Why the hell not." He punches the gas a little harder than usual and pulls into the school parking lot. "Why the hell not," he says again. He parks a few rows from Sawyer's car and looks over his shoulder at Rowan as he turns off the car and pulls out the keys. "You're going to be the one who actually survives this family, aren't you. The only one."

Rowan just stares at him, and then he's out and slamming the door, shoulders curved and head bowed to the wind.

We get out. "What was that all about?" she asks as Sawyer gets out of his car, sees me, and heads toward us.

I shrug, but I think I know, because I used to feel it too. Trey's jealous. "I think maybe he wishes he had something you have," I say. But I don't take the time to explain, because Sawyer is standing on my shadow and his ropy lashes are about to lasso me in.

Gag. That was bad.

Ten

Rowan melts into the sea of students and Sawyer is pulling me to the side of the school building. "When," he says.

"What?"

"When can I see you? I need to see you. After school? Say yes. Say yes. Say yes."

"I—" I begin, and the rest of the automatic sentence, *have to work*, drops away. His cheeks are flushed with the cold. "Okay," I say.

"Okay?" He sounds shocked.

"Yes," I say, grabbing some of Rowan's boldness before it dissipates. "I—I'll join a group. Volunteer."

"What?"

"Nothing. Alibi. Just thinking out loud. Don't you have to work?"

"I switched with Kate."

Kate. The cousin in college. Kate with the funky blond hair whose life I saved. "Right. Excellent. Rowan will cover for me. Okay." I take a breath and decide specifically not to think about what my father will do to me when I don't come home. Trey will help. As we walk into school together I start reading posted signs on the walls for the first time in my high school career. "Pep Club? No, no way. Too much Roxie and BFF Sarah. Psych Club . . . a-ha-ha-ha, no comment." I keep looking. And then I turn to see Sawyer watching me, that little smile on his lips. "Do you play chess?" I ask.

"Um, why? Is this a trick question to determine if I'm too awesome for you?"

"No no no, I'm just looking for a club to join so I have an excuse to see you. I could tell my parents I'm in a chess club, but then I might have to, you know, eventually, um, prove that I know how to play."

He's still smiling at me. My brain turns to fuzz.

"Yes," he says. "I play chess." We stop at my locker and he says, "In fact, I was thinking about starting an exclusive chess club for offspring of pizza proprietors."

I grin. "Oh my dogs, I believe I qualify."

"We'll have a lot of meetings," he warns.

"I'll be there—as often as I can." I ignore the nervous quake in my gut that taunts, *Your parents will find out.*

His face is close to mine. "Tonight's launch meeting is from three to five thirty. I'll have you back at the restaurant by then. Will that work okay?"

I nod. Whisper, "We'll get this vision thing figured out, Sawyer. I promise."

The bell rings. Sawyer's smile turns reluctant and he caresses my neck, one slick motion that makes my hip sockets burst into flames.

Trey promises to tell Mom that I joined a chess club (dotcom, he says wickedly, so I have to kick him), and that I'll be home by five thirty. And that I would have called her myself but I still don't have a cell phone. Not one she knows of, anyway.

I load up my backpack more slowly than usual, letting the halls clear around me. Sawyer saunters up to me and we walk down the hallway together. Ever so casually he takes my hand, entwining his fingers with mine. And then my eyes get all misty. Stupid, I know, but you know what? I remember thinking there would never be a time when I'd hold a boy's hand in the hallway at school, much less the love of my life's. It's all a little emotional there for a second, because here I am, and it feels even better than it looks. I squeeze his hand

and he squeezes back and looks sidelong at me, and I am so in love.

He opens the car door for me, which feels so incredibly awkward that I hurriedly ask him not to do that again, unless I'm, like, carrying a six-foot sheet cake or something. And then we set out for somewhere, I'm not sure where. He takes my hand again and puts it on the stick shift with his. When he pushes in the clutch I change gears for him, and we're flying out of town, away from Melrose Park, away from people who frown at us for stupid reasons. After a few minutes Sawyer pulls into a community college parking lot and parks by the gymnasium. Without a word we get out and he pulls me through the snow to the side of the building. There are a few cubbyholes in the wall and I can hear fans running. I catch a whiff of chlorine and feel a blast of humid air on my cheeks.

Sawyer and I duck inside one of the indents and suddenly it's warm. "Pool fan," he says, facing me. "My brothers told me about this trick."

I stare at him. We are alone.

At last, at last.

I lunge for his coat, unbuttoning it, and I slide my hands to his neck, pull his head toward mine, trying not to scrape him with my clunky cast. His hands suspend in the air for a second, and then he buries them in my hair and we're kissing and panting and touching each other, starving and lusty and steamy hot, and soon he's wrenching my coat off and pulling off his own, and he presses against me, his chest against my chest, our feet finding spaces every other, and his thighs squeezing mine. And suddenly I realize that what's pressing against me is not all thigh, and I am secretly amazed and a little shocked by it being there, doing that. He moans and drags his lips to my neck, and my hands flounder at his hips and slide over them into his back pockets, like my fingers are someone else's expert sexy fingers and I'm the lucky one who gets to feel through them, because dog knows I don't know what I'm doing, I'm just going with it, intoxicated by his fervor and the overwhelming electric, psychedelic aching in my loins.

"Oh my God," he whispers after a few minutes, breathing hard, and he lifts heavy hands one by one and slaps them against the wall behind me, pushing away, forcing space between us. He leans forward, arching his back, and rests his forehead on my shoulder, panting. "Shit. You are dangerous."

I pet the back of his head, my lips tingling. "Are you okay?"

He lifts his head and looks at me, and it's a look I don't recognize. Desire and heat and I don't know what else. "My God," he says again, shaking his head a little. "What the heck was I thinking all those years?" He mops his face with a hand and looks at the coats on the cement pad at our feet. "I mean, it's—" He looks around, distracted, like he forgot where we are. "It's not just the *this* stuff, but the *this* is . . . probably . . ." He nods to himself. "Yeah. It's going to kill me. For sure."

I am intrigued by his random candidness, and I think how funny it is that I can make ball jokes until I'm blue in the face (dot-com) but I'm sooo inexperienced in the actual *this* of things, that I'm not quite sure what should or should not be happening on what I'm starting to think of as our first date. Which is also *my* first date ever. I'm pretty sure coats on the ground is far enough, though.

I reach up and kiss him again, lightly this time, and then turn my head and rest it on his shoulder, holding him. But those last words from him ring in my ears. *Yeah. It's going to kill me. For sure.* And that reminds me of something else entirely unsexy, which makes my stomach clutch. I glance at my phone to check the time, and my brain totally changes gears. "Sit with me," I say. I slide down the wall and sit, enveloped in the warmth from the swimming pool circulation fan. He hesitates and eases down to sit too. And then, together, we sigh. The fun is over, and we turn our attention to the urgent matter of the vision that is taking over Sawyer's life.

Eleven

He pulls out a folded wad of paper from his pants pocket and opens it. The late-afternoon sun glows orange through nearby branches as he looks at his notes.

"First of all, this sucks," he says. "Making out was way more fun."

"Making out is my favorite," I say glumly.

"Right?" He folds the papers with one hand and puts his other to his forehead, rubbing his temples. "Okay, so here's how it goes."

I link my arm in his and scoot my butt closer.

"We're in a classroom. You asked me how I knew before, and I couldn't tell you back then, but now I know. In a couple of the frames, as my view—or whatever—pans the room, there's a whiteboard on the wall and a few tables and overturned chairs."

"I always thought of my view as the camera angle," I say. "You see what the camera sees, right? And the angle changes a few times? Mine did, anyway."

He nods. "Yeah, it does. That's totally how it looks." He rests his hand on mine, absently traces my fingers. "So the first scene, I guess, is from a back corner of the class-room. The camera does a fast pan of the room and lands on a person—the gunman. He's wearing dark-wash jeans and a black fleece jacket, and he's got a floppy knit cap on his head." He turns toward me a fraction. "Any questions so far?"

"Yeah," I say. "About a hundred. Was there a clock or calendar anywhere?"

"Not that I saw."

"Any writing on the whiteboard?"

"Yes, but I couldn't read it."

"A lot?"

"A few lines."

"Like math equations or like sentences?"

"Sentences. Outline form. Ish."

I rummage around in my coat pockets for a pen. I always used to keep a few handy for when I was doing deliveries. I find one in an interior pocket and pull it out. Sawyer hands me the notes, and I start jotting down things on the back of one page. "Okay, so probably not a math class, right?"

"Hunh. I guess that's a reasonable assumption."

"Did the guy have any snow on his shoulders or hat?"

"Um, I didn't notice. I don't think so."

I start a second list on a different sheet of paper—things for Sawyer to look for next time.

"Did you get any view of the windows?"

He squeezes his eyes shut, thinking. "You know, I think maybe I did, but I don't remember anything about them. The windows felt . . . dark. I'll look again."

I write that down and ask, "How tall was the guy?"

"Kind of short."

"How could you tell?"

He pauses. "In relation to the tables, he seemed short. Thin build."

I nod. "Boots or shoes?"

His mouth parts and then closes again, and I write that one down for him to check on.

"It was dark, you said the other day. Darkish, anyway, because you could see the muzzle whatever fire thingy."

"Yeah. Not totally dark. More like . . . dimly lit."

"So it could just be from the shades being drawn? Like they were doing something with a projector? Or maybe it was stormy outside?"

"Maybe. I don't know." He sets his jaw. "I don't know."

"I'm sorry."

"No, it's okay. You're asking great questions. It's just . . . hard."

I nod. After a minute I ask, "What about the next scene?"

He looks at his notes. "Okay, so the angle changes. The camera, I mean. I think it's at the front of the room, because the wall I can see in this next scene doesn't have a whiteboard and the tables are on the left instead of the right. I—"

"Wait. Is anybody sitting at the tables or are the chairs empty?"

"Empty. Disorderly. Some of the chairs are tipped over."

"There are no people? Just the shooter?" I watch his face. He stares straight ahead.

"There . . . are people." His eyes glaze.

A shiver rolls down my back. Finally I whisper, "Where are the people, Sawyer?"

"They're . . . in the back corner."

"They're standing in the back corner of the room?"

"Not standing." His voice is wispy under the grumble of the fan. His eyelids droop shut and his face grows pained. "They're . . . they're on the floor. And there's . . . stuff . . . everywhere."

My stomach turns, and I don't want to ask. "Stuff?"

He nods. "I don't want to tell you."

I can barely breathe. "You mean blood."

"Yes. Blood."

"More than blood?"

He takes in a sudden breath and blows it out through his mouth. "Yeah. Guts and brains, I guess. And . . . that's all."

I pull my hand out from under his and rub my forehead, almost feeling sick. I know how real the vision must look to him. And I know he's looking at me to say something that can give him some hope. But it's a long reach. "The thing is," I say in a quiet voice, "is that if we get this right, and we find this classroom, and we stop this gunman, that scene will go away. It won't happen. They won't get shot, and they won't die. Right?"

He's frozen.

"Right," I answer for him. "So we focus on finding the date, time, and place. And we don't focus on the bodies and the blood and the . . . the stuff."

This time he nods, and after a minute he looks at me. "The only time I think there's any chance at all to save them is when you're with me."

I give him a grim smile. "Oh, there's definitely a chance." I think about it for a minute—the vision police, or the president of scenes, whoever or whatever controls this beastly mind game—and I say, "I don't think we'd get this chance to save people if it was hopeless."

As I say it, I try to convince myself that I believe it.

Twelve

Five things that you can never truly understand
unless you live through them:
1. Hoarding
2. Visions of dead people
3. Driving a giant meatball truck to school
4. Depression
5. Love
6. Sexy time

Okay, so that was six, but I could probably come up
with even more. Shall I elaborate on said list? I say no on
numbers one through four.

Number five—I just really had no idea how painful
love is. I mean, my love is different for Sawyer than for

anybody else I love. If Trey was the one going through this vision thing, I think I could handle it better. Oh, it aches, the love. Gah. I hate my pathetic overdramatic self.

Number six. Sexy time—I guess I'm trying to process this one. Let's just say that weird things happen when you get all sexy with somebody. I seriously didn't understand this even from reading some of the skanky books my dad brings home from yard sales that Mom forbids us to read. Like, during sexy time, stuff happens physically and mentally and emotionally *all at the same time*, and you kind of lose your mind a little bit. Let's dissect.

First, you're just minding your own business one day when something inside you randomly decides that you are attracted to a certain person, and you really have no control over it. Like, one day he's just some guy in your math class, or some boy you played plastic cheetahs and bears with in first grade. And then before you know it, he's like a freaking sex magnet and you can't stop thinking about him. What the heck? He says something or does something that changes absolutely everything. You used to think he had a big nose, but now it's perfect or whatever. Or you thought you'd never like a person with zits, but then you totally change your mind and decide zits aren't so bad after all. And if you kind of look at them in a different, intense way—and I seriously did not factor in the power of all the possible ways to look at someone—it makes your body get all electric and wilty inside, and so you decide, hey, I wanna suck face with that person. What?

Seriously? I mean, I care about germs. I do. I work in a restaurant, and we have rules upon rules, and I am a stoic follower of germ rules. But if Sawyer Angotti wants to put his germy tongue (GERMY TONGUE NOT RELATED TO HAIRY TONGUE) in my mouth, I will welcome it. What has happened here?

Yeah, I took health class–slash–sex ed, and I learned all that textbook stuff, like that the first sign of pregnancy is missing your period and that whole "point of no return" and shit like that. But they do not, I repeat, they do not teach you about that delicious, delirious, buttery, melty feeling between your legs.

I'm not trying to be gross or weird here. I'm just saying there is no teaching or describing this in any possibly accurate way. Parents do not tell their children about this, even the hippie parents who are all like "sex is beautiful" and stuff. There is only discovering it when you are going through that whole rationalization scene—how you used to think other people's tongues were disgusting, and then suddenly in *one instant* they're, like, the best thing ever and you want it in your mouth, like, *now*.

And let's talk about the boys. And how things like penises are so weird and awkward and probably superugly, and then they, like, *react* to things like they are alive and living their own little life in your pants—I don't know. Like a freaking barnacle or something. And as a girl, I'm sorry, but I have never really thought about this penis factor as it pertains to me. And boys? I have to say that I am very sympathetic. Because what if, like, my boobs or my elbow or something totally wigged out into the shape of the Eiffel Tower whenever I started kissing someone I liked? I mean, seriously. How embarrassing. But guess what? Because of number six, suddenly it's not embarrassing, because we're in some sort of bizarre temporary world where such things are acceptable.

And I'm not talking about *actual* sex, okay. I mean, I just had my first kiss, so it's not like I'm experienced enough to address that. I'm talking about the attraction thing and the mushy gut stuff that goes with that.

And it's those feelings that I am most shocked by. Indescribable. Which means, of course, I want like hell to describe it.

I think I might even write my next psych paper about it.

Poor Mr. Polselli.

But the last thing I need to say about this is that I should not, not, not be thinking about sexy time when Sawyer is having a vision portraying a freaking homicidal maniac who blows people's brains out. I mean, how awful am I that my mind and my dreams return to sexy time again and again? Pretty freaking awful.

But here's the thing that's even worse. What if Sawyer can't save those people, and he dies trying? Seriously, what if he dies? I don't know if I can handle it. After all I did to save him with my vision, I have to go through this all over again, only somehow, now that we are together, it's a hundred times worse. Because I'm the one with a crazy, endlessly depressed father and these crazy psycho genes, and I infected Sawyer with this vision that he has no choice but to obey.

If he dies? It'll feel like I killed him myself.

Thirteen

"Chess club," my dad says from the single uncluttered chair in the darkened living room. The blue haze from the muted TV hangs low in the room, making his hoards of junk look even weightier somehow.

Tonight I did my first shift of deliveries since the crash. Somebody had a late-night craving that we agreed to satisfy even though technically the restaurant was closed. By the time I got back the place was dark.

I take off my coat. "Yeah," I say.

"They start a new club in the middle of the second semester?"

My left eye starts to twitch. "No, it's been going on all year." I hang my coat up and start down the hallway.

"Come back here," he says.

I stop in my tracks and turn around slowly and walk to the doorway of the living room. "It's late, Dad," I say. "I'm exhausted."

"Chess club will do that to you." He's not looking at me.

My stomach is clenched. But I'm mad too. "No, actually, working a six-hour shift after chess club on a school night will do that to me."

"You don't know how to play chess." It's a challenge.

"That's why I wanted to learn," I lie, and I'm surprised how easy it is to lie to someone you've lost all respect for. "I was thinking about trying out for a sport, but with the cast, my options are limited."

"Is that Angotti boy in chess club?" He turns to look at me for the first time. He hasn't shaved in a few days.

I meet his gaze. It would be so easy to just tell the truth and say no. Instead, my big mouth shows up. "Why don't you call his parents to find out?"

His eyes flare and he squeezes the arms of the chair. He looks like he's going to ream me out, but he holds it in.

After a moment I force a smile. "Night," I say, and turn around, heading back down the hallway to my room. Once inside I let out the breath of fear I'd been holding. Note to self: Learn how to play chess. Now.

"I need to learn how to play chess," I say when I see Sawyer the next morning.

"Yes, yes you do."

"Like, for real."

He nods seriously. And then he narrows his eyes. "Wait. You mean literally."

I grin. "Yes, you horn dog. My dad's suspicious."

"Oh. Well, then." He contemplates this as we walk in the direction of our first-hour classes. And then he stops outside his classroom and his face brightens. "No problem. We'll do it at lunch. I just remembered—there happens to be an app for this situation."

I laugh. "Wouldn't it be cool if there was an app for figuratively playing chess?"

His green eyes bore holes in mine. "No. I only like the real thing." He pulls my hand toward his mouth, never taking his eyes off mine, and lets his lips linger on my thumb knuckle. Then he gives me that shy grin and disappears into his classroom.

Big sigh, Demarco.

At lunch Sawyer downloads a chess app on his phone and starts explaining the game pieces and what they do. Trey looks on, mildly interested. After a while he says, "Maybe I should join chess club."

Sawyer and I look at him.

He frowns. "Not your euphemistic club. Duh. I'm not into incest, thank you. However . . ." He raises an eyebrow at Sawyer. "If you ever, you know, want to experiment . . ."

I punch Trey in the arm.

Sawyer grins. "Maybe I could bang all the Demarco siblings."

"Ack! This conversation is so inappropriate," I say, and I feel my face getting hot. "Now I can't get that image out of my head, you losers. Don't drag poor, innocent Rowan into this love triangle, please."

Trey pipes up. "It would be a quadrangle—a love rhombus. Not pretty. And two equal teams would end up in a draw. But at least two of the Demarcos would be—"

"Stop," I say, putting my hands over my ears, and they stop, finally. Guys are so weird and gross. But it's good to see Sawyer having a little fun in the middle of this mess.

Sawyer's fun doesn't last long. After school he's waiting for me outside with a serious look on his face. I glance at Trey and Rowan, who stop with me. "You guys go ahead," I say to them. "Tell Mom I had to go to the library." I turn to Sawyer. "Can you drop me off later?"

"Yeah, of course."

"Cool." I turn back to Trey. "I'll be home before five. We just need to talk about . . . some stuff."

Trey and Rowan glance at each other and then back at me. "Okay," Trey says. He shrugs and they get in the delivery car.

When they leave, I look at Sawyer. "What happened?"

"Had a film in biology today."

"And?"

"Supposedly it was about amphibians."

I wait.

"All I saw was twenty minutes' worth of the vision on constant repeat. Gunshots in my head every four seconds." He taps out the rhythm on the car door.

"Sorry." I cringe, thinking of the gory mess he described. "Did you see anything else?"

"Yeah. There's new stuff."

"Helpful?"

He shrugs. "I don't know. It's so quick. But then something else happened."

I narrow my eyes. "What?"

"After the film was done, we opened our textbooks, and all I could see was the vision." He brings a gloved hand to his eyes and shakes his head a little. "I think I'm losing it, Jules. I'm not sure I can handle this. Not sure at all."

Fourteen

We go to the library and sit at the computers. I tell Sawyer to pull up a video while I take some notebook paper and a pencil out of my backpack.

"Are you seeing it?"

"One sec," he says, pushing play. "Yeah." He presses pause, rewinds, and hits play, then pause again.

"Okay. What do you see?"

"Hey—can't I just print—"

"Ah, no. Tried that. Doesn't work."

He frowns. "This is one of the new pieces. It's our guy walking. He's outside, wearing the same clothes."

"Bonus. Finally. Is it dark or light out?"

"Dusk."

"What do you see?"

"A sidewalk. Grass. A bare tree."

"Grass?"

He nods. "Brownish-yellow grass, all flat and wet."

"Any buds on that tree?"

"No. Eh . . . wait. Yes, tiny buds. It's blurry."

"Any snow at all?"

"No, just wet grass and wet sidewalk."

I look out the library window. There's snow on the ground a couple of inches deep, but huge honking piles of the dirty kind along the road and the sidewalk. On my computer I check the weather report. The ten-day forecast shows a quick warming trend with rain on the weekend and temperatures reaching the sixties by next Tuesday. One week from today.

"Shit," I mutter. "Rain plus warmth equals snow melted by this weekend." I look at Sawyer. "How bad has the vision been, exactly?"

Sawyer stares at the computer. His hand shakes on the mouse. "Bad. It's everywhere."

"Car windows?"

"Sometimes."

"Mirrors too?"

"Yes."

I stare at him. "Why didn't you tell me?"

"I—I thought I was telling you."

"Well, yeah, but you didn't say it was getting so

intense. That means it's happening soon!" My whisper is on the verge of breaking decibel records.

He turns to me, his eyes weary and red rimmed. "I know. But there's no fucking information here, okay? I can't *do* anything unless it tells me how to find it!"

"Sawyer, there *has* to be something there. That's the way it works! You have to look for stuff!"

"That's the way it worked for you," he says, no longer whispering. He pushes his chair back. "You keep telling me I'm doing it wrong, but you don't see it. You don't know. There are no body bags, no faces I can recognize, because the faces are all blown to bits. Okay? There's nothing there that I recognize. You had a building that you could figure out. You had a face you recognized, and that helped you put it all together. Me? I don't have jack shit."

I stare at him. He stares back. And I think about what I just said and close my eyes. "God, you're right," I say finally. "I'm sorry, Sawyer, I don't know what I'm saying."

The intensity on his face wanes a little, but he leans forward and adds, "Don't treat me like I'm stupid just because my vision is different from yours. I get what we're trying to do here. I'm doing my best."

I hang my head. Dear dogs. What am I doing to him? Nothing like adding another layer of pressure—as if the vision wasn't enough. "Sorry," I say again.

He gives me a rueful smile. "S'okay. I know you're worried too. You must feel pretty helpless."

I nod. "Anyway," I say.

"Anyway," he agrees. "Okay, so I liked the questions you were asking earlier. That was helpful."

I nod again. And I like that we just talked this out. No big fight, nobody getting all hurt feelings or acting passive-aggressive or whatever . . . it's nice. As nice as it can be, anyway. "In this frame, are there any buildings?"

"No. But there's a road. More like, um, not a public road with painted lines or anything—it's like a private paved road."

"Like a school would have. Makes sense. Any signs? Street signs, big cement block signs, school marquee-type signs in the distance?"

"There's a little stop sign down at the end of the road. Not like full size."

"Can you see the sky?"

"The sky? Yeah, I guess. It's dark, cloudy."

"No sign of a sun or sunset or anything?"

"No."

I take a few notes. "Any idea what kind of tree that is?"

He squints. "It's got really thin branches. The trunk is sort of squat and rounded and the branches are like long, narrow fingers going everywhere."

I frown. "Like a weeping willow? All hanging down like hair?"

"No, more like . . . hmm. Like the kinds of trees that line downtown streets, you know? They aren't like hulking oaks or maples; they're daintier, low to the ground, like a big bush."

"A flowering tree, maybe?" I tilt my head, trying to picture it. "Here, can you draw?"

"Not well." But he takes the pencil and tries.

"What if you hold up the paper to the monitor and trace it?"

He glances sidelong at me. "Smart." He does it, and it's so weird to see him tracing something I can't see. The bare branches look like fish skeletons. "I don't know what good this will do."

"I know. Probably none. But at least we're accomplishing something. How's the vision now—if you look out the window, is it there?"

He turns his head and looks. "No, not at the moment."

I smile. "Good."

"So we're doing something right?"

"I think so."

"About time."

We go through the vision frame by frame until it's almost five and I have to go. Sawyer drops me off a block from the restaurant. "Thanks," he says. "It's nice talking things through, you know? My family always just yells."

"It was really nice. Sorry I was in your face."

He leans over and we kiss, slow and sweet, and then I get out and head to work, wondering if Depressed Dad is oblivious to my nonappearance or if Angry Dad will be waiting by the back door for me.

Fifteen

Lucky for me, no one notices me slipping in because my parents are too busy admiring the shiny new ball truck in the back parking lot. I dump my coat and backpack, throw on an apron, and go out back to join them in the cold. The giant meatballs are the same, but the lettering and logo on the side of the truck are fresh and bold. Inside it's pretty much brand-new, customized to Dad's requests, with all-new cooking equipment and fixtures and extra storage from what we were used to. It's actually pretty nice, as food trucks go. Here's hoping it puts Dad in a better mood.

"I hear it's warming up this weekend," I say, trying to pretend I've been here all along. "Can't wait to try it out. There's a food truck festival in the city. Heard about it on Twitter."

Trey snorts and gives me a look.

I grin and shrug, rubbing my arms to keep warm. My cast snags my sweater, not for the first time. Annoying. I frown and poke the yarn into the new hole with my pinkie. "I'm going inside to see if Aunt Mary needs help," I say.

"Me too," Rowan says.

We run in together.

"Is Dad pissed?" I ask.

"No, he didn't say anything. Giant balls saved the day," Rowan says. We clear the snow from our boots.

"Sorry to put you guys in an awkward position again."

"Don't worry," Rowan says, hanging up her coat. She looks over her shoulder at me and fluffs her hair before she puts it up into her usual work ponytail. "I'll get you back."

The first customers are arriving as we check in with Aunt Mary, and my mind strays to Sawyer and the new scenes. It's frustrating, not being able to see the vision. I feel like I'm removed from it in a big way. Like it isn't really happening because I can't see it, and this is just a puzzle I need to solve. Like eleven gunshots are just ricocheting in some movie I haven't been to.

But it's real. It'll happen to real people, and to their real families, whether we're there or not. It's the kind of horrendous tragedy that makes national headlines. And somehow, in my mind, a guy with a gun that could go off in any direction and end lives in an instant seems so much more random and dangerous than a single snowplow hitting a single building. Like the snowplow is easier to control than one person's arm.

Around nine we have a lull, so Mom and I are starting cleanup in the kitchen. When I feel my phone vibrating under my apron, I grab the bags of trash and run them out to the Dumpster.

"Hey," I say. "I have about ten seconds."

"Okay. Something wasn't sitting right, so I went back to the library after I dropped you off. I watched the vision again, then rewound all the way and realized there's a single frame so quick I missed it—it was just a little flash right after the short scene with the grass and sidewalk. And it took me forever to land on it just right, but finally I did, and there's a building."

I suck in a breath. "Okay?"

"It's an old building with ivy on it. I can only see part of it. I sketched it. I'll bring it tomorrow."

"'Kay. Gotta run. Good job." I slide the phone into my pocket again as Trey pulls up after finishing deliveries. I toss the trash into the Dumpster with my good arm and meet Trey on the way to the door.

"Slow night," he says. "Nothing new come in?"

"Nada. You get to help us clean up." I grin.

Before we go inside he pauses, his hand on the knob, and turns to look at me. "Is there something going on with you and Sawyer besides . . . you know. The usual kisskiss stuff?"

I try to stop my eyes from darting around guiltily, but I've never been good at lying to Trey. "Well, I'm not pregnant, if that's what you're wondering. Again. Be sure and tell Dad and everyone."

He laughs. "No, I wasn't thinking that. Sawyer just looks . . ."

"Hot?"

"No. Well, yeah, but—"

"Sexay?"

He sighs. "Stressed out."

I just press my lips together in a grim smile and shrug.

After a minute, Trey nods. "Okay." He starts up the steps to the restaurant and turns. "Well, if you ever need an ear." I can tell he's trying not to look hurt.

"Thanks, big brother," I say, and reach out to squeeze his arm.

He messes up my hair. "Dork," he says. He turns the handle and we go inside.

At night, when I lie in bed staring at the ceiling and watching the blinking lights from the sign outside, I think about what schools might be composed of old-looking buildings with ivy on them. The last thought I have as I drift off: *Probably in the city.*

Sixteen

In the morning I'm on the computer early, researching Chicago's oldest school buildings still in use. I scribble notes to myself—"Lincoln Park. Old Chicago. Survived the big fire? Grass. Bushy trees. Private road. Small stop sign."

Not all of the older schools I can find have pictures online, and besides, our stinking slow connection makes it impossibly hard for me to load anything, so I give up on that and start to list school names on a different paper. "Drive by: Lincoln Park HS. Lake View HS. Wendell Phillips Academy. Robert Lindblom Math/Science Acad."

And then I add questions.

1. Victims are presumably high school age, not
   middle school, right? Can tell by clothes/

dress/size? Maturity—boobs/facial hair?
Note clothing of each victim—for identifying before.
2. Close-up of whiteboard—forgot to tell you
about zooming the pic to read the writing.
3. . . .

It's right about here that I realized these notes could
be vastly misunderstood, maybe even peg me as plotting
a school shooting if they end up in the wrong hands, and
I nearly choke at the thought. What a kick in the teeth. I
debate ripping this up and swallowing it vs. burning it, and
then decide I'm being irrational and just fold it up and put
it in my pocket.

In the five seconds that remain before Rowan drags
me out the door, I leave a note on the kitchen counter by
the sink. "Going to library after school for tree research.
Our lame Internet connection is too slow—can't get my
homework done."

"Tree research?" Rowan asks as we three climb into
the car.

"Yeah. It's for a . . . project."

Trey turns his head sharply to stare at me. "I don't
remember having to do any tree project in tenth grade,"
he says. He looks back at the road, but I can feel an accusa-
tion in his posture.

I shrug. "Maybe it's new." My hands start to sweat.

"Look," he says, glancing in the rearview mirror, "I know something's up. You're a terrible liar. And you're starting to piss me off."

I sigh. "Nothing's up. Not with me. Okay? Sawyer needs my help on something."

Tension strains the silence.

"It's not my thing to tell," I say.

After a few quiet minutes, we're at school and Trey parks the car. We all climb out.

"Go ahead, Ro," he says.

She rolls her eyes. "You'd better include me this time if it's something exciting and dangerous, that's all I can say." She shrugs her backpack strap higher on her shoulder and walks toward the school.

Trey comes around the front of the car and stops me, a shock of his sleek dark waves falling over one eye. "After all I did for you, *and* for him, I think I deserve to know what's going on. Or you can forget about me covering for you like this day after day. Okay? I'm done."

He stares at me for a long moment, black eyes piercing into mine, and then he turns on the wet pavement and strides through the parking lot, leaving me standing there looking at the rivulets of water migrating from the shrinking piles of crusty, dirty snow.

• • •

Inside, Sawyer hands me a folded piece of paper, and I hand him one in return. We both open them and read them, standing together at my locker. I skim his long, detailed outline, my eyes growing wider as I read. When I get to the bottom, I look at him. "Seriously?"

He nods, staring blankly at the paper I gave him, and then he looks at me. "There's no way we can do this alone," he says in a low voice.

"I've been thinking about that. What about . . . Trey?" I ask.

He nods again. "I don't know who else to go to." His voice is hollow, and his hand drops to his side like he's too tired to hold the paper any longer.

"No, this is good," I say. "Really. He already knows something's up." I fold the notes he gave me into a tight square and put them safely in my pocket. "I'll talk to him and see if we can figure out a time to meet up so we can explain—"

Just then Roxie and BFF Sarah come up behind Sawyer. Roxie slaps Sawyer on the butt, and when he turns, Sarah grabs the paper from his hand.

"Ooh, a love note!" She laughs.

Sawyer tries to grab it but Sarah hands it off to Roxie. And because of my paranoia this morning, and because it's so stupid rude anyway, I lunge for the paper, grasp Roxie's shirt collar with my good hand, and pull the paper from her with my other hand, leaving only a tiny bit between her fingers and, unfortunately, a large scratch on her neck from my fingernail.

"Ow, you bitch!" she shrieks, holding her neck like it's way more than just a flesh wound, and then she lunges back at me, going for my neck rather than the paper, which I manage to shove into my pocket.

People around us start shouting and I can't see anything but Roxie's flaring nostrils in my face. I think frantically about how this all will lead to nothing good, namely parents being called, and I sink to the floor, deadweight, praying that somebody pulls her off me as she follows me to the floor, because I'm not going to fight back. In an instant, she digs her knee into my stomach and rakes her fake claws down my neck. I close my eyes and keep my flinching as invisible as possible, hoping she doesn't totally fuck up my innards after they've been trying so hard to heal. Instinctively I bring my good arm up to her rib cage to try to lessen the weight she's putting on me, and she jabs her elbow into my biceps, giving me a wicked charley horse.

"Stop!" I hear, and realize it's my hoarse voice yelling.

The whole thing lasts about five seconds, maybe a few more than that, but it feels like an hour before her knee is off my gut. I'm not quite flat on the floor; my head is against the lockers and my neck is twisted. I open an eye as Sawyer kneels down to see if I'm okay and help me up, and I look at Roxie, who is being held back by the guy whose locker is next to mine. Mr. Polselli stands between us, his hand on Roxie's shoulder, his eyes on me.

"Are you okay?" Sawyer asks.

I nod quickly and scramble to get to my feet, embarrassed. We're surrounded by students eager for a girl fight. "Sorry to disappoint," I say to them, catching my breath. I hold my cast in front of me and my good arm pressed against my stomach and make a pained face. Hey, I'm not stupid.

"My classroom," Mr. Polselli barks at both of us just as the bell rings. "Everybody else get out of here."

Sawyer tries to come with me, but Mr. Polselli gives him the hairy eyeball. Sawyer says how sorry he is with his eyes, and then he frowns and grabs his books, watching at least until we're out of sight and inside the psych classroom. Mr. Polselli's papier-mâché bust of Ivan Pavlov stares at me.

"Roxanne, you start," Mr. Polselli says.

"She attacked me and cut my neck," Roxie says. "I can feel it. See?"

"Why did she attack you?"

"Because she's a paranoid freak," she says. "She can't stand that I'm friends with her boyfriend."

"I did not *attack* you. You *took*—" I begin, but Mr. Polselli holds a hand up to me. Students start to come into the room, and they send curious looks in our direction.

"So she scratched you, and you scratched her back four times. And pushed her to the ground?"

"No, she fell." Roxie won't look at me, but her eyes are brimming, and I feel strangely sorry for her for the briefest moment.

Mr. Polselli turns to me. "Julia, did you attack Roxanne?"

"No, I was reaching for something and I accidentally scratched her. I wasn't trying to do that."

"What were you reaching for?"

"A note. Her friend Sarah pulled it from Sawyer Angotti's hand and gave it to her. They think it's a love note. It was something private I gave him, and she was just, I don't know, goofing around or whatever, and I reacted, trying to get it back." I pause, setting my jaw so I don't cry. I have never been in trouble like this before. "I'm sorry I scratched you, Rox. I didn't mean to. I just wanted the paper back." My fingers go to my own neck, which throbs now, and I wonder how bad my scratches are. I can feel the raised welts.

My biggest fear is that Mr. Polselli asks to see the paper, but I'm prepared to say no—it's not like we got caught in class passing notes or something. School hadn't even started yet. But he doesn't ask for it, and I breathe a silent sigh of relief.

"Roxanne?" Mr. Polselli asks. "Do you have anything else to say?"

"No."

"It doesn't look good for you, frankly," he continues, still looking at Roxie. "What I saw was you kneeling on a girl who has a broken arm and just had surgery last month. She's got four scratches, you've got one, and yours is not that bad." He fishes around in his drawer and, after a minute, pulls out a rectangular glass mirror, handing it to Roxie. "I don't think we want to take this to the principal, do we?"

"God, no. Please," I say.

Roxie looks at her scratch. I agree, it's not that bad. Mr. Polselli digs around a bit more in another drawer and hands her a small square packet containing an antiseptic wipe. He gives me one too.

Roxie sets the mirror on his desk out of my reach and glances at me. I avert my eyes and fold my arms as best I can with the cast. "Fine," she says. "Sorry."

Mr. Polselli looks at me, then picks up the mirror and hands it to me. "You don't want to go any further with this either?"

I train the mirror at my neck and study the scratches, four neat lines, the first three pretty heavy and the fourth just a light scratch like the one I gave Roxie. Thankfully, there's no dripping blood. It's going to be interesting explaining this one at home. "No, it's fine," I say. "Just a misunderstanding."

Mr. Polselli nods. "Okay, then." He scribbles a note on

a small pad of paper and hands it to Roxie.

She takes it. "Thanks," she says. And without another glance, she weaves through the aisle of students and goes out the door, eyes still shiny, biting her lip.

Mr. Polselli scribbles a note to get me back into class, and then he says, "She was on your stomach. Any need to get you checked out? You had some internal injuries from your crash, right?"

I smile, and now my eyes fill with tears because he's being nice, and because the danger and fear of the moment just caught up with me. "I'm okay. She wasn't pressing too hard or anything."

He looks down at his desk as a tear spills over the edge of my lower lid and I swipe it away. "Did you get your letter back?" he asks.

I freeze. "Yes."

He smiles. "Good." He hands me the excused note as the second bell rings and the students in his classroom start to sit down. "Take a few minutes to clean up. I added ten minutes to the excused time on your pass."

I take the pass and the antiseptic pad. "Thank you," I say. "A lot." And before another tear can leak out, I turn and barrel down the aisle, hoping nobody's looking at me and my big ol' neckful of scratches.

Seventeen

"Jeez," Trey says when he sees me at lunch. "What happened to you? Looks like Sawyer's got either a well-oiled hinge on that jaw or some retractable incisors."

I sit down next to Trey as Sawyer finds us and sits across from us.

"Random feline incident," I say, waving him off. "One of my fans got a little too close."

Sawyer examines my neck, then glances at Trey. "For the record, I did not do that." He looks at me. "Does it hurt? Any repercussions?"

"Yes, and no, thankfully. Polselli's cool. He kept it small. Good thing nobody threw a punch." I pull the crumpled note out of my pocket and hand it to Sawyer.

Trey swipes it.

"Seriously?" both Sawyer and I exclaim.

Trey stares at us like we're insane. "Calm down," he says. "Take a moment." He slowly hands the paper to Sawyer. "It's just a lingering adolescent attention-grabbing behavior. We all do it. It's human nature."

I start laughing softly, insanely, at the plate of lard-filled fats on the table in front of me.

"Trey," Sawyer says, and then he grabs my hand and squeezes it so I stop acting crazy.

I look up.

Trey's eyes narrow slightly. "Yes?"

"We—*I*—need your help."

Trey bats his eyelashes. "Oh?"

Sawyer flashes a grin despite the intensity of his thoughts. "No, not like that. It's, uh . . . God, this is going to sound insane, but—"

Trey grows serious again. "Oh, no." He leans forward. "Did you just say the magic word?"

"He did," I say.

Sawyer looks over his shoulder, making sure nobody's paying attention to us, and then he leans in. "Trey, ever since the crash, I—"

"No," Trey says. "Shit."

"Ever since the crash, I've been having this—"

"No." Trey sits back. "No, you haven't. No."

Sawyer sits back. "Yes."

Trey shakes his head. "Not funny. It's not quite April Fools' Day. Good practice joke, though." His mouth is strained. I know this look. It's the *I'm pretending I'm not freaked out right now* look. A classic Demarco face.

Sawyer digs the heels of his hands into his eyes and then rests his arms on the table and looks back at Trey. "I wish it was a joke."

Trey throws a nervous glance my way. I don't smile. He looks back at Sawyer. "No. You are mistaken. You are not having a vision. It's just PTSD or something. You've been through a lot."

Sawyer sighs. "Okay. Well. You would know." He stares at his lunch and shoves a forkful of by-product into his mouth. His eyes get glassy and he won't look at either of us. He chews a few times and then just stands up and takes his tray to the guys in dishwashing.

"He's serious?" Trey says.

"Yeah. Thanks for making him feel like crap."

"Fuck. What did you do to him?"

The guilt pang strikes again. I get up as Sawyer comes back this way. "Yeah, I don't know," I say. "Come on. We need to talk to him."

Trey sighs and gets up. "Okay." He grabs my tray and his and takes them away while I meet up with Sawyer.

"He knows you're serious now," I say.

Sawyer just shakes his head. "Maybe this was a bad idea."

"I don't think we have a choice. Let's just get it out there to him, see what he says. Please—I think he'll help us."

He presses his lips together. "Fine."

I beckon to Trey.

Trey catches up to us and we leave the cafeteria together. The clock says we've got about twelve minutes before the bell rings. We walk down to the trophy hall-way, where only the memories of students linger—almost nobody hangs out here; they just pass through.

When we reach a quiet corner, Trey stops and faces us. "Okay, explain. How the hell did you start seeing a vision? What is this, some sort of contagion? A virus? What? It's like a bad B movie."

"We don't know. All I know is that I don't have my vision anymore, but Sawyer has one now."

"So what is it—a snowplow hitting *our* restaurant this time?"

I look at Sawyer. "You should explain everything. Including what you said in your note."

Sawyer begins. And I watch the two guys I love most in the world talk to each other. They are almost exactly the same height, a few inches taller than me. Trey's eyes are black and his hair is darker than Sawyer's, almost black, but they both have natural waves. Sawyer tries to fight his hair by keeping it short, while Trey coaxes his longer locks to curl every morning. I almost smile as I watch them. They are both so beautiful.

But the story Sawyer tells is not beautiful. I tune in, watching Trey's face go from shock to disbelief. "A school shooting," Trey says. "God, that's my worst nightmare." He shivers.

I didn't know that. "Mine's a toss-up between burning and being crushed," I murmur.

"Drowning," Sawyer adds. "Stampede. Or . . . being shot in the face by a fucking maniac or two."

That brings us back. "So we have two shooters now," I say, opening up the note Sawyer gave me this morning. Trey shushes me as a group of freshmen walk by. One of them eyes us in fear.

Sawyer waits until they're gone. "Yeah."

"And you don't know what school," Trey says. "That's . . . impossible."

"We need help, man. You're the only one who will believe us."

I watch conflict wash across Trey's face.

"Guys," he says, "look. I'm not trying to be all superior or grown up or whatever, but this is insane. *Insane.* How bad . . . I mean, the visions—I guess they're pretty bad."

"They let up a little when I manage to figure something out. But yeah. It's about fifty million times worse than having the theme song from 'Elmo's World' stuck in your head for a month straight."

Trey glances at the clock. "I think . . ." He gives me a guilty look, and then his gaze drops to the floor. "Look. I think it's too big for two teenagers. Or three. And, Sawyer, you should try and just get through it until it happens, and then hopefully it'll go away."

The bell rings.

"But, Trey," I say, "it's a lot of people. It's their families. Their lives."

"You don't know them."

"We don't know that for sure," I say, my voice pitching higher. "Besides, I feel like it's my fault. I mean, Sawyer didn't do anything to deserve this stupid vision, except somehow he caught it from me. I have to do something—" I grab his shirtsleeve as he turns to go to class. "Trey, come on."

"Come on, what? It's too dangerous. You're being irrational. I'm sorry about the noise in your head, Sawyer, and I hope it goes away soon, but, well, we almost died once already. If we manage to survive this, it won't be for long, because our parents will murder us." He starts walking quickly. "Get to class," he says over his shoulder to me.

Sawyer and I look at each other. "I'll work on him," I say.

"No. It's cool. I'll . . . I'll see you."

"I'm planning on the library if you can make it."

Sawyer's face sags. "I—I don't think so. Not today."
He turns and goes toward his next class, and I go to sculpting. With Trey.

Eighteen

"Let's just talk about it a little more before you decide," I whisper once the teacher lets us loose to work on our own. Trey and I share a table, which is, according to our stunned classmates, something no brother and sister have ever before done willingly in the history of education. I don't get why not, but whatever.

Trey pretends I'm not there.

I don't know how to handle him when he does the silent treatment—it may be a stereotype, but we Italians aren't exactly known for our ability to keep our opinions quiet. All I know is that if I poke him a little, he'll start in on me, and that's when we can actually accomplish something.

"What if we *do* know one of the victims?" I whisper. "Does that change anything?"

He frowns at his misshapen bowl, then scrunches up his nose and smashes the clay into a ball and starts over.

I try again. "What if you save someone and he turns out to be the guy of your dreams?"

He turns toward me. "For shit's sake, Jules," he hisses. "This is not a romantic situation in any possible way. Grow up."

Yow. I stand abruptly and walk over to the paint shelf, pretending to pick out colors for the fake fruits I've been making to go in Trey's dumb lopsided bowl that he keeps destroying, all of which will one day be buried under a sea of bullshit crud collected by my father. I think about painting my fruit Day-Glo colors so they'll be easier to find when my mother's looking for something to put on top of my casket after I get shot to death. And then I start thinking about actually getting shot if things don't go well, and I really start creeping myself out.

I'm pulled back to reality when I realize somebody's calling my name. I whirl around, and it's the art teacher telling me and Trey to go to Dr. Grimm's office—the principal. Yeah, that's his real name. Thank dog he's not an oncologist.

Trey's puzzled glance meets mine, and then in an instant my heart clutches, because I realize if they want both of us it's not just because of my stupid scratchfest with Roxie. It's got to be something serious with Rowan or Mom or—or Dad. Fuck.

I stumble out of the room after Trey, and I feel like the world is coming up around my head like water. When we're alone in the hallway, both of us walking faster than normal, I say it. "Do you think Dad . . . did it?"

Trey's teeth are clenched and he replies in monotone. "I don't know."

How awesome is it being a kid who's always wondering if one day she's going to come home from school to find out her dad offed himself?

We round the corner near the office, and inside, through the glass wall, I see a cop. "Oh, Christ," I say, and I feel all the blood flooding out of my head. "Do you see Mom anywhere?"

"No."

We reach the door and Trey pushes it open and I stare at the cop and then at the secretary and I can't help it. "What's wrong?" I say, breathless. "Is Rowan here?"

The secretary, Miss Branderhorst, frowns at me like I did something wrong.

Trey whips his head around as somebody enters the office behind us.

It's Sawyer.

He looks as puzzled as we are.

The cop asks us our names, and then the principal comes

out, and they make us go back into his office, and the only thing I can think of is that my dad went postal and took out Sawyer's parents and *then* killed himself. *Mom*, I think, and now I'm freaking myself out and telling myself to calm down.

We sit in chairs, and none of our parents are there, most likely because they're dead, and then the cop says, "Where were you at lunch today?" And this is weird, but right then I realize he's the guy who fills in once a week for our regular beat cop, Al, by the restaurant, and somehow knowing that makes me feel better.

"Wait." Sawyer holds his hand out. "Um, did somebody die? Why are we here?"

Principal Grimm interjects. "Mr. Angotti, kindly answer the question."

Trey sits up, his eyes sparking. "You're not going to tell us if somebody died?"

"Nobody died," the cop says.

"Jeeezabel," I say, slumping back in relief. "You gave us a heart attack."

The cop and Principal Grimm exchange a look. And then the cop repeats the question. "Where were you at lunch today?"

"We ate lunch in the cafeteria. Together," Trey says. "And then we wandered the halls until the next period started like everybody always does. Are we in trouble or something?"

The cop looks at me. "What did you talk about?"

"What?" I ask, confused as hell, and then my blood runs cold. Somebody overheard something. I sense Trey stiffening in the chair next to me.

"We received a 911 call from a student who says he overheard you three talking about something suspicious. Do you want to tell me what you were talking about?"

I keep the puzzled look on my face. "Let's see, we talked about the weather warming up, we talked about our work schedules—me and Trey at Demarco's Pizzeria, and Sawyer at Angotti's Trattoria—" I add, in case it helps. "And, gosh, I don't know," I say, looking at the boys on either side of me. "My psych project, maybe? TV shows, video games?" I start throwing out random things, hoping one of them will save me.

"Call of Duty," Sawyer says. "You ever play?" He looks at the cop. "It's kind of violent, but . . ."

The cop doesn't answer. He looks at me and my cast, and then at the scratches I almost forgot I have on my neck. "You're the Demarco kids who saved this guy's parents' restaurant," he says, flicking a thumb at Sawyer.

"Yes," Trey says. "Well, it was mostly Jules."

I blush appropriately, for once. "You're our beat cop when Al has his days off, aren't you?" I ask.

"Police officer," Principal Grimm corrects.

The cop grins for the first time, rolls his eyes without

the principal seeing. He pockets his little notebook and adjusts the gun on his belt. "Yeah, I'm your fill-in beat cop," he says to me, and then he turns to the principal. "I think we're done here."

The principal's eyes flicker, but he nods. "Thank you, Officer Bentley."

The cop leaves, and then the principal looks at us. He clasps his hands together. "Well. You may go."

We all stand up and file out to the reception area. Principal Grimm flags down Miss Branderhorst to write us excuses to get back into class.

Once we're in the hallway and my heart starts beating again, I let out a staggered breath. I don't dare say anything or even look at Trey and Sawyer. When we turn the corner, Sawyer puts his arm over my shoulders, and then Trey puts his arm over my shoulders and Sawyer's arm, and I reach around both of their waists, and we don't talk. Not a word.

Except for when Trey says, "All right. I'm in. But only to keep you bozos from getting killed."

Nineteen

After school Trey and Sawyer head to the library while I drive Rowan home.

She observes me loftily. "Are you going to tell me what happened to your neck?"

My fingers automatically reach up to touch the scratches. "Oh. Stupid Roxie took something and I accidentally scratched her trying to get it back, so she lunged at me and scratched the hell out of my neck."

"Wow. Well, I guess she's probably jealous."

I raise an eyebrow, check my speedometer, touch the brakes just slightly. "Of what?"

"Come on," Rowan says. "Pay attention for once. She's been in love with Sawyer for years."

"Years? How would you know?"

"The same way you sophomores know more about the junior class than you know about the freshman class. Everybody watches up."

I'm a little surprised at how delicious this news feels. "I thought they were just friends."

"Please. Is *anyone* just friends? There are always other motivating factors in relationships. Maybe not constant, but consistent."

I look at her.

She looks back at me, her face certain.

I shrug, wondering how she became such a philosopher all of a sudden.

"So now what?" Rowan says.

"Now what what?"

"Now what are you guys doing? You, Trey. Sawyer. Something's up."

"Nothing. Don't worry about it."

She flips the visor down and examines her face. "My flight is Sunday morning," she says. She rummages through her backpack and pulls out a pair of tweezers, then starts plucking invisible hairs from her perfect eyebrows.

I haven't thought about her flight. Or about her secret visit to see Charlie. I haven't thought about her at all lately.

She continues. "So I'll need a ride to O'Hare Airport while Mom and Dad are at mass." She's never flown before, and she says it like she's bored.

"Impeccable timing. When do you come back?"

"I'll be back Friday before dinner service. You're welcome."

I laugh. Sometimes Rowan just leaves me speechless. "Okay," I say. "What do you want me to, like, *say* to Mom and Dad when they get home from mass to find their youngest child missing? I mean, can I tell them the truth? Are you going to give me all the information about where you'll be and stuff?"

"I'll have my cell phone with me. That's all they need to know. But yeah, I'll give you the address and stuff too in case Charlie is secretly an ax murderer. But don't give it to them. Please." She licks her pinkie and smooths her eyebrows, then deposits the tweezers back into her bag as I turn down the alley behind our home and park a few buildings away so nobody sees me—I don't want my dad to force me to come inside. "Maybe we can talk tonight." She gets out and waves, then saunters down the alley toward the restaurant like she owns the world.

And I totally want to be her.

I meet Trey and Sawyer at the library. They're up in the loft on the corner couches where you can see everyone approaching but still have a private conversation. I plop down next to Sawyer, kick off my shoes, and curl up into him, and he slips an arm around my shoulders and kisses the top of my head. And I feel like this exact moment right here, this feeling of warmth and love, is what I have been waiting for my entire life.

Trey watches us. He smiles a small smile and doesn't look away. And then he sighs and leans forward, elbows on his knees, and says, "All right. Number one: Nobody here gets hurt." At first I think he must have new information from Sawyer that I haven't heard yet, but then I realize it's a command.

Sawyer nods. "I hear you, bro. We hear you. No crazy stunts. No matter what."

"Of course," I agree.

While I was gone, Sawyer filled Trey in on a few of the minor but important details—the tree, the grass, the tiny stop sign, the old building with ivy on it.

I pull the note Sawyer gave me this morning out of my pocket and hold it out. "We need to destroy this or something," I say. "Yours, too."

Sawyer pulls his note out and takes mine. "We have a shredder in the office. I'll take care of it. From now on, only verbal communication, and we don't talk about g-u-n-s in school. Does Trey know about your secret phone?"

Trey raises an eyebrow.

"It's just a temporary throwaway," Sawyer says. "Don't bother trying to text her."

I give Trey my new cell number and watch him enter it

into his phone. "Sawyer, can you get away from the propri-etors long enough to drive by some schools? The list is in your hand—can you memorize them before you shred that?"

"Yeah," Sawyer says. "I'll drive around tonight and tomorrow morning before school." He looks at the addresses. "Some of these are way out there."

"Are you safe to drive?"

"So far." Sawyer squinches his eyelids shut and rubs them. "The vision keeps playing in the windows down there, though, and it's giving me a headache." He points to the wall of glass on the main floor below us. "And in the face of that clock." There's an old school clock on the wall opposite our couch.

"What about your windshield and mirrors?" I ask, worried, knowing how distracting that is, and how much worse it could be for Sawyer going out into city traffic.

"Not bad," he says lightly. "But . . . things are getting worse. The noise is driving me insane. I think—I feel like it's happening very soon."

Trey lifts his head. "I'll go with you to look at schools," he says. "I'll drive."

I bite my lip. I want to go, but I haven't been pulling my weight at the restaurant. "That's a great idea," I say. I glance outside and then at the clock. "Maybe you guys should go now before it gets dark. Do the close ones. It's rush hour."

Trey gets up and blows out a sigh. "If we're going to do this, let's do it hard, fast, and often."

"Dot-com," I mutter, getting up. "Okay, be safe." I give them each a hug. "Talk it through from the beginning, maybe. Trey might have some good questions that will trigger something—anything—about day, time, place. Maybe identifying features of the . . ." I almost say "shooters," but now I'm scared to use the word. "Bad guys," I say. And that triggers my memory. "Oh," I say, turning to Sawyer. "Can you zoom in on a close-up of the, ah, weapon *and* the whiteboard? I'm not sure if the weapon's information will help anything, but I thought of it earlier when Officer Bentley was at school. I could see a logo on his. Is there a way to trace something like that? Or, like, figure out how many bullets a . . . thing . . . can shoot just by looking at it?"

Sawyer looks at me with this face dotted with little hints of surprise—in his eyes, the corners of his lips. "Good one, gorgeous," he says. "I'll check them both out in slo-mo tonight when I get home and I'll call you."

Big sigh.

And a question. Why does danger make love so much more intense?

Twenty

I hit the computers after Trey and Sawyer are gone so I can do my tree research, and my best guess is that the bush-tree in Sawyer's vision is a redbud. I pay to print a few pages of examples and take off. I make it home before five and get to the restaurant early to help set up for dinner.

"How was your tree research?" Dad booms when I glide through the kitchen. He looks good today. Clean shaven, a smile on his face. At school a few hours ago I thought he might have killed himself, but staring at him now, it's hard to imagine he's ever depressed.

"Good. Successfully identified a redbud tree. But teachers are hitting hard with assignments. I'm going to have to spend more time at school and at the library, where I can use decent computers." I cringe, hoping he doesn't see that as a slam, because it's just a fact. Our computer sucks. And I need to establish that I'm going to be gone more. But bringing up chess club again is a bad idea.

He lets it go. Even makes a joke about typewriters. Today he is my favorite kind of dad. I realize just how seldom this dad comes out these days, and I wonder what triggers it. When I catch a glimpse of Rowan, I know my dad's up days are numbered. As soon as he realizes what she's doing, it's going to be shitty again.

Part of me wants to tell them what she's up to. But I can't. I owe her. I owe her big, and she is well aware of that. In fact, she probably planned it that way. I shake my head and watch Rowan with new respect. She arrives on time every day. She kisses Mom and Dad on the cheek when she sees them, and greets Tony the cook like he's family. She tells them just enough about her day that they never say "You never tell us anything" to her. She treats everyone with respect and she's the one who gets the most customer love on the restaurant comment cards.

And it's all a big screen. A ruse. Well, that's not really fair to say, because she truly is a thoughtful, respectful, punctual person. But she also knows how to use her strengths to her advantage, and when she goes to New York, Mom and Dad are going to be absolutely gobsmacked—they'll never see it coming. Because if anything, Mom and Dad are looking at me to be the one to disappoint them again.

She's a freaking genius.

With Dad working at 100 percent tonight, Mom sends all three of us upstairs early. I grab Trey and drag him into his room, which is mildly messy. He has posters of famous people on his walls and weird gadget-like stuff between the books on his bookshelves.

I close the door. "Well?"

"Nothing. We got to three of the schools on your list before dark, and I thought of another one on the way home, but none of them looked right."

I flop down on his unmade bed. "Crap."

"He's picking me up at dark thirty and we're going to try to get out to Lake View and Lincoln Park and back before school starts."

"Ugh, that's going to be horrible at that hour."

He shrugs and sits next to me. "We don't have a choice. He thinks we're running out of time."

We both lie back on the bed and stare at his ceiling. "Anything new?"

"Still no. I asked him some questions that he thought he could find answers to in the vision." He sighs.

"Thanks for doing that."

"No, it's cool. He's a great guy."

I smile and look over at his face. "You sure you're not in love with him?"

That gets a laugh. "I'm in love with something, I guess, but not Sawyer, though I still think he's a total hottie. I guess I'm in love with this cute little relationship thing you guys have." His lingering smile is wistful. "And, like, you know, Rowan and . . . what's his name?"

"Charlie."

"Yeah, Charlie. I heard more about him the other day when I drove Rowan home. Seems like they've got something good too."

My throat catches a little. "You'll have it too. You will. I mean, maybe just not in high school. Maybe college. For sure college—things will be better."

He folds his hands behind his head. "I hope so, Jules. I really do."

There's a soft knock at his door.

"Come in," he hollers.

Rowan peeks her head in. "Hi. I heard my name and came running." She comes in and closes the door. She wrinkles up her nose and sniffs tentatively as she surveys Trey's mild clutter, and then she approaches the bed.

I sit up and shove Trey over so Rowan can sit too. "The only way you could have heard your name is if you were standing with your ear pressed against the door."

"It was a short run," she says agreeably.

My eyes grow wide and meet Trey's alarmed look. What else did she hear?

She sits down and lies back on the bed next to me. "So, guys," she says. "Isn't it about time you fill me in on this whole vision thing?"

Twenty-One

"Um," Trey says.

"Um," I say, and then add in a weak voice, "What?" I lie back down again.

She sighs. "Oh, please. Just come out with it already." She looks at her cell phone clock. "I'm leaving in a few days."

"Maybe we should talk about *that*," Trey says.

"Nice try." She sits up and scoots back so that she can lean against the wall between Trey's posters of Johnny Depp and Adele.

I tilt my head back so I'm looking at Rowan upside down. "What exactly do you think you know?"

"Well, I know you have a phone, I know you talk to Sawyer at night when you think I'm sleeping, I know somebody's having a vision of some kind of . . . shooting, and you all seem to think you have to do something about it."

Trey snorts and sits up. "Well, that about sums it up, Ro." He shakes his head, laughing. "Thank you and good night, everyone—I've got an early morning, so, uh, Jules? You wanna take this one in your office?"

I just stare dumbfounded at Rowan.

"Oh!" Trey adds, standing and fishing inside the pocket of his jeans. He pulls out a familiar key chain. "Just remembered. Great news. Dad says it's time to start advertising at school again." He gives me a patronizing smile and hands the keys to the new meatball truck to me. "Don't crash it. Have a ball."

"Har har. Don't forget my ten bucks," I mutter, taking the keys, and then I get up and shuffle toward the door, dragging Rowan by her pajama collar. "Come on, you little weasel," I say. "Girls' quarters. Immediately."

Mom and Dad are still in the restaurant. Ro and I go into our room and close the door. Rowan pulls her terry cloth robe from the closet, rolls it up, and presses it against the crack under the door as a sound barrier. I stand at the closet, take off my clothes, and put on some booty shorts and my "Peace, Love, Books" shirt, which I got from this dope bookshop called Anderson's. Ever since the visions, I started wearing it to bed because it made me feel calm, and bed plus calm equals sleep. Which I can always use more of.

Rowan turns out the light so when our parents come upstairs there's no chance of them seeing any light through the door cracks and barging in, and we climb into her bed. I lie on my side and sling my arm over her waist like I used to do when we were younger, and we talk about what the hell she's about to do.

"I guess I want to meet him," I say. I feel like the mom.

She's quiet for a moment. "Well, come to the library during second hour, then. Tomorrow. I'm always in that little study room with the door shut."

"I have class."

Rowan sighs. "Honestly, Jules. You're supposed to be the bad child."

"What, you want me to skip class? They'll call home."

"Not if you have a note from Mom."

"Right, and that'll be easy."

"Oh, Jules. Tsk."

"What, you forge her signature too? Do you even go to class at all?"

"I'm pretty good at it, actually."

I shake my head in Rowan's pillow and almost laugh. "One day you are going to get so busted."

"Nope," she says. "Because I have you taking the focus away."

"At least you admit it."

"Why wouldn't I? I'm nothing if not grateful."

I pinch her upper inner arm in the soft spot that hurts about fifty times more than it should, and she stifles a yelp and jabs her elbow into my boob.

"Ow, loser," I mutter.

We nurse our injuries. "Okay, fine," I say. "Write me a note and I'll find you."

"In my mind it's already written," she says.

"Okay, Gandhi."

"That was Yoda."

"Not even close."

"Yeah, well, I'm a little young for *Star Wars*."

"You're a little young for having a long-distance boyfriend."

"*You're* a little young for stalking a serial killer."

"It—he—they're not serial killers," I say. "It's a school shooting." I spend the next ten minutes giving her the whole explanation of the past months, including my crash vision and how everything happened with that, and everything that's now happening with Sawyer.

And she just listens and doesn't seem surprised or incredulous or anything. All she says is "I wonder what the shooters' motivation is?"

"So you believe it?" I ask.

"Why wouldn't I? You, Trey, and Sawyer can't all be nuts."

What a relief.

Later, when I'm in my own bed, falling asleep while waiting for Sawyer to call me, Rowan whispers, "Jules?"

I open my eyes and stare at the blinking neon light on the wall. "Yeah?"

"You said Sawyer thinks it's happening soon, right? And the weather forecast has the snow gone by early next week?"

"Yeah."

"Next week is spring break for *all* public schools around here. Nobody's in school. Every classroom in Chicago will be empty."

My heart clutches and I suck in a breath. And then my pillow starts vibrating.

Twenty-Two

"Hey," Sawyer says, his voice a husky whisper that slides down my spine. "Sorry it's so late. Did I wake you?"

"No, Rowan and I were just talking."

"Hi from me."

I look up and see Rowan propped up on one elbow in the dim light. "He says hi."

She grins, and then falls back on her bed and puts her pillow over her face and says, muffled, "Go ahead and do your oogy talk, I can't hear you."

I breathe out a laugh and put my mouth against the phone again. "Rowan knows," I say.

He hesitates. "Um, okay . . . ?"

"She was onto us for a while. Don't worry, she's good

with it. And she just discovered something big for us."

"Oh. Well, in that case, cool. What?"

"If this thing happens early next week, or anytime next week, it won't happen at a public school because we're all on spring break at the same time."

He's silent, and for a minute I think I lost the connection. And then, "Well. Damn. How did we not think of that?"

"Fresh ears and eyes are good," I say, remembering. "And don't worry about her. She keeps more secrets than a tomb."

"I'm not worried," he says, and his voice totally has me convinced that he's got this whole thing under control. But I know better.

"So that leaves private schools?" he asks.

"That seems to be the logical conclusion, though I imagine some of them have the same spring break as us."

"How many private schools are there?"

"I'm not sure. But instead of wasting time in the morning going to check out the two public schools you were planning to look at, maybe we three can meet somewhere to do research?"

"Four," Rowan says, still muffled.

"I thought you couldn't hear me," I whisper.

"What?" Sawyer says.

"Nothing. I mean, Rowan wants to help, if it's cool with you."

"Hell yes. I'll take all the help I can get. Meet me at the coffee shop, North and Twenty-Fifth. Five thirty?"

"Sure." I turn to Rowan. "You're in. We're leaving here at five fifteen in the morning. Don't be late."

She lifts her arm from the blankets and gives a thumbs-up.

I turn away from her and face my wall. "We're going to figure this out," I say, softer.

He's quiet. I picture him in his bed, nodding.

"Jules," he whispers.

"Yeah?"

"Thank you."

I smile. "Sure."

"Jules?"

"Yeah?"

"I wish you were here with me so I could hold you."

My eyes close and a wave of longing rises through me. I remember middle school and my Sawyer pillow. "Hold your pillow. Pretend it's me. I'm here. Right here with you."

I hear a muffled sound like he's actually doing what I suggested, which almost brings tears to my eyes, because what guy does that?

"Jules," he says once more.

"Yeah?" I say again.

He's quiet for a long time. And then he says, "I'm really very insanely much in love with you."

And I can't speak, because this big ball of tears and air is blocking my words, and finally I sniffle and I manage to squeak out, "That is the best thing anybody has ever said to me, ever. And I am insanely really very much in love with you, too."

We sit on the phone all quiet for a minute.

And then, from below Rowan's pillow, a snicker.

I freeze. And she snorts.

I twist around. "Oh my God, Rowan, shut *up*, I hate you!" I grab my pillow and chuck it at her head, but her bed doesn't stop shaking until after Sawyer and I hang up.

In the morning I stumble out of bed at four thirty and kick Rowan in the butt to wake her up. Trey is just emerging from the steamy bathroom when I get there, and he looks at me with surprise.

"What's up?" he whispers. "You going with us?"

I tell him Rowan's discovery and our latest plan. He gets out of my way so I can take a quick shower. Forty-eight minutes later we three are headed out into the darkness.

When we get to the coffee shop, Sawyer's got a table staked out and is leaning over his laptop. We join him.

I look at Rowan. "Spinach-and-feta wrap and a tall coffee, blacker than black," I say.

Rowan nods primly and turns to Sawyer. "May I take your order?"

He gets a cute puzzled grin on his face. "Iced coffee and a sausage-and-egg sandwich." He reaches for his wallet.

Rowan puts her hand out to stop him. "That won't be necessary," she says. She looks at Trey. "Well? What would you like?" Her tone is annoyed.

"What's going on?" Trey asks.

Rowan looks at me.

I shrug. "Tell him."

She clears her throat, clearly not wanting to tell. "I'm buying everyone breakfast today on account of how I disrespected Jules's love."

Sawyer chokes and Trey laughs out loud. "I see. Well, in that case, I'll have a hot vanilla chai tea, yogurt, and granola. With whipped cream. On everything. And a brownie. And—okay, I guess that's enough."

Rowan gives me a condescending sneer and I respond with my superior smile. She goes up to the counter.

Sawyer recovers and starts typing again. I pull my chair closer so I can see, and Trey looks around the other side of him. "There's a ton of private schools," he says under his breath.

"The oldest schools might be mostly Catholic around old Chicago," I say.

"Here's one, Saint Patrick. Over a hundred and fifty years old," Trey says.

Sawyer pulls up the map and zooms in until he has

a street view. "Nope. The building is wrong." He looks up at me. "You know, you might be onto something. The scene of the building in the vision has a tall section. Reminded me of a church." He digs further, and Trey and I keep track of the schools he rules out. Then he finds a list of private schools by neighborhood all within the city limits. There are dozens of them.

It's frustrating. "We need a better computer at home," I say. "This is crazy. I think we're the only kids in the entire city who don't have laptops." I drum my fingers on the table.

Sawyer gently places his hand over mine, stilling my fingers, but his eyes never leave the screen and his other hand moves swiftly around the keyboard. "We can go to school at seven when the doors open and try—" He shakes his head. "Oh, that's right. We're not breathing, typing, or speaking a word of this there."

Rowan finally comes back with a tray of food, then retraces her steps and returns with the coffees.

She joins us as we work and eat, and sits quietly, respecting our love, listening as we talk through the various options and why they don't fit the puzzle in front of us. When seven o'clock rolls around and it's time to head over to school, we have nothing.

Nobody talks as the four of us walk into school, dejected shoulder to dejected shoulder: Trey, Rowan, me,

56

Sawyer. As we reach the freshman hallway, Rowan peels away from our sad little group, but not before shoving a folded note into my hand.

"Second hour," she says. And then she frowns. "Put some makeup on or something, sheesh."

Twenty-Three

Five things Rowan rocks at:
1. Writing fake notes from our mother
2. Disrespecting my love
3. Being on time
4. Flying under the radar
5. Picking gorgeous boyfriends

There are many things Charles Broderick Banks is not. He is not Italian. He's not grumpy. He's not hard on the eyes. He's also not American born. He's South African–Irish-English, he says. The lilt in his voice is swoony. No wonder Rowan is in love.

Rowan and I huddle at a cubicle computer desk, and I take him in: his deep umber eyes, his sun-bleached blond hair, and his tanned, lightly freckled skin that makes him look as if he just came home from a trip to the tropics. He has an adorable little scar on his head that looks like an inch-long part in his hair. His smile is warm and sweet, and I watch my little sister's face come to life when she talks to him. He and Rowan chitchat awkwardly at first with me there, but soon they are bantering back and forth.

He seems to know only the nice things about me, and he asks me pointed questions. "How's your arm? Do you get your cast off soon?"

"Soon," I say. "Next week. It doesn't hurt at all anymore. I practically forget it's here except when I need to, you know, bend that wrist or something."

He grins. "Rowan says you're very brave."

I blush. "Oh, really?" I glance at her and she smirks.

"She's also very mean," Rowan offers. "She made me buy everyone breakfast this morning."

"I'm sure you deserved it," he says.

"Okay, I approve of this boy," I say.

"Approved!" he says, doing an English version of the Target Lady from *Saturday Night Live*. And then he turns his head away from the camera, distracted by a distant voice.

I look at Rowan. "Uh-oh? Or no?"

She shakes her head and listens. "No, it's his tutor.

Oops, my bad. It's his mom." She watches for a second until a tall blond woman appears. "Hi, Mom B!" She waves at the screen.

"Hey, Ro," the woman says. She's wearing designer workout clothes drenched in sweat but still somehow manages to look gorgeous and radiant. "Who's this?"

I wave weakly. "Hi, um, I'm Rowan's sister."

"Oh, Jules. Cool—heard a lot about you."

I nod and smile. *So it seems.*

"We're excited to see Rowan again. Thank your mom and dad for us—I left a message the other day but I know they're really busy."

I glance at Rowan as her face turns red. The little weasel erased it, I'll bet.

Mrs. Banks continues. "We'll be waiting at Baggage Claim, and it's a direct flight so there's no way she'll get stranded somewhere. Just follow the signs to Baggage Claim, hon."

"And I'll call you when I land," Rowan says, like they've rehearsed this.

"And me," I say.

"Yes, I'll call you, too."

Charlie gives his mom a look, and she waves. "Okay, gotta go. See you Sunday."

Rowan calls out her good-bye, and she and Charlie share a private joke I don't get, and they're all just . . .

carefree and having fun, and the biggest stress weighing on them is wondering if rain will delay the flight.

I sit back in my chair, working my fingers through a tangle in my hair, and just watch them. And I can't wait to have so few worries. I can't wait to have fun again. I can't wait to have that kind of light, easy banter with the guy I love.

After a while I excuse myself to let them do their mushy talk in private, ahem. On the walk back to class, I find myself wondering if something horrible will happen while Rowan is gone. Worrying that my parents won't know where to find her or how to contact her. I clench my jaw and force the thought away. Because that can't happen. It can't and it won't.

My stomach hurts.

Twenty-Four

At lunch we don't talk about anything much. We all just sort of sit there feeling glum. Sawyer holds his spoon in front of him, staring at it.

"It's in your spoon?" I ask.

He nods. "It's upside down, though, because of the scientific nature of spoon reflections or whatever."

Trey grunts like he knows what that's called, but he doesn't offer up a term, and I don't care enough at this moment to put forth the effort to ask. Instead, I ask the broken-record question, "Do you see anything new?"

"Actually . . ." Sawyer trails off and keeps looking at the spoon. "Hm."

I sit up, watching him, and Trey raises an eyebrow.

"It's weird," Sawyer says. "My eyes focus on different parts of it than they did before. I think . . . I think . . ."

Roxie and BFF Sarah come up to the table. "Admiring your reflection?" Roxie asks. Her neck scratch is practically gone. Mine are still ugly. They stay hidden under my collar.

Sawyer doesn't look up, so Roxie sticks her boobs out, being way obvious, and I almost laugh at how stupid it is to do that, like a peacock making sure everybody sees his feathers. Only they're not beautiful, colorful feathers, they're just boobs. Trey actually does laugh, in a snorty fashion, and he rolls his eyes. But he can get away with that. He's a senior. He has nothing to fear from her.

Sawyer turns his head and looks at Roxie's boobs, seeing as how they're practically in his face, and, well, because he's a guy. He wears a slightly bewildered look and then raises his eyes to meet Roxie's. "Oh, hey," he mumbles. "What's up?" He scoots his chair over so he doesn't actually get an eye poked out, and he glances at me with a worried expression like he thinks I might punch him in the face.

Body language is so interesting, isn't it? We're learning about it in Mr. Polselli's class. I observe. Roxie takes the tiniest step back and her shoulders relax. "Not much. Just haven't seen you in a while." The boobs deflate slightly, which makes me stop worrying about one of them accidentally bursting. And neither Roxie nor BFF Sarah so much as glances at me, but they both look at Trey and Sawyer. I smile at Sawyer when he catches my eye, and he relaxes. And it's weird. I think I'm supposed to be jealous, but I'm not. I don't think I'm very good at being a stereotypical girl.

"I've been pretty busy," Sawyer says coolly. He shrugs and takes a small bite of his burger. "Attack anyone today?"

"Well, let me tell you," Roxie says, ignoring his disdain. She shoves her butt against Sawyer in an attempt to get him to slide over so she can share the edge of his chair. He stops chewing but doesn't move over, leaving Roxie and her butt hovering weirdly. I just keep watching, and it's like I'm invisible or something. Like I'm not even there. I glance at Trey, who is now finishing up his lunch and ignoring the girls.

"Can you see me?" I ask him.

He looks. Narrows his eyes. "Only if I squint really hard."

I nod. "That's what I thought."

"It's kind of a cool superpower, if you ask me. Invisibility."

"Yeah, you know? You're right. Right, Roxie?"

No response.

"I don't think she can hear invisible people," Trey says.

I shrug. "So that's two superpowers for me, if you really think about it."

Trey chugs down the rest of his iced tea and wipes his mouth with his napkin. "I'll give you that."

"Thanks."

"Who's the other one again?"

I glance up. "That's BFF Sarah."

"BFF is her first name?"

"Ah . . . yes. Yes, it is."

"Interesting."

"Not much different from a name like J.T. or R.J. or C.J."

"Except there's no *J*."

"True."

Sarah turns sharply and frowns at us. "You guys are beyond weird."

My eyes open wide. "You can see me?"

She shakes her head, disgusted, and tugs at Roxie, who, after being denied, is now leaning over the table, talking to Sawyer about Spring Fling, which is like prom but not really, because it's only for freshmen and sophomores and it's lame.

"So you want to go with me?" Roxie asks him. "I got my license. I'll pick you up."

"Um . . . Rox . . ."

"It'll be like old times, you know? We can make out behind the bleachers like when we were a couple." She's speaking really loudly. And finally the jealous factor kicks in. And it kicks in hard. Because I don't know what she's talking about.

"Roxie, what the heck—" Sawyer begins, and I hear anger in his voice.

I stand up and push my chair back, the heat rising to my face.

Trey touches my arm. "I think we need to just sit and watch this, don't you?"

BFF Sarah crosses her arms, bored.

Roxie smiles at Sawyer.

Sawyer looks at me, his lips parted, eyes apologetic. "Please don't go," he says.

I sit down again. "Yeah," I say to Trey, "you're right."

But I can't concentrate on what anybody else is saying right now, because all I see is Sawyer and Roxie making out behind the bleachers. And I feel like a stupid fool. Because I thought somehow Sawyer would have waited for me like I waited for him. I thought our first kiss was our first kiss. And it's not; it was just my first. And even though it's ridiculous for me to expect that he hasn't kissed anybody else, because we're sixteen, for crying out loud, it still makes my throat ache.

When I can focus, I watch BFF Sarah grow impatient and walk away.

And I see Sawyer's mouth moving, and Roxie scowling and getting angry. But I can't comprehend anything.

After a minute, I look at Trey. "I really need to go," I say in a low voice.

"If you leave now, she'll feel like she won something. Just stay here and talk to me. Ignore them. She's looking to get a rise out of you, so don't let her. You and Sawyer will work this out. He's a good guy, remember?"

"I know." But he made out with Roxie. He was a *couple* with her. How did I not know this? Maybe because I'm a freaking outcast, huh? Pretty stinking likely.

"So, about that other thing," Trey says, keeping my gaze locked on his. "Let's meet up after school and do the library again. I need to do some research for a term paper anyway. Sound good?"

"Sure," I say, my voice hollow. They're talking about me now. I stare at Trey, and he keeps talking. And then he laughs, and I think it's because Roxie just suggested Sawyer was gay and having a secret relationship with Trey, and I was acting as his beard. I can't help it—I have to tune in.

Sawyer looks hard at Roxie for a long moment. And then he says, "Yes, okay, I admit it. I'm gay, and I'm in love with Trey."

Roxie stares at him. "You are not."

"You just said I was. And, well, it's true."

"I made out with a *gay*?"

The immediate area goes silent. Heads turn, everybody looking to see who the newly outed gay guy is. I hate this. I glance at Trey, who seems to be enjoying this immensely.

"Well, I'm not just any old *gay*, I'm Sawyer the gay." His lip twitches. "That's what we call each other."

"True story," Trey adds. "But I rejected him."

"He did, yes. Multiple times, in fact."

"But he's still very much in love with me, and I like that, because it kind of feels like I have power over him. It's a form of torture, and it's fun."

Sawyer nods. Then he shakes his head. "Not fun for me, I mean. For him."

A few people around us start snickering.

Roxie's face turns red. I think she figured out they're teasing her and sort of throwing her own actions in her face, but she says through gritted teeth, "So are you gay or not?"

Sawyer drops the shtick. "Really? You're asking me this?"

"Obviously."

Sawyer gives her an incredulous look. "Okay, well, then I . . . I am."

Her eyes bulge. "Were you gay when we made out?"

Sawyer holds his straight face. "Not before, but after . . . well, then I was."

A few people laugh, and Roxie falters, and I feel sorry for her. Not because she's gullible. But because it means so damn much to her to know if she made out with *a gay*.

"Okay, that's enough, guys," I mutter.

The bell rings. People around us turn back to gather their stuff. Trey squeezes my shoulder and slips away. Roxie stomps off, and I stand there, looking across the table at Sawyer, who is searching my face with his eyes. And I don't know what to say, except "I guess I'll see you at the library after school."

He sighs and looks down at the table. "Yeah. Okay."

I stand there a second more, and then I take my tray away. I have to run to make it to class on time.

Twenty-Five

And here's the thing. I hate that junk. I hate that whole whatever you want to call it—the misunderstanding-slash-thing-between-us story line. It's on every TV show, in every book you read, every movie. Something always happens to put this stupid wedge in the budding relationship, and the people don't talk about it so they just keep being misunderstood, and by the end of the movie, maybe it all works out and maybe it doesn't, but I hate it and I wish this kind of crap didn't happen. Why can't the two lovers just be together? Why can't the fucking *plot* of the fucking *story* of everybody's *life* just be like, hey, you finally find the person you want to *be* with, and you just be with them, and that part is the good part? And the conflict is something else, like a crash and an explosion, or a school shooting, but you're just still together with that person as a team and you both fight *together* against some *other* enemy? Why does this have to happen? Because it's very clear to me that we just. Don't. Need this. Right now.

"So, uh, that got a little out of hand," Trey says when he gets to our table in sculpting class. "Sorry about that. It was all in fun."

"I know."

"Why are you being so quiet?"

"I'm not sure."

He nods, and we sit there in silence for once, working side by side making a bowl and painting fruit, both of us knowing that scary junk is coming, and the world is so much bigger than this place, and these people, and a stupid rivalry.

We meet up at the library after school and Trey wisely goes to look for books for his research project, leaving me and Sawyer alone on the couch in the library loft.

And the dude, to his credit, looks way more distraught about what happened at lunch than he is over the visions that are driving him crazy. "I'm sorry I never told you I made out with Roxie," he says. "We were never a couple, I don't care what she says. We made out twice at the beginning of ninth grade, more just to experience things and mess around."

I listen and say, "You didn't have to disclose any of that to me, you know. People have pasts. It's not a big deal. I mean, I guess my reaction was more because of the way she was approaching it, and approaching, um, you. And just pretending I wasn't there and throwing it in my face."

"Boobs first?" He laughs.

I smile. "Yeah, you noticed? It's kind of sad, actually."

He nods. "She has no self-confidence. And . . . I think I took the joke too far. I kept expecting her to get it, but she got so hung up on whether she'd—well, yeah. You were there."

"Yeah." I shrug. "Well, thanks for explaining, and, you know, I'm not mad or anything, I just don't like her. She used to be my friend and now she's just . . . sad. And mean."

"So . . . you still like me?" he asks with a grin. He slips his hand in mine.

"A little," I agree.

By the time Trey comes back, Sawyer and I are both on computers. I'm researching private schools; Sawyer's trying to get close-ups of every frame in his vision. "When I was watching it in my spoon and everything was upside down," he says, "I thought I saw something through the window."

Trey looks at Sawyer's screen automatically, even though he and I both know we can't see anything. He laughs. "You picked 'Surprised Kitty' as the video to channel it?"

Sawyer is concentrating too hard to laugh. "Yeah. I mean, why not entertain you guys?" He hits pause and stares, then takes a screen shot that only he can see and starts enlarging it.

I go back to looking up schools and start bookmarking them so I can show them all to Sawyer at once. And then he mutters, "Yesss," and starts scribbling things on a notepad. "There's the road in relationship to the building. Now I'm getting a bigger picture."

Trey and I look over and wait for him to finish. We haven't had a "Yesss" in forever. I squeeze my eyes shut and hope for a major breakthrough.

But when I open my eyes again, I see Trey looking at his phone and muttering, "Shit," and I see Sawyer looking at the stairway and getting to his feet.

Because guess who's here? Yay, it's my dad.

Dad reaches the top of the stairs and spies us. Trey types something quickly and stashes his phone, and he stands up, so I stand up too.

"Hey, Dad," Trey says. He puts his hands in his pockets. "What's up?"

Dad stares at me, and then he looks at Sawyer.

"Hi, Mr. Demarco," Sawyer says. His voice is calm.

I don't say a word.

Dad looks like he's trying to hold it in. His face is red. But he won't make a scene in a public place. Not in front of potential customers. He doesn't answer Sawyer, which feels kind of jerkish to me. Instead, he looks back at me and says, "Tree research. Is that the same as chess club?"

"Dad—" I say.

"Don't bother," he says, and I'm a little freaked out that his voice is so quiet. "Both of you, it's time to go. Julia, you're coming with me. Trey, come on. You take the truck."

"No, sorry, Dad. I'm still working—" Trey begins.

"You'll get home in ten minutes or you're grounded too, like this one."

"Dad, I'm eighteen," Trey says. "I'm graduating from high school in two and a half months." He sits back down. "You can't ground me."

"Watch me."

"No, you watch *me*. Watch me sit here and do my homework like an excellent student. What the heck is wrong with you? I'll be home when I'm finished with it, and I'll get a good grade like I always do, and then I'll go to work for you and do a good job there, too. But right now, I'll sit with Sawyer Angotti if I feel like it, so don't even go there. This stupid rivalry ends with your generation. It doesn't exist in mine."

Dad's face twitches. He gives Trey a long, hard look

that scares the crap out of me, and then he looks at me. "Come on, Julia."

I stand there. And my face is hot, and I feel like yelling, and my stomach hurts.

"Julia," my father says again, his voice ending on a strained note, and I can tell he's about to blow a gasket.

I press my lips together and swallow hard. I shake my head. And I don't move. We stare at each other for the longest five seconds of my life. And then Trey says, "Jules, go with Dad."

I glance at him and frown, but his face is set. I look at Sawyer, and he nods in agreement with Trey.

And I'm like, what the heck? I can't even think clearly. I feel like a total baby. I know I'm going to get reamed the whole way home. And I have a life too—why should I have to go with him?

"Julia!" Dad barks, and now people around us are looking, which I'm sure Dad will blame me for later.

"Fine." I throw the meatball truck keys at Trey's face, grab my backpack and coat, trying to shove my arm through the hole but my stupid cast keeps catching on it. When I give up and move around the table, Dad tries to take my arm. I yank it away from him and run down the steps, leaving Dad following me, and Trey and Sawyer standing there watching over the loft railing. I can't even look at them because I don't want them to see me cry.

• • •

We get into Dad's car, and I'm immediately aware of how seldom I ride anywhere with him. I can probably count the number of times on my fingers. He hardly ever goes out, and when he does, my mom almost always drives.

He leans forward, squinting at the windshield and muttering under his breath as he eases out of the parking space. And for a split second, his mannerisms are so familiar. With a chill down my spine, I realize he reminds me of *me*, trying to drive when I had a vision clogging my windows and mirrors. I watch him in horror. Could it be?

And then he starts in on me. "I don't know what to do with you," he says. "You lie to us about everything. I told you that you weren't allowed to talk to that one."

"Will you stop calling him that? Sheesh, Dad."

"Don't talk when I'm talking!" he roars, his booming voice taking over. "You need to go back to respecting me!"

"You mean being scared of you?"

"Dammit, Julia!" He slams his hand into the steering wheel and for a second I'm scared he's going to drive us off the road. He comes to a hard stop at a light and I'm tempted to just jump out, but that would only prolong this and make it all worse.

I sit there, silent, so he can talk more. Yell more. Like a big hypocrite, he hollers about trust, trust, trust, until I want to throw up, because he has never trusted me, and I no longer trust him. I close my eyes and rest my pounding head on the window. And he goes on and on about what a bad child I am.

And the truth is he's right about the things I did. I lied to him and Mom. I saw Sawyer when I wasn't supposed to. I faked some school projects so we could find time to work on saving some lives. But as long as my parents are being overprotective nutcases, I will have to continue disobeying them, I guess. Because I'm not able to let people die when I can stop it from happening.

Now, shall I try and explain that to Dad?

We pull into the parking lot behind the restaurant. I get out without a word and close the door. It seems like he's done yelling. I stopped paying attention. But before we walk into our apartment door, he says, "I'll talk to your mother about what your punishment will be. Be back down for work in five minutes."

And I look at him. "You're not even going to let me say anything?"

His jaw is set. "What do you want to say that I don't already know? That you're pregnant, too?"

I almost laugh, because he just can't let that idea go, but it also makes me furious because he thinks he knows me, and he thinks I'm out there banging people left and right, and he's just so wrong and that's so not me in any way, and it hurts. "Three things, Dad," I say, winding up. "I want to say three things."

He folds his arms and waits like he's doing me a big favor.

I plunge into the rage headfirst. "One," I say, "I'm not pregnant. I'm not sure why you constantly think I am, but I am not sexually active, so you can just knock it off with that." I can't look at him. "Two, I know about your affair, so it's kind of hard to take you seriously on this whole trust thing. And three?" I forgot what three was. And then I remember. "Three. Find yourself another slave. I quit." And before I can allow the shock on his face to poke into my conscience and make me feel bad, I turn on the wet cement step, open the door, and run up the stairs and into my room.

Twenty-Six

Trey knocks on my bedroom door ten minutes later. "It's me," he says.

"Come on in."

He stands there. "You okay?"

"Yeah, but I'm in deep shit. You're home early."

"Sawyer was worried Dad was going to hit you or something. I told him Dad has never done that, but Sawyer was pretty jittery. I think he feels bad we told you to go with Dad."

"Yeah, what the hell was that?"

"Sorry. I suggested it because I figured it might save you a little grief in the end."

"Well, it didn't."

"We're not at the end yet."

"Let me know when we get there, will ya?"

He laughs softly. "I will once I take my metaphorical beating. He's pretty pissed at me."

I don't say anything. All I can think about is Dad and his stupid affair, and how Trey and Rowan don't know, and I don't know if I should tell them. And I wonder if Dad will kill himself now that he knows I know.

It's the constant question. And then I worry that Dad's going to think Mom told me and be mad at her. I flop down on my bed, finally beginning to realize the scope of what I've done. "I quit," I say.

Trey looks at me like he didn't hear me.

I answer his look. "I quit. My job, I mean. I told Dad I quit."

"Holy shit."

"I know."

"What did he say?"

"I didn't really give him time to answer. He yelled the whole way home." I sigh deeply. "At least now I can work with Sawyer more. If Dad doesn't chain me to the house."

Just then we hear pounding up the stairs. It's not our parents. Three seconds later the bedroom door flies open and Rowan is standing there in her work clothes, bug-eyed. She looks from me to Trey to me again. "What the heck?" she asks. "Dad's on a rampage. Sorry I couldn't warn you in time. I didn't know he'd left until later."

Trey explains. "Rowan texted me that Dad was on his way, but by the time I got it he was already coming up the library loft steps." He looks at Rowan. "Who's working?"

"Dad's in the kitchen. Mom and I are in the dining room. Aunt Mary's up front." She looks at me, her face showing hurt for the first time. "How could you quit? I'm leaving Sunday. Now who's going to cover for me?"

I shake my head. "I'm sorry, Ro. It all happened really fast. Dad went nuts and I just lost it, I guess."

"He's superpissed at you, too, Trey. What did you do?"

Trey rolls his eyes. "I think I humiliated him in front of an Angotti. He told me to go home. I said no. He tried to ground me." Trey laughs bitterly. "He's really losing it. He can't get a handle on that stupid rivalry. Okay, so somebody stole your recipe. Get over it. Make up a new, better recipe."

I bite my lip and look at the floor. I know it's more complicated than that. And I'm starting to wonder if there's even more shit going on with Dad. But as mad as I am about the way he's treating me, I don't think I should say anything, especially about the affair. I've made enough messes for now.

Rowan looks at her phone. "I gotta get back down there," she mutters.

"Hey, Rowan?" I say as she turns to leave.

"What." She's still upset with me.

"They'll figure something out. I'll help them if they need me. If Dad'll let me. They can get Nick or Casey or hire somebody else—they're business owners. Stuff like this happens. But I'm still sorry for letting you down."

She scowls. "It's fine. I don't actually blame you." She pauses once more. "Dad told Mom that you're not pregnant. I take it he accused you of that again."

I nod.

"Well, I understand why you'd quit."

"Thanks."

"What did any of us ever do to make Dad not trust us? I don't get it." She disappears, nimbly zigzagging through the cluttered hallway, and then we hear her feet on the steps once more.

Trey stands up. "I should go down too."

I look up at him. "Everything's such a mess."

He nods. "You should call Sawyer. He was figuring stuff out, remember?"

I'd forgotten. "Yeah, okay," I say.

When he leaves, I pull out my phone.

Twenty-Seven

Sawyer's working and can't talk. We make a plan to meet at the coffee shop again before school. I hang around feeling useless, getting all my homework done in record time, making a veggie omelet for dinner, and getting on the computer to research more schools since that's all I know to do to help Sawyer.

When I've exhausted everything I can think of, I sit down in the living room chair and watch TV. Local Chicago news pops on and I watch it idly. There's something about the food truck festival this weekend, so I pay attention, wondering if Dad signed us up. And then I remember I don't work at Demarco's Pizzeria anymore, and I feel really lonely all of a sudden.

When the segment is over I mute it and stare at the

screen, thinking about how I've messed everything up. My eyes focus on the TV when there's a piece on the University of Chicago, which is where Trey once thought about going until he found out how expensive it is. A reporter stands on the grounds, talking about who knows what, and then the headline pops up. "Vandalism over Spring Break." The camera pans wide and some of the campus is visible, and then my eyes open wide. I lunge for the remote and hit the record button, begging it to get the whole segment. Then I fumble for my phone and call Sawyer.

"Hey," he says.

"Where are you?"

"I'm—"

"Come over. Right now. Can you?"

"I, um, are you kidding me?"

"No. I think I found the school. I have it on my DVR. It's not a high school, Sawyer—it's the University of Chicago!"

"The—okay, but what about your parents?"

"They won't be upstairs before eleven. Come!"

"I'm—I'm turning around. I'm five minutes away. Meet me at the door to your apartment."

"Awesome." I hang up and run to the bathroom to make sure I look okay. And then I go back to the TV and rewind to make sure I actually got what I need. I do—I have the whole show. While I wait, I cue it up so Sawyer can be in and out of here quickly. And then I look around the living room like I'm seeing it for the first time.

"Oh, dear dog," I say. "Oh. Dear dog." It's mortifying. No one has ever seen this. No one.

"Whatever," I mutter. This is more important. And I head downstairs to wait.

Sawyer comes out of nowhere, a sudden face in the door's window. I open it quietly and wave him inside.

"Two things," I whisper as we creep up the stairs. "We have to hurry. And . . . my dad is a hoarder. I'm not sure if you knew that. It's a train wreck in here, I'm just warning you, and I'm really embarrassed, but I want you to know the rest of us don't live like that. It's part of his . . . illness."

He nods. "It's okay," he says. "I knew. You mentioned it in the hospital."

We weave through the apartment, Sawyer pretending like it's the most normal thing in the world to have piles of Christmas lights and bulbs in the dining room but nowhere to put a tree.

In the living room I grab the remote. "Watch," I say. "About a minute in, the camera pans and there are buildings with ivy and a whole row of those trees along a street." I turn on the sound for the first time and hit play. And the segment runs. "Say stop if you need me to," I say. "Can you even see it, or is it the vision?"

"No," he says. "I can see it." Sawyer stands there, coat

still on, and watches. The reporter is talking about recent vandalism—graffiti painted around campus. The students are on spring break this week. She's talking about having time to clean up before school is in session again. And then she says something about the beautiful campus's botanical gardens and redbud trees that are just about to burst into bloom. The camera pans, and Sawyer leans forward, staring, straining as if that'll make the camera go where he wants it to go.

"Stop," he says.

I press pause.

"That's it," he says. He stares at it, taking it all in. "This is it. It's one of those buildings for sure—look at the ivy. These are the right kinds of trees. The snow is almost gone." He looks at me. "And the road. You're a genius. How did you know?"

"By your description. And because of the spring break headline. Is there graffiti on the building in your vision?"

"No. They must have it cleaned off by the time this happens." He rubs his eyes. "I can't believe it. You figured it out. I never thought we'd get it." He turns to me and pulls me into a hug, which feels superawkward here in my house, but I'm not complaining.

Still, the risk is large and I pull away. "Let's get you out of here. We'll figure out what to do in the morning."

He nods and we're snaking back down the steps when the door at the bottom rattles and opens.

Twenty-Eight

Thankfully, it's Trey. He startles when he sees Sawyer in our house, but he recovers quickly and holds a hand up in warning. He turns to look behind him, and I can hear him talking to someone outside. Sawyer and I stand so still I don't even think we're breathing.

"Okay, good night, Tony," Trey calls. He comes inside like nothing's up, then presses his back against the door. "I'm going to murder you both," he says.

Sawyer and I nod.

After a minute, Trey opens the door a crack and looks out. "Okay, get the hell out of here," he says to Sawyer.

Without a word, Sawyer makes a break for it, and Trey scoots me up the stairs.

"What the—" he starts, and he's so stunned he can't even finish.

"I'll show you," I say. "Come on."

He follows me and I show him everything. When he's done watching it, he looks at me. "It's not a high school."

"Not a high school."

"You figured it out by accidentally watching the news."

I nod. "I do watch the news on occasion," I say in my defense. "But I didn't have much time back when I had a job."

He laughs. "Oh, Jules . . . your job misses you."

"Did Dad yell at you?"

"Of course. He also suggested that since I'm eighteen I might want to consider moving out and feeding my own mouth."

"He—he did? He really said that?"

"Yes."

My stomach twists. "Are you going to?"

"I—no, not this time. But if he doesn't stop, I might."

This scares the hell out of me. "But where would you go?"

He looks at me. "Aw. Don't worry. I'm not going anywhere." He punches me in the arm. "Do you think I'd leave you and Rowan here? Come on. Not until I go to college in the fall. And even then, I might have to commute." He pinches and rubs his fingers together. "Money.

Though now I'm starting to rethink things again. I need to decide soon."

He goes into his room, and all I can do is think, *Don't leave me here with them!*

Later, Rowan comes in, and I can hear Mom moving around the kitchen. I'm not quite sure what will happen next, but Trey and Ro and I are all planning on going to the coffee shop to meet Sawyer like this morning. The three of us sit around my bedroom, talking quietly. And it occurs to me that the reason we're so close is that the weirdness gene maybe skipped a generation, and we all get along because it's the only way to survive.

Rowan tells us about her trip and gives us all of her flight information, Charlie's address, his phone number, and his parents' numbers too. And even though I feel kind of odd about letting her go and not telling Mom, I feel very good about where she is going to be now that I've seen Charlie and his mom and their non-hoardy, non-tense house. And besides, I couldn't possibly stop her from going.

We hear Dad lumbering around and I make Trey stay in our room even though he's falling asleep. I don't want to face Dad. But he doesn't come in. We hear their bedroom door close like it's the door to a crypt, and we know he's down for the count. Whether it's just for the night or for a few days, no one ever knows. But we think this latest problem will put him in the sack until Rowan leaves.

And then Mom knocks.

She looks at us all—Rowan on her bed, Trey on the foot of mine, and me on the floor in between, and she gets this melancholy look on her face. I think she's going to say something, or yell at me, or tell me what my new punishment is, but all she does is stand there looking at us, like she didn't realize we were all so grown up. She massages her weary eyes. And then she says, "I am so glad you have each other."

"Aww, Mommy," Rowan says, and gets up off her bed to hug her.

Trey says, "You have us too, Mom."

And I just watch her grow old before my eyes, and I smile at her and hope she knows I love her.

If she has a punishment for me, she doesn't issue it.

Friday morning rolls around quickly. It's the last day of school before spring break, and I half expect Dad to be standing outside our room, waiting to catch us going to school early, but he's not there. We three leave by six and sit at the same table we sat at yesterday, but Sawyer doesn't come. After a while I call him, wondering if he slept through his alarm, but he doesn't answer.

We hang out, unable to do anything without computers

or smartphones, and finally we just go to school, not sure what's going on.

Sawyer is not by my locker. He's not in school. There's no sign of him. And I'm worried. By lunch, I've tried calling him three times, and he doesn't answer.

"I'm freaking out a little," I say in fifth hour with Trey. "We should have gone to look for him at lunch."

"Where the hell would we look?"

"We could at least see if his car is home."

Trey shrugs. "He's probably got the flu or something."

"He looked fine last night."

"Maybe he's skipping. Heading over to University of Chicago to see what he can find out."

"Why wouldn't he answer the phone, then?"

"That . . . I don't know. Okay. We'll drive by after."

The warming trend has continued throughout the day, and there are dirty puddles filling potholes everywhere. I try Sawyer's phone once more after school as Trey abandons a ride from his doucheball friend Carter again and the three of us climb into the meatball truck. And this time Sawyer answers.

"Hey," he says.

I pause and hop back outside the truck so I can have some privacy. "Hey, are you okay?"

His voice is quiet. "So, remember back when my dad called your dad after you stopped by our restaurant?"

My eyes fly open. I look at Trey and Rowan, who are peering out the windshield at me. "Yeah."

"I'm guessing you don't know that your dad returned the favor last night."

I bow my head and press it against the truck. "Oh, God."

"The proprietors were not amused."

"What happened? Where are you?"

"I'm pulling into the school parking lot now. You got room in that ball truck for one more?"

"Hell yes," I say. "We'll make room. We're going to drop Rowan off and head to the university. Trey and I told Dad about the food truck festival this weekend, so he wants us to—" Sawyer pulls up next to us and parks the car, and I just end the call rather than standing there next to him wasting phone minutes. He opens the door, gets out, and slowly turns to face me.

His left eye is swollen, black and purple.

He eases out of the car like he's in pain.

Trey and Rowan burst out of the truck when they see him, and all I can do is stare. "Holy shit."

"Nice, right?"

I go to him. And nobody has to ask what happened.

"Your grandfather didn't seem to care about hiding it this time," I say.

Sawyer shifts his gaze like he doesn't want to talk about it. "It wasn't my grandfather. Let's just get out of here."

Twenty-Nine

We leave his car in the school parking lot—it's safer in case his parents go looking for him, he says. And we drop Rowan off. She knows she's got to stay the model obedient child for a few more days, so she doesn't even pout about it.

Trey drives and we go straight to the University of Chicago. We find the building we need, park the balls in a nearly empty parking lot, and wander the grounds until we find a whole huge section with mostly old buildings—Trey says it's the main quadrangle.

Sawyer walks slower than usual, so we let him take the lead. He talks us through the vision—as much of it as he can.

"I only see one gunman in the outdoor scene—the

short, slight one. I don't know where the other guy is. He's bigger and blond. Maybe he's there next to the smaller one and I just don't see him because he's not in the shot, I'm not sure. So if this is the right sidewalk," he says, pointing to the one we're on, "he walks in this direction, I think."

"Do you know which building it happens in? Can you tell?" I try to sound easygoing. Sawyer doesn't need anybody else harassing him, especially me.

"I don't know."

Trey points. "Look, there's some graffiti. Those two guys are trying to remove it from the stone."

Sawyer and I follow his finger. "I'll go talk to them," Sawyer says.

Trey and I exchange a look and stay back as Sawyer approaches the two painters in front of an old, ivy-covered building. He talks to the guys for a minute and returns to us.

"The vandals were some haters writing slurs at one of the college equal rights groups or something," Sawyer says. "They didn't really know." He frowns, gazing over the grounds, and starts walking through the campus, lost in thought.

Trey and I follow, acting casual when security drives by in their carts. I look at the trees. Definitely budding, and with the warming trend happening, they'll be growing quickly, changing daily.

Sawyer stops, closes his eyes, and massages his eyelids, deep in thought. He covers his ears, then looks up and all around. He walks a few paces up a path between a road and a building and looks all around again. He frowns and mutters something.

"What are you looking for?" I venture.

"The little stop sign. I haven't seen it. It should be here . . . somewhere." He rubs his temples. "The vision is in all the windows. Fucking gunshots won't stop. I can't even think."

Trey and I start looking for the stop sign too.

"It should be there," Sawyer says. "I guess I have the wrong building." He emits a heavy sigh and runs a hand through his hair, gripping it in frustration. "But everything else is right. That building with the ivy," he says, pointing to a gorgeous old building on one side of the quad near where we stand. "The redbud trees. The sidewalk. And suddenly now, believe it or not, the noise and everything stopped. I can't seem to conjure up the vision at all—not in any windows or signs or anything."

"It's because you're doing something right," I murmur, hoping he can find some encouragement in it, but knowing how helpless he must feel.

Trey walks in the direction of where Sawyer pointed. "Maybe we're just on the wrong side of the building," he says over his shoulder. "I'll run around to see if it looks the same from the other side." He starts jogging down the path. I go over to Sawyer.

"Is there anything I can do?" I ask.

There's a distant look in his eyes that's not due to the punch he took to the face, but he focuses in on me and relaxes into a half smile for a moment. He reaches one arm around my neck and pulls me close, kisses the top of my head. "Just don't leave me."

As we stand there together, two girls and a guy all dressed in black pass by us silently, and I think it must be sad to be stuck at school during spring break. And then I think about me going to college someday, and wonder if I'll ever want to go home. Only if Trey and Ro are there too.

Sawyer's arm tightens on my shoulders and his whole body tenses. He puts his lips to my ear and whispers, "I think that's them."

I turn my head and look at their backs. One girl has dark brown hair in a ponytail. The other has short blond hair, a pixie cut. The guy has blond hair too. He's wearing a black knit cap. My heart races, but I'm confused. "I thought you said there were two guys?" I say in a soft voice.

"Come on," he says, and we start to follow leisurely behind them. "I thought they were guys, but I never see their faces and they're wearing black. The guy I see with the gun in the classroom is slight and short. It's that girl, the one with the ponytail."

I bite my lip. Has Sawyer started losing it?

"In the vision she's wearing a knit cap and her jacket collar is up. I'm guessing her hair is tucked into the cap. That's her, I'm sure of it."

"But, Sawyer," I say, "school shooters are never girls."

"Don't be sexist," he says, and I actually hear a little bit of the old, nonstressed Sawyer teasing in his voice, and I know he's sure we just stumbled on a big clue. But he turns serious again as we follow, trying not to look like we're trailing them.

Trey is standing at a crossroads, looking at the ground. The three in black pass him, and the girl with the ponytail gives him a long stare, long enough for Sawyer and me to get a good look at her profile before they continue walking.

"I'm going to follow them," Sawyer says. "I'll meet you back here."

I almost protest, but then I notice the expression on Trey's face. I nod instead. "Be careful." And he continues on without me. I make a beeline to where Trey is standing.

I squint as I approach. "What's wrong?" When I'm close enough to whisper, I tell him, "Sawyer thinks those people are the shooters."

"No way." Trey looks startled and cranes his neck to get a better glimpse. I look down at the ground next to where he's standing. And there's the stop sign that's missing, lying in the grass, a fresh black dirt hole near the base of it. But it's no longer a stop sign. Underneath the word "STOP" is another word in black spray paint.

"'Stop fags,'" I say, reading it, and the anger wells up inside me. I press my lips together and blink back the gritty tears that spring to my eyes. "Wow, the haters are so clever these days."

"Aren't they?" Trey murmurs. "At least we found the stop sign." He tries to shrug off the slur but I know better. I know it hurts him. Then he points to a little blue flag stuck in the ground next to the hole. "Looks like it's flagged to be replaced. I'm sure they'll have it up before school starts again."

"Well, that'll satisfy the evidence in the vision. I think that means the crime scene is somewhere near this building. We'll have to ask Sawyer." Trey and I both look at the sprawling structure, several stories high, with spires and gargoyles adorning it and green ivy creeping up its walls. Trey takes pictures with his phone. I count windows, trying to figure out how many rooms are in there, but it's impossible to tell.

Trey shakes his head a little and looks at me, then looks back at the enormous buildings around us. "Somehow this seems just a little harder than stopping a snowplow," he says.

Thirty

Sawyer comes back after a few minutes. We show him the stop sign and the structure Trey and I guess to be the gorgeous, ivy-colored building in Sawyer's vision where the shooting will take place. Sawyer cocks his head and looks at it through narrowed eyes, taking in the turrets and spires. He glances beyond it, and then he turns to peer along the stretch of buildings the other way. "I don't know. I think it's this one," he says, pointing to Cobb Hall, but he doesn't sound very sure.

"What happened to the shooters?" I ask, making sure nobody else is in earshot.

"They went to the parking lot, got in a car, and took off. I got the car info and license number. Not that it'll do us any good."

"Don't you think we should call the police?" Trey asks. "I think we have to. Isn't it the law or something?"

"Come on, Trey," I say. "We went through this last time. They're going to ask how we know. And then what?"

He's quiet for a second. "Why can't we leave an anonymous tip?"

I think about that. "Okay, that's not a bad idea. Is there a way to do that?"

He shrugs. "Easy enough to find out with Sawyer's phone."

Sawyer is already looking it up. "Yeah, there's an anonymous text line called TXT2TIP. It doesn't give the cops your number."

"So . . . we just say we think somebody has plans to shoot down a bunch of students sometime in the near future?" I think about it for a minute. "I suppose it would be better than nothing."

"Yeah, I guess." Sawyer looks up. "You think I should do it?"

We look at each other and nod. "We need all the help we can get," Trey says. "It would make me feel a lot better about everything."

"Me too," Sawyer says. "Okay, here goes nothing. I sure hope this isn't a trick." His fingers fly over the screen. He stops, reads what he has, and shows it to us.

"That looks good," I say. Trey nods in agreement.

Sawyer takes a breath and lets it out. He presses send. And now the police know there might be a shooting in the near future near Cobb Hall.

There's not much else we can do. We try to peer into windows on the first floor, but none of the ones we can see into look anything like what Sawyer described. We try the doors to the building all the way around, but they're locked.

"You know," I say after we come full circle around the buildings, "we might not want to be seen here. We look kind of suspicious since there aren't very many students. Especially with the graffiti stuff that was happening, and now that the police have our tip . . . I mean, they could be on their way over. Maybe we should get out of here."

Absently, Sawyer touches his puffy eye. "Yeah, that's cool, but how are we going to monitor things to figure out timing? The buds on the trees are near where they're supposed to be. The ivy is . . . well, it's hard to tell if it's the same as in the vision. I don't think ivy changes much from day to day. The new stop sign will be up soon, I'm sure. But maybe there are other stop signs. And the vision doesn't actually show the shooters walking into the building by the stop sign—they're just walking near it. So I don't know." He looks around and we all start heading toward the meatball truck. "How are we supposed to know when it's going to happen?"

Trey shrugs. "All we know is that it isn't happening tonight. And that's the best we can do."

We stop by the food truck festival grounds to check it out like Dad's expecting Trey to do. Trey takes care of booking a spot tomorrow for the meatball truck, and finally we're on our way back home to Melrose Park. We don't say much, but we're all wondering. What day? What time? What building? What room? And I remember the way it was with the crash. Everything pointed to Valentine's Day, but at the last minute I realized it was happening the night before. It was all about observation, noticing the littlest things in the vision, that made the difference. It's unbelievably frustrating that I can't see this thing myself.

"How are the visions?" I ask. It's dark now, and we're out of the city, heading back to school. Trey's driving, I'm in the middle seat. Sawyer's by the window, staring out, tapping out the sound of eleven gunshots on his thigh.

"They come and go." He winces and closes his eyes, and his fingers stop tapping.

"Were you able to decipher any words from that whiteboard once you did a close-up?"

"No."

I look at my lap, cringe, and ask another question. "In

the vision, when you see the shot of the building, is there any particular part of the building that seems to be, like, the focus of the scene?"

He's quiet. Trey glances at Sawyer and then at me. I shrug. He frowns and looks back at the road.

"Yeah," Sawyer says after I've already given up on him. He shifts and stares out the window, and I realize he's looking into the side mirror of the truck. "I mean, not any specific window, but there's a section of what I think is Cobb Hall that gets a close-up."

Without a word, Trey slips his phone from his pocket and hands it to me. I look at him, puzzled, but then remember he took pictures of the building. I go through them until I find a shot of Cobb Hall. I touch Sawyer's arm. "Which part?"

He startles and looks at Trey's phone for a long moment. And then he looks at me. "I can't see the photo," he says.

We stop talking.

Trey pulls the truck into the school parking lot. "Jules, I think you should drive Sawyer home. I'll take this ball bus home and pick you up from Angotti's back parking lot on my first delivery. That'll give you two a little chance to . . . do . . . whatever it is you do when you're alone."

Sawyer doesn't argue, and he and I get out. I wave my thanks to Trey as he takes off again.

We stand face-to-face in the warm, wet air as every-thing around us melts. I look up into Sawyer's eyes, and he cringes and looks away. "Dammit."

"What is it?" I ask.

He doesn't look at me. "It's in your eyes," he says. "The vision. It's playing in your eyes."

It makes my stomach hurt. I close my eyes, reach up to touch his face, turn his chin back toward me. "Better?"

I feel his breath on my face a split second before his lips touch mine. A thrill runs through me, from my toes up to my throat and ending in a low moan. Sawyer sucks in a breath and kisses me hard, his hands sliding around my neck, under my hair. I lean back against the car door and he presses against me, setting me on fire.

My fingers explore his chest inside his jacket and he flinches once, just barely, just enough to remind me that his father beat the shit out of him last night. I lighten my touch and slide my good arm around his back, pulling him close, chest against chest, legs clenching legs, wishing I could pull his entire body into mine. Wishing I could fix him.

His lips find my neck and I can't think straight. I reach up and slide my fingers through his hair, whisper his name in his ear. His hot breath rakes over my collarbone and his fingers tremble at my shoulder, his other hand sliding down my side and finding the hollow of my back, and then our lips are together once more, softer, gentler, and we're breathing hard.

Sawyer reaches around me for the handle of the door to the backseat, fumbles with it, and then lets it go. "No," he says like he's reprimanding himself. And then, after a deep breath, "No," again. And then he lets the breath go, his cheek against mine and his sigh in my ear. "Jules Demarco," he says, "you scare the hell out of me."

I smile against his earlobe. "I know," I say.

Truth is, he scares the hell out of me, too.

Thirty-One

Saturday dawns clear, sunny, and unseasonably warm, and all I can think about is that we're running out of time and there's nothing I can do. I have no job for the first Saturday in years and I don't know how to occupy my time. I hawk over the weather report, put on my wellies, and sneak out for a walk, studying tree buds and pining for Sawyer, closing my eyes as I slosh through puddles in the elementary school playground nearby, remembering the melty feeling I get when he touches me. But every time my mind goes there, reality slams me in the face and I remember all the shit we're in.

And I think it's so ironic that as grounded as I supposedly am right now, I have never felt freer to wander around and not tell anybody where I am. After I test out all the swings, I start walking, trying to figure out what we have to do. What I have to do to solve this mystery, to finish the puzzle. Because it still feels like it's my fault—or at least my family's fault for passing down the crazy gene—and I can't *not* take responsibility for it.

By the time I've walked an hour, I realize I'm not far from the Humane Society. I hesitate at the door and go inside, look around, but I don't see Sawyer. The employees are busy with adoptions, so I wander into the dog room and look at all of them, some begging for love, others having given up, still others faking it, pretending they don't need anybody. And I see myself in all those dogs.

Five weird thoughts I've had in my life that I would never admit to having:
1. Um, *that* one
2. That I'm not really me, but I'm sort of just floating above myself watching my body do things
3. That there's something really stable and comforting about hoarding
4. That there's probably an opposite me some-where in a parallel universe doing everything right, and my job on earth is to make her look good by messing everything up
5. That monster spray secretly invites more

monsters to hide under the bed rather than
repels them

And while I'm standing there thinking weird thoughts and watching this sweet-looking boxer mutt named Boris, and all the dogs are barking as loud as they can at me and the other people walking through, I feel somebody's gaze boring into my skull. I turn around, and there's Sawyer watching me through the wire-mesh window to the cat room. He's got two black kittens crawling up his sweat-shirt, and he's just standing there with this amazingly sweet, kind look on his face. I raise my hand in greeting, and he mouths the words "I love you."

I smile and blush, and weave my way back through the dog room to the lobby and into the cat room, because when a boy with two kittens says he loves you, you do whatever you can to get to him as quickly as possible.

"Hey," I say.

"You found me," he says. He pushes a lock of hair out of my eyes and looks away quickly.

My heart sinks. "Still with the vision in my eyes?"

"Yeah. And all the kitties' eyes too."

"Dude," I mutter, because I never had that. It was never that bad. "How did you get here?"

"Took the bus. I—there's no way I can drive."

I study his face, and even excluding his black eye, he

looks exhausted, and I know he's been keeping the intensity from me. "Sawyer . . . I just don't understand. The times when it got really bad for me were when I had things wrong or the crash was imminent. I just don't know why it's not letting up on you when we're making progress and figuring things out."

And then we both stare at each other. Sawyer says it first. "Maybe we have things wrong."

My heart clutches. "Or maybe it's imminent."

"Shit."

"But it can't be. There are hardly any students on campus. It's spring break."

"Yes, but they've got to come back sometime before classes start Monday."

"You mean, like, today and tomorrow? But who would be using those buildings?"

Sawyer puts the kittens back into their cage and goes to the next cage, pulling a single gray kitten out and handing it to me. He reaches in for another one—a blue tortie, according to the label on the door—and cradles it. "I don't know. But colleges aren't like high schools, are they? I mean, they might have meetings. . . ." He strokes the kitten's back and it mews and tries to bite his thumb. Sawyer readjusts the kitten and gazes down at it, then back at me. "Can you try a search to find out? I've got my laptop with me, but I'm scheduled here until two today."

"Sure. There's got to be Wi-Fi around here somewhere."

"Meet me back here at two?"

I nod. We put the kittens back in their cage and he whispers, "I'm scared."

My spine tingles, and not in a good way. "Me too," I whisper back.

I return at two with no information on any classes meeting this weekend but with a lot more info about U of C and a possible clue to the actual motivation of the shooters. "I think we need to go back to the campus," I say. "Like, now. There has to be a clue. Something."

"What's Trey doing today, working?"

"He and Rowan are at that food truck festival."

Sawyer washes his hands at the sink and says goodbye to the other volunteers and employees. We walk out. "I have to work tonight," he says. And then he frowns and shakes his head. "No, I don't." He pulls out his phone.

He dials and waits. "I'm taking the weekend off," he says in a dull voice, a voice I've never heard.

"Yeah, well, if you make me come in, I'm telling everybody who asks how I got this black eye."

He listens for a second, and then, with no emotion, says, "Fire me, then. I really don't care." He hangs up. "Jesus," he says as we reach the bus stop, his face gray and dead. "I can't deal with this. I really can't."

"I know."

"I mean it, Jules." He rakes his fingers through his hair and cusses under his breath. "My family is a mess. The visions and the gunshots are killing me. I don't have anything . . . left. . . . Shit." He jams his fingers into the corners of his eyes and lets out a shuddering breath, and he turns toward me. I wrap my arms around him, feel his shoulders tremble.

He can't stop. "I mean, what the hell are we supposed to do? We're teenagers. We have no weapons or magical powers here. What are we going to do, Jules? Can you tell me, please? Because we're going to fucking get our heads blown off."

"No, we're not. And today is the day we figure it out. Right now. You and me. And we're not going home until we know what's happening."

He sniffs and clears his throat, like he doesn't want me to see his emotion. But I understand tears, especially about this. Hell, I wish all guys could just cry and not have it be such a big stupid deal. Shed a tear. Be a man. Whatever. But I guess when you live in a house where your father and grandfather beat the crap out of you, maybe you have a different mind-set on that topic.

We get on the bus, trying to figure out where to pick up the transfer that will take us to U of C, and then I open Sawyer's laptop and click on one of the tabs of the web pages I left open. I show Sawyer the history of the school and its beginnings, involving John D. Rockefeller, Marshall Field, and—what I think is the most interesting fact that I didn't know before—the American Baptist Education Society.

I point out the highlights. "So it's this private college with that big Rockefeller Chapel we saw, started by Baptists, yet totally secular from the beginning, I think. The dorms have coed floors, and there's a strong LGBT community."

Sawyer looks puzzled. "I'm not getting why any of this matters to the shooting."

"Rowan said something off the cuff the other day—she wondered what the motivation of the shooters might be. I couldn't stop thinking about it. And if you think about what happened here this week with the graffiti and what the workers told you about a protest over equal rights, and the defaced stop sign that Trey found, it's pretty obvious that somebody's upset with this school or some of the organizations in it, and it has something to do with equality. Since the slur "fag" was used, I'm guessing that it's gay rights that are being protested."

"Okaaay . . . but . . ."

"Hang on," I say, looking up, realizing it's time to transfer.

We change buses and keep reading. Sawyer sets his

phone up to be a Wi-Fi hot spot so I can get online on his computer and he can search for more news on his phone, but it's no use for him. His screen is just a medium for the vision. He leans back and closes his eyes. "I don't know how many more piles of dead bodies I can see before I lose it completely, Jules," he says. "What are we doing wrong?"

I pull up the Wikipedia page for U of C. Normally I don't trust Wikipedia, but this page has a bunch of great photographs, so I browse through them. I locate several of the buildings we saw on the main quadrangle and study them. There's a ton of great detail about the insides of the buildings too—stuff I never expected to find. "Hey," I say, looking over. But Sawyer's eyes are closed, his head nodding against the window. Sleeping. Thank dog. I have a feeling he's going to need it. I go back to scouring headlines.

What I find next stops my breath.

Thirty-Two

I can't help it. I have to wake him up. He blinks
and looks around, like he forgot where he was.

"I found something," I say, jiggling my foot impatiently.

"Whoa," he says. "Power nap." The sleep confusion
clears, and his face grows concerned. "What is it?"

I turn the computer screen toward him. "Can you
see?"

"Yeah. At the moment."

"Cool. Look here, where I researched other local news
and protests," I say, clicking over to another tab. "There's
that local cult preacher dude who always hangs out by
Water Tower Place—you know the one, right? Same guy as
always. Anyway, he's been shouting about gays taking over

the government again, and he's been ragging on U of C lately because their rights groups have been picketing the guy.

"See this article, 'A Call to Arms Goes Too Far: Free Speech at All Costs'? The dude has been riling up his followers, saying God wants his cult to rid the country of homosexuality, and that the local Chicago universities are the heart of the nation's problem and the leaders of the so-called gay uprising." I look up. "Isn't that insane?"

Sawyer takes it all in. "There's a lot of insanity these days," he mutters. "So you think our shooters are some outsider cult followers of the raging lunatic, coming to campus to . . . do God's will."

"I don't know. But seeing that, plus the graffiti, and the timing of this . . ." The whole idea of it turns my stomach. Who would want to believe in a God like that? If God is not, like, totally in love with *all* the people he created, why would anybody want to believe in him?

Five things a real God should be:

1. Not a hater
2. That about sums it up

After a minute Sawyer nods. "It fits. It's fucking sad, but it fits." He looks at the window for a long minute. He's watching the vision again.

• • •

The bus stops near the college and we walk to campus. There are more people wandering around today than yesterday. The stop sign has been replaced, all the snow piles are melted, and the tree buds are just noticeably more in bloom than yesterday. The grass is sodden and the botanical gardens on the property look pretty bedraggled, but spring is clearly on its way. And the vision clock is ticking.

"How do the buds and ivy compare today?" I ask. We wander around the quad, really looking at each building now that we have a good feel for the lay of the land.

"Really close," Sawyer says.

We go to the other end of the quad to make sure we haven't made any mistakes, and sure enough, there are old, ivy-covered buildings, streets, little stop signs, and sidewalks on this side of things too. Sawyer stops in front of a gorgeous ivy-covered building as a few people come out of the wooden door. He stares at it. I read the words above the door. It's a dormitory—Charles Hitchcock Hall.

After a minute, Sawyer looks all the way down toward Cobb Hall, and then he looks back at the dormitory in front of us. "I wonder if I have the wrong building," he murmurs. "I mean, just because I see the stop sign in the vision doesn't mean it's near the scene of the shooting— they're different frames." He puzzles over it some more. "No. It can't be a dorm room. There's a whiteboard and tables." He shakes his head like he's reprimanding himself. We start walking.

A cute guy wearing funky glasses comes out of the dormitory and sticks a flyer to the building wall. He walks into the quad, heading toward us, handing out more flyers. He looks at us, hesitates, then holds one out and smiles brightly. "GSA is teaming up with the Motet Choir for our final spring food drive and fund-raiser. Meeting in the Hitchcock green room tomorrow night. You should join us."

I reach out and take it, and the guy moves on, heading toward the next dorm. I read the info. Eight o'clock tomorrow night. "GSA. Gay-Straight Alliance," I say, looking up.

Sawyer nods, his voice taking on a trepid tone. "Sounds like this could be the group we're looking for. Plus the time is after sunset, which would make the room naturally darker. Though they'd have lights on, presumably." He frowns.

"I wonder where this green room is."

"Let's go find it."

But the door requires a student ID to unlock it. We wait until someone exits, and Sawyer catches the door before it closes. We walk into Hitchcock Hall and to our right is a large room with brick walls, portraits, couches, and a piano. "Green room?" I guess. I see one of the flyers with "HERE" written over the location in black marker.

"That was easy," Sawyer says. "But it's not the room in the vision." He looks all around, as if hoping to find the items from the scenes. "I mean, I guess they could bring tables and chairs in here, and a whiteboard, but . . ." He looks at the windows and shakes his head. "No. This isn't it. The walls are wrong."

I flop down in a chair, suddenly weary of it all. Nothing is lining up. "How are the visions," I say, barely even a question, just a repetition of every other time.

"Bad."

I lean forward and rest my face in my hands. And for the first time, I feel like we've completely run out of ideas. "And there's nothing new?"

Sawyer sighs sharply and I know I've asked him that once too often. I cringe, not that he can see it, and follow up with a muffled "Sorry" before he says anything. We go back outside to wander aimlessly around campus again.

Before we can figure out what to do next, my cell phone vibrates in my pocket. I look at Sawyer to see if he's screwing around, but he's not. I pull it out and look at the number, and it's Trey. I answer. "What's up?"

"Um, like, where the hell are you?"

I look at my watch, and it's after six. No wonder my stomach is growling. "Sawyer and I took the bus to U of C."

"Mom and Dad are freaking out. They keep calling me

and Rowan and we're trying to run the stinking truck. It's a nightmare. We could actually use your help . . . if you hadn't quit, you know."

I shrug. "Maybe if they buy me a new cell phone they could get ahold of me. You may want to mention that."

"I'm going to tell them that you called me from . . . shit. What do you want me to tell them?"

I look up at Rockefeller Chapel and see a door open, inviting in the spring air. I step inside and see a group of adults wearing choir robes, rehearsing. "Tell them I took a really long walk, looking desperately for a pay phone."

"Whatever. Did you figure anything out?"

I glance at Sawyer, who is sitting on the chapel steps with his head in his hands. "No." I pause, and then I say, "Tell Mom I'm coming to help you. We're only about twenty minutes away."

I hear Rowan utter a muffled swear word in the background. Trey sighs. "Thanks, Jules."

We hang up and I go back outside and hold my hand out to Sawyer. "Hey," I say with fake enthusiasm. "Wanna go run the giant truck o' balls with team Demarco?"

He looks up at me, and despite the situation, a slow grin spreads across his face. "That actually sounds awesome," he says.

Thirty-Three

Trey's eyes light up when he sees us. "Thank the gods," he breathes. "Did you see the line?"

"How could we miss it?"

Rowan's hair is stuck to her forehead with sweat. She grabs a towel and wipes her face, then throws the towel into the dirty bin. "Blown away," she says. "I do not understand why you guys enjoy this truck so much."

I give Sawyer a hasty tour, show him how we do our orders, and set him up filling bread bowls with meatballs and sauce so we can catch up on the backlog. I make him taste everything. "This is excellent," he says, his mouth full.

"Don't be stealing our recipe now," Trey says as he hands an order through the window to a customer.

Sawyer laughs, but he shoots me an anxious look that says, *Does he know about our parents?*

I shake my head and start grating fresh mozzarella like it's going out of style. "No wonder you're blown away. You've got no *mise en place*. You're out of everything."

Trey gives me a scornful look. "Oh, we had everything prepped, I assure you. Again, I refer your gaze to the line out front and ask you to kindly note that it's been like this for four hours."

"Point taken. We'll set you back up. Right, Angotti?"

"Yes, boss," Sawyer says.

I look around and it feels a bit too crowded in here. "Ro, you want to go outside and take orders and hand 'em through to Trey? That way you can go down the line a bit and we can get things moving faster."

"Good call," Trey mutters.

"Gladly," Rowan says. "It's fucking hot in here."

I look at her as she leaves. "When did she start cussing?"

"Mmm. Yeah. That would be today," Trey says.

Sawyer laughs. He works really fast, and once he's caught up with the bread bowl orders, he looks for other things to do. "How can I help?"

I grab bunches of fresh spinach from the cooler and shove them at him. "Rinse, spin, steam two minutes, and rough chop. Got it? Then garlic and onions over in that cooler—you okay chopping onions?"

"Pfft. Of course," he says, like I just insulted him. And I freaking love that he knows everything I'm talking about. I remember my dreams of leaving love notes made of green peppers for him on the cutting board and laugh under my breath.

Once I have the cheese tub filled, I chop tomatoes, and then the orders start getting filled again and the line begins moving.

"Okay," Trey says when we have a good rhythm going. "Catch me up. Are we still looking at Monday or Tuesday for the thing?"

"Don't know," I say. "For a while we were actually thinking tomorrow night, but now we're not sure. Still, Sawyer's visions are so bad he can't drive, and he's seeing them everywhere."

"Tomorrow night."

"Yeah."

"Great."

"At least if it is tomorrow, it'll be over soon," Sawyer says, moving to get onions. He looks in the caddy to see how we dice them and starts in. His knife skills are pretty great, and I'm freaking in love all over again.

"So what's the plan?" Trey asks. "Do we have one?"

"Um . . . ," I say, and I feel really helpless, because we

don't have a plan at all, despite my promise to Sawyer that we'd have one by now.

"I think what we need to do is forget about the classroom," Sawyer says decisively. "And focus on the sidewalk and the shooter guy—girl—walking there. If we stop her, the rest of the plan doesn't come together for them. If she doesn't show up, I bet the other one—or two—abandon the plan."

Trey gets backed up, so Rowan pops in to help with a stack of new orders. "You guys better not die while I'm gone," she says. "I mean it."

"Shit," I say, remembering. "I've got to get you to the airport."

"Yes, you do. You ruin this for me, and I ruin your face, bitch." Rowan smiles sweetly and hands off another order through the window.

"Wow." I glance at Sawyer and he's grinning. He looks at me. "I freaking love you guys. Can I work at your place?"

"Um . . . ," we all say, knowing it was a joke, but I change the subject back to what Sawyer just said. "Anyway, I think you're right, Sawyer—we don't have enough information, so we go with what we know. We know the shooter walks down the sidewalk by Cobb Hall. So we plant ourselves there around sundown in the next few days, or whenever the weather looks like the skies could be dark."

"And that's so easy to predict in Chicago in spring," Trey says. He hands off another order. "Nice, too, that the campus is just around the corner from our house." His sarcasm is evident.

"But we're on spring break, so that's easier."

"But we have jobs."

"Some of us do," pipes Rowan from outside the window.

"This is more important," I say.

"Your face—" Rowan says.

"Shut it," I say. "Inappropriate at this time."

"I love you all," Sawyer says.

"Well, let's just get through this before you go spouting off with your overemotional diatribe," Trey says. "Sheesh. You're even scaring the gays."

"I don't think you understand," Sawyer says, scooping up his diced onions and putting them into the onion bin. "At my place, it's a bunch of old ladies, my parents, my older brothers, who are almost never there, and me. And my cousin Kate—she's cool. But she's in college so she only works a couple shifts a week."

I frown, glancing at Trey, who looks horrified. "That sounds awful," he says.

"It is, trust me."

"And then you also get punched in the face."

There's an awkward pause. Sawyer tries to blow it off. "Yeah. Just one of the many perks of the job."

I shoot Trey a warning glance, but he chooses not to see it. "You know," he says, "once this whole thing is over, we're going to talk about that." He looks at his ticket. "One salad, one balls minus cheese, one heart attack," he calls out. "Come on, step it up back there."

And there's something comforting about Trey being there, knowing he'll be with us tomorrow and the rest of the week too. Once we get Rowan out the door, we're home free.

Thirty-Four

My parents are strangely silent about my being gone all day, probably due to Rowan handing over gobs of money and telling them how I went out to save them when they were blown away. My mother thanks me for helping out, and I respond kindly, coolly, and that's the end of that.

Sawyer and I talk on the phone until he falls asleep. I toss and turn all night, and so does Rowan, making me think she's actually nervous about flying for the first time, all alone.

Sunday morning dawns, and I hear my mother moving around the apartment, getting ready for mass. Rowan has already begged off mass after the long, arduous day on the food truck, and Mom said she could skip today, which was the plan all along. Rowan goes through her duffel bag for the millionth time. By eight thirty, I think I hear Dad moving down the hall, but when Mom leaves, I strain to hear Dad's footsteps on the stairs too and I don't hear them. Rowan looks at me and mouths a cuss word.

I sit up and shrug, hearing his door close again. "Meh. No worries. It's not like he's going to notice us."

Once we're ready, Rowan gets her bag and we sneak out to the pizza delivery car. I have directions printed out and Rowan goes through her purse nervously. "Photo ID, ticket, toiletries," she mutters. She tells me her airline and we head out to the glorious world of O'Hare Airport, a slithering ant farm of a place where even really seasoned drivers choke and get lost. After missing the correct terminal, almost getting plowed over by a bus, and more swearing by the innocent fifteen-year-old I once knew, we finally find the right place, and I do what everybody else seems to do—park any old where I feel like it.

She puts her hand on the door handle and looks at me. "Thanks," she says.

I smile. "Have a blast, okay? And if it's not what you expect, call me. I will come and get you."

She laughs. "You have a few other things on your mind."

"You're my number one," I say. And then I have to

punch her in the arm before things get mushy. "You know what signs to look for inside?"

"Yeah. Don't do anything stupid."

"You either." I pinch her knee, which she hates, and then she's opening her door, slipping out, and she's gone. A second later I roll down the passenger window and yell out, "Call me when you get there!"

She looks over her shoulder and smiles. "I will," she says. She lifts her hand in a wave. And she looks so damn excited it makes me cry.

On the way home I can't get my stomach to settle down. I know our parents are going to freak, and if they find out I drove Rowan to the airport, they'll probably have me arrested or something—I wouldn't put it past them. My dad, anyway. And you know what? I'm trying really freaking hard not to care. Before I head back inside the house I call Sawyer to discuss the plan for the day, which is to get the hell out of here before my parents figure out Rowan is gone.

Inside I can hear the TV, which means Dad is out of his room and hopefully getting ready to open the restaurant rather than sit in the blue TV haze all day with the shades down. They're going to need him down there without Ro and Trey. I feel a twinge in my gut, but I have to ignore it. Today is not the day for that. I slip past the living room and knock lightly on Trey's door.

He opens it and lets me in, closing it behind me.

"You ready?" I whisper. "Mom will be home any minute."

Trey sighs. "Yeah, about that," he says. "I think I need to stay here, for the afternoon at least. You're pretty sure this thing is happening in the evening, right?"

I nod.

"I'll meet you guys out there before dark. I just think I should be here for when they find out about Rowan, you know? So they don't call the cops."

I sit down on his bed and rub my temples. He's right, of course. And he's the best one to handle them.

"Yeah, okay," I say.

"If anything crazy happens, call me. I'll be there as fast as I can."

"Okay," I say again. On an impulse I reach out and hug him around the neck. My cast clunks against his head.

"Ouch. When are you getting that stupid thing off?" he asks, laughing.

"Friday morning. If we all live that long."

"And we have multiple opportunities to die," Trey says. "Death by exploding heads. Er, I meant Dad, not . . . the other." He cringes.

"That was bad."

"I know. Sorry."

I rap on his chest with my knuckles. "We'll be in the quad. I'll call you if anything changes."

His lips press into a wry smile. "Be careful," he says. "It's not worth dying for, okay?"

I nod. And I know. "We're calling the police as soon as we have an idea of what's happening, and when, and where."

I open Trey's door and almost run into my dad. "Oh. Sorry."

He startles too and hits one of the stacks of Christmas tins. Finally, after years of waiting, they come crashing down, making way more noise than something so light-weight should make. I stoop down and help pick them up, putting them back on the precarious pile as best I can with my dad blocking the hallway. I hand the last one to him, not quite looking him in the eye.

"Thank you," he says.

I nod and back into Trey's doorway again so he can get past me.

"And thank you for helping your brother and sister yesterday," he says gruffly. "Mom will add those hours to your final paycheck."

"That's fine."

He doesn't ask me if I want my job back. And I'm too proud to ask for it.

Scary how much like him I am.

Thirty-Five

Dad goes into his bedroom, and I duck into mine, grab my backpack, make sure I have my phone, and scoot out of there. As I descend the stairs, I hear my dad calling for Rowan, and I can't run away fast enough. "Trey Demarco, you are a saint," I mutter under my breath. I owe him big for handling this.

The sky is dark. Occasional giant drops of rain splat on the pavement in front of me, and I wish I'd thought to bring an umbrella. I grab the bus to Sawyer's neighborhood, call him to let him know I'm coming, and just miss a wave of pouring rain. It's only spitting by the time I hop off. And when I look down the street toward Angotti's Trattoria, I see Sawyer walking toward me.

"Okay, so here's what I know," he says in greeting.

"Main shooter girl is holding a Glock 17 Gen4. It holds at least seventeen bullets. She doesn't have an additional magazine on it."

"Hmm," I say. This information means nothing to me, other than the fact that the killer woman can shoot at least seventeen times. Which is more than eleven.

Sawyer grips my hand as the almost empty bus pulls up and he buys two fares. We grab a seat in the back. "Also, I finally managed to figure out a few words on the white-board. Musical terms and composer names." He flashes a triumphant smile.

"How did you manage that?"

"Every time I tried to zoom, the pixels went nuts and I couldn't read anything. But I finally thought to use my mother's reading glasses to magnify the words—she's, like, totally farsighted—and I got these words: Rachmaninoff, Vespers, E A Poe, The Bells."

I frown. "Edgar Allan Poe is a writer, not a musician."

"Right, but I looked up 'The Bells,' which is by Poe, and Sergei Rachmaninoff turned it into a symphony."

I feel a surge of hope for the first time in a long time. "So it's a music classroom, you think?"

"That's what I think."

"So, wait—the victims are not the Gay-Straight Alliance people? It's, like, a regular music class?"

Sawyer's breath comes out heavy, and his face is

strained. "All I know is that the GSA is meeting in the green room, and the room in the vision is a regular music classroom. So the two events don't appear related."

"But that means . . ."

"We've got everything wrong. But at least we know it's probably not going to happen today—there are no classes in session until tomorrow."

I think for a moment. "But the weather is supposed to be sunny tomorrow, and you said it's cloudy and the pavement is wet in the vision."

He shrugs. "Maybe there are sprinklers on the quad. Or maybe it rains when it's not forecasted—wouldn't be the first time."

"True." I look out the window. "So, wait. Why are we going there today, then?"

"To see if we can find the music classrooms and figure out which ones have evening classes. Hopefully the buildings will be open now that students are returning from break." He pulls out a map of the entire main quad, and it's like he's been energized.

"Are you . . . feeling okay?"

He looks at me. "Actually, for once, yeah. The vision calmed down after I figured out the music thing. So I feel like I got something right."

We stop for an early dinner near campus at Five Guys and spend a couple of hours talking everything through.

Sawyer tells me the entire vision one more time, using the map to point out where he thinks things are. I borrow his phone to check the weather, but it still calls for sunny skies tomorrow.

"Question," I say. "In the vision, when you see the, uh, girl," I say, looking around to see if anybody can hear me, "do you see other students around? Like, do you get a broad view of the quad?"

"No other students, no broad view. Just the sky and tree, then the grass and pavement and little stop sign. We zoom in to the building, then out to see the back of the girl's body, and then we're in the classroom."

I look more closely at the map, seeing the individual buildings labeled. "Do you think the music building is in the main quad?"

"That's my guess."

I frown and start googling the names of the buildings around the Snell-Hitchcock Halls. "These are mostly sciencey. Like labs and stuff." I keep going. "Cobb. That's the building with the ivy that we thought the vision was focusing on the other day, right?"

"Yeah." He's got his laptop out and is searching too.

"Here," I say. "Music. It's this one next to Cobb. Goodspeed Hall. Offices, music classrooms, and practice rooms all on the bottom four floors. Practice rooms open seven days a week."

"Sweet." After a minute, Sawyer looks up. "Is Trey coming?"

"Oh, crap," I say. "Yeah. Does he need to? Are you sure it's tomorrow?"

"It's a classroom, Jules. It'll be tomorrow."

"Okay, well, that's probably better timing. . . ." I whip out my phone and call Trey.

He answers and says in a curt voice, "Not now. I'll call you later."

"Oh," I say, but he's already hung up. I look at Sawyer. "He's handling the Rowan thing." I drum my fingers on the table, suddenly nervous about that. She should have called me by now. Hours ago, in fact. I call her cell phone.

"Are you alive?" I almost yell when she answers.

"Shit," she says. "I forgot, I'm sorry, I'm sorry. I figured you knew I made it since Mom's been screaming at me on the phone for the last two hours."

"Yeah, well, I'm not at home. How's it going?"

"Good. I think Trey has them settled down enough not to call the cops, and poor Charlie here is kind of pissed at me for doing this without them knowing."

I hadn't thought of that. "Ack. Do his parents know?"

"Not yet. Hopefully not ever." She hesitates and I hear her talking to someone. "I gotta go, Jules. Love you."

"Love you, too."

"And, Jules?"

"Yeah?"

But she doesn't say anything, and I figure one of us hit a dead spot or she's got to answer another call from our parents. I bite my lip and hang up. And then I look at Sawyer. "I think I'd better head home."

He smiles. "Yeah, you definitely should. Poor Trey." He gathers the wrappers and we get up. "I'm going to go to the campus and see if I can figure out the classroom situation."

I feel terrible leaving him here alone. "Are you sure you're cool with that?"

"Hundred percent."

I glance at my watch. There's a bus in twenty-three minutes. "Okay. Call me whenever you find out anything. And when you're on your way home. And when you get there. And if anything weird happens."

He grins. "I'll call you every five minutes just to let you know I'm still alive."

I grin. "That sounds perfect." I look outside, and it's sprinkling again. The sky is a roiling cauldron of dark, angry clouds. We go outside and I reach up to kiss him, and then we split up, him to campus, me to the bus stop.

As I stand there under the shelter of a nearby overhang, the rain pelting down, I grip my phone, waiting for it to ring. Waiting to hear from Sawyer. Or Trey. And I think about my parents, and Rowan, and how everything we're doing feels so underhanded, and I kind of don't like myself much these days. It's way too easy to lie. I have an argument with myself, telling me that there's no other way to go about it. That all the superheroes have to lie to hide their true identity, and this is a lot like that.

"Except you're not a superhero," I mutter. "You're a not-quite-seventeen-year-old kid with a contagious mental disorder." I bounce on my toes, waiting for the stupid bus, which is most certainly late. "Come on. Somebody call. I'm anxious." I pause, and then I say, "I'm so anxious I'm talking to myself."

Finally, ten minutes late, the bus pulls up just as the heavens open. I watch the people get off and prepare to make a mad dash for the bus door.

And then I see her getting off the bus.

It's the girl. The girl with the gun.

Thirty-Six

Her black hat is pulled down over her eyes, and she looks like a guy. She's alone. I think. She's wearing dark-wash jeans and a black jacket, and she's gripping a little backpack so hard her knuckles are white. And on the backpack is a button with a picture of a rainbow with a line through it. My heart thunks around in my chest and I almost can't breathe. *So it* is *the GSA they're after?* I'm so confused.

The bus driver inches forward and cranes his neck at me. I shake my head and wave him off. And after a second, I follow the girl. I let her get a few dozen feet ahead of me and inch my phone from my pocket. I dial Sawyer's number, but nothing happens. No signal. I try him again, and then I look at the phone battery. It's not dead. But there's a little notice in the corner in the tiniest print that says "minutes used: 250."

"Shit," I mutter. And then it really hits me. My prepaid minutes are used up. I have no phone. No wonder neither of the boys has called me.

I have no phone.

I look up to make sure the girl is still in sight. At the corner where we'd turn to go to U of C, she stops and waits for traffic. I pretend to look in a shopwindow, and then when the light changes I begin to follow again. And I don't know what I'm going to do. I don't know what she's going to do. For all I know, she's just doing one more stakeout of the campus in preparation for tomorrow. But the way she's gripping that little bag tells me otherwise.

Thankfully, the rain keeps her from looking around. She scurries along, head down, and when we cross a street, she's joined by the blond guy who she was with the other day. They barely say two words to each other, and then they walk together but not very closely. And I realize this is really it.

My hand finds my phone again and I try a few more times in case I'm wrong and the minutes haven't expired, but it's futile. My phone is useless. I want to run ahead, try to find Sawyer, but I don't want them to see me, and I don't want to lose track of them. I follow the two into the quad as the rain stops, the only drops now coming from the trees.

"Where are you?" I mutter. The quad is huge, and there are a lot of buildings. And the campus is alive again with students running through the rain, transporting their suitcases, bags, and backpacks back to their dorms. I want to go toward the hall we determined was the music building, but the two people in black go to the opposite corner of the quad toward the Hitchcock Hall dorm. I strain my eyes looking for Sawyer, but I don't see him anywhere.

My chest is tight. I hear a distant church bell chiming the hour as we near Hitchcock Hall. Eight bells. The two in black stop at the side of the big wooden door and stare at something as people dash in and out of the building. The guy looks panicked for a moment, but the girl shakes her head slightly and says something. I stay by the road, trying to look like I'm waiting for someone, trying to hide that I'm praying my brains out to whoever will listen that Sawyer is okay.

The two stand there whispering for a minute, and then they come back toward me. I freeze, and then I pull a notebook from my backpack and rip a page out. I fumble for a pen and keep my head down as they pass by me, pretending to write things down. And then I walk as fast as I can to the Hitchcock door to see what they were looking at.

It's the Gay-Straight Alliance flyer. But the green room meeting place is crossed out and instead it says, "Moved to Goodspeed 4th Fl!!"

The blood pulses in my ears. That's the music building. And suddenly everything I can remember from Sawyer's vision is coming together and making sense. It's all happening right now, and Sawyer doesn't know. I look at the torn sheet of notebook paper in my hand, write, "Call 911—Goodspeed 4th Fl!" and take off after the shooters at full speed, shoving my paper into the hands of a surprised student as he enters the dorm.

I race across the quad to Goodspeed, splashing through puddles, soaking wet, watching the shooters enter the music hall. When I reach the door I dash up the stairs to the fourth floor, trying to look casual, as others move through the short hallways, some carrying backpacks or musical instrument cases. And I don't even care about the massive deaths right now. All I can think of is that I need to find Sawyer and get him out of here. We're not ready. We can't do this. We need to bail. Just call the cops, get the hell out of the way, and hope for the best.

A few students wander the fourth floor, some of them peering at closed office doors or into classrooms, and I'm guessing they are looking for the same room I am. And then I spy the cute guy with the glasses who handed us the flyer yesterday. He's down the hallway, standing in front of an open door, frowning at his watch. "Come on, people," he says.

He takes a look at my wet clothes and hair. "Now that's

dedication," he says with a grin. "Hey—I remember you. Your boyfriend is inside."

My eyes bug out. "I—he—what?"

His kind eyes crinkle. "Oops. Did I get that wrong? I thought you were holding hands the other day. I'm sorry."

"No, I mean . . . never mind. Thanks." I push past him into the room and look around, spying the two shooters immediately at the front table. Sitting at the table behind them is Sawyer, whose normally olive complexion is alabaster now. He stares at me. I walk in like I don't know him and go to the window.

A minute later, he's next to me. "What happened?" he whispers.

"It's now," I say back.

"No shit. You could have answered your phone!"

"Ran out of minutes. Couldn't call you either. Now what?"

"Ohh," he says. "Crap. I should have thought of that." He glances over his shoulder. "I texted the tip hotline. Can't exactly call."

"We can get out of here. There's time."

Sawyer grips my arm. "No, we can't. It's changing. The vision. Us being here is changing it. Fewer gunshots, fewer bodies. Down to seven. We have to stay and try to stop it."

"But what if the bodies are *us*?"

"Jules," he says, and he grips my wrist. "Remember how it was with you. You have to trust me." There's no time for him to explain—the cute guy clears his throat loudly and announces that it's well past eight. Sawyer gets a text message and responds quickly as we sit down at the table. I question him with my eyes. "Trey," he mouths.

My eyes widen, begging for more information. But Sawyer glances at the shooters and shakes his head. He puts his hands below the table and holds out nine fingers, then one, then one again.

"Oh," I breathe, relieved. *Trey's calling the cops.* Everybody continues to make small talk except for the shooters, who sit there stone-faced.

From the doorway, the cute guy asks the students to finish up their conversations. He looks down the hallway once more and closes the door. "Okay, everybody, settle. Sorry about the last-minute venue change—the green room was too noisy with everybody coming back from break with all their luggage and parents and junk." He looks around the room and grins.

"If you don't know me, I'm Ben Galang, freshman, next year's secretary of the alliance, and this is my first time organizing a charity event, so yeah. Help a guy out, will ya?" He laughs. A few people smile. "Okay, well. Welcome to the choir members, some of whom are already part of the GSA here at UC. It's great to work with you all and to see some new faces." He smiles at somebody on the other side of the room, at Sawyer and me, and at the shooters.

I can't smile back. I don't dare to turn my head to see who else is in here. I'm freaking out. I can't even focus on what this guy Ben is saying. All I can do is stare at the shooters in front of me, stare at the girl's black bag, at the bulge on the blond guy's hip, under his jacket. I glance at Sawyer and he's sweating, watching the glass in the door, and I know from experience that, one, he's watching that vision *very* closely and, two, all I can do is trust him and follow his lead, because he's the only one who knows how this is all going down. And if I mess with it, it could change everything. I dare a quick glance around the room at the faces, all these faces that Sawyer has been seeing for weeks with bullet holes in them, but my mind can't even record them—they are all a blur of one victim's face.

Sawyer's elbow touches mine, and I look at him. He points to the clock above the door. "New scene," he whispers. Does that mean he knows the time this will happen? He points to the table and mimics flipping it. Then he points to the girl and looks at me.

I nod. He scratches his knee and looks at me again. I swallow hard and panic—I don't know what that means. He points to their legs, his fingers shaking, and finally I understand what he's trying to say. I nod again. And then he spreads his hand out on his thigh, five fingers, and before I know it he hides his thumb, and then his first finger, and I realize that he's counting down, and this is happening in two, one . . .

The shooter girl pulls a gun from her little black backpack, stands up, and whirls around, yelling, "All you fags to the back of the room!" The blond guy follows her lead, pulling his gun out and shoving their table out of the way, but at first nobody else in the room moves. Nobody understands what's happening. They're in shock.

It all goes in slow motion. Sawyer and I flip our table, trying to give others something to hide behind. Ben, smile fading, turns to see what the commotion is all about. Sawyer springs forward from his chair, stays low, hops over the table, and tackles the blond guy at the back of the thighs, making his knees crumple. A shot rings out, hitting the ceiling light fixture. The whole row of lights goes out, leaving us in semi-darkness, and that wakes me from my frozen state. I dive from my seat and tackle the girl the same way Sawyer tackled the guy. She loses her balance and lands on my back as two more shots pierce the air and shatter my eardrums, along with a chorus of screams.

"Run!" I yell from under the girl, pulling sound from the depths of my lungs. "Go! Get out! Run!" I hear tables and chairs scraping and crashing, people screaming, almost everyone running for the door as a few more shots ring out.

Sawyer gets on top of the blond guy and starts pounding his wrist, trying to get him to let go of the gun, and it goes off again, but I can't afford to look at what, or who, it hits. I struggle to get the girl off my back, rising quickly to my hands and knees to throw her off balance. I can feel her weight shift, and she teeters, grabbing my hair and yanking it, trying to hold on. I reach deep, finding some other inner strength, and try to buck her off me, digging my cast into the floor like a cane to push me up. The girl's gun hits me in the head as she loses her grip on my hair and falls to the floor.

I scramble aside and turn to look where she is. She kicks me in the face, and I see stars. As she gets to her feet she starts screaming over and over, "Die, you sick fags!"

My cheek throbs. I try to grab her around the ankles, but all I get is her pant leg, which she rips from my grasp, taking parts of my fingernails with it. She stumbles off balance and kicks me again. Awkwardly I reel away from her kick, then try to catch her foot, but instead I trip over a chair and I'm back on the floor once again as she catches herself and stares at me like she hates me. I roll to my stomach and cover my face like a coward because I think this has to be the end for me.

I hear three gunshots and I don't know if anybody's hit. I freeze in place, cringing and crying, figuring she'd be shooting at me, but she isn't. At least I don't think so, anyway. When I dare to look, she's grabbing Ben, who is stoically trying to drag a bloody person out of the room. The shooter girl shoves him, makes him turn around to face her, digs the gun into his forehead, and backs him up against the wall just as Sawyer and the blond guy, rolling on the floor, bump into me. I can hear Sawyer cussing, trying to stand but slipping on a smear of blood, twisting crazily and falling hard. With the momentum, Sawyer manages to extend his arm, slamming it down across the shooter's chest.

The blond guy's gun goes flying. I get to my hands and knees and crawl after it, trying shakily to get to my feet, but the guy grabs me and yanks my legs out from under me, making me land hard next to him. I hoist myself up with my good hand, swing my cast around awkwardly to block his fist, and slam my knee into his groin before he can choke me. He gasps and shrivels up, his face telling me I nailed him just right, and I'm free. But my muscles are in shock and I can't get them to obey me. I roll away, out of his reach, searching desperately for Sawyer.

Sawyer's got blood on his face and he staggers to his knees, crawling around desks and chairs and broken equipment, trying to get to the guy's gun, while I refocus on the girl with the gun to Ben's forehead as she screams in his face, and for the first time I feel like we have failed. I am helpless to save him. I know he's about to die, and there's nothing I can do. "No," I whisper, and I can't even hear the word come out because of the screaming. But Ben is silent, stiff, gun jabbed between his eyes, facing the girl and barely flinching. Something about his bravery gives me the weirdest sense of courage. I grab the edge of a table and stagger to my feet once more.

Then the door bursts open. It hits the wall hard, the glass window shattering and sprinkling shards everywhere. The girl turns her head at the noise, and Ben—the new, desperate leader Ben—slams his fist into her gut and she doubles over. Her gun goes off. And just as Sawyer staggers over to grab the blond guy's gun, I fling myself at the girl and start flailing my arms and legs, feeling like I've got no plan but nothing to lose. I kick the crap out of her arm that holds the gun, and I whack the shit out of her face with my cast, once, twice, three times, until she drops, and I kneel on her fucking head as she screams.

With a ragged breath, I look up at the door, suspecting it was the police who shattered the window within it, but all I see is my brother's startled face, his body leaning against the wall.

"Trey! Thank God!" I shout. And then I watch him sink to the floor, leaving a streak of red on the wall behind him.

Thirty-Seven

"Trey!" I scream again, but I can't let up on the girl. I move my free leg around and step hard on her arm as she screams out in pain, screaming her hatred, calling me a sick fag, calling me an abomination, telling me I belong in hell. Telling me God hates me. Ben comes running to kick the gun away from the girl, and finally, finally, the police come.

It takes them a few minutes to sort out the good guys from the bad, especially with the girl screaming at us. As soon as they've got her, I crawl over a slippery floor to Trey, where another cop is trying to talk to him, telling him to stay awake, telling him help is on the way.

"Back off," the cop says, holding his arm out to push me back. "Give him some room."

"He's my brother," I cry, my voice ragged, and the guy lets me near him again. "Is he breathing?" Blood spurts out from somewhere around his shoulder.

"Yes. What's his name?"

"Trey. Trey Demarco."

Within seconds the paramedics are there, assessing all the injured, and I follow their gazes around the room, suddenly remembering Sawyer again in all of this. Two of the paramedics run to a girl who is lying against the back wall, eyes glazed, holding her side as blood spills from between her fingers, and I don't want to see that, but I can't look away.

On the other side of the room, the blond shooter gets shoved to the floor and handcuffed, and the girl shooter still hollers hate speech as she's being held by two cops. And then there's Ben Galang, glasses knocked off, face bleeding. Ben Galang, who almost surely should be dead, reaching out and helping Sawyer to his feet.

There's one more guy near the door who cries out, trying to scrape himself along the floor, his foot bleeding profusely.

That's it. That's all. Everybody else made it out.

I look at Sawyer as the paramedics take the girl with the stomach wound away first, and then they load Trey onto a stretcher. Sawyer stares back at me, his face as stricken as mine feels. I turn to the paramedics. "He's my brother. Can I go with you?"

The paramedic looks at the cop, who nods. "Just her."

"What hospital?" I ask.

"Down the street—to the UC ER. Let's go." They hoist him up until the wheels click into place.

I check to make sure Sawyer hears it, and he nods. And then, with tears in his eyes, he mouths, "I'm so sorry."

Later, after Trey has been wheeled into the ER, a doctor checks me over. He gets an intern to cut my blood-soaked cast off, and we decide there's no reason to put a new one on since I was getting it off later in the week anyway.

While I'm sitting there, the cops arrive to interview me and the others who have trickled in. I tell them what happened, my voice getting shaky all over again. "We were sitting in chairs," I begin, "and Ben was leading the meeting. The girl and blond guy got up and pulled guns out. My friend Sawyer and I both reacted—the shooters were right in front of us so we saw them. The girl was yelling hate speech against the LGBT students. I dove for the girl's legs to knock her off her feet. Her gun went off a bunch of times . . . I'm not sure how many. I saw that Sawyer had the other guy on the floor." I tell them how the girl got away from me and held the gun to Ben's head, and then how my brother burst in and broke the glass in the door, and how that distracted the girl and Ben punched her and she shot Trey instead.

And when they ask me how I knew to react so quickly, I just look at them. "I don't know," I say. The cops seem satisfied, and they're gone before my parents arrive.

My parents.

Yeah.

Five things I don't want to talk about:

1. Why the heck Trey and I were getting shot at when our little sister was missing

2. Why we were clear on the other side of the city when we were supposed to be grounded

3. How on earth their good son could be with them one hour and shot in the arm the next

4. Why we want to give them so much grief, because first the crash and then Rowan and now this

5. How that Angotti boy fits into all this mess

And all I can think to say in response is "At least I didn't wreck the balls."

They are not amused. But thankfully, they have a lot of other stuff on their minds.

And after the docs get a good look at Trey and fix him up, they tell us we are very lucky, because the bullet passed through the muscle of his arm and didn't hit any bones and barely nicked an artery. And while there may be some nerve damage, he should regain full use after a few months. They're going to keep him here for a couple of days.

Once I get to see that Trey's all right, I wonder where Sawyer is. I leave Mom and Dad in Trey's room and venture out to the waiting room. And there, either stupid or stoic, is the boy I love. The blood on his face is wiped clean, and he has a couple of stitches on his forehead. Sitting next to him are two guys. One I don't recognize, and the other is leaning forward with his face in his hands, and I don't realize who he is until he looks up. It's Ben.

Sawyer stands up fast when he sees me. He looks me all over. "You okay?"

I nod. I have some bruises, a few cuts, but that's it. "You?"

"Fine. How's Trey?"

"Trey's okay," I say, and it's clear by the look on Sawyer's face that he hadn't heard anything yet. "I'm sorry, I thought they'd tell you."

"No."

"Have you heard anything about the others?"

"They're alive," Sawyer says.

Ben glances at Sawyer with a puzzled look. "How do you know?"

"I mean, I guess I don't know," Sawyer says, giving me a look that says he really does. Because the vision changed,

I'm sure, like mine did, right there at the end. "But they were alive when the paramedics took them. So I hope . . ."

Ben stands up and comes over to us. "Hey," he says to me. "I don't know if you remember. I'm Ben Galang—"

"Freshman," I say. "Just voted in as next year's secretary." I smile. "Your first charity event ever."

Ben's face crumbles, and I feel terrible. Because he doesn't know everybody lives. He doesn't know how bad it could have been.

"Shit," I say. "I'm sorry. I'm stupid. I'm just a stupid non-college student who is, um, stupid."

He holds back his emotion, and then he says, "You guys saved our lives."

And you know what's funny in a not-funny way? I almost forgot that part, because I got so wrapped up in the clues that none of the tragedy seems real. And I hate that about me. Sawyer shrugs and says, "We just had the clearest view of what was happening." He looks at me. "Gotta stay on your toes when you run with danger girl's crowd."

I squelch a smile. "You guys want to check on the others? I should get back to my family. See if I can get my parents to stop freaking out."

Sawyer gives me a sympathetic smile, and then we hold each other for a long minute, unable to talk about it all right now, but both of us saying everything we can with a kiss to a forehead and one to the lips.

When his arms stiffen, I turn around, and he lets me go. My mother is there in the doorway. She shakes her head and opens her mouth to speak, and then shakes her head again, like she can't believe my gall. And then she closes her eyes and sighs heavily. "Hello, Sawyer," she says.

"Hi, Mrs. Demarco."

"You're not too badly hurt?"

"No, ma'am."

"Your parents . . ." She looks around.

"They're not here."

She nods, unable to hide her relief. "Well."

"We were just leaving," Sawyer says. He looks at Ben and the other guy, who now rests his hand on Ben's shoulder, and I wonder if he's Ben's boyfriend.

"I'd like to thank your son," Ben says. "He saved my life. He . . ." Ben stops talking.

"Now's not a good time," my mom says. "Tomorrow, when Antonio isn't here. That would be better."

Ben nods. "I'll come by. Thank you."

My mother smiles grimly. "I'm glad you're all okay."

Sawyer and the others file out of the waiting room and go down the hallway to the elevator. I look at my mother, waiting for her to yell at me some more.

And all she says is "Your father told me you know about his affair."

It takes me a second to change gears.

"Yeah," I say. "I do. I told him that."

Her face is pained. "Do the others know? Trey and Rowan?"

"No."

She looks away. And then she says, "Do you know where in New York Rowan is?" Her voice is broken and weak for the first time, and I realize she's trying to hide her tears from me. "That's all she'll tell me."

"Yes. She's safe, Mom."

She puts her hand to her eyes like a shield, a brim for the tears, and she breaks down, unable to hold in her sobs. And I stand there, scared, in shock, watching her cry for the first time, and I don't know what to do because we're not exactly a hugging family, and I don't think she probably wants me to. So I watch her, dumb, cold, as she sobs into her hand. And I hate that. I hate myself for not hugging her. I hate that the Demarcos can yell like crazy but that's the only emotion in our tiny repertoire of feelings that we're allowed to express.

Mom drives, and we ride in silence once Dad gets the clue that I'm not speaking to him no matter what he says to bait me. When we get home, I go straight to my room, the only Demarco kid left, and I have no phone. No way of talking to Trey or Rowan without my dad eavesdropping. No way of calling Sawyer without Dad checking the numbers, because he's so controlling and paranoid. So all I can do is lie on my bed in the dark, alone, and stare at the flashing light that pulses on my wall, thinking about the horrible event that happened today, and wondering why I'm so fucking cold inside.

Thirty-Eight

In the morning I grab my savings money, leave a note for my parents telling them I'll be with Trey all day at the hospital, and head down the stairs. The sky is still cloudy, but it's not raining. I debate taking the delivery car, but that'll just piss my parents off more, so I'll take the bus. I descend the steps and go outside.

"Hey," says a voice.

I whirl around, and there's Sawyer standing next to the back door. "You scared me," I say. "Guess I'm a little gun-shy."

He cringes. "Too soon."

I nod. I don't know what my problem is—I feel like I just finished playing a video game or something, like everything that happened yesterday wasn't real. And I don't know what's wrong with me.

We walk to his car and get in. "Are your visions gone?"

"Completely. It's insane."

I laugh, and he frowns again. "It's not funny."

"I know." On the seat is the newspaper, and on the front page is a picture that looks familiar. I pick it up and open the fold, and stare at the students in the quad outside the door to Goodspeed Hall. In the foreground paramedics are loading somebody into an ambulance, and students' faces are in agony. And then I read about it. The whole story, plus some quotes from witnesses: "Two students—I don't know their names—they, like, tackled the shooters and screamed for us all to run . . . and we did. We left them there and we just ran."

I read that there were two other injured students who managed to make it out and down the elevator, and they directed the police to the right place. And I read about a guy who said, "Some girl ran by me and shoved a note in my hand that said to call 911, so I did. I didn't know her. I'd never seen her before."

I look up and realize we're still sitting in the parking lot, and I can't read any more because tears are streaming down my face. And I look at Sawyer and he's crying too, and he reaches over to me and he holds me and we cry together for a very long time. And it's real now. Suddenly it's really freaking crazy real. *That* happened. And we were sitting right in the middle of it. And Trey could have died.

"You're sure you're not seeing any more visions?" I ask after I've wiped my eyes and we're on the road, heading for the hospital.

"I'm sure. It's gone."

"Thank God. It's really over." But the relief I want to feel isn't coming.

He glances at me. "How did you decide to come back?"

I'm not sure what he's asking at first, but then I realize what he means. "The girl with the gun—she got off the bus I was going to get on, so I followed her. When did you figure it out?"

"I ran into Ben in the quad as he was changing the location. He recognized me from the day before and asked where I lived. I told him I was still in high school and checking out the campus for the weekend, thinking about going there for college. I told him I thought what he was doing was cool. He latched onto that and sort of dragged me with him, but then I realized we were headed for a music classroom. That's when everything came together. I tried calling you but you didn't pick up. . . . I figured you were on the bus asleep or something." He glances over his shoulder as we merge. "I'm sorry about your phone. I never thought about you having it long enough to run out of minutes. I guess I figured your parents would get you a new phone when you started doing deliveries again."

"They made me take Rowan's on the few times I did deliveries." I pause. "It's my fault. I should have been keeping track of the minutes." That was a dumb mistake, and I cringe to think about how it could have wrecked everything. "I almost freaked when I saw you sitting in that classroom. Wasn't that strange to finally be there—to see it?" I ask, remembering how it was when all of my crash vision stuff fell into place.

"It was spooky and horrible." He adjusts his hands on the wheel and I notice his knuckles are all scraped up.

I think about all the things that could have happened. "One of the reasons I feel so weirdly detached from this is that I wasn't seeing it like I was last time. I mean, this time I was focused on the clues and figuring them out. I wasn't seeing body bags or dead students. I knew I had to trust you and do whatever you said. And that was really hard at first, but in the end, especially in those last seconds, I knew that was the only way to go. You were, like, navigating, and all I could do was listen and follow." I glance over at him. "And you did it."

Sawyer sighs and puts his elbow up next to the window. He scratches his head and smooths his finger over his stitches. "No, I didn't, Jules. That's the problem. I didn't stop them. They still managed to hurt people. They still managed to get attention for their hateful shit."

I shift in my seat to look at him. "Sawyer, you don't even know what you're saying. You saved almost a dozen lives! You're one guy, and you stopped this tragedy from being major. I wish I could've stopped that truck before we hit your building, or stopped it down the street before the guy had the heart attack, and saved him. But we can't do everything—the vision isn't a total fix; it's a chance to change a bad thing to something less bad. But there's no guarantee that everybody turns out fine. Come on, Sawyer," I say, my voice softening. "Don't be so hard on yourself. The vision's gone. You did what you were supposed to do. Maybe . . . maybe those people needed to go through that experience in order to become the people they're going to be, you know? Maybe that experience triggers something inside of them that will help them become great."

"And maybe it'll make them dependent on prescription drugs, or want to kill themselves." His voice is bitter.

My mouth falls open. "Are you serious right now? You think the vision gods, or whoever, gave us these chances so we can end up watching the people we save turn into drug addicts?"

"How the hell should *I* know?" he yells. "How the hell do *you* know? Are you just rationalizing it to make yourself feel better about almost getting killed?"

"I don't know what I'm doing!" I shout back at him. "I'm just trying to live my life and get through it, okay? So what if I'm rationalizing. So what? At least I'm dealing with this freak thing!"

"Just because it's over doesn't mean I'm ready to deal with it!"

We're both quiet for a long time. And then Sawyer asks in a softer voice, "When we're acting on a vision, do you ever wonder if we're invincible?"

And it's so almost funny in a superhero cartoon sort of way. But really, it's not funny at all. Because I've thought it too.

Thirty-Nine

When we come in, Trey is sitting up in the bed, his arm in a sling and a shadow of stubble on his face. "It's about time," he says. He's got the look of a stoner on his face, and I see he's got a morphine drip going. Guess Mom and Dad don't think *he'll* get addicted. Eye roll.

"You could've gotten shot a little closer to home."

He screws his face up. "Yeah, about that. What the hell happened? I don't remember anything."

Sawyer and I pull up chairs and tell him the story. Before we can finish, there's a knock on the door. A nurse pokes her head in. "Trey, a few of the students you helped save are here. They want to say thanks—is it okay if they come in?"

Trey looks at me. I nod, and Sawyer and I slide our

chairs back to get out of the way as Ben and his friend come in. I stand up and introduce Ben Galang, and Ben introduces Vernon, the guy he was with yesterday, who apparently was at the meeting, though I don't remember him.

Ben looks like he slept in his clothes. His hair is disheveled and his self-repaired glasses can't hide the dark circles under his eyes. He reaches out his hand and carefully shakes Trey's hand. "I don't know how to thank you."

Trey looks up at Ben and gives him a goofy, drugged smile. "I'm not sure why, but okay."

Ben glances at me, confused.

"We haven't quite gotten to the part of the story where Trey came in and busted up the party," I explain. "I don't think he knows what he did."

"That, and he's a little drunk on morphine," Sawyer adds.

Trey frowns. "All I remember is someone screaming 'Die, fag!' in my face, which really, you know, sucked. Then I took one look at the blood spurting out of my arm and I was like, 'Wuh-oh, check, please,' for the rest of the event." He blanches just thinking about it. "Doesn't sound very heroic to me, but whatever."

Ben brings his hand to his mouth and I can see his chin is trembling, his eyes filling up. And then he pulls his hand away and says, "The girl had a gun to my forehead.

I have a scrape here where she dug it into my skin. I was a split second away from getting my brains blown out. And then the door flew open, glass went everywhere, and the shooter was distracted." He pauses. "I got the gun off my head. And she turned and it went off. She shot you instead of me." Ben's lips quiver. He presses them together.

Clearly Trey doesn't know what to say. He opens his mouth and closes it again, and lets his head fall back against the pillows. And then he says in this hilarious Clay Aiken voice, "Well. That was right nice of me."

For a second, nobody moves, and then I snort, and everybody else sort of relaxes, and before I know it Sawyer has found more chairs and Ben is giving us updates on everybody. The girl who was shot in the abdomen, Tori, was the worst off. She made it through five hours of surgery and the doctors are cautiously hopeful. And the guy who was shot in the foot is doing okay, but the bullet shattered a bunch of bones and he won't be walking anytime soon.

Back at UC, Ben says, classes are canceled and there are counselors helping students cope. There are also reporters everywhere. Because the police caught the two alleged shooters immediately, they didn't close down the school, but a good portion of the quad is blocked off around the crime scene and a lot of students went back home. "And seriously, you guys are the unnamed heroes.

You're, like, becoming a legend," he says to all of us, but he can't stop looking at Trey, his true hero.

"Please don't give anyone our names," I find myself saying. "We don't want a bunch of reporters in our faces. We just want to, you know, get through it and move on. Our parents are sort of freaking out. I'm sure you can imagine." And then I add, "I'm only in tenth grade."

"Me too," Sawyer says. "Jules and I just want to disappear, if that's cool with you." He looks over at Trey and grins for the first time since everything happened. "Trey, on the other hand . . . he's a senior and he could really use some attention."

Trey pushes his morphine drip. "Indeed," he says, adorably loopy.

Ben smiles and turns to me. "I'm not quite sure why you guys picked this weekend to check things out at UC, or how you managed to spring to action that fast, but you really did save a lot of lives. And if you don't want your names out there, I can totally dig that. Just watch it when you're wandering around here—there are some reporters in the lobby."

"Here," Trey says, fumbling for his cell phone on the bedside table. "You should call me."

Ben turns and looks at him, a small smile still playing around his lips. "Oh, should I? What's your number?"

Trey tells him, and Ben enters it into his cell phone, and

then he takes Trey's and enters his number. "Okay," Ben says a little cautiously, "well, we'd love to have you come for a meeting. Are you seriously considering U of C? Even after what happened?"

"Oh yeah. I totally am. What's your name again?"

Ben laughs and tells him.

I frown. Trey knows U of C is a private school. Mucho big bucks. But hey . . . there's always the power of morphine to make you forget about the minor details of your life, like living above a restaurant that struggles monthly to pay its bills, and considering returning to the place where some lunatic outsider came in and fucking shot you because you're gay.

When Ben and Vernon leave, Trey looks like he's about to fall asleep. My parents will be along soon, I'm sure, so Sawyer and I go to the nurses' station to try to find out the status of the others. We learn that Tori is still in intensive care, so we're not allowed to see her, and the guy with the injured foot is asleep. So we head out a side exit and take a walk on a sunny, windy spring Monday.

I push up the stretched-out sleeve of my hoodie and look at my pasty-white arm. I was so glad to have that cast—it was like a weapon. It did way more damage than I could have done with my fist alone.

Thinking about that makes me wonder briefly what

kind of pain the shooters are in today. Trey will be proud that I kneed the guy in the meatballs. I shove my hands in my pockets and Sawyer and I walk in a somewhat awkward silence now that we're alone. I feel like we're in the middle of a fight, but we're fighting about different things.

After a while he says, "What are you going to do about your parents now that this is all over?"

And I don't know the answer, because something keeps buzzing around the back of my mind. I swat it aside. "I guess maybe try talking to them. I mean, it probably won't work, but it's actually something I haven't tried before, so who knows. We're just not really great at that." I tilt my head to look at him. "The words never come out right, you know?" He nods and I ask, "What about you?"

"I don't know."

"I hate it that you're getting hit, Sawyer."

And normally I'd expect him to get a little defensive and say something like *I don't exactly like it either.* But this time he doesn't. This time he's quiet for a long time. And then he says, "I'm leaving."

Everything inside me stops working. "What?"

"It's toxic living there. I'm moving out."

I have no pulse. My words come out as weak wisps of air, and without warning the tears pour from my eyes. "But where are you going?"

He hears the blubbering child in my voice and he turns

sharply to look at me. The hardness in his face melts and turns to surprise, then realization. "Oh, baby," he murmurs, gathering me in his arms. "God, I'm sorry—I'm not leaving you, or Chicago, or school. Just my parents and grandfather. I'm moving out. Not sure where yet, but I have a few options."

I'm flooded with relief. "You big jerk," I say, sniffling in his chest. "You don't have a fight with a girl and then say you're leaving. Even though I'm really glad you're getting away from them."

He holds me closer and I feel his breath as he laughs silently into my hair. "We had a fight? I thought that was just, you know, talking. Loudly. The Italian way."

I put my arms around his waist and raise my head to look at him. "I don't like talking loudly with you."

"I don't either. Let's not do that again." He gazes at me until I'm lost in him, and says, "Your eyes are so beautiful. I've missed them." And then we're kissing on the sidewalk in front of the University of Chicago hospital.

Forty

Five things I finally manage to get done over spring break:
1. Buy a cell phone. Myself. I even give my parents my new number because I'm responsible like that
2. Call my sister to see if she's doing more making out than I am (she's not)
3. Get my job back and make it seem like I'm doing them a favor while Trey's out, when really I just kind of miss it
4. See Sawyer every day, and find out being in love, with no stressful visions, is way more fun than anything
5. Scare the hell out of Trey when I tell him

that he totally threw himself at a college boy
while under the influence of morphine

It was hilarious, that last one. I have never seen Trey
so mortified. But you know what? Ben came back to the
hospital to see Trey once more. Alone, this time, and he
stayed for over an hour. I'm just saying.

And on the morning Trey was being released, Sawyer
and I pushed him in a wheelchair to see the other victims,
and everything hit hard once again, reminding me that
solving the mystery of a vision is not the real part. The
real part is the people and the way their lives are changed
forever.

It's weird how hatred can make people do such terrible
things to other people. It kind of makes me think about
my dad. And I wonder, is his anger a form of hatred? I
think about my anger—at Sawyer's family, at the people
who want to kill other people because of who they are, at
the vision gods who put us through all of this. Is that anger
really hatred in disguise?

Or is only irrational anger actually hatred—the kind
of anger and hatred my dad has over a recipe, and toward
a family with whom he made a big mistake. Is his hatred
really aimed at them? Or is it reserved for himself, because
he's pissed about what he's done—or what he didn't do?
And does he even know that his anger affects the Angottis'

anger, and that's why Sawyer gets punched in the face by his own father?

Selfishly, I want to excuse myself, reward myself for having the proper kind of anger. The kind that helps make the world better, not the kind that festers and makes people bitter. But I don't know.

I don't know.

It's late Friday night of spring break when I run into Sawyer at the Traverse Apartments. We're delivering to different buildings this time, but I park next to him so he sees my car and waits for me when he comes out. Which he does.

"Hey," he says. "My last weekend."

I nod. He told his mother on Tuesday that he would finish the weekend to give them time to find a replacement, and that he was moving in with his cousin Kate for a while, maybe forever, and taking a part-time job at the Humane Society.

He says his mother cried. And that makes me furious. I think, where the fuck are the tears before it's too late, you moms? Where are they? Why does it have to go this far before you let yourself break? But I don't say anything. That's my own battle, and my family is walking on eggshells until somebody (me) decides it's time to deal with it (just . . . not yet).

"How's Rowan?"

"She had a blast once our parents calmed down and got distracted with Trey. But she said she wasn't sure it was worth lying about. Now she's the one Dad's eyeing, asking her if she's pregnant." I laugh a little, but my mind is elsewhere, on my dad, wondering things I don't want to wonder but I know soon I'm going to have to ask him about. I lean against my car and pull on Sawyer's hoodie strings. "You doing all right?" I ask. "After the vision, I mean."

He shrugs. "I think so. Considering."

"Trey tried to be hilarious today," I tell him. "He came into my room this morning and told me he had a vision."

Sawyer's eyes open wide. "That's so not funny."

"My heart totally sank—I mean, I almost started bawling, you know? I don't know if I could do this again." I look at him hard.

"Oh, God," he says. He looks away, picturing it, I suppose. He shakes his head. "I really am glad that we had a chance to save people, but I'll tell you what—I can eliminate police officer and firefighter from my list of things I want to be when I grow up."

"I just hope . . . ," I begin. "No. Never mind."

He narrows his eyes and focuses in on me. "What," he says slowly.

I shrug. Bite my lip. "I mean, obviously I had a vision and somehow I passed it to you. And now, who knows? Maybe it's done. Or maybe . . . it's not."

Sawyer grips the back of his neck and leans against his car door. "What are you saying?" he says, like he knows what I'm saying.

"I'm just . . . I don't know. What if you got your vision because I saved you, and now you saved people, and one of them is having a vision, only we don't know it."

"Oh my God, Jules," Sawyer says, and I can see he's straining not to raise his voice. "This is not our problem. Are you kidding me? You are not responsible for saving the whole fucking world. Besides, where'd you get your vision from, then?"

I look down at the pavement. And I wonder, not for the first time, if my father's illness is responsible for this. And my grandfather's, too. Maybe these visions have been a Demarco family curse for generations, and I just unleashed the curse to the rest of the world. Back when I was feeling sick out of my mind, seeing that explosion and Sawyer in a body bag, I almost asked Dad if he'd ever had a vision. Maybe I should have. Because what if he's been having a vision for years, but he doesn't know what to do? And what if my grandfather had a vision too, and it got so bad that he killed himself—because it was the only way he knew to be free of it? Maybe the Angottis actually have very little to do with my family's history of depression, and it's been *this* all along. What if all the visions started with Demarcos and stayed with Demarcos, and none of us figured out how to get them to stop, so the visions festered inside of people until it ruined them. And then I came along and stopped mine. And by stopping my vision, I passed the curse to someone I saved. And by stopping Sawyer's . . . Well. I just have to find out.

"It started with me," I say. I glance up at Sawyer. "But that doesn't really matter, does it? It doesn't change anything. It's what happens next that matters. We're talking about people's lives—what if Trey hadn't helped me save you? What if Trey and I hadn't helped you with the shooting? I can't let some traumatized shooting victim handle the next thing alone." I shrug. "I can't. I unleashed the beast."

Sawyer stares at me. And then slowly he shakes his head, and I can tell his mind is made up. "No way," he says. "No way."

One look at his set jaw and I know he's not going to change his mind. I hold his gaze a moment more, and then I nod and attempt a smile, because this is not his battle. He's a victim of the Demarco curse, like everybody else.

"Okay," I say. "I understand." I pull the keys from my pocket, and then I reach up and caress Sawyer's cheek, pull him close. Kiss him until the tension between us melts away. And when we pull apart, I tell him I love him. And that I have to do this—I have to find out if anybody else is having a vision. And if someone is, I have to help. That's the way it's going to be, that's my responsibility, and I'm going to do it. Invincible or not, I started this, and I'm in it until I see a way out.

He just stares at me like I've lost my mind again.

I hope I can't find anyone with a vision. With all my heart, I hope this mess ends with us, but frankly, I doubt it does. And I can't rest until I know for sure.

When I get home it's late. Rowan's fast asleep. I lie on my bed, eyes closed, trying to picture the music room. Trying to count the people in there. Wondering where to start, how to track them all down. What to say when I do. Eventually I get up and find Trey watching late-night TV in the living room. He's got his bad arm in a sling, the other hand in a bowl of popcorn.

"Hey. You have Ben's phone number, right?" I ask.

He shoves popcorn in his mouth and nods, eyes narrowing. "Why?" he asks, his mouth full.

"I need it."

He stares at me, chewing slowly. He swallows and pauses the TV show. "Why?" he says again, suspicious.

I drop my gaze, studying a stack of board games, trying to decide if I should tell him. Finally, I say in a softer voice, "I just do. I need to make sure nobody new is . . . affected."

His hand drops to his lap. His eyes close, and he sighs heavily. "Shit," he says. "You gotta be kidding me."

I stare at the floor.

He sits up, his voice suddenly concerned, like he's just realizing what I'm saying. "Wait. If Sawyer passed the vision to Ben," Trey says, "I swear I'll shoot you both in the face."

"I know. Just give me the number. I'll call him in the morning."

He hesitates a moment more, like he can't believe this is happening, then sets the popcorn bowl on a pile of magazines next to the chair and pulls his phone from his pocket. He forwards Ben's contact info to my phone. "Try not to sound like a total psycho. And, you know. Don't make me look bad."

"Yeah, sure. No problem."

He attempts a reassuring smile, but his eyes are worried when I say good night.

At three in the morning my cell phone buzzes, and at first I think it's a dream. I finally wake up enough to answer. It's Sawyer. "Hey," I whisper, propping myself up on my elbow. "What's up?"

The line is quiet, but I know he's there. I can almost feel his chest move as he breathes, see his earnest eyes adorned with those ropy lashes, sense the trepidation in his voice before he speaks. And all he does is whisper three simple, beautiful words that I've come to love hearing.

"Okay," he says. "I'm in."

gasp

For the Midwest, with love

One

It's been a week since the shooting, and we're back on the University of Chicago campus. Ben Galang's eyes light up when he sees us, and he opens his dorm room door wider to let us in. Sawyer and I step inside and stand awkwardly in the crowded space while Trey eases in after us, taking care not to bump his injured arm on the skateboard that hangs from the ceiling next to the doorway.

Ben and Trey exchange greetings, and Trey's face floods with color.

"I didn't know you were coming with them," Ben says to Trey. He sounds genuinely happy to see him.

"Jules talked me into it," Trey says.

Right. Like I *had* to. I try not to laugh. "Yeah, I made

him. He needed to get out of the apartment and get some fresh air. Thanks for getting up early on a Sunday."

"Thanks for saving my life, guys," Ben says.

"Okay," Sawyer butts in, "dude, you gotta stop with that."

"Sawyer is a rather uncomfortable hero," Trey explains.

"Sorry, man—I won't mention it again." Ben grins and points to our seating options.

Trey steps around a pile of laundry to a love seat and carefully picks up a bra from the seat cushion. He glances at Ben, eyebrow raised.

"Roommate's girlfriend spent the night. It's awesome," he says, sounding like it's totally not awesome. He snatches the bra from Trey's hand and tosses it on the bottom bunk bed. "They're slobs. You guys met my roommate—Vernon. He was with me at the hospital. Have a seat. How's the arm?" He perches on the armrest opposite Trey as Sawyer and I sit in the two desk chairs.

Trey shrugs with his good shoulder. "Eh," he says. "It's all right."

Ben presses his lips together but says nothing more.

"So," I say, glancing around the room. Bunk beds, two desks, the love seat, a small TV balancing precariously on milk crates. One desk is fairly neat, and there's a map of the Philippines on the wall above it. "Um," I start again, turning my gaze back to Ben, "you're probably wondering why I wanted to talk to you."

He's wearing different funky glasses, I notice, and I remember that his got broken in the shooting. He smiles. "Kind of. What's up?"

I stare at the carpet, knowing that even though I practiced what I was going to say, this is going to sound so ridiculous. I lift my head and catch Sawyer's eye. He nods, giving me encouragement. My boys are on my side. I'm not alone. But it's still insanity, and I have to be careful. I turn my head toward Ben, who waits, puzzled.

And then I just blurt it out. "Any chance you've started seeing visions recently?"

Two

I expect Ben to laugh, but he doesn't. He studies me a moment. "No," he says slowly.

"Oh," I say. "Um, okay." I peer more closely at him. "You're sure?"

He frowns and looks at Trey. "I'm not sure I understand what's going on here."

"Sorry," Trey mutters. "Yeah, it's a weird question, but she's not insane, I swear."

Sawyer nods in agreement.

"See," Trey continues, "Jules, well, see, it all started . . ." He falters and looks at me.

"A few months ago," I say. "I got this vision of a truck hitting a building and exploding, and I kept seeing it, and it got more and more frequent, interfering with my life, and I kind of felt like I had to do something to, you know, *stop* the thing from happening, or whatever. And it turned out that the building was actually Sawyer's family's restaurant, and the truck was a snowplow with a dead driver—"

"Not like ghost dead—he had a heart attack while driving," Trey adds.

"Right," I say. "We're not *that* nuts. So in the vision the snowplow crashes into Sawyer's family's restaurant, and there's a huge explosion and nine body bags in the snow—"

"Including me in one of those body bags," Sawyer interrupts. "And Jules tried to warn me, but I wouldn't believe her. But she, and Trey, of course," he adds, "ended up stopping the truck from hitting the gas line, so our restaurant didn't explode, but that's how Jules broke her arm . . ."

"And then I thought the whole vision nightmare thing was over and we could just go back to normal, but apparently I, like, *gave* it to Sawyer, and then he—"

"And then I," Sawyer continues, "started seeing a vision too, of . . . of . . ."

The room is suddenly silent and we three glance at each other, and then at Ben, who is looking like a cornered feral cat right about now, wondering if there's a way out of this room, and probably willing to use force if necessary to achieve it.

Trey clears his throat and says quietly, "Then Sawyer started seeing a vision of a mass shooting. At a school."

Ben's eyebrows twitch.

"For the past few weeks," Trey continues, "Sawyer heard eleven gunshots in his head. And reflected in windows, on billboards, on TV screens and other places, he saw the music room on the fourth floor of that building, and he saw . . . bodies. Piles of bodies. And so that's why two high school sophomores were hanging around here last weekend, when the University of Chicago wasn't even officially in session. They weren't checking out the school. They were here to stop a mass murder—or at least keep it from being as horrible as it was in the vision." Trey smiles grimly. "That's why, Ben."

Ben's face is strained. He looks from one of us to the next. "This isn't funny," he says. "It's not funny."

"It's not a joke," I say. "I promise we wouldn't do that to you. I promise."

Ben glances at Trey again, like he trusts him more than us.

Trey nods.

Ben turns to Sawyer and studies him for a moment more. "Piles of bodies?"

Sawyer meets his gaze. "Yes."

Ben stands up and paces in the tiny space. He stops. "Me?" he asks, stabbing his thumb into his chest. "My body?" His voice wavers.

Sawyer drops his gaze to the floor. He doesn't answer.

Three

Trey interrupts the silence. "So you're not having any visions, then?"

At first Ben doesn't appear to hear him, but then, after a moment, he looks at Trey and shakes his head. "What? No. I'm sorry."

Trey leans back and lets out a sigh of relief. "Don't be sorry. This is a good thing."

I catch Sawyer's eye. He looks relieved, but I'm even more stressed, because if it's not Ben, that means we have to keep looking. "Ben," I say, "here's the thing. Just like I passed the vision to Sawyer, I'm worried that Sawyer might have passed the—the curse of the vision on to somebody else." I frown, thinking "curse" sounds too whackjob, but I can't think of a better word. "Like, maybe somebody else who was in that room is now infected, or whatever, and they're seeing a vision of something else—the next tragedy. So . . . um . . . I need to find out. So we can help them."

"*We* need to find out," Sawyer says.

Ben looks at us like we're speaking a foreign language.

"So," I continue, "can you remember everyone who was in the room at the time of the shooting? Do you know them all?"

Ben's face clears slightly, like he's beginning to understand what I'm asking. "I—I know most of them," he murmurs. "Some just by face—it was a combined event with the Motet Choir."

"Can you, like, I don't know—find out everyone's names?" Ugh. I hate this.

Ben bristles. "Okay, this is really getting weird. I'm not sure that's a good idea. I mean, it's pretty strange, what you're asking."

"I know."

"And even the people who haven't left school over it are still pretty shaken up, you know. It's only been a week."

"Totally, totally—so are we," Sawyer says, nodding emphatically. "And, well, if one of them is having a vision of the next disaster waiting to happen, they will definitely stay shaken up, because the visions are—well, they're just horrible, Ben. So yeah, anybody with the vision will stay *very* shaken up, until either they go insane or they die trying to save the next victims." Sawyer adjusts his jacket like he's getting defensive, ready to argue. Just the other night he said he wasn't going to help me with this. Now he's totally invested. I heart that guy.

Ben leans back and sighs. He takes off his glasses and rubs his eyes. "This is so insane."

I give Trey a pleading look.

Trey sits up. "Please," he says, his voice soft and earnest. "We all know how weird this sounds. We just—we don't really have any other choice, you know? We feel like we can't let somebody struggle with this thing alone."

Ben absently starts to clean his glasses with his shirt. "Why don't you call the police or something?"

Trey, Sawyer, and I all wilt. We've been over this before, having vetted this option time and time again. "Because," I begin, but Ben stops me.

"No, it's okay," he says. "I get it. They'd think you're nuts." He frowns as if he's still considering that point himself, and puts his glasses back on.

I close my lips and press them into a defeated half smile, and just look at him, waiting.

Finally he shakes his head. "All right. Fine."

I breathe a sigh of relief as Ben gets up and goes to the clean desk, muttering, "This is so weird," and pulls a few newspaper articles from the desk drawer. He brings them back to us. "We can start here."

Four

From the newspaper articles we glean nine names of students who were actually in the room at the time of the shooting. Ben jots down several more, and then he stops. "This is crazy," he mutters, and looks up. "How do you plan to explain this vision thing to everybody without looking totally nutballs?"

"Very carefully," I say. I actually haven't figured it out yet. "I mean, I know I can't go around asking them all if they're having visions. But I was thinking . . ." I pause as an idea forms. Blindly, I go with it. "I was thinking that maybe we could call a sort of support group meeting for the victims to all get together and talk. And see if anything comes out of it." I glance sideways at Sawyer, who nods.

Ben tilts his head. "That's not a bad idea. We did a

candlelight vigil thing outside the building a few nights ago for the whole campus, and there have been counselors around all week, but maybe I should organize a group with just the victims . . ." He looks at his phone, checking the time. "Actually, tonight would be good, since it's been a week. Kind of like a bad anniversary." He taps his finger to his lips. "I can get contact info for everybody. Can you guys be here at eight?"

"Yeah, no problem," Sawyer says. "The sooner the better."

I glance at Trey. "I think I can get Rowan to switch shifts with me."

"She will. We'll be here," Trey says. He looks at Ben. "I can stay through and help you make phone calls if you like."

Ben smiles. "That would be great." The two hastily look elsewhere, like they're sixth graders crushing on each other, and my heart pinches a bit—could my brother finally have found a nice boy to like?

"Thanks, Ben," I say. "I mean it. You're amazing for . . . well, pretty much everything." I stand up, and Sawyer stands up with me. "I've got to get back if I'm going to take the lunch shift for Rowan. Let us know what's up. We'll see you around eight."

Sawyer and I walk out of Ben's dorm and across the ominous quad that haunted Sawyer's waking hours up until a week ago. Now it only haunts his dreams. I look over the familiar grounds, thinking about last Sunday when we stopped a couple of gun-carrying gay haters from killing eleven people. "I hope they plead guilty," I say in a low voice.

Sawyer nods. "Yeah. I don't exactly want to testify."

My stomach hurts like hell at the thought.

Five things I hate about my life:

1. Apparently there's no end to this insanity
2. The tension at home is probably giving me an ulcer
3. Spring break is over and it pretty much sucked balls
4. I just realized it's my birthday tomorrow. *Tomorrow.* Who forgets important shit like that?
5. It's like things aren't funny anymore

My lunch shift is boring and slow, and Rowan, under slightly heavier surveillance after her little escapade to New York, hangs out in the dining room doing her spring break homework that she wisely waited until the last minute to do. With everything that has happened lately, I'm surprised our parents haven't locked either of us up or gotten suspicious, but they have their own problems, and my dad mumbled something about bad things coming in threes, so I guess with that attitude, he was sort of expecting Rowan's delinquency.

The lull gives me time to fill Rowan in, which makes her even madder than usual that she's missing out on something. I tell her for the millionth time that this isn't something she wants to be in on. She disagrees, and we leave it at that. At five thirty we switch out, and I sneak outside to the alley and find Sawyer waiting for me. We stop for dinner and we're off to UC once again.

We find Ben and Trey in Ben's room a little before eight, Ben at his desk and Trey leaning over Ben's shoulder as he types on his computer.

I knock on the open door and poke my head in. "How many?" I ask.

"We spoke directly to twelve and left messages for the others," Ben says.

"And you didn't forget anyone?"

"I don't think so. Though we didn't bother Tori. She's still in the hospital."

Trey pipes up. "We asked each person we called if they could remember who else was there that night. We're all meeting in the green room in two minutes." He and Ben get up, lock the room, and head in that direction. Sawyer and I follow.

There's a handful of students in the green room already. The guy who was shot in the foot walks in on crutches, and I grab him a chair to put his leg on. A girl sits in a corner of a love seat, clutching her backpack.

Ben's roommate, Vernon, is there, sans braless girlfriend. More people straggle in over the next quiet minutes. "We should have brought refreshments," I say under my breath.

"It's not exactly a party," Sawyer whispers back.

A few people look expectantly at Ben, who glances at his phone and then stands up. "It's been a week," he says with a small smile and a heavy sigh. "And I thought it would be a good idea to just check in with each other, you know?"

A few heads nod.

Ben asks us all to go around the room, introducing ourselves. Trey checks people off his list. I catch his eye and smile, and he smiles back.

Then Ben explains that we don't really have a format; we're just here to talk without any counselors or reporters around to analyze us or judge us or whatever, and I can see people relaxing. I wonder what it's been like here.

Ben looks at the guy with crutches. "Schurman, how's your foot?"

Schurman shakes his head and looks at the floor. "Not great."

"What did your coach say?"

"He's being cool, but obviously I can't play anymore this year. I don't know if, you know, if I'll ever be able to run the same again. I might not be able to play." His voice contains no emotion, like he's become a robot. Like his dreams for the future are over and he's pretending to accept it. I wonder what sport he plays, but I don't ask.

Ben presses his lips together. "I'm sorry, bro."

Schurman shrugs and looks at the floor.

Ben turns to the girl in the love seat. "Sydney? How's it going?"

Sydney's face is strained. "It's going," she says.

"Are your parents . . . handling things?"

"They let me come back here," Sydney says with a shrug. "It's weird. I didn't think . . . you know. That seeing the building, and all that yellow tape . . ."

Someone else nods. "Yeah, I don't ever want to go back in there."

More chime in now, and I sit quietly, watching, feeling the same things they're all feeling, yet somehow I must keep myself distant from those things and stay focused. I know Sawyer is watching too. Looking for signs. Is anybody distracted? Looking out the window, watching a vision play out? It might be too early in the cycle—it's only been a week.

When things quiet, Sawyer says, "I keep having weird nightmares . . . only . . ."

I look at him. So does everybody else.

"Only . . . what?" Trey asks.

"Only, they're not about the shooting. And I'm not . . . actually . . . asleep."

I hear a little shuffling in the room, but I keep my gaze fixed on Sawyer. When no one says anything, Ben says, "You mean like a daydream, only it's scary?"

Sawyer looks at the floor. "I guess. But . . ." He shakes his head. "Never mind. It's not exactly normal. Just . . . trauma, or something."

"What happened to us isn't exactly normal," a girl says. "I guess we can expect weird shit to happen."

I look at her, then back at Sawyer. "What's your . . . daymare . . . about? You said it's not a shooting?" I think I know where he's going with this, and I hope I'm helping.

"No. Something completely different. It's a . . . a truck. Crashing into a building. An explosion," he says. "It's, like . . ." He runs a hand over his eyes. "It's, like, not a dream at all. It's like . . ."

"More like a vision?" Ben asks.

Sawyer laughs weakly. "Well, I'm not—I mean, I wouldn't say that . . . exactly . . . but . . ." He shrugs. "But yeah. I guess that's pretty accurate."

No one chimes in with a similar story. No one appears to be uncomfortable in his silence on the matter. No one flushes or blanches or reacts with their limbs or eyes or anything to indicate they can relate to what Sawyer just described. But they are sympathetic.

Sawyer deserves a Tony Award for that performance. Too bad there's nothing admirable about being a fraud. It's even less admirable when a few of the students hang back at the end of an hour of sharing, giving Sawyer the names of their therapists and urging him to call. Soon.

Five

The truth is, we could all probably use some therapy right now. Hell, we're a mess.

"Well, that was good for everybody, I think," I say later, making myself at home in Ben's room by curling on the foot of Vernon's bed. "I mean, we didn't get what we needed. But at least we've established contact with everybody and they've got our phone numbers."

"Yeah, you can't expect somebody to come forward in front of everybody to say they're seeing visions too," Trey says. He sinks onto the love seat, and Ben sits next to him. Sawyer takes a desk chair.

"How many victims weren't able to come to the meeting, Ben?" I stare at the underside of Ben's mattress. This room smells gross, like a sack of armpits.

GASP

Ben takes the list from Trey. "There are three who have left the school completely, one still in the hospital, and one who lives here in this dorm but either couldn't come or didn't want to."

Sawyer looks at me. "How are we going to handle this?"

I think about it. "Start here and work our way out to the ones who left the school, I guess. Who's the guy in this dorm?"

"His name is Clark."

"Should we go up and see him since we're here? I mean, he might have avoided the meeting because he thinks he's losing it." I sit up and slide off the bed.

"I suppose we should," Sawyer says. "But can we just ask him outright? I feel like a big cheat playing things like I just did in the green room."

"Yeah. Let me take this one." I look at Ben. "Will you show us where his room is?"

Ben's already getting up. "Of course."

We knock on Clark's door, but no one answers. Ben hollers down the hallway to some guys toilet-papering the doorway to somebody else's room. "Have you seen Clark?"

They shrug and shake their heads. One holds his finger to his lips to quiet us, and points to the toilet paper.

"Yeah, because no one else will notice what you're doing there if we're quiet," Ben mutters, and I'm kind of

505

digging his sarcasm, which we haven't really seen before today. He looks at us. "I don't know what to tell you. You can hang around and wait if you want."

I look at Trey and Sawyer, and then check the time. "We should go if we want to hit up the hospital tonight, guys."

Sawyer nods. "Yeah. Okay, thanks, Ben. We'll have to come back later this week." He grabs my hand and tugs, but I want to see what Trey does. Watching my big brother have a crush is the only fun I have in my life right now.

Trey smiles at Ben. "Yeah, thanks. I, um, I left my jacket in your room . . ."

I squelch a grin and Sawyer squeezes my hand, probably hoping I'll behave. "We'll go to the hospital and see if Tori is up to having visitors," Sawyer says. "Meet you at the car in thirty minutes? I'm parked on Fifty-Seventh, in front of the bookstore."

Trey waves in acknowledgment.

Sawyer drapes his arm over my shoulders and we walk down to the quad and then out to the street toward the hospital. When we get outside in the dark, he twirls my hair around his finger and smiles at me. "Five bucks says they're making out in Ben's room."

"Dogs, I hope so," I mutter. I lift my chin and we kiss while we're walking, and I feel like even though everything is such a mess, I can actually handle it because Sawyer's here with me.

Six

Tori is awake. It's the first time she's had her eyes open when we've visited her. She doesn't know who we are, but her mom explains and introduces us—we've talked to her a few times before.

Tori's face is unmarred from the shooting. Her dark brown skin is flawless and beautiful. Her hair—a gorgeous mess of tiny black braids—undisturbed. Only her guts were ripped up, and the shreds sewn together. She still has tubes going into her arm—pain meds and antibiotics, her mom says.

My mind flashes to the music room again. The black-and-white checkerboard floor streaked with red. Tori looking dazed, lying against the wall, holding her hand to her stomach as blood poured out between her fingers. . . . Gah. She was the most seriously hurt. I grab the back of a chair as a wave of nausea rides over me. Half the time I feel like I'm still in shock. Like one day, when this is all over, I really will need to be committed.

It feels awkward, us knowing her but her not remembering us. I'm thankful for her mother, who has heard the story no doubt countless times by now from Ben, from us, from others who have visited.

My cell phone vibrates in my jeans pocket, but I ignore it and focus on Tori. "How are you feeling?"

"Terrible," Tori says in a soft voice. "Mostly terrible." She looks at her mom. "Sorry. I'm tired of saying I'm fine."

Tori's mom shrugs and smiles. "Nothing wrong with telling the truth," she says lightly. She turns to us. "It's been very difficult."

"I'm sure it has," I say. "I'm so sorry this happened to you."

"So am I." Her bottom lip trembles the slightest bit. "It sucks."

I reach out and rest my hand on her forearm, and she lets me keep it there. "I'm really sorry. What else is happening? Are you having any nightmares . . . or anything?"

Sawyer leans in. "Jules and I have had some really weird side effects. Just mind tricks, I guess. The psychologist says it's normal."

Tori narrows her eyes at the ceiling. "Nightmares, sure. I think the pain meds are messing with me."

I glance at Sawyer, and I can tell we're wondering the same thing. "Every once in a while Sawyer was seeing a . . . like a vision, I guess. Right?"

"It really helped me to talk about it, though," Sawyer says.

My phone vibrates again in my pocket. Tori doesn't respond.

"So do you want to talk about it or anything?" I ask, trying not to sound odd about it.

"Not really," Tori says. She looks out her window, frowns, and looks away.

Sawyer sits up straight. "Okay, well, is there anything you need? Any homework or stuff from your dorm or whatever?"

She looks at us like the weird strangers we are. "No. My roommate is handling that kind of stuff." She yawns. "And I'm really tired now, so . . . ."

Tori's mother stands up on cue. "Thank you both for coming by to visit," she says.

Sawyer and I stand too, somewhat reluctantly. "Sure," I say. I spy a notepad and pen by the bed and ask, "Is it okay if I give you my phone number in case you ever want to talk?"

"Sure," Tori says, but there's no enthusiasm behind it.

I write my name and number on the notepad and sigh inwardly. "Okay. Well. I guess—"

Suddenly there's a flurry of activity outside the room. I turn to look. Trey is running down the hallway toward us like a total lunatic, something he would never do under normal circumstances. I spring to my feet.

"Jules," he calls out in a way that makes my heart clench. He sees me and lunges into the room, face flushed and breath ragged. Tori's eyes widen in fear and Tori's mom rushes over to stand between Trey and her daughter as a nurse comes running in to see what's happening.

"Who are you?" Tori's mom demands.

"What's going on?" the nurse asks.

"He's my brother," I say, grabbing his arm. "Trey, what's wrong?"

"Why don't you ever answer your fucking phone?" Trey shouts, and I feel his breath hit my face. He stares at me, his face breaking. "We have to go."

My stomach twists. "What? What is it? What happened?"

"It's not Dad," he says quietly. "It's . . . it's worse. Come on!"

Seven

"What is it?" I nearly scream as my brother races down the hallway to the elevator. I chase after him.

Trey stops in front of the closed elevator doors and turns so we're standing face-to-face. His dark eyes are pooled with fear and he works his jaw like he does when he's trying not to cry. "It's a fire," he says.

I stare. "What?"

"The restaurant," he says, his voice cracking. "It's on fire."

My throat is closed. I am unable to choke out a single word. I hear Sawyer swear under his breath from somewhere behind me. I didn't hear him approach. I didn't hear anything. And then he's explaining things in gibberish to the interns and security guards who have followed us, apologizing, and then when the people stop crowding around us he's ushering Trey and me into the open elevator and pushing the buttons.

The elevator door closes and my senses return.

"Holy shit," I say. "Oh my God—Rowan?"

"She's fine. She's the one who called me."

"What about Mom and Dad? Tony? Aunt Mary?"

Trey shakes his head, dazed. "I don't know anything else for sure. Rowan was pretty hysterical. She and Tony and Mom were the only ones in the restaurant, and when she called me she was standing outside with Tony. She said she thought Mom got out but now she can't find her. . . ."

"Oh my God, Mom!" I scream.

The elevator door opens to a few curious stares. Sawyer pulls us out of the hospital and points in the direction of the car. We start running, blindly snaking around buildings and down car-lined streets. I pull my phone out of my pocket and see I have three messages. One from Rowan, two from Trey.

"Shit," I say, nearly tripping on a crack in the sidewalk. I dial Rowan, and she answers.

"Rowan! What's happening?"

"Did you find Trey?" She's sobbing.

"Yes, he's with me now. Is Mom okay?"

"I don't know!" Rowan screams. "Just get here!"

"Oh my God," I say as I climb into Sawyer's car. "What about Dad?"

"I don't know! I haven't seen him, and the firefighters won't let me get any closer. Tony's running around to the front and he told me to stay here and watch for them." Her voice hitches in a sob. "Just hurry up!"

"We're driving. Sawyer's going as fast as he can. We'll be there in less than an hour."

"Forty minutes," Sawyer says.

"Forty minutes," I tell Rowan. "Just, whatever you do, stay safe! And call me when you find Mom and Dad."

"I will."

I hang up. "I can't believe this is happening."

From the backseat Trey says, "She told me it was just her and Tony in the kitchen and Mom was out in the dining area. There were only a couple of customers . . ." He trails off. "Tony must have spilled some oil or something."

"Or it could've been a pan on the stove. . . ." Only three of them working. So Dad must have been upstairs. Neither of us says it.

Sawyer grips the wheel and stays silent, concentrating on the road. If we talk, I don't remember any of it. All I need to focus on is that Rowan is okay.

When we get close to home, we can see the lights of police and fire vehicles. The whole block is cordoned off and the sky is filled with smoke, lit up by spectacular, horrible flames. Sawyer parks as close as he can, and Trey and I jump out of the car, pound the pavement, and dodge onlookers, searching for Rowan in the back parking lot.

And she's there, a stranger's blanket draped around her. Trey and I run to her and fold her in our arms and hold her. Her phone shakes in her hand and her face is streaked with tears. "They're okay," she says. "They're on the other side. Dad was on a delivery . . . I didn't know . . ."

"Mom and Dad?" I ask, making sure before the hope can rise too far. "Both of them are okay?"

"Yeah. Tony just called me—Mom twisted her ankle helping customers get out. She crawled out and has been stuck on the other side all this time trying to find me and calling me from other people's cell phones because she left hers in the restaurant. But I wasn't answering because I was trying to call her and you guys and Tony and Dad. Dad was doing the last delivery, which I didn't even know about, and he's back now, and they're both fine." She releases a shuddering sigh. "Tony and Dad are helping Mom walk around the block to meet us here."

"Thank God," Trey says. He hugs us both again. And then we hear warning shouts from firefighters who have been spraying down the buildings on either side of ours—a florist on one side and a bike shop on the other, with apartments above, just like ours. Their buildings are so close to ours that there's no possible way the entire block hasn't gone up in flames, yet there they are, bricks scorched but no sign of interior flames so far. We turn back and stare at our restaurant . . . and our home.

The firefighters' shouts grow louder. They begin to push back from the building, and with a roar and a rush of gasps, the roof falls in on everything we own, everything my parents have worked their entire lives for, everything my father has collected and hoarded for the past ten years. The sparks fly like shooting stars into the night sky.

We stay all night.

Not because we have nowhere else to go. We stay because our parents won't leave, and we won't leave them.

My father's face is like an old worn painting, gray and cracking. He looks eighty years old today as he watches, mourning his business and his precious hoards of recipes and treasures. My mother fusses over us for a while, telling us not to worry. Telling us that we'll get more clothes, of all things—right there in the middle of the parking lot, with her whole life crashing down in front of her, Mom is worried about us being upset that we have nothing to change into. How does one become this person? I don't know.

I don't think my father even notices that Sawyer is there, bringing blankets and food and water and collapsible sports chairs from neighbors and I don't know where else so we can sit down on something other than the cold cement curb of the parking lot. My mother notices, though. When he shows her the chair, she puts her hand on his arm, thanks him with her wet eyes, and sits. He nods and presses his lips together, and I realize how much it means to him to have her approval.

Sawyer hovers nearby. Rowan, Trey, and I all sit together in birth order, thinking about all the things we'll never see again, and every once in a while stating the obvious: "Everything is gone." But it's not everything. It's weird. I have my boyfriend, my siblings, my parents. I'll miss the pillow I pretended was Sawyer. My favorite pajama shirt. My hairbrush and clothes and makeup. But I realize there isn't much else up there that's all mine. Certainly there was no space up there that was all mine. These people—this is what's mine.

I look around, realizing Tony has gone home. "How did it start?" I ask Rowan after a while.

"I don't know," she says.

"But you were in the kitchen, right?"

"Yeah. But it didn't start there, or we might've been able to put it out. Tony and I grabbed fire extinguishers as soon as we heard the smoke alarms, but it was already too late and we had to get out of there."

Weird. I heard my parents warning us about fire hazards in the galley so often that I figured restaurant fires must always start in the kitchen. "I guess they'll investigate."

Rowan shrugs. Nothing is important right now. I look at Trey and he looks at me, and I don't know what to say or do. Nothing is adequate to express how I am feeling. As we turn our eyes back to the smoldering remains of our lives, I hold his arm and rest my head on his shoulder, and we speak at the same time.

He says, "Happy birthday."

And I say, "Did you make out?"

And we look at each other again, absolutely beside ourselves with the strangeness of this all.

"Thanks," I answer. "Best one yet."

"No," he says. "But he touched my face and kissed me."

And that's the thing that makes me start to cry.

Eight

In the morning, Sawyer reluctantly leaves to get ready for school. Neighbors and people from my parents' church come with clothes and food, and we don't know what to do with it all. We put it in the meatball truck and try to figure out where to go from here. There have been offers, but no one is able to put all five of us up together for more than a few nights. I guess hoarders don't tend to have a lot of friends.

Is it wrong that I'm okay with that?

Is it wrong that I don't want to go live in some other person's house?

Now that the fire has been mostly out for hours, the lack of flames helps Dad focus. "We'll go to Vito and Mary's," he says. My uncle Vito and aunt Mary, our hostess, have four kids. The oldest, my cousin Nick, occasionally works—worked—for the restaurant on the pizza holidays. Night before Thanksgiving, New Year's, Super Bowl, prom. Days like those. Nick has three sisters. It's hard to keep track of how old they are, or even which one is which—they're a lot younger and they all look sort of the same. And I'm sorry, but there's not enough room in their house.

"I'll stay with a friend," Trey offers.

"Me too," I say. Yeah, right. I have none.

Rowan frowns. "I'll go with Jules."

"We're all staying with Mary," Dad says, and it's clear that now is not the time to argue. "At least for now."

When it's finally clear to my dad that the firefighters aren't going to let him poke around in the still-burning embers, we pack up the meatball truck and the delivery car and drive away with everything we own. We park in the elementary school parking lot across the street from Aunt Mary's house. We drag our bags of random donations inside and crash in Aunt Mary's living room while her kids are in school.

When I wake up, it's two in the afternoon. I have a crick in my neck and for a minute I can't figure out where I am. But then I hear my mom and dad talking about insurance and it all comes back to me.

Five things that rush through your brain when you wake up midday in a strange place after your house burns down:

1. It feels like somebody died.
2. I wonder what the losers at school are saying about this.
3. I guess that's one way to get rid of all Dad's shit.
4. My hair absolutely reeks.
5. Oh yeah, it's my birthday.

Wait. One more thought:

6. Um, why didn't anyone have a vision to help prevent this?

From the reclining chair I've been sleeping in, I watch my parents talking at the kitchen table. My dad looks like he got hit by a truck. His hair is all messed up and his face is gray leather. I don't think he slept much. Mom looks tired, but not as bad as my dad. She's always been stronger than him. I get up and venture over to them.

Mom looks up and sees me. She smiles and points to a chair. "Did you sleep okay, birthday girl?"

My lips try to smile, but for some stupid reason I'm overcome by the fact that in the midst of this mess, my mother remembers it's my birthday, so I do this weird screwed-up face instead. "Not bad, considering it's a lumpy chair. I just want a shower."

"You've got about an hour before your cousins get home," she says. "Aunt Mary has everything you'll need in the bathroom."

I get up, and she grabs my hand. I stop.

"We had gifts for you," she says through pinched lips.

I swallow hard and feel dumb that I'm so emotional about this. The whole house and restaurant is gone, and I feel sorry for myself because my birthday presents burned up. "I don't need anything," I say. "I wasn't even going to mention it."

"I know." She squeezes my hand. "We'll all go out for dinner—the five of us, I mean. For your birthday."

I glance at my dad, and he nods. He pats his shirt pocket. "I have my delivery tips to pay for it."

It's a joke.

My dad made a joke.

And I remember when I used to love him.

Nine

Sawyer calls when I'm putting on some stranger's donated clothes.

"Happy birthday," he says. "I love you. What do you need most for your birthday?"

"Besides you?"

"Besides me."

"A phone charger."

"That can be arranged. What else?"

I think about this stranger's bra I'm wearing that doesn't quite fit, and cringe. "Some . . . you know. Embarrassing schtuff."

"Ahhm . . . ," he says, and I can tell he has no idea where to begin. He guesses. "Like panty liner shit? And whatever else? 'Cause Kate's got like a whole drawer full of that stuff and she said I could bring you whatever." Kate is Sawyer's college-aged cousin who he moved in with after his dad gave him a black eye.

"Thankfully, no." I think about how much it would suck to have your house burn down on the night before your birthday and also get your period, and I realize things could actually be worse. "Like underwear." I blush. Apparently we haven't gotten to the underwear-discussion stage in our relationship.

"Hey, that's perfect—according to my sources, underwear is the five-week-dating anniversary gift," he says. "Can we go shopping today? Or are you too busy with . . . uh . . ."

"With wearing a stranger's underwear?"

"Yeah." He laughs.

"I can probably sneak out of here for a couple hours. I'll need to be home in time to do my birthday dinner, which should be a wild party." I search through Aunt Mary's bathroom cupboards for a hair dryer. "Can you pick me up in thirty minutes?"

"Aren't your parents around?"

"I don't care. I'm getting out of here for a while, and I'm leaving with you, and it's too bad if they see me. They have enough other stuff to get ridiculous about."

He hesitates. "I don't want to cause them any more stress."

I pause. "No, it's cool. I'll talk to my mom. She's starting to dig you a little."

"She is?"

"Don't tell her I told you."

I can hear the smile in his voice. "Okay, well, if Trey and Rowan need to get out, they can come along. If you want."

I think about it for a moment. I want to be alone with Sawyer, but the bratty cousins will be home soon, and Rowan and Trey need underwear as much as I do. "Yeah," I say reluctantly. "I'll ask them. Even though I just want to be alone with you."

"Me too, baby," he says, and I can hear the longing in his voice. It makes my chest hurt. "But they could probably use a break too."

"Yeah. Make it forty-five minutes." We hang up.

Forty-five minutes later, Mom and Dad are sitting at the table with a woman from the insurance company. Trey and Rowan are ready to go, and my mother seems distractedly relieved to hear we're going shopping for underwear. Sawyer comes to the door with two paper sacks full of stuff from him and Kate, like fingernail clippers and tampons and hairbrushes and razors and crazy hair product and a huge bag of makeup samples from Sephora, which is a store I'd totally shop at if I gave a shit about makeup and had a million dollars. Rowan squeals when she sees it.

My father looks up from the kitchen table, pulled from his thoughts, and his eyes travel from Sawyer's shifting stance to Rowan's delighted expression. Mom watches Dad, but Dad doesn't say anything. He turns his attention back to the insurance woman, and we're home free. "Be back by six," my mom calls after us. "Don't eat any junk."

I almost cry at that. I don't know why, other than it sounds so normal.

We stop at the ATM to get money, thankful all three of us deposited our latest stash of tip money on Saturday, so we didn't lose much. We head to the underwear section of the local everything store. Over the course of thirty minutes, Sawyer transforms from suspicious-looking ladies' department fringe creeper to active participant in camisole and bra fetching. I think it helps that as soon as Trey grabs his boxer briefs and a few other necessities from the men's department, he begins roaming our section, letting everyone know how he feels about the various "design collections." We get some clothes, too, but not very many, because, as Trey points out, we're not really sure if we're going to need our savings for other things . . . like a place to live. Because we definitely don't want to live in Aunt Mary's living room forever.

In electronics we pick up phone chargers for the whole family, which Sawyer insists on paying for. We buy a few snacks to replenish Aunt Mary's cupboards, and then we go. When Sawyer drops us off at five forty-five, Trey and Rowan take the bags inside. And Sawyer and I finally get a few moments of privacy in the car.

Sawyer reaches for my hand. He kisses each knuckle and looks at me with his sweet, sweet eyes, and then he slides his free hand through my hair and leans in, kissing me, our entwined fingers trapped between his chest and mine, our hearts beating through them, and I feel like the fire is inside me now.

After a moment we break apart and I glance nervously at the house windows, but nobody's spying. Sawyer traces my wet lips with his thumb.

"Let me know if you need anything," he says.

"I will."

"You going to school tomorrow?"

"Yeah."

"Good. I felt weird being there without you today."

I nod and look down. "Does everybody know?"

"Yes. It was pretty much the topic of the morning. People are sorry. Mr. Polselli wanted me to tell you he's glad your family is okay."

"That was nice of him." Suddenly I don't want to go to school. It's going to be awkward, not for the first time this year. I glance at the dashboard clock. "I should get inside before my dad starts in with the pregnant bit," I say.

Sawyer smiles. He releases my hand, reaches behind my seat, and pulls out a package with a bow. "Here," he says, handing it to me.

I look at him. "But you paid for the phone chargers and a bunch of other stuff."

He shrugs. "So? You think I want to be known as the guy who got his girlfriend a phone charger and underwear for her birthday? You think I want that hanging over my head the rest of my life?"

The rest of his life.

He catches himself and adds, "I mean, when you're famous and you're out there telling your first-boyfriend stories . . . well, I don't want to be remembered for that."

I laugh, but it sounds hollow in my ears. "I guess I don't want you to be that guy either, since it would only make me look bad when it comes to my choice in boy-friends." I shift my eyes to the package and start opening it, letting the distraction of working the taped corners ease the awkwardness of the moment.

Under the paper is a plain brown rectangular box. "Perfume?" I guess.

"No guessing."

I shake it.

"You might not want to do that."

"A can of soda?"

"Which is somehow better than a phone charger? Open it."

I can't imagine what it is. It's too heavy and big for jewelry, and it's clearly not a book. What else do boys get girls for their birthday?

I open the box and pull out something in bubble wrap. I ease the tape off and unwind it to find: a superhero bobblehead. In my own likeness. And on my cape is a giant letter *I*. I crack up and tap my bobblehead. "Best present ever! How did you do it?"

He looks relieved. "Through a website. I sent them a photo of you."

I examine it. Dark hair, brown eyes, skeptically arched eyebrow. "Yep, that's me." I point to the letter *I* on the cape. "Is that for 'interesting'? 'Intelligent'?"

"No," he says quietly.

"'Important'?" I guess, batting my lashes.

He shakes his head.

"No, wait, I know. 'Insane.'"

"No," he says. "It's for 'invincible.'"

"Invincible," I repeat.

He nods and looks away. "Because I need you to be."

For the first time since the fire, I think long and hard about the vision curse.

Ten

Mom, Dad, Trey, Rowan, and I pile into the delivery car, which no longer has anything to deliver, so I guess it's just a car. We go to one of those Japanese teppanyaki places where the chef does all those spatula and knife tricks and makes an onion volcano and tosses food into his hat and at your face, and we all try really hard to have a good time for the sake of everybody else. It's weird, actually, the five of us all eating dinner together like today is Christmas Day or something. And when I think about how life could be like this for who knows how long, it makes me feel like I'm suffocating.

During a lull in the chef action, Rowan makes a paper airplane with her used napkin and gives it to me for my birthday. Trey presents me with his soup spoon and three mints that he swiped from the register area while we were waiting to be seated. And Mom and Dad slip me twenty bucks, no card or anything—they haven't had time to do more. The chef finds out it's my birthday and does the fake ketchup squirt trick on me—where a red string comes out of the bottle when he squeezes it—and tosses me an extra shrimp, and then after we're done eating, the server brings me a free dessert with a candle in it, which is pretty cool.

When we get back to Aunt Mary's, she and the younger two cousins are frosting a birthday cake for me, so of course I'm forced to eat a piece of that—what a shame. But for once I can't even finish it. My stomach feels like lead. Being here at Aunt Mary's is like a glaring reminder that our home has been destroyed. And finally, as eleven Italians sit around in rare quiet eating cake, Trey asks the question we've all wanted to ask but didn't quite know how.

"So, Pops, what are we going to do now?"

It's startling. My dad looks at him, and at first his face goes to that normal sternness that we've gotten so used to recently, as if Trey was acting up. But then it softens. "We have insurance," Dad says. "We're going to be okay."

"Well, are you going rebuild the restaurant or what?" Rowan asks.

Dad looks at Mom.

"We don't know yet," Mom says. "We're trying to figure that out."

I sit up. "What would you do if you don't rebuild? Do you know how to do anything else?"

Mom laughs and looks offended.

"I didn't mean it like that," I say, even though I think I did. I can't imagine my parents doing anything else. Especially my dad. I'd like to see him get his butt out of bed for a regular job day in and day out.

"And what about our house?" Rowan asks. She glances at Aunt Mary. "I mean, we love you and all, but we can't live here forever."

"We're working on it," my father says. "We'll know more soon. We're trying to figure everything out."

The room erupts into loud conversation about our options, with the cousins giving animated ideas of what my parents could do for a living instead of running a restaurant, such as joining the circus or being professional birthday party clowns. Trey and Rowan get into it, and the house turns back into a typical boisterous family gathering once more. When the doorbell rings, I get up to answer it like I live here.

And it's Ben.

I stare at him, at first confused by how he knew where to find us, but then I gather my senses. "Come in," I say, and a delighted grin spreads across my face. "It's really great to see you."

"Hey," he says. "I'm so sorry. Sawyer called me. I'm—I can't believe it."

"I know." I usher him in. He looks a little frightened by the noise coming from the dining room. "Don't be scared. This is our typical decibel level whenever the family gets together."

"I don't want to intrude."

"You're not. In fact, I think you will lift the spirits of more than just me by your presence." I grin, and he blushes.

I drag him through the breezeway and into the kitchen, which is connected to the dining room, and when Trey notices us, he stops talking midsentence. He shoves his chair back and stands up. His face betrays just how much it means to him to see Ben. Everybody stops talking and turns to look at what Trey is looking at. Ben waves nervously.

"Hi, um," he says, not sure which of the adults to address.

"This is our friend Ben," I say. At the name, Rowan perks up, and I remember she's never met him. I introduce everybody.

"I'm sorry about the fire," Ben says. "You must be, uh, really shocked and sad . . ."

Trey springs to life and comes to Ben's rescue. He

rushes over and turns Ben around and guides him back to the breezeway so they can talk, and Rowan whispers, "He's so cute!"

"I know," I say.

"Why can't you go out with him instead of that other one?" my father booms too loudly, but for once there's no anger in his tired voice.

I stare at him. "Seriously? There are so many things wrong with that question that I don't know where to start," I say.

"What is that supposed to mean? It's just a question."

"He's gay, Dad," Rowan says, licking the frosting off her fork.

"Oh. Well, why didn't you just say that?"

"He's not Italian," Uncle Vito remarks.

"So?" Mom's eyes flash. She turns to me. "Is he—are he and Trey—?"

I shrug. It's not for me to say.

However, there's Rowan. "They made out."

"God, Ro," I say, and I start laughing. "They didn't, actually. Poor Ben."

"Why poor Ben?" Mom says, bristling. "We're good people. What's wrong with us? Is he too good for us?"

"No, he's just scared to death."

"He's not Italian," Uncle Vito says again.

"Exactly, that's why he's scared."

"That's what I'm saying," Uncle Vito says. He picks his teeth. "So what is he, Mexican?"

"Vito!" Aunt Mary and Mom say together.

"What? It's just a question!"

"It's racist," Aunt Mary says.

"Oh, for crying out loud. It is not. People ask me that all the time."

"They do not," Aunt Mary says. "It's too obvious with you."

"Either way, it's rude," Mom says. "He's American like everybody here."

"How do you know?" Uncle Vito asks. Aunt Mary slaps him.

"He's Filipino-American," Trey calls out from the breezeway in an annoyed voice. "So knock it off already. Hey, kids, have another piece of cake, why don't you?"

I grin at Rowan as our younger cousins start shrieking and grabbing more cake and Aunt Mary shoots a look of mock disgust in the direction of the breezeway. It's good to be laughing.

I hear the screen door slam shut and hope it's not Ben running for his life.

And if it is, I hope Trey is running with him.

Eleven

School is weird but we get through the first day, and the second, and the third. People are being nice—for now. But I know how this goes. In a few more days, when their pinprick-size moments of sympathy run out, they'll be talking behind my back again.

After school on Thursday I find Sawyer and we linger outside the meatball truck for a minute while Rowan and Trey climb inside.

"Anything you guys need?" he asks me, like he's asked every day this week.

"Nah. We're good." He's already done enough. "Do you have plans tonight?"

He shifts. "I was thinking about going back to UC to talk to the guy we missed. Clark, I think his name is." He hesitates. "You probably can't come along, right? I mean, I totally understand if—"

"Yeah," I say. "I mean no, I can't. Whoever has the vision curse is going to have to wait." I can't believe I'm saying that, but that's just how it is right now.

"I figured. You don't mind if I just try to keep things moving while you handle your family stuff, do you? I'm just . . . getting a little anxious about it."

I frown at the ground. I want him with me. It's selfish, I know. "Yeah," I say. "Go." I try to sound like I really mean it. Because I should really mean it. Just because my whole life burned up doesn't lessen my responsibility for this vision thing. "I wish we knew how to stop the visions," I say.

Sawyer looks at me. "Do you? Because if we stop it, chances are more people will die."

"Yeah." I scrape the toe of my new used shoe along the asphalt. "I guess I'm just full."

He seems to know what I mean by "full," even though I'm not quite sure myself. Full of shock, full of sadness, full of stress. Too full to deal with the vision. He brushes my hair from my shoulder and caresses my cheek like his hand belongs there. "It's okay. I'll keep searching." He lifts my chin and puts his soft, cool lips on mine.

And then he's gone, and I'm in the food truck with

my siblings, riding to Aunt Mary's. I lean my head against the window as we pass the Jose Cuervo billboard, which looks just as it should.

When we walk into Aunt Mary's breezeway, I can hear the cousins running around, arguing. Trey presses his eyelids shut and shakes his head slowly. Rowan flashes an annoyed look. We have nowhere to hide, and this is getting old. Our home is the living room. I try to be thankful for Aunt Mary and Uncle Vito for opening up their house to us, and for keeping their kids mostly out of the living room so we can feel like we have someplace to call our own, but it's hard.

We venture up the two steps into the main part of the house and around the corner into the kitchen and see a stranger sitting at the table with Mom and Dad. Mom's lips are pressed together so firmly that they're gray, and Dad is staring straight ahead, a vacant look in his eyes. It's frightening.

"What happened?" Trey asks them above the noise of the cousins.

Mom snaps her chin toward us. She looks right through us and shakes her head ever so slightly. Dad doesn't blink.

I stare, and then I grab Trey and Rowan by the elbows and push them toward the living room.

"What the hell," Trey mutters.

"No idea," I say.

"It looked bad," Rowan says.

Later, when we're trying to do our homework, I look out the window and see Dad driving off in the delivery car. Mom comes into the living room, fists clenched like she's going to lose it. She looks at us, and we look at her, and she says, "They believe the fire began upstairs, not in the restaurant."

My eyes widen. Nobody says anything, waiting for Mom to continue.

She does. Her voice is low. "It looks like it started from a worn extension cord in the living room next to some of Dad's . . . stuff."

My heart leaps to my throat.

"With all the hoards of newspapers and books and recipes," she continues, her voice straining, "well . . . there was no chance of saving anything."

I drop my homework and stand up, Trey and Rowan right behind me, and we wrap our arms around our mom. Her tears fall now, and a groan from deep inside her chokes its way out in a coughing sob like I've never heard before. I glance at Trey, and his eyes are as scared as I think mine must be.

Mom cries for a minute, and then she sniffs and wipes her eyes with her sleeve and tries to laugh, embarrassed for losing it in front of us, I guess.

"We're sorry, Mom," Rowan says.

"He feels just terrible." Mom's laugh disappears. She shakes her head. "He walked out in a daze. I don't know where he's going." She lets out a shuddering breath and runs her index fingers under her eyes, absently checking for mascara smudges, and for a split second, in her vulnerability she reminds me of Rowan.

"Do you want me to go find him?" Trey asks.

Mom nods. Her voice cracks when she says, "I don't know what he'll do."

Five things I want to say right now:

1. He's a douche for making you worry.
2. Maybe it would be best if he does just go kill himself, so we can get on with our lives.
3. Okay, those are the only two things I can think of, but dammit, I'm pissed.
4. And now I remember why I don't love him anymore.
5. Because I can't.

Twelve

Rowan stays with Mom, and I go with Trey to find Dad.

"Back home, you think?" Trey asks as he pulls the meatball truck out of the parking lot across from Aunt Mary's. He winces turning the wheel, and I know his shoulder must hurt, even though he doesn't like to admit it.

"Home would be the logical guess," I say. And then I let out a huge sigh. "Now what?"

"I don't know."

"Do you think he's going to . . ."

"No." He puts on his sunglasses when we turn west. "Mom wouldn't send us if she really thought he'd do it."

We drive in silence as the sun sets. Trey pulls into the alley and goes toward the restaurant's back parking lot.

There's a portable fence now around our plot of destruction and there are NO TRESPASSING signs posted. Trey parks next to the delivery car and we get out. He glances in the delivery car's window, probably to make sure Dad didn't blow his brains out in the front seat or something.

The substitute beat cop, Officer Bentley, is doing his rounds. He sees us and comes over. "I'm so sorry about your place," he says.

"Thanks," I reply. "It pretty much sucks."

Officer Bentley turns to Trey. "How's the arm?" he asks. "I heard you took a bullet over at the UC shooting."

I can't quite read the tone of his voice, and maybe it's the uniform, but I think I detect a hint of suspicion. I glance at Trey.

"It's not bad," Trey says lightly, which makes me think he's detecting it too. "I was lucky. It's healing nicely. Starting physical therapy soon." He looks beyond Officer Bentley and changes the subject. "You haven't seen our dad, have you?"

Officer Bentley points his thumb over his shoulder toward the fence. "He's in there." He gives us a grim smile, and he doesn't mention what a coincidence it is that we were hauled into the principal's office a few weeks ago for talking about a shooting at school.

"Thanks," Trey and I say together.

Officer Bentley hesitates, eyeing us, and then he

nods briskly and smiles. "Take care, kids. And stay out of trouble. We've seen your names in the paper more than enough lately."

"Yes, sir," I say. "We'd really like things to calm down too."

He smiles and continues walking.

When he's out of earshot, I mutter, "I was worried he was going to ask a few more questions."

"Me too," Trey says. "We need to stop getting hurt. And be invisible."

"You're telling me."

Trey and I walk over to the opening in the fence and look through it. And there's Dad, on his haunches next to a long, slanted hunk of whatever the roof was made of. Delicately he picks up a nearly unrecognizable scorched book and wipes the ash from it, straining to see in the dying light. And then he sets the book on a pile of other books and pokes through a layer of ash, picking up something else. Something small. He wipes it off and holds it up to the last weak rays of sun, and it glints silver.

"It's the thimble from a Monopoly game," Trey says softly. "Dear God."

Dad slips the thimble into his pocket.

My stomach hurts.

I look at Trey. He looks at me. We drop our eyes and walk away.

• • •

Later, after we've debriefed Mom and everybody else is either in their bed or in a sleeping bag on the floor, I find her again in the dimly lit dining room, sitting at the table holding a cup of hot chocolate, staring out the window into the darkness.

I pull out a chair. She turns at the noise and smiles at me.

"Are you feeling okay, sweetie?" she asks.

"Yeah, I just wanted to see how you're doing."

She puts her warm hand on mine and squeezes. "I'm fine. It's just a house. It's just a business. Replaceable things."

I nod and contemplate that for a long moment. "Waiting up for Dad?"

"Yep," she says, trying to sound upbeat. Trying to sound like the old Mom we're used to.

She takes a sip from her mug and turns back to the window.

After a minute I ask, "Aren't you mad at him? I mean, it's kind of his fault . . ." The words aren't coming out right, so I stop talking.

For a moment I think Mom doesn't hear me. But finally she turns again to smile at me. And then she nods. "Yes, Julia," she says in a measured tone. "I'm very mad. I'm mad that your father won't get help. I'm mad that I can't make him. I'm mad that he can't see . . ." She trails off.

Maybe it's the darkness, maybe it's the circumstances, maybe it's because I'm seventeen now. I'm not sure. But it's the first time she's been so honest with me about her feelings. And I think it's the first time she's treated me like an adult, rather than protecting me because I'm her kid.

"Maybe he'll get help now," I say. But knowing what I know about the Demarco curse, I don't really believe it. He's been in the hospital before for his mental illness, and he won't go near anyone who could put him there again.

I don't think my mom believes it either.

Just then my phone vibrates. I frown and look at it. It's a text message from a number I don't recognize. When I open the message, I almost drop the phone.

It reads: *I want to talk about the vision thing.*

Thirteen

"Are you all right?" my mom asks.

My heart is racing. I look up from my phone. "Yeah," I say. I close the message, slide my phone back into the pocket of my sweatshirt, and yawn. "No big deal. I'm going to bed. Or . . . to sleeping bag, that is." And then I add, "I'm sure Dad will be home soon."

Mom gives my shoulder a squeeze. "Me too."

We say good night. In the living room I hunker down inside my sleeping bag and pull out my phone again.

Sure, let's talk. Who is this? I type in response. It could be anybody. We gave our numbers out freely at the meeting Sunday night.

I wait for a response. It comes: *Tori Hayes.*

My heart races. "It *is* her!" I whisper.

Rowan kicks me and I emerge from my sleeping bag.

"What are you doing under there?" she asks. "Sexting with Sawyer?"

Trey is looking at me too, propped up on his elbow. "Gross," he says. "That's Nick's sleeping bag. You don't know what other body fluids could be in there."

"Yick. Don't be disgusting. I thought you guys were asleep," I say, pushing the sleeping bag off me. My hands are sweating and I'm suddenly nervous about what to say to Tori next. I just need to keep it cool. "One sec," I say, and then I type: *Oh hey Tori. Sorry, didn't have you in my phone. Can Sawyer and I come see you tomorrow after school?*

Tori's response is quick: *I'll be here. Like always.*

I look up and explain in a whisper, "It's Tori. She wants to talk about the visions."

Trey's attitude changes fast. "Oh, wow," he says. "For real?"

"Which one is Tori?" Rowan asks.

"The one still in the hospital," I say. "She got shot in the stomach."

"You were right," Trey muses. "Sawyer passed it on."

I smile grimly. "Looks that way."

Rowan screws up her face. "How's a girl in the hospital supposed to help you figure out the tragedy? She can't even get out of bed."

I shrug. "All she needs to do is tell us what's going on

in her vision. We can figure out the rest. It's not her problem. It's ours."

Rowan and Trey exchange looks, but they don't
disagree—this is their problem too. Just because I was
the one who apparently took it from Dad doesn't mean
we're not all responsible. Me more than them, maybe,
because I'm the one who passed it on, but Dad is their
dad too. They've got the same crazy genes.

Rowan nods. "I'm helping this time," she says. "Besides,
I don't have anything else to do now."

Trey frowns. "I suppose, but you'd better freaking listen to us. This isn't a joke, Ro."

"I know, sheesh. Don't you think I've figured that out
after all the times I visit you guys in the hospital?"

"She has a point," I say.

Trey shrugs. "And we could use her since Tori isn't
able to help."

We're quiet for a minute as I text Sawyer, letting him
know what's up.

"I wonder what her vision is," Trey whispers, just as
we hear the breezeway door open and Dad's footsteps in
the kitchen.

"Me too," I say. An involuntary shiver races up my spine
as I try to force my brain to stop thinking so I can sleep.

That never works, you know.

Fourteen

After school on Friday, as I wait for Sawyer so we can visit Tori, my psych teacher, Mr. Polselli, comes up to my locker. He hands me an envelope.

"This is from the teachers," he says. "For your family." He shrugs and smiles, the laugh lines around his eyes crinkling. He's like the under-the-radar teacher of the year. To me, at least. I don't know why he likes me, but it's been pretty awesome having him on my side. Maybe with all his psychological knowledge he can tell I'm batshit crazy and he feels sorry for me.

"Thanks." I take the envelope and realize it's too dense to be a letter. It's thick. I look up at him as he shoves his hands in his pockets and turns back toward his classroom across the hall.

I slip my thumb under the flap and peek inside. It's money. "Hey!" I say.

He looks back over his shoulder.

"This is money," I say, flustered. We're not charity types.

"Very good," he says with a grin.

"I can't—you don't need to do this." I hold the envelope out.

He stops walking. "Julia, I think you know why you have to take it."

I think hard. Is this a psych question? A life lesson based on book facts? I figure it is. He's that kind of teacher.

"Because it makes *you* guys feel better?" I guess. And I know it's something like that. "You felt helpless to fix the real problem—i.e., make our house and restaurant not burn down—so . . . you do what you are capable of doing to help us and appease your inner . . . whatever?"

"Close enough," Mr. Polselli says. "An A for the day." He slips back into his classroom, leaving me standing there, kind of in shock, when Sawyer finally comes.

We decide that it's best not to have Trey with us when we visit Tori since he acted like a crazed madman the last time Tori and her mom saw us. And they don't know Rowan, so we leave her home as well to help Mom and Dad search for an apartment for us. Sawyer and I make the familiar trek up to Tori's room.

"Hey," I say, lightly knocking on the open door. I poke my head in.

"Come in," Tori says, her voice listless.

Tori's mom frowns when she sees us, like she's not expecting us. I glance at Sawyer.

"We're really sorry about what happened last time we were here, Mrs. Hayes," Sawyer says, looking at Tori's mom. "Trey—Jules's brother—had just run here all the way from campus to let us know that there was a fire at their restaurant."

"Oh dear," Tori's mom says, her face softening immediately. "Is everything all right?"

"It's fine," I say. I don't want them to have to pity us too—they have enough to worry about. "But yeah, I'm sorry for the way Trey came screaming in here, scaring everybody."

"It's understandable," Tori's mom says, and Tori nods.

Sawyer and I pull chairs to the side of the bed, across from Tori's mom. We sit, and I give Tori a reassuring smile. But I'm worried. Will she talk in front of her mom? Does her mom know why we're here? We talk for a minute about how Tori is doing with her slow road to recovery. And then, after we run out of small talk topics, I say, "So, I got your text."

"Yeah," Tori says. She looks uncomfortable, and I don't know what to do. Tori's mom is paging through a magazine.

I mouth the words "Do you want to talk about this now?"

Tori's eyes flit over to her mother and then back to me. She nods. "Yeah," she says. "She knows." It's impossible to read her face. And she's not giving us anything.

"Okay, so if I remember correctly," I say, "we told you about Sawyer seeing a vision as a sort of aftereffect of the shooting. Right?"

Tori nods.

"Are *you* seeing a vision?" Sawyer asks.

"Maybe. I don't know."

"But you're seeing something? Like, a reflection, or on TV, or in the windows?" Sawyer leans forward.

Mrs. Hayes looks up. "The doctor believes it's a side effect of the drugs," she says in a firm voice. "And I agree."

"Mom, please."

Sawyer sits back. "Well, um . . ." He looks at me, scrambling, not knowing what to say.

I don't know what to say either. I wish Tori's mom would go away so we could talk. But we've never seen Tori without her mother here. She never leaves. She even has a cot set up. I take a breath. "Um," I say. "I—I—I think I need to give you some information that is going to sound really weird." I bite my lip and glance at Sawyer.

He shrugs.

"You see," I say, "it really started with me." And I give

her the entire story, even going into the part where Sawyer got his vision, and how we saved people because we prevented the shooting from being worse.

And that's when Tori's mom stops us. She stands up and says, "That's enough."

I swallow hard.

"My daughter has been through a tremendous amount of pain and stress. You are not making her any better with your crazy theories and your—your—making light of the fact that my daughter almost died. This isn't a joke, and if you two really are seeing things, I think you should tell your parents and go to the doctor immediately so you can be treated."

"Mom, I just . . . ," Tori whispers, but then she gives up, like she knows it's futile. She sinks into the pillows and puts her arm over her eyes.

We are motionless, absorbing the words. After a moment, Sawyer stands. He touches my shoulder. "Come on, Jules," he says in a gentle voice. He turns to Tori's mom. "We're really sorry to have bothered you, Mrs. Hayes."

I get to my feet too. "Yes, we're sorry. It was a mistake." I look at Tori. "I apologize if we upset you."

"You didn't. It's fine," Tori says. She lifts her arm. "Mom . . . don't."

Mrs. Hayes ignores the plea and ushers us to the door.

"There's no need for you to visit again," she says, as if she's the decider of what we do.

I mask the panic in my eyes and nod. "All right."

She closes the door behind us and we walk in silence to the elevator and out to Sawyer's car.

"I totally blew it," I say once Sawyer is navigating the streets once more, heading home. "Now what?" I lean back against the seat's headrest.

"I don't know. I'm pissed off. It's not like we forced her to listen to us. She contacted you. And you gave her an opportunity to not talk about it because her mom was there, but she didn't take it."

"How are we going to figure this one out?"

"We're not," Sawyer says. He steps hard on the gas to merge onto the highway.

"But we have to!"

"It's over, Jules. There's nothing we can do. We're not allowed to come back. She's not going to talk to us. Not now. We don't even have a hint of what this one's about."

I scrunch down in my seat and scowl. "I do not accept this."

"Okay," Sawyer says with a wry grin. "But there's still nothing we can do. Your responsibility has ended. We are done."

Funny how I don't feel at all relieved.

Fifteen

I gaze through the car window as we get closer to Melrose Park. And then I text Tori: *Can you at least tell me what happens in your vision? I promise I'll leave you alone.*

She doesn't respond.

Sawyer and I meet up with Trey and Rowan at the library so we can get our homework done in relative peace, even though it's a Friday night. I think we're all tired of hanging out at Aunt Mary's, and besides, I need something to read now that my books are all burned toast. And it's there at the library that I get a response: *I don't know if I can stand this. It's been going on since I woke up after the shooting.*

"Guys, look." I show the message to the others.

"What the heck," Sawyer mutters. "I don't get it."

"It seems obvious," Rowan says. "She can't talk in

front of her mom, so she can only tell you important things via text. Like when her mom is in the bathroom or asleep, probably."

"But why would she make us go all the way over there if she wasn't going to talk anyway?" Sawyer asks.

"I don't know," Rowan says. "Maybe she's sneaky, and she thought she'd be able to get rid of her mom for a little bit, but it didn't work."

"Spoken like a pro," Trey remarks.

Rowan sticks out her tongue at him.

Sawyer tilts his head, thinking. "Yeah, maybe Rowan is right. Tori realized she doesn't have the support she thought she had from her mom, and now can only text when her mom isn't around. It wouldn't surprise me if Mrs. Hayes looks over Tori's shoulder and reads every text she sends." He pauses. "I mean, don't get me wrong. It's great Mrs. Hayes has dropped everything to be at her daughter's side. It just seems like she's gone a little overboard."

"So what should I reply?" I ask. "Just tell her we can stop the visions but only if she tells us everything?" I shake my head, trying to imagine getting all the info we need from her text messages.

"Yeah," Trey says. "Don't waste time asking her what's up with her mother. Just get right to the point."

I type: *We can help but we need to know everything about your vision so we can stop the tragedy from happening. It's a tragedy of some sort, isn't it?* I look up, my finger hovering over the send button. "Okay?"

Everybody nods. I press the button.

Yes, comes the reply.

Sawyer groans. "Come on, Tori. Give us something."

"Hold on, she's typing more," I say.

We stare, breathless, waiting to find out what our next impossible mission will be.

"I think I'm going to throw up," Sawyer whispers.

"Me too," I say.

And finally: *Must hurry—there's a house. Sirens. Ambulance. Paramedics taking bodies out on stretchers.*

I read the text aloud, and then type: *Do you see any street signs? What kind of house? Is there a house number? How many bodies? Can you tell what's wrong with them?* I look around the group. "Okay?"

They nod. I send. And we wait.

She doesn't reply.

After a few moments of silence, all of us willing my phone to vibrate, willing Tori's name to show up on my screen, we give up and try to do our homework for a while.

"This is agonizing," Rowan says as the "Library closes in ten minutes" recording breaks our concentration. We pack up and make our way through the teen section, each of us grabbing a few books to borrow, and stop at the checkout desk.

Once outside, I look at my phone again to make sure I didn't miss anything. I echo Rowan's words. "It *is* agonizing. It must be for Tori, too. Especially since it seems like she thought it was okay to talk about this in front of her mom." I think back to my vision—how horrible and alone I felt. And that helps strengthen my weakened resolve to help Tori.

I say a quick good night to Sawyer in the parking lot and head home with Rowan and Trey.

"I wonder what happened to the people on the stretchers," Rowan says. "Do you think they were murdered?"

Trey frowns. "I don't think paramedics are supposed to move bodies if they're dead. So there must be some hope of them surviving if they're carrying them out to the ambulance." He pauses. "Of course, there could be dead people inside the house."

I look at Tori's description on my phone. "She didn't give us much to go on. I hope she has a chance to text me again soon. 'A house.' That's about all we've got. Hello, this is Chicago, land of many houses."

On Saturday morning I send Tori the longest text known to humankind: *Tori, I think we can help you but we need more information. Can you please answer the questions I asked? Tell us everything you can. Please. The only way to stop the visions from driving you crazy is for you to stop the tragedy from happening. But since you can't, we will do it for you. I'm sure the vision is getting worse every day. Believe me, I understand. I want to help.*

My phone is so silent I think it must be broken. I forward the message to Sawyer just to make sure my phone is actually sending text messages. He replies in a nanosecond: *Good job.*

The hours crawl by as we go out as a family to look at some houses for rent. By midafternoon my parents think they've found the one they want. Even though the rent is a little higher than they'd planned, it's really close to our pile of ashes, and I guess they find that comforting. They go back and forth in quiet voices about the rent being seventy dollars a month higher than they had budgeted based on the insurance money, and after ten minutes of that I want to butt in and tell them I'll give them the stupid seventy bucks a month . . . except I forgot I no longer have a job.

But then, in a flash of brilliance, I remember the envelope Mr. Polselli gave me yesterday. When we get back to Aunt Mary's I race to the living room, pull it from my backpack, and present it to my dad. "This is from the teachers at school," I say.

With a puzzled look on his face, he opens the envelope and pulls out a wad of twenties. He counts the money—all eight hundred dollars of it.

"Holy moly," I say. I feel so weird about it. Teachers

don't have a lot of extra cash. I bet most of them sacrificed something pretty important in order to chip in, like, I don't know, bifocals or cat food or whatever teachers buy.

"That's incredibly generous," Mom says. Her eyes are shining.

And my dad grips the cash like somebody just threw him a lifeline.

Sixteen

On Saturday night Sawyer comes over, and Dad still doesn't yell at him, not even when I say we're going out for a while. Together. Alone.

"Definite progress," Sawyer says later in the car. "Is he just distracted, or do you think he's actually starting to like me?"

I grin. "I wouldn't go that far. I think it's a combination of having too many other things to worry about plus realizing the inevitable—that I'm going to see you whether or not he approves. I think he's given up. At least for now. And as long as I behave."

Sawyer gives me a sidelong glance and slides his hand on my thigh. "Oh?"

And just like that, my whole body tingles. It's been a

while since Sawyer and I have had some time alone. I try to swallow the instant desire in my throat but it rushes up again. "I guess what he doesn't know won't hurt him."

I lean toward Sawyer and watch him driving, the outline of his profile lit up by streetlights. I resist the urge to trace my finger down his sexy chin, run my hand through his thick, dark hair.

He turns to look at me. His lips part when he sees my face, and I hear him take in a short breath. "Jesus, Jules," he says, and his grip on my thigh tightens and inches up.

"Pull over," I whisper.

His Adam's apple bobs in response and he peers ahead, looking for a place to stop. He pulls into the parking lot of a closed factory and parks in the shadows of the building.

I unlatch my seat belt and climb over the gearshift to straddle Sawyer's lap as he adjusts the driver's seat as far back as he can. And then I'm touching his face, nipping his lip with my teeth, drawing the tip of my tongue across his. His seat belt unlatches and I slide it out from between our pressed bodies, between our hot lips, and fling it aside, barely flinching as the buckle hits the window.

Sawyer kisses me hard, and when I move my lips to his neck he moans and reaches up under my shirt, his cool hands on my bare sides, and I can't think, I can only breathe and taste his skin and fumble with the buttons on his shirt with fingers that are shaking. Finally I rest my face against his hot bare chest and imagine us naked together. For the first time, it doesn't seem too weird. A thrill rushes through me from my thighs to my throat. I guide his hand up my side and press it against my bra, and through the fabric his thumb stumbles over my nipple. I suck in a breath.

"Oh, God," he says, and his body convulses under me. I bury my face in his neck and kiss him, run my tongue along his collarbone and my fingers up and down his sides under his shirt. He adjusts again and I grip the waist of his jeans and kiss him full on the mouth as he pushes against me, breathing hard. His hands pull me toward him and he searches with blind fingers for the clasp of my bra.

"It's two hooks in the back," I whisper, my lips against his ear. I don't even know what I'm saying, only that I want him to succeed, I want him to touch me. He finds the clasp and wrestles with it until I help him, and then his hands are cupping my breasts and his hips are grinding, pushing up against me, and I feel mostly euphoric and a little scared as something deep inside me builds.

I rake in a breath and move my jeans against his, like I'm controlled by some other force of nature, and then Sawyer's breath turns ragged and he wraps his arms around me and holds me to him, thrusting his hips and gripping mine, and I find his rhythm and try to match it, feeling weird about it but also wondering if this is a little bit like what it would be like if there weren't any clothes between us. But I don't want to stop and analyze that now.

Waves of lust rush through me and I want to be closer to him, touching him, my body becoming one with his body. I open a few buttons of my shirt, as much as I feel comfortable with, and press my chest against his, roll my hips with him, and I feel so beautiful and free. His breathing grows deeper, heavier, and it's thrilling and scary all at the same time to watch him react to me in this way.

But then he buries his face in my shirt and gasps, "Oh. Oh, shit. Oh, shit. Oh, SHIT." And then his torso jerks and shudders and his gasp turns into a low moan. "Oooh. Faaahck."

I don't know for sure what's happening at first, but even though I'm not an anatomy expert, I think I have an idea. I ease back against the steering wheel and peer at him. "Are you okay?"

His eyes are closed and there's a pained look on his face. "Shit," he groans, and lets his head fall back against the seat. He brings his hand up to cover his eyes, takes a deep breath, and lets it out. "God, Jules. I'm so sorry. I didn't even know that could . . . you know, happen, without actually, you know. Touching it."

I bite my lip, not sure what to do now. Sawyer shifts and gingerly slides his hand into his jeans. He cringes. "Well, that's awkward," he mutters. I ease off his lap and

LISA McMANN

back into my seat, twist my jeans back into place, turn aside, and hook my bra. My lips tingle. I button up my shirt. And I'm not exactly the Sahara Desert in my pants either.

I'm not sure how I'm supposed to feel about what just happened. Flattered? Disgusted? I definitely don't feel disgusted. I feel . . . smarter. Like I'm beginning to figure things out. Applying book knowledge to real life, like Mr. Polselli says, except, ew, let's not think about him right now. But I like knowing what happens. I like knowing how things work. Cause and effect. That's probably weird, isn't it? But I feel like if I understand what's going on with this whole sex thing, I can figure out how much of it I want to take part in, and I can plan better.

I glance at Sawyer to see if he's done doing whatever needed to be done. He's buttoning up his shirt. And then, from his still reclined position, he lolls his head sideways and gives me a sheepish grin. "That was not in the plan," he says. "I'm sorry." He raises his seat back to an upright position. "So, um, basically," he says, like he needs to explain, "I don't know if you are aware of this, but being within, like, fifty feet of you makes me want to have sex with you pretty much all the time. I think that's normal. And I guess even just the hotness and nearness of you combined with the amount of, um, friction and stimulation that occurred," he continues in a scientific voice, his

564

face flushing, "through no fewer than two hearty layers of denim protection, well . . . I guess that was enough to just wake everybody up down there and have 'em throw a party."

I laugh. "No need for sorry." I kind of want to ask him how it felt, but I'm too self-conscious.

He sits up and reaches out to smooth my hair. His fingers linger on my jawbone, and he says, "I love you, Jules, and not just because you make my thing happy. I love you because you make *me* happy."

I grin.

He goes on. "I don't want to push you into having sex, and I don't want to push myself into it either. And I don't want to do it until we are both ready for that, and I don't know when that is, but I'm pretty sure it's not today. So I hope you can forgive me for letting things get a little out of hand."

He chuckles at his pun, and then grows serious again. "I mean it about the love thing, Jules. And I know it's true, because every time I think about you getting hurt trying to stop one of these visions . . ." He drops his gaze. "Well, I can't stand it. I can't lose you. I can't."

My eyes well up. And the thing that is so big inside my chest spreads through my body. I have never felt like this before. I lean over and kiss him softly, gently, on the lips.

And then I smile and sit up and pat him on the chest. "Dude," I say, "I just have to tell you that you buttoned your shirt wrong."

Which, in JuleSawyer language, means "I love you, too. Maybe even forever."

Seventeen

When Sawyer drops me off, I go inside and find Rowan sitting at the table playing Clue Junior with the three younger cousins. She gives me the stink-eye. I wipe my chapped lips with the back of my hand to hide my grin and hope I don't look like I've just been tumbling around a steamed-up vehicle with my bra undone for the past forty-five minutes.

"Where's Trey?" I ask.

"On a date." Rowan clips the words.

"Oh, cool. What about Mom and Dad?" I ask.

Rowan replies through clenched teeth, "On a date."

I laugh.

"I'm serious," Rowan says. "It's like Trey inspired them. After you left, Mom said they haven't been on a date in twenty years, and she made Dad go. Then Aunt Mary decided she and Uncle Vito haven't had a date in eighteen years, so they left too." She smiles evilly at the kids. "Nick was supposed to babysit."

"Where'd Nick go?"

Rowan glares, one eyebrow arched. "On. A. Date."

"Oh my." I snort.

"Yeah." She looks at her cards and writes something down. "So why are you home so early?"

"Um . . ." I try to think of something other than *Sawyer spooged his pants so we called it a night.* "I don't know. Probably because I could feel your agony."

Rowan laughs.

The cousins look at me like I'm a jerk. "She's not in agony," the oldest of the three announces. "She's having fun, aren't you, Ro?"

"Pssh. Yeah, of course. Tons. Gosh, Jules."

"Sorry." I retreat to the living room, stare at my phone, where I have no messages from Tori, and pick up one of the library books and try to read it. I have a little trouble concentrating on the story, though, since I keep thinking about Sawyer and getting this goofy smile on my face. I'm kind of pathetic right now. Even the cousins' yelling doesn't bother me.

A half hour later Rowan makes everybody go to bed. She comes into the living room and sits on the piano bench next to my chair. And she's all business. "Any word from Tori?"

"No." *In fact, I kind of forgot all about her for a while.*

"You should call her."

"But her mom might see it's me."

"Call the room phone. I'll call, in case her mom answers. She doesn't know my voice."

I tilt my head. "Well, that's a brilliant idea."

"See?" she says, stretching into a yawn. "This is why you need me."

"Isn't it too late to call?"

"It's, like, nine fifteen on a Saturday night. Don't be ridiculous."

"But she's not exactly able to be out having fun."

"Stop stalling."

"Fine." I look up the number for the hospital and give Tori's room number to Rowan.

She calls, and after a listening for a second, punches in the room number. She looks at me. "Ringing," she whispers. Then her eyes light up. "Hi there, Tori?" She waits. "Oh, sorry. Is Tori able to come to the phone? This is her friend Rowan from UC." Rowan pauses, then gives me a thumbs-up. She lowers her voice. "Hi, Tori, this is Jules's sister. We know you can't talk because of your mom. Maybe now would be a good time to smile or laugh like I said something funny."

Rowan pauses. "Yes, your head hurts because of the visions and we can help you stop them if you just tell us what's happening. Is there a good time for me to come by to see you when your mom isn't there?"

Rowan listens for a minute. Her face grows puzzled. "Oh. I see. Maybe you could e-mail—what's that?" Rowan frowns. "You're welcome. Wait. Hello?" She looks at me. "She said she had to go and hung up."

"Nice going, Demarco."

"Shut it," Rowan warns. She hops off the piano bench and lies down on the living room floor, splaying her limbs in all directions. "She must really be under some kind of freaky surveillance over there."

"I told you. Her mom is really protective. She rarely leaves."

"Clearly."

I don't know what else to do but wait. All I know is that some people in a house in Chicago—presumably—are going to be hurting pretty soon.

When Trey and Ben walk in, Rowan and I look at Ben. And then we both look at each other. And I turn back to Ben and say, "Help me, Obi-Wan Galang. You're my only hope."

Eighteen

Trey, Ben, Rowan, and I decide to brainstorm before the parentals begin to trickle in, but we can't come up with anything that we haven't already thought of. We determine that Ben could go visit Tori, but they still wouldn't be able to talk about anything.

"What if I bring her a notebook and hide questions in the middle of it?" Ben suggests.

"Her mom will see her answering," Trey says. He slips his hand into Ben's. "Nice idea, though." Ben smiles at Trey, and all around the world millions of puppies are caught being almost as adorable as them.

I flop back in my chair. "I think all we can do is wait. The more things we try, the bigger risk there is that Mrs. Hayes will confiscate Tori's phone. We just need to chill.

I feel like I need medication to get through this. Or some comic relief."

Ben picks up one of the cousins' picture books and starts reading to us. I forgot how hilarious some picture books are. The laughter takes the pressure off the Tori situation, and by the time Uncle Vito walks in, yelling, "Hey, it's the Filipino!" we're already in various fits of giggles over this book about a bear who wants his hat back.

Ben leaves around midnight—I sneak a peek of him and Trey kissing in the driveway—and our parents stay out even later. Trey has stars in his eyes, and finally, when Rowan can't take all the blooming love any longer, she wakes up her long-distance boyfriend, Charlie, who lives in Manhattan, and Face Times with him. He's funny when he's sleepy. Or maybe everything is funny tonight so that it doesn't have to be tragic.

I drift off eventually, my bones aching from sleeping on this hard living room floor for almost a week, and when I wake up, it's still dark, and my phone is vibrating with a text message.

2 bodies outside w/ambulance, 2 inside dead, no blood, no house number, Loomis St. OMG my head! Visions everywhere I look, sirens wailing, won't stop. Can you help me?

I look at the time. Six fifteen in the morning. And I remember when I was in the hospital after the meatball truck crash. Right around 6:00 a.m.—that's when they come to poke you and hand out meds and check your temperature. Maybe Mrs. Hayes sleeps through it. I text back quickly, trying to be really encouraging: *Great info! This helps a lot! Are there any clues about what day this happens? And what time—sunny, cloudy? Look hard. I know it sucks. You're doing great! What else is nearby? What's the house made of? Color/style? 1 story or 2?*

And then I wait. Again.

I manage to get a couple more hours of sleep, waking up only when I hear Mom and Dad leave for mass. Trey is up too, eating cereal. I show him the text, and he gets on his phone immediately, looking up Loomis Street.

"Did she say North or South Loomis?"

"She just said Loomis. I'll ask her to look again."

Trey scrolls down his screen, again and again. "It's a really long street."

I lean over to see. Trey zooms in and scrolls. "Lots of houses. Like, miles of them. See if she can narrow down what side of the street it's on. And we really need a house number or at least a cross street."

I doubt I can get any of that info out of her. "I'll ask," I say. I start a new text with these additional questions and send it. "She said she sees visions everywhere she looks. That's not a good sign."

"Is that because we haven't figured things out?"

"Well, Loomis is a big clue. If the vision is still constant and not letting up, I think that means . . . it's imminent."

"Crap," Trey mutters. "That's what I thought."

We look at each other, both thinking the same thing. *We're not going to make it.*

Nineteen

Tori doesn't respond, and she doesn't respond, and she doesn't respond. On Sunday afternoon Sawyer, Rowan, Trey, Ben, and I pile into Sawyer's car and we find Loomis Street. We drive up it slowly. There are nice sections of Loomis Street and not so nice sections. I take notes on the kinds of houses on the street in hopes that Tori will give me a clue, and I text her again. *Big or small? Nice or run-down? Brick or siding?* Anything. ANYTHING.

If we only knew how the people died, we might be able to go door-to-door . . . or something. Send out a flyer warning of a homicidal maniac on the loose or whatever. But there's nothing more to work with.

By Tuesday we're all really on edge.

By Wednesday we're freaking out.

On Thursday we break down and send Ben to visit her, just to make sure Tori didn't die or something. We sit around our spot at the library and wait for Ben to call. When he finally does, Trey runs outside so they can talk, and we all follow.

Trey puts Ben on speakerphone.

"Okay," Trey says. "We're all here and you're on speaker."

"Hey, everybody," Ben says. His voice has lost the funny/sarcastic edge for the moment, which does not reassure me in any way. "I went to the hospital and tried to see Tori. The nurse stopped me at the door and said I should wait, that Tori wasn't feeling well today but maybe I could go in after her meds kicked in. So I waited. After about an hour, I figured everybody had forgotten about me in the waiting room, so I snuck back down the hallway and tried to peek in the window to her room but the shade was drawn. Still, I could hear something in there. So I was really quiet and I opened the door a crack, and all I could hear was Tori moaning over and over, 'Make it stop! Make it stop!' and her mother on the phone yelling at somebody, telling them to come immediately or she'd sue for malpractice."

There's a pause while we let the words sink in. Finally Trey says, "Holy shit."

"Yeah," says Ben.

"What happened? Did you get caught?" Rowan asks.

"No. I closed the door and slipped away. I didn't want them to see me in case you guys need me to do something else."

I catch Trey's eye and grin despite the situation. Ben is definitely a keeper.

"Okay," I say, realizing everybody's looking to me to call the next play. "Great job, Ben. Seriously. We couldn't do this without you. Thank you. I guess . . . I guess we just wait. I don't know what else to do. We have no date or time, no exact location, not even a reasonable vicinity." A sense of doom descends over me, and unexpected emotion clogs my throat. "So, I don't know." My voice squeaks at the end, and Sawyer and Rowan both put their arms around me. "I guess I failed on this one."

"Stop it," Trey says, and his eyes flash. "You didn't fail. The victim failed you. It's not your fault. We are not God." He pauses. "Or dog."

I half smile through watery eyes and nod. But I can't help it. I still feel like a failure.

The next morning, as I'm drying my hair, Sawyer texts me. *I'm outside the front door. Can you come out?*

I set down the hair dryer with a clatter, slip past Rowan, and run down the hallway and through the dining room and kitchen and breezeway, and fling open the door. I go outside in my bare feet to Sawyer.

Sawyer, with the thick hair and green eyes and ropy lashes.

Sawyer, the boy I love.

Sawyer, who is holding a newspaper.

He looks at me, solemn, wordless. And he points.

I don't want to look. But I do it anyway.

On the local news page, one headline reads: TWO DEAD, TWO CRITICAL FROM CARBON MONOXIDE POISONING NEAR ADA PARK.

I look at him. My lip starts trembling. "Are you sure it's the right house?"

He nods. And then he reads for me, "'Emergency response teams were called to a home on South Loomis Street late last night after a Boston man's repeated, unsuccessful attempts to reach his sister and brother-in-law and their elderly parents. The older couple were pronounced dead at the scene, and the younger man and woman remain in critical condition. It is unknown . . .'" Sawyer trails off. He lets his arms drop heavily and looks at me.

". . . if they'll survive," I say softly, finishing the report. I sink to the step and bury my face in my hands. Sawyer sits next to me and wraps his arms around me. But I cannot be consoled.

Twenty

By the time I look up, Sawyer has magically summoned Rowan and Trey, and they're staring at the news like they can't believe it. And then they say it. "I can't believe it." And I almost want to shake them, because I told them this would happen. They know this. But they don't understand the coarse reality of the visions like I do. Like Sawyer does.

I collect my racing thoughts and stand up. "I need to get ready." Without another word, I march inside and finish my hair, feeling numb. Those people could've been fine. That man in a distant city, so concerned about his sister, his parents, that he called 911. That man who has to bury not only both parents at once, but also grieve for his sister and brother-in-law, who could die any minute.

That man could've been fine too, going about his business, but not now.

All this because Tori wouldn't tell me the information I needed. And I realize that if I'd only known the cause of death, we could have gone door-to-fucking-door up and down Loomis Street with a carbon monoxide detector a *week* ago, and saved their lives.

"It would have been so *easy!*" I yell at myself in the mirror, and I slam down the brush and take off down the hallway, shoving past Nick and Rowan on my way to grab my backpack, and then I go outside, where Sawyer still remains like I knew he would, waiting for me. I climb into his car and we go to school like good little students, and all day my fury grows. And grows. Kind of like the fire that burned down my family's life. And I'm not sure if I can contain it.

After school I don't even have to say it—it's like Sawyer can read my mind.

"You want to visit Tori?" he asks.

"Yes, please."

And without trying to stop me or suggest I wait a day until my anger dies down, he drives me to the UC hospital. And I am so furious I can't wait for the elevator, so I take the stairs two at a time, and Sawyer follows. We go down the hallway to Tori's room, and for a split second I worry that maybe she's not there. Maybe she's been discharged, and I won't get to yell at her after all.

But my split second of worry is for nothing, because when I get to her room and open the door, there she is, sitting up, talking to her mother. Looking beautiful. I want to kill her.

They look up at me when I come in, and I almost falter, but I can feel Sawyer right behind me, and I know I have to do this. For me. For that poor man and his family. Then I almost falter again when I realize I forgot to bring the newspaper in, but Sawyer slaps it into my hand just before I make an ass of myself, and I walk over to Tori with it and shove it in her face. "Does this look familiar?" I ask, pointing to the photo of the house with the ambulance outside. I shake the paper a little to get her to look at it instead of me.

Mrs. Hayes gets to her feet and starts pointing at me, protesting my presence, but then she catches the look on Tori's face and stops. She goes to look at the article too.

As I watch the look of horror grow in Tori's eyes, I start to shake. "You did this," I say in a low voice. I look at Mrs. Hayes. "It's your fault they died."

They are stunned. "Is that the house you . . . you saw?" Mrs. Hayes asks Tori.

She nods. She won't look at me.

Mrs. Hayes will, though. "The vision is gone," she says. "It's over."

I want to punch her in the face. "That's because *this*

happened! There's no saving anybody now. They're dead! You both had the power to help stop this, but you didn't help. You didn't believe me. You wouldn't let Tori talk to me." I stop to breathe, to try to keep my voice low so no one comes in.

"I couldn't see my phone screen anymore to read your texts or respond," Tori says, distressed. "Plus, I was so sick from the constant movement. But now it's gone. No more vision." It's like she doesn't grasp what happened.

"Tori," I say. "Listen to me. If Sawyer had done what you did—if he hadn't believed me, or had refused to do anything about what he was seeing, *like you did with your vision*, you would be dead. You. Would be dead. And ten others in that music room *would also be dead*. You are alive because Sawyer acted on his vision. These people are dead because you wouldn't act on yours." I slap the newspaper. "Do you get it now? Do you?"

Sawyer puts his hand on my shoulder and I stop talking. Tori weeps into her hand, teardrops falling between her fingers onto the newspaper.

Mrs. Hayes at least has the dignity not to kick me out. But I don't need any encouragement to leave. I've had enough. And I think I said enough. Probably just a little too much.

On the way home my anger begins to subside. But

there's still something that infuriates me. Something I can't let go of.

"Her vision," I say after a while, "it just went away. Just like it did for us after we risked our lives. Only she didn't have to risk anything except motion sickness and her mom being mad at her."

Sawyer nods. He's worn a thoughtful expression since we left the hospital. "I noticed that. I'm not sure what I think about it either. Like, I should feel relieved, but really I'm kind of pissed off about it." He drums the steering wheel with his thumb. "It sure might have been easier to just ride it out and pretend like people weren't dying. If we'd only known . . ."

I look at him. "It wouldn't have been easier for me."

The corner of his mouth twitches and his eyes don't leave the road. He reaches over and takes my hand.

Twenty-One

I don't want to go to my aunt Mary's. I don't want to talk to anyone. I feel bad that I'm ignoring Trey and Rowan when I know they're probably reeling from all of this too, but I can't help it—I need an escape right now. It's like everything's closing in on me and I can't breathe. Sawyer takes me to his cousin Kate's apartment. She's not home.

It's a cute little place near the community college where she goes to school. Two tiny bedrooms and an even tinier bathroom. But a big kitchen. Isn't that how every home should be?

"Sit," Sawyer says with an Italian accent, sounding eerily like his grandfather Fortuno, magistrate of the evil Angotti empire. "I cook for you."

I grin for the first time in days, sit down on the sofa, and relax, reading Kate's fashion magazines while Sawyer bangs around in the kitchen. I text my mom so she knows where I am. And it occurs to me just how much more freedom I've had since the restaurant burned down. Not only because I don't have to report for my job but also because my parents have had too much stuff on their minds to keep up their reign of terror over us. Our whole family has been forced to adapt, and that part, at least, has been in my favor.

I look up and watch Sawyer cook, and I think how wonderful it is that we have this thing in common. How we learned to feed people from our parents, and they learned from their parents and grandparents, and so on down the line. Sawyer hasn't spoken about his parents since he moved out. I guess I've been hogging all the attention these days.

"Have you seen your parents lately?" I ask.

"I stopped in to see my mom the other day. She's fine."

"That's good. I bet she was glad to see you."

"Yeah." He doesn't elaborate, and I don't press him on it. I can tell he doesn't want to talk about them.

"So," Sawyer says after a while, "do you think your father still has visions? Or do you think he had one and it stopped after its tragedy happened, like Tori's did?"

I've been thinking about that. "I guess I don't know. I

mean, I believe he's had one for sure, obviously. But . . . I don't know." I frown, puzzled. Something doesn't add up.

"Maybe it's not a repeating vision that's been driving his depression all this time," Sawyer says lightly, pulling toasted raviolis from the broiler and plating them with a small bowl of marinara and freshly grated cheese—from here it looks and smells like Pecorino Romano, but I'm not sure. "Maybe it's the guilt of not having saved people."

I think about that. And I don't know. I might never know.

But I do know that I'm hungry and this bad boy in the kitchen can cook.

When Sawyer drives me home, I invite him to come inside. And he does. He offers a nervous hello when I officially introduce him to Aunt Mary and Uncle Vito, but they greet him with warmth. When my mom comes up to him, he plants a kiss on her cheek, which makes her smile, and my dad doesn't yell or kick him out. He just leaves. Probably heading to the ash heap to find some more treasures. I still think that's progress. The Sawyer part, not the treasures part.

Once Sawyer and I migrate to the living room with Trey and Rowan, I ask them, feeling a little ashamed, "You guys doing okay? I'm really sorry I blasted out of here."

"It's just weird," Rowan says. "I feel so bad."

Trey nods. "It sucks. It's like we had this power to do something good, and we didn't use it."

"Not *didn't*," Sawyer says. "*Couldn't*. We did our best. We did everything we could think of to stop it. But we can't force some stranger to give us what we need."

"And now it's over," I say softly. I still can't believe it. "I mean, I think so. There's nobody for Tori to pass the vision curse to."

"Tori told us the vision is completely gone," Sawyer explains, and he fills in the others on our visit.

And it's a boring Friday night for the first time in forever. None of us are working. There's no vision to ponder. Ben shows up after a while and we all hang out in Aunt Mary's living room, even the cousins, and we play this game called Apples to Apples, and after months of stress, it's like I'm finally starting to decompress. It's over.

It's really over.

When my dad comes home around nine, he doesn't have pocketfuls of scavenged burned junk. He has ice chests and ice and bags of groceries. We stop our game and look up as he stands in the kitchen, arms laden.

"Two things," he says in his old familiar, booming voice, and it shocks me to hear it again after so long. "First, our new landlord just called and said we don't have to wait until the fifteenth—the house is ready and we can move in on Sunday."

We try not to cheer too loudly because we don't want to seem ungrateful, but we are all ecstatic over this news.

"And second," Dad continues, holding up a bag of groceries, "Paula and I are taking Demarco's Food Truck out tomorrow. And next week, and the next, and every day until we open the doors of our new, improved restaurant!"

The household breaks into applause, and I cheer too, at first, until the doubt creeps in and all I can do is clasp my hands together and stare at my dad's flushed cheeks and triumphant smile, and wait for the cracks to come back and ruin it all.

Twenty-Two

Mom and Dad start preparing the sauce on Aunt Mary's stove for tomorrow's big day in the meatball truck. We go back to our game, eventually forfeiting so the little kids win, because Aunt Mary says they have to go to bed as soon as the game is over, and we just want to get rid of them because we're selfish teenagers like that.

Nick sticks around and hangs out with us because all his friends are working tonight. He doesn't say much. We don't really have anything in common, even though he's between Trey and me in age and we played together a lot when we were little. We haven't been close since I started elementary school, even when he spent an occasional day working for the restaurant.

So things are somewhat quiet, and we can't talk about

what happened with the vision even if we want to. And strangely, I don't want to. I snuggle into Sawyer and he drapes his arm over my shoulders, and it feels wonderful to be safe and stress free for once.

I think about the man who has to bury his parents. I look up at Sawyer and murmur, "Should we go to the funeral?" And I love that he immediately knows what I'm talking about.

"We can do that. I'll try to find out when it is."

I nod. He smiles.

When I get a text message, I look at my phone. "It's from Tori," I say. I open it and read: *I'm so sorry.*

That's all there is.

I raise an eyebrow and mutter, "Jules is not impressed." I shove the phone back into my pocket.

"What was that?" Sawyer says near my ear.

"Tori says she's sorry."

"Good. Maybe she understands it now. What did you say back?"

I grunt.

Sawyer shifts so he can look at my face. "Jules," he says, "I know how you feel, but there are a few factors here that you're not really considering. One, she couldn't see the phone screen because of the vision playing out on it. Two, her mother dictates absolutely everything."

"Her mother ought to be the one saying sorry," I mutter.

"And three," Sawyer continues in a louder voice, pretending he didn't hear me, "Tori has been heavily medicated this entire time. Do you even remember when you were on your pain medication in the hospital? Do you happen to recall Trey on pain meds?"

"I do," Ben offers from across the room. "He was . . . *emboldened*."

"Whoa," Trey says. "We agreed not to talk about that."

I glance at Nick, who is playing some game on his phone and ignoring us.

"Anyway," Sawyer says, "you can't judge her equally with someone who can actually stay awake for a four-hour stretch and doesn't appear to be stoned all hours of the day and night."

I sigh. "You're right, I know. I just don't want to forgive her."

"That's up to you, I guess," Sawyer says.

"Yes, it is," I say. But I know Sawyer is the one being reasonable here. "I'm sorry," I say. "I'll think about it."

Dad and Mom say they can't afford to hire us to help them quite yet. We say we'll work for free, but it's like they're having some sort of weird bonding time or something and they don't want us along. So while they head off to the public market Saturday morning, Trey bolts for the shower, and Rowan and I are supposed to pack.

"Pack what?" Rowan asks from the middle of the living room floor, where she's sitting like a pretzel with her hair all messed up from sleep. She's cranky. "We don't own anything."

I look around the living room, realizing we've managed to collect a good deal of stuff since the fire. "I don't know. All this stuff, I guess."

"What are we supposed to put it in?" she whines.

I glare at her. "How about we shove it in your face hole?"

"How about we cram it up your butt . . . nose."

We stare each other down. Finally I concede. "Buttnose is funny."

"Thank you. It was an accident."

"Oh, really?"

"You can cut the sarcasm." She gets up and kicks me in the shin with her bare foot.

I snort my mockery in her direction.

She kicks me again and I grab her by the back of the neck and shove her to the couch and sit on her.

She pokes her fingers at me, trying to find a sensitive spot, so I'm forced to bounce up and down on her while giving her a noogie. Then she hits her mark. "Whoa!" I yell, and jump off of her. "Out of bounds, loser. That was totally my buttnose."

She sits up and smooths her hair, trying not to laugh.

I back my way toward the kitchen in case she plans to try something else, and scrounge around for some shopping bags to pack our junk in.

Somewhere during the scuffle I got another text from Tori. I glance at it: *I really am sorry and I need to talk to you.*

I groan and shove the phone back into my pocket. "Great. Tori's feeling guilty now," I call out to Rowan. I skirt a small cousin in the dining room and head back to the living room with the bags. I throw a few at Rowan's head.

"How can you tell?" she asks.

"She just sent me another text. Says she really is sorry and that she wants to talk."

Rowan puts her clothes into a bag. "What did you tell her?"

"I haven't responded."

She shrugs. "She's probably trying to deal with the shock of it."

I feel a twinge in my gut, but I'm not giving in. "She could have prevented all of this."

"Yeah, I think she probably knows that now," Rowan says with a smirk.

"How would you know? You don't even know her."

"It's a logical guess. Besides, you two aren't exactly BFFs either."

"Yeah we are. We're BFFs. I know everything she's thinking and you know nothing."

Rowan rolls her eyes. "I'm just saying you're not being very gracious. She practically died. This is a lot to take on from a hospital bed."

I put my index finger in the air. "But! She didn't die. Because Sawyer and I risked our lives for her. And she did not do the same for her fellow humans of Chicago."

Rowan sighs and gives up. And for some reason I don't feel very triumphant about my win.

Twenty-Three

Sunday is a day of joy. We have a new place. Not just an apartment—a whole little house in a neighborhood across from my old elementary school. And there's no restaurant attached. It'll be months at least before I have to go to school smelling like pizza. Mean people will cease to recognize me. I may survive high school after all.

Ben and Sawyer show up at the new place, surprising us with a pickup truck full of used furniture. My dad stares from the garage (yes, we have a little garage!) as they start unloading it onto the driveway (because yes, we have a driveway, too!), and walks over to them.

"What's all this?" Dad says.

"We brought you some furniture," Ben says. "Thought you could use it. Is it okay if we show you what's here?"

Dad's stern gaze sweeps over the scene.

"You don't have to keep any of it," Sawyer replies. He stops unloading, looking uncertain. "We just thought . . ." He wipes a bead of sweat from his temple and stops talking, likely scared to death.

My dad shakes the hard look off his face and clears his throat. "We can use it. At least for a little while until our new stuff comes." He lifts his chin slightly. "Thank you." But we all know our "new stuff" hasn't even been decided on, much less ordered. We're being extra cautious with the insurance money since we don't know how long it'll take to get the new restaurant running.

I leave Sawyer outside to bond with Dad (har har) and follow Rowan into our new bedroom, where we each currently have two bags of clothes and toiletries and basically nothing else. We will have new beds to assemble later today, and I'm hoping there's a dresser on that pickup truck.

"Where'd they get all that stuff?" Rowan asks.

"No idea," I say. I'm not sure I want to know.

By evening, the house is starting to feel like a home, and the best part is that there are no little cousins running around. It's a little bit bigger than our old apartment above the restaurant. Or at least, it feels that way without all the piles of junk. I worry that this place will fill up too. And I don't know how to prevent that from happening, but I'm sure as hell going to try.

Sawyer returns later in his car, having taken the truck away, to see if we want him to pick up some burgers, and then he's gone again with our orders. When he returns with the food, I watch him as he ever so slowly works his way into the good graces of my dad. And I think that makes Sawyer a good, quality guy. I will just have to keep him.

Before Sawyer heads home for the night, he and I sit together in the dark on the front step of my new house, and he tells me that he found an updated article about the carbon monoxide poisoning. He says the old couple who died were both receiving hospice care, which means that they were already dying. And that the man's sister is fine now, and her husband is improving and should be okay.

I'm quiet for a moment. And then I say reluctantly, "It doesn't excuse what Tori did, but I guess that's a pretty good outcome under the circumstances."

"You know, there's a chance that this even spared the old people from a pretty miserable ending to their lives," Sawyer says. "I mean, I don't know that for sure. But it's possible. And maybe it's okay to think of it that way."

"Maybe," I say. "Is there a funeral planned?"

"Just a private memorial service for the family."

"Well. I guess that's that." I draw in a deep breath of

the fresh spring nighttime air in my new yard (because I have a yard!) and I blow it out, trying to get rid of all the anger that was stored up inside me. I imagine it escaping my lungs and leaving my fingertips. And it feels like all the negative crap is finally beginning to clear out.

"It's like a fresh start," I say, more to myself than to Sawyer. "We have a nice new home. My dad is getting out of bed every day. The parentals are back to work with the meatball truck. I no longer smell like pizza. We experimented with sexy time."

Sawyer laughs. "Is that what we're calling it?"

"Yeah."

"And let's not forget that there are no more visions to deal with."

I smile in the darkness. "Right on," I say. I squeeze his hand and he squeezes back. And for the briefest of moments, I feel like all is well in the world.

When my phone vibrates, I am reluctant to pull it out of my pocket for fear of disturbing this new perfect universe. And when I see who's calling, I'm tempted to ignore her. But I don't. Maybe it's because the old people were already dying, and maybe it's because I'm feeling fresh and full of love, and maybe it's because I know deep down I've been too hard on her, but this time I decide to answer.

"Hi, Tori," I say.

"I'm so sorry," she says. She's crying.

"I know. I get it. It's in the past."

"No," she says. "Let me explain—"

I sigh. She needs to say things. She needs to help herself heal. I can handle that. "Go ahead."

And for the second time in a month, three little words change everything. "Jules," she says, her voice faltering, "it's happening again."

Twenty-Four

My mind doesn't compute what Tori is saying.

"Hold on," I say. "I'm putting you on speaker so Sawyer can listen too, okay?"

"Okay."

Sawyer's face is a question. I press the button. "Go ahead. Start from where you said 'It's happening again.'"

"Well, it is. And I'm so sorry—"

"I know you're sorry," I say impatiently. "What do you mean—are you seeing the vision again? How is that possible?"

"It's not the same one," she says. "It's a new one now. Totally different."

"What?" Sawyer covers his face with his hands and shakes his head slowly, swearing under his breath.

"Wait. How are you suddenly allowed to talk to me

now?" I demand. "What about your mother?"

"She's right here—she's the one who made me call you. I knew you'd be mad, but—and she's sorry too. She wants me to tell you that."

I roll my eyes to Jesus in the sky. "Sure. Of course. You're both sorry now. Little late for that."

"I *know*," she says. "Just please, you have to help us. I promise we'll do everything right this time. I mean it! My mom says she won't interfere."

I stand up and start pacing along the sidewalk. What am I supposed to do here? Say no? I can't. I'm ethically bound. Personally responsible.

I close my eyes and rub my left temple, where a sudden headache has sprung up.

"Jules?"

"I'm still here," I say. "I'm just processing."

"Sorry."

She needs to stop saying *that* now too. I take a breath and blow it out, and then sink back to my spot on the step. "Okay. When did this start?"

"Saturday, I guess."

"Is that why you sent me the apology text message?" My blood starts to boil.

"No, I sent that text on Friday night. I swear. I feel terrible about the people dying. I wish I could go back in time and fix it. I mean it."

Sawyer pats my knee. "Let it go, Demarco," he whispers.

I shoot him a look, but I know he's right.

With a whoosh of air from my lungs, I let it go. "All right. Tell me what's happening. Sawyer's going to take notes on his phone, so please try to be very specific about everything." I glance at Sawyer, who quickly gets his phone out. "Let's hear it."

"Okay," she says, and I hear her mom saying something encouraging in the background. "There's a ship."

"A ship?" both Sawyer and I exclaim. We look at each other in alarm. "Wait. Where? In Chicago?"

"I—I don't know. It's in the water. It looks like the ocean."

"The ocean?" Sawyer and I exclaim again. We need to stop doing that.

"I mean, I don't know. There are huge waves and rocks. And the ship is sinking."

This time Sawyer and I are silent. "Are there people on board?" I ask after a pause. *Of course there are, dumb shit.*

"Yes. Lots of people. And they're jumping and sliding and falling off . . ." She chokes on a sob. "Some are hurt. A bunch of them are going to drown."

We are silent.

"The looks on their faces . . . ," Tori says in a near whisper. "The panic and fear . . ."

Sawyer springs to life after the initial shock and starts typing everything into his phone. I wait for him to catch up, and I try to pull my thoughts together.

"How big is the ship?" I ask, my voice more gentle now. I know how horrible it is to see death over and over.

"I don't know. Pretty big. Not like a giant freighter or cruise ship or anything, but yeah. Kind of big."

"What color is it?"

"White. And some blue."

"How many people do you see?"

She's quiet for a long moment, and I think she might be counting. "Twenty or thirty," she says. "It's hard to count them because the scene goes by so fast."

Sawyer mutters an expletive.

"And do they all . . . drown?"

"I—I think so."

"Dear God," I say. I slump against the step and stare blindly at the phone. I can't comprehend. How are we supposed to save that many people? "Hey, Tori?" I say after a minute. "I'm going to have to call you back once I come up with a list of questions for you. Okay?"

"Yeah."

"You okay? I know this is horrible." All my anger toward her and her mother has now evaporated.

"I'm okay," she says. But I hear her crying.

"Tori, if you help us, it's going to be okay. Why are you crying?"

It takes her a minute. And then she says through sobs, "I don't want this to be my fault too."

Twenty-Five

When I hang up, I hear a noise behind me, and for a second I panic. What if my parents heard everything? How would I explain this? But when I turn to look, it's Trey. Rowan's there too, behind him.

"You gave me a heart attack," I say. "How long have you been standing there?"

"I had the bedroom window open and I could hear you guys talking," Rowan says. "So I got Trey and we came out."

"We heard almost the whole thing," Trey says, his voice grim. He glances over his shoulder at the house and says, "Let's take a walk. I'm pulling Ben in on this over the phone if that's okay."

"Yeah, definitely," I say. We head across the street to

the elementary school and walk the sidewalks around the property while Trey updates Ben, and then he keeps him on the line to listen to our conversation.

Sawyer begins by recapping the notes he took. "White-and-blue ship, ocean, high waves, rocks, twenty to thirty people, some injured, in the water, all going to drown." He stumbles and sucks in a breath. "Geez," he mutters, shoving his phone into his pocket.

"You okay?" I ask.

"Yeah. Just . . . just blinded for a minute by the phone's backlight."

I frown, because his breathing is a little too heavy and his hand a little too clammy in mine for that to be the problem. But I push it aside. We need to figure this out.

"Okay," Trey says. "I'm really not excited about this at all. So let's start with this ocean bit. I'm telling you guys right now, we are not going to any freaking ocean. If this thing isn't local, it's out of our hands. That's my decision, and I'm the oldest, and I can, like, vote an' shit, and I'm telling you that this is the way it's going to be." He sounds like he thinks we're going to argue.

"No, you're right," I say. "I'm on board with that." I cringe at the unintended pun. "Anybody want to challenge Trey and his self-appointed authori*tay*? Nobody? Okay." I look at Trey. "Hey, I think you just defined us as being strictly local superheroes."

"There's only so much a superhero with no actual powers can do," Rowan says matter-of-factly.

"And we're a picky, demanding bunch," Sawyer adds, apparently feeling better now. "We put our foot down whenever we decide a tragedy is on the wrong side of the local boundary line."

"*Feet,*" I say. "Our foot? Like we all have one big collective foot?" I shake my head. "I don't think so."

"Thank you, grammar whore," Rowan mutters.

"I also have feet, not foot," Ben contributes through the phone.

Sometimes this is just how we do our best thinking.

We come up with a list of questions and call Tori back. Her phone rings and rings, and finally someone answers—Tori's mother. I get a sick feeling in my stomach, like I'm about to be yelled at, but all she says is that Tori is asleep, and can we maybe text the questions instead?

I agree and she actually thanks me, and we hang up. I start typing.

Five things to ask Tori:
1. Are the rocks in the middle of water or part of a shoreline or what?
2. Do you see any land?
3. Are there any markings on the ship—name, numbers, logos, designs?

4. What's the weather like?

5. Time of day? Sun position?

I look up and show everybody.

"That's enough to start with," Sawyer says. "We don't want to overwhelm her." His uneasy look is back, and I wonder if he's changing his mind about this.

We head back home and stand in the driveway. I make everybody gather around, and I say, "I wish we didn't have to do this, guys. It was so nice there for a couple days, thinking it was all over and we could go on with our lives." I watch Sawyer's face as he stares at the ground. "You can all walk away, you know. This is my deal. And I don't want anybody here who doesn't want to be here. I can't handle that hanging over my head." I look at them. "Think about it and let me know."

"I don't need to think about it," Trey says.

"Me neither," Rowan adds. "I'm in."

"I'll go where Trey goes," Ben says. I forgot he was still on the phone with us.

Sawyer looks up. "We're all in, baby," he says. "Sink or swim." He chuckles uneasily.

Trey groans and pats Sawyer on the back. We say good-bye to Ben and hang up, and make our way to the house. Rowan and I walk together, while Trey and Sawyer fall behind and linger by Sawyer's car. And I hear Trey say, "It'll be okay, bro. We'll get through it together."

I glance at them, puzzled. And I realize Sawyer's not following us to come inside.

"Later, guys," he says. "Night, Jules." He gets into the car, starts it, and pulls out of the driveway. I knit my brows, then lift my hand to wave, and watch him go.

Twenty-Six

In the morning, after the traditional jockeying for the bathroom at 6:00 a.m. (I lose due to phone-checking distraction), I'm relieved to find a lengthy message from Tori:

1. Rocks are in the distance along (I think) the shore.

2. Can't really see much land per se though because of weird angle, spray, and chaos but I think it's there.

3. Ship is mostly white, but blue on bottom. Didn't catch any markings—everything goes so fast.

4. Weather is stormy. I think it's raining but could be spray.

5. Some light low in sky like early midmorning and maybe a glimpse of a far-off building? Could just be a weird shadow. It's just a flicker. Is there a way to stop this crazy thing so I can actually look at it?

I reply: *Great stuff here. Will check in with you soon. We'll teach you how to pause it. Let me know if anything new shows up—it usually does.* As she probably already knows.

There's another text message, from Sawyer this time. *Sorry I left all weird. Wasn't feeling well. Better today. Ready to tackle Tori's vision. See you at school. <3*

I smile. Maybe that's all it was.

At school Sawyer acts completely normal, and I think I must have seen something that wasn't really there regarding his weirdness yesterday. Trey, Sawyer, and I meet up for lunch as usual, and for the first time since the fire, Roxie and BFF Sarah give me a long stare as they walk by our table, and Roxie says something immature about my ugly, hand-me-down fire clothes.

"Ahh," I call after her, "an insult! Finally! Now things are really starting to feel like they're back to normal. I knew I was missing something in my life."

"You're welcome," Roxie says.

Trey and I look at each other. "She was actually funny," he says.

"I was just going to say that," I say. "Jules is impressed!"

"So is Trey," Trey says.

Sawyer looks at us. "Is this the latest Demarco thing to do? I'm just trying to keep up here. I thought we were still doing dot-com jokes."

"Please," I scoff. "Dot-com jokes are so two visions ago. Stay on your toes, Angotti, or you're off the team."

"You can be on my team," Trey tells him with a wink.

Sawyer shakes his head and grins. "Aw, man. I thought Ben would cure you of this desire to force homosexuality on me for your own selfish whims."

"Ben's not here," Trey says. He leans toward Sawyer. "Come on. Kiss kiss. Huh? Yeah?"

Sawyer laughs out loud. "Trey, my friend, if you can keep me from drowning, I'll give you a kiss you'll never forget."

"Aaand, here we go." I fold my arms.

Trey sits back and looks offended. "How dare you, Sawyer. Really. I'd never cheat on Ben."

Sawyer just shakes his head.

I change the subject. "So, what are we going to do about Tori? Should we head over there after school, or what?" I'm personally getting really sick of the drive to UC. The traffic makes me crazy.

Trey and Sawyer sober up and we toss around the options. "There's not a huge hurry, is there? All the visions have had time frames of at least a few weeks, right?" Sawyer asks.

"Yeah. Mine was more like six or seven weeks. Longer than yours," I say.

"And mine was longer than Tori's first one," Sawyer says.

Trey knits his brows. "So it appears that the time from first vision to the day of the tragedy is growing progressively shorter. I wonder if that's something to note or just a coincidence."

"Good question," I say. I consider it for a moment. "But in all instances, or at least in Sawyer's and mine, the vision gave us more information as time progressed. A hidden frame exposed here, an extra scene there," I say, remembering the moment I discovered Sawyer's face in the body bag.

"And in all cases, the visions appeared more frequently as the event became imminent," Sawyer says. He taps his chin. "I can't believe I'm saying this, but the way it works, it really seems like the vision gods want you to succeed."

I give a sarcastic laugh. "They're on our side, all right."

"You know what I mean."

I nod. "Yeah, I do. The vision really does give you the clues you need and the urgency to find all the answers. You just have to work at it to see them all."

As the bell rings, Trey concludes, "So maybe we should wait a few days to visit Tori, in hopes that she gets more information or some new scenes in the vision."

Sawyer and I look at each other and nod. "Let's shoot for the weekend, then," I say. "I'll let everybody know if anything changes. But I'm sure we're safe to wait until then."

Twenty-Seven

Tori gets discharged from the hospital on Tuesday to finish her lengthy recovery at home. All week I stay in touch with her, coaching her and keeping her calm despite the fact that the vision is growing more intense every day. "Even though it seems like everything is out of control, it's okay," I tell her. "You'll see more soon, and as long as you are telling me everything, we'll know when we can start to act. But right now, we just don't have enough information." I pause. "You got more information over time with your last vision, right?"

"I guess," she says. "Yeah. But this is horrible, going through it all over again. And this one is so . . . gruesome. It makes me sick to my stomach."

I rise above the urge to say she should have listened to

me last time, and instead I tell her, "Just try to stay sane. And let me know if anything changes. You can call me anytime, day or night. I mean it."

"Thanks," Tori says.

"Is your mom still being cool?"

"Yeah. No worries. She gets it now."

Friday morning Tori texts me: *It's getting worse, and I think there's something new.*

I write back: *We'd all like to come to your house tomorrow. Is that okay?*

She gives me her mom's address, and thankfully it's much closer to our house than UC is. We were going broke paying for gas.

On Saturday, Trey, Ben, Rowan, Sawyer, and I sprawl out in the Hayeses' living room, surrounding the recliner where Tori rests wearing loose-fitting sweats.

"You look fancy," I say. "No hospital gown."

"Finally," Tori says. She smiles for, like, the first time ever. "I'm so glad to be out of the hospital."

"I'll bet." I tell her about my recent time in the hospital after the crash.

"So, wait—you got hurt doing your vision thing?" Her face is troubled.

"Totally," I say. "And obviously you know Trey got

shot in the arm during the one at UC, and he was helping. He knew about the vision. He was lucky, though. He's
doing physical therapy stuff now."

"Wow, that's terrible," Tori says. "I didn't realize that
you guys could get hurt while doing this. That's not fair."

I glance at Sawyer, who is looking at me. "Invincible,"
he says decisively, and I give a reluctant half grin. I turn
back to Tori. "We try not to think about that."

I officially introduce Trey and Rowan to Tori, and then
I make sure Tori knows Ben since I don't know if she was
at the meeting from the Gay-Straight Alliance side or the
choir group side of things. Ben assures me they are well
acquainted.

"Great," I say. "Let's get moving, then."

I pull out my smartphone while Ben and Sawyer set up
their laptops. Tori gives us the Wi-Fi password, and within
a minute we're online.

"It's like Command Central in here," Rowan says,
looking around the room.

Sawyer props his computer on a small table next to Tori's
chair and directs his browser to a video page. I pull out some
tracing paper and a pencil that I bought from a craft store a
few days ago for this purpose and set it on the floor next to
Sawyer for later. We're starting to get good at this.

"Everybody ready?" Sawyer asks, looking around.
We're all poised to take notes and research anything that

is researchable. Sawyer starts the video. "Do you see your vision?" he asks Tori.

"Oh, yeah," Tori says. "Question is, when do I *not* see it these days?"

"Okay, good," he says. "So here's what we're going to do. I'm going to start this video from the beginning and pause immediately, which should pause your vision. Then I'm going to need you to talk us through what you're seeing little by little, scene by scene, and tell us everything. Don't leave any detail out, even if it seems unimportant. Got it?"

"Got it," Tori says.

"And then after we talk through each frozen screenshot, I'll have you do a little tracing of the scenes, if that's okay."

"Yeah, totally," Tori says. She seems very eager to redeem herself, and I'm glad. I'm actually starting to like her. She walks us through the vision.

"The first thing I see is the ship. It's all white where I'm standing, but later from a different angle I can see it's blue on the bottom."

"What's your point of view in this scene?" I ask. "Are you, you know, standing *on* the ship, or looking at it from a different spot?"

"For the first scene, I'm on the ship. Like I'm standing on a deck," Tori says. "The ship is rocking and there's a lot of spray and big swells like you'd find in the ocean. There are benches out here, and then there's a door that leads to . . . like a giant glass room, and I can see a bunch of empty seats in there. Rows of them, like in an airport terminal. Some tables, too. There's stuff strewn all around."

Ben looks up. He tilts his head, eyes narrowed, but says nothing.

"Can you see any land in this frame?" Sawyer asks.

"Not this one. Just sky. Cloudy, possibly raining, windy. Slight bit of yellow behind low clouds, like it's morning."

"Anything else? Any writing on the ship that you can see?"

"The benches have words indicating there are life vests inside. That's all I notice."

"Any people in this shot?"

"Only blurry images far inside that glass room. Nobody's sitting—if they're not on the floor, they're all in one place, crowding around."

Sawyer hands her a piece of tracing paper and the pencil, and she holds it up to the screen and quickly traces what she sees.

Tori slides the video play bar slightly to the right, narrowing her eyes and trying to get it in just the right spot. "Okay," she says. "The next scene is from farther away, like I'm not on the boat, because I can see the whole thing and a vast expanse of water behind it. There are words on the side, but I can't read them—I'm really far away, like maybe my view is from land. When this scene is in motion, there's a very sudden jolt or something. I can't really describe it, and there's no sound or anything. It's like the vision has a glitch in it. . . ." She stares at the computer and we all look at her quietly.

"Oooh," she says softly. "That's why." She looks closer at the screen. "There's something in the water, and I think the ship hits it. I never realized what that bump in the vision was until now." She touches the screen and slides her finger across it, as if we can see what she's pointing at. "There," she says. "It's like a seawall sticking out." She looks up. "It's almost invisible because the waves are so high."

"Good job, Tori," I say. "That explains a lot."

She traces this picture and Sawyer passes it around the room.

"Are the people on the floor before or after the little jolt?" I ask.

"Hmm. Before. That's weird."

I write everything down.

As Tori goes on to find the next frame, Ben studies the sketch. He looks up. "Am I allowed to ask questions or . . ."

"Please," I say. "Yes."

"Tori," he says, "I'm just curious. Have you spent

much time on the water? Sailing, fishing, swimming, anything like that?"

"No, hardly at all. I mean, my mom and I went to this little cottage once on a lake that was more like a pond, and I've spent a few hours at the beach now and then, but I'm not really a beach fan."

He smiles warmly. "So you won't be offended if I correct you?"

She laughs. "Heck no."

Ben nods and holds up her sketch. "Technically, this isn't what I'd call a ship. It's a ferry. I wondered that at first when you mentioned all the rows of seating and the glassed-in observation deck." He points to the vessel drawing. "See how stout and flat it is? Unless the computer stretched the image, I'd say this might even be a car ferry."

Sawyer looks at Ben. "Sawyer is impressed," he says, and glances at me. "Did I do that right?"

I grin. "Perfect." I turn to Ben. "Great. So, Ben, have you been on the water much?"

He scratches his head. "I have."

"What's your experience?"

"Well," he says, almost sheepishly, "my family owns a marina. And I'm also a lifeguard."

Twenty-Eight

I blink. "Seriously, Ben?"

"Yep."

"I think I'm in love right now."

"Me too," says everybody else in the room.

Ben laughs it off.

"No, I'm serious," I say. "This whole impossible feat just got a little bit easier, thanks to you. I mean, as long as it's not in an ocean somewhere." I press my lips together, forgetting that I hadn't mentioned that little caveat to Tori. If this happens in the ocean and we bail, we don't save Tori from going insane.

"My guess is it's right here in Lake Michigan," Ben says. "You can't see across it, so Lake Michigan can very easily look like an ocean, especially in a storm. There were twenty-foot waves when the remains of Superstorm Sandy pushed through here—remember that one? And that's not even the record."

"What's the record?" I ask, suddenly curious.

"Oh, heck, I don't know. Twenty-three feet, I think."

"Ben, I had no idea you were such a geek," Sawyer says with sincere admiration in his voice.

"Back off, Sawyer," Trey mutters as he types frantically on Ben's computer.

Tori moves on to the next scene, and the next, and the next, all of which offer no additional clues, though the progression of the drawings of the ferry listing and sinking lower and lower in the water is frightening.

She goes to the next. "This one I'm really curious about," she murmurs, adjusting the slide on the screen. "Right around here there are the rocks and a little glimpse of land, I think. If I can only . . . just . . ." She sticks her tongue out of the corner of her mouth as she tries to land on the scene just right.

"There," she says. She squints at the screen. "In this scene my point of view is from the other side of the ship— I mean, the ferry—as it begins to tip in the water. On the right there's a splotch of orange and I can see people on it. I think that's a lifeboat."

"Interesting," I say.

"And looking over here," she says, pointing to the

other side of the screen, "I see the top of a building." She looks closer and shakes her head. "I can't tell for sure, but I think that's what it is."

"Hang on," Sawyer says, and he rummages through his computer case. "I just remembered I snagged my mother's reading glasses back when I was going through this, and I never gave them back. This is what helped me read the stuff on the board in the classroom at UC so I could figure out which room it was."

Tori takes the glasses and puts them on, magnifying the bit of a building. "I take it back," she says after a moment. "It's the tops of two buildings. And something red over here."

"Hmm," I say. "Two buildings. The edge of a skyline, maybe? Could it be Chicago?"

"I can't tell." Tori lifts her gaze. "I'm sorry." She looks exhausted.

I check my phone clock and see we've been here for two hours. I reach out and touch her hand. "Don't be sorry. You're doing great."

She smiles. "If you say so," she says, taking a deep breath and letting it out. "Let me see what else is here."

She slides the vision forward ever so carefully. "Here's the one that makes me sick." She studies it for a moment. "The ship is half sunk, almost lying on its side, a big wave behind it. There are two lifeboats with people in the water clinging to them. And a third lifeboat that's empty, floating away, while the remaining ferry passengers fall and slide over the railing and into the water below."

She stares at the screen, and then slowly picks up a fresh sheet of tracing paper and starts another outline.

I look down at my notes, not sure what to say. It's probably better just to be silent and let her do what she needs to do.

When I look up again, Sawyer is leaning forward, eyes closed, a bead of sweat dripping down his temple. I open my mouth to ask if he's all right, but then I close it again. Because I finally realize what it is that's affecting him.

I think back to a conversation he, Trey, and I had in the school hallway about our biggest fears after Trey had said his worst nightmare was a school shooting.

"Suffocating," I remember saying mine was.

And then there was Sawyer. Who said drowning.

Twenty-Nine

Trey looks up from Ben's computer. "There are two ferry services that cross Lake Michigan," he reports. "One sails round-trip from Manitowoc, Wisconsin, to Ludington, Michigan, and the other goes between Milwaukee and Muskegon, Michigan."

Rowan, looking at her phone, chimes in triumphantly, "And the second one is white on top and blue on the bottom."

I turn to see her phone. "That's the Milwaukee one?"

"Yes." She shows it to Tori. "Is that it?"

"Wow," Tori says. "Yes, that's totally it. You guys are good."

I look at Trey. Milwaukee is a good hour-and-a-half drive from home. "So, Milwaukee. Is that within our, um, jurisdiction?"

Tori turns sharply, a look of fear in her eyes. "What do you mean? Can't you guys help me? Is there another team of you vision-solver people up there?"

Trey gives me a dirty look. "As far as we know, there aren't any other weirdos like us anywhere," he says to Tori. "So of course we'll go to Milwaukee."

And as much as I wanted to call this one off at one point, I'm glad Trey isn't going to give me a hard time about going forward. Because deep down I am fully committed, and there's no way I can let Tori deal with this on her own when the reason it's happening to her is because of me.

We pack up our things to leave and let Tori get some rest. Before I go, she asks, "Did I do all right?"

I lean down to her in the chair and give her a hug around the shoulders. "You did great," I say. "We've narrowed down one of the most important components—the *where*. Now all we need to figure out is when it happens." I groan inwardly, because the *when* has been a constant difficulty in this process.

"And how you're going to save everybody."

"Right." I haven't even thought about that part yet— the impossible part. "So if you have any ideas, feel free to pass them along." I manage a weak smile.

"I will."

"And play around some more with the vision. If you

have a DVR, you can pause, rewind, and fast-forward whenever you catch it on TV too, you know. Let me know if you find anything new." I turn to join the others outside, but then hesitate. "Where's your mother?"

Tori grins sleepily. "I told her that if she hung around during this meeting, I was going to hitch a ride with you guys to UC to recover in my dorm room."

I laugh. "I don't know how you handled it, being in the hospital with her there all the time. Did she ever leave?"

"Not often," Tori says. "I tried to get her to go to the cafeteria when I knew you were coming, but she decided she wasn't hungry." She rolls her eyes. "But," she adds, with a kinder smile, "I'm pretty much all she has. My dad died when I was a baby, so . . ." She shrugs. "I cut her some slack on the smothering."

"I'm sorry," I say.

"It's okay. I don't remember him."

"Well, I'm glad today worked out."

"Me too. Because if my mother finds out what you said about getting hurt while you're trying to save people, she'd stop everything." She emits a hollow laugh. "I guess since you and Sawyer didn't get shot, we figured you had some mystical protection or a guardian angel watching over you or something. It just doesn't seem fair otherwise."

I flash a grim smile. "No, it doesn't."

There is nothing more to say. I wave and wind my way out of her house to the car, where the others wait. I look at Ben and Trey and Ro, and I wonder how the hell I got so lucky to have people actually sign up for this.

Thirty

On Sunday, everybody's got major stuff to study for, so we decide to abandon the hive-mind approach and instead come up with ideas individually, thinking that we might even be more effective problem solvers without being steered in one group direction. We plan to meet up at Sawyer's on Monday night since he and Kate have wireless Internet.

Through it all, we hardly see my parents. They are seemingly making business work with the big truck o' balls. They've got a calendar of events stuck to the refrigerator, showing the various food truck lunches and market/food truck tie-in events, which seem to be a thing now that we're heading toward the summer months. People buy local homemade goodies, spices, and fresh produce, and then support the local food truck vendors too. And Mom and Dad have managed to book a couple of private party events in the community, which they probably wouldn't have gotten if the restaurant hadn't burned down. That last bit was Mom's look-on-the-bright-side take, actually, not mine. They're gone almost every day. And so far, since the fire, my father hasn't spent a single day in bed.

We don't quite know what to make of it, but Mom looks like she's ten years younger. So Monday morning, while I wait for Trey and Rowan for school, she happens to get up early, and I tell her that.

She smiles her beautiful smile. "Well, thanks. It helps having Dad around more," she admits, and then confides, "You know, he really likes the customer inter-action through the service window. If I'd known that would give him some spunk, I'd have had him waiting tables years ago."

I laugh. "Spunk."

"What? That word's no good anymore? I can't keep up with your lingo."

"It's totally a good word. It's cute, Mom. I'm going to start using it."

"Stop teasing me." She kisses my cheek when we hear Trey and Rowan stampeding through the living room. I grab my backpack as they drag me to the not-delivery car.

"You guys are so spunky today!" I say, loud enough for Mom to hear.

"I mean it," she calls after me.

I grin and wave.

"You're weird," Rowan says.

After school we head over to Sawyer's and arrive just as Kate is leaving for her shift at Angotti's Trattoria. She's probably the cutest person I've ever seen, with this funky short bleached-blond hair and cool piercings and gorgeous tattoos. She's kind of like a rock star to me, I guess. She's twenty-one and goes to college and has, like, a *life*, you know? Plus she took Sawyer in. So that makes her a hero, too.

I met Kate before, though I don't remember it. It was after I crashed the meatball truck into that snowplow in the Angotti's parking lot. I remember the seconds before the crash, how she was standing outside having a cigarette and our eyes locked for just a second while I screamed through the closed window at her to run.

After the crash happened, she called 911 and came running over and apparently stayed and talked to me and Trey while we waited for help to come. I don't remember that, but Trey does.

And I guess she came by the hospital to see me once, but my dad wouldn't let her in because she's an Angotti, so

Trey and Rowan hung out with her in the waiting room.

So now Trey and Rowan say hey to Kate like it's no big deal to see her again. But I get all nervous. I guess . . . I guess since I'll never talk to Sawyer's parents, I want her to like me. To have someone in Sawyer's family approve of me.

"Hey," I say. "Thanks for the bags of stuff after the fire. We all really appreciated it."

"No sweat," she says, and she gives me a hug. "Nice to see you."

I think I'm in supercrush mode with this girl. Not really, but yeah.

Sawyer introduces Ben to her, and then she's out the door, yelling behind her, "Don't eat the prosciutto or salami, I need them for a charcuterie plate!"

And that does it. Because nobody should get between a girl and her pork. I'm in love.

But there is a time for crushes, and that time is not now. And maybe not ever, if we don't figure out how to survive this sinking ferry.

Thirty-One

I bring out the sketches from Tori, and we take turns discussing our findings so far.

Trey starts. "The good news is that the sinking ferry isn't going to happen this week."

I look over from the well-stocked refrigerator, skeptical. "Because?"

"Because the ferry service hasn't started for the season yet. It starts a week from today, and there are only two ferry departure times per day. Six in the morning and twelve thirty. Since Tori sees a dim spot of light low in the sky, and the sun rises in Milwaukee ten to twenty minutes before six over the next few weeks, I deduce that this disaster happens on the early morning ferry. No idea what day, but I think this narrows down the time of day pretty nicely." Trey looks up from his notes.

"What about the Muskegon departures?" I ask, checking the fridge for snacks.

"Too late in the day to line up with the sun's position."

"Wow," I say. "Have we ever known the time of something this early on? This is huge. Good work, Trey."

Trey leans back in his chair, looking smug. "I know," he says.

I slice some chorizo and two apples and assemble a little Kate-inspired charcuterie plate of my own, adding cheese, crackers, and some walnuts I find in a cupboard, and bring it to the table for everybody to share. "What else do we have?"

My little rookie Rowan raises her hand, which is kind of adorable. "I checked the ten-day forecast and there are small chances of thunderstorms next Monday through Wednesday. That's all I can get so far. I'll keep an eye on it, though."

Ben adds, "I've done some more Lake Michigan and ferry research. There's definitely an issue with riptides in the lake, especially in relationship to breakwalls, which is what I'm guessing the ferry hits and what eventually causes it to sink. The riptides might pull down individuals in the water. Added to that, water temps are still in the forties this time of year, and anybody who doesn't make it into a lifeboat is in serious trouble."

He continues. "As for the ferry, I think it would have to hit that breakwall with quite a bit of force to damage it enough to eventually sink it. With the waves that high and visibility low, I could see it happening, but my guess is that Tori's vision isn't showing something. No little bump or glitch, as she said, would be enough to have that kind of effect."

"She said there were people on the floor of the ferry before the bump," Rowan says. "Maybe it hits more than once, and hard enough that people would be injured."

"That's what I was thinking," Ben says. "Speaking of lifeboats, the ferry has plenty of them, with more than enough room for a full-capacity voyage. But something must go wrong for one to be floating away empty. Could be the ferry's tilting—that would make it hard to exit from one side."

I glance at Sawyer, who is quiet at the stove, sautéing onions and garlic and chopping up several Roma tomatoes.

"Okay," I say. "I just have to tell you that it's such a relief not to have to do all of this myself. Thanks to all of you for putting so much work into this. We're making a lot of progress here."

"Sure," Ben says.

"You're welcome," says Rowan.

Sawyer turns around, agitation clear on his face. "Yeah, it's all really helpful, but what I'd like to know is how the hell we stop a ferry from hitting a breakwall and sinking during high seas." He rips his fingers through his hair, which he does when he's frustrated—I know that well enough by now.

"We're working on that," I say coolly. "In fact, that's what I'd like to talk about next."

He doesn't reply, so I go on. "Ben, do you have access to a boat that you'd feel comfortable driving—or sailing, I mean—in weather like that?"

Ben knits his brows. "I have access to boats, yes. But I'm not qualified to sail safely in those conditions."

"Okay, that's what I figured. No problem, it was just a thought. Next, I don't think we try to stop the ferry from hitting the breakwall. That's impossible. We can try to stop the ferry from sailing, but that kind of action never seems to work for us, right? Making strange claims of future disasters will only get us in trouble. I mean, I couldn't stop the snowplow driver from driving. We couldn't stop the shooters from attacking. So I'm assuming rather than wasting time trying to get the captain to stop the voyage, our job is to keep people from dying in the confusion that follows the impact." I pause and look at the solemn faces looking back at me. "Right? That's been our job all along. We do our best to stop people from dying." I glance at Sawyer, who is half turned, listening.

"Okay," he says. "And?"

"And so we need to be on that ferry."

The only sound is a wooden spoon scraping the bottom of a stew pot. I smell fresh basil.

After a moment, Sawyer says, "How do we save twenty or thirty people from drowning when we're on a sinking ferry?"

"By organizing the passengers and keeping them calm. Handing out life vests and helping the crew with the lifeboats. Taking charge of the situation and trying to make sure that the runaway lifeboat doesn't get detached from the ferry until it's full of people."

"And when the ship sinks?"

"We . . ." For the first time I falter. "We get into a lifeboat too."

"And then?"

"We get rescued," I say. I look down at the table, staring at the remains of the charcuterie plate, no longer hungry.

Sawyer pulls an electric hand blender from a cupboard and pulverizes the contents of his stewpan into soup while the rest of us imagine ourselves in lifeboats, crashing into breakwalls and splitting our heads open on rocks.

Or maybe that's just me.

Thirty-Two

I stay at Sawyer's when everybody else leaves.

"The soup smells delicious," I say, trying to get a peek at it over Sawyer's shoulder. "Looks great too." I wrap my arms around his waist and he pours a splash of cream into the pot. I can feel his muscles tense as he stirs.

"Almost ready," he says. He takes a clean spoon and dips it in. "Wanna test it?"

"Of course," I say. I blow on it and take a sip, closing my eyes to savor it. "This tastes like a cold fall day," I say. "I forgot it was April. *Delizioso*."

He turns off the burner and faces me. I put my arms around his neck and he slides his around my waist, and he looks into my eyes, not smiling.

I look into his eyes, and I don't smile either. "Talk to me," I say softly. "What happened to you?"

His eyes narrow a fraction. "Nothing," he says.

I tip my head slightly. "So what's going on?"

"What do you mean?"

Our faces are inches apart.

"What is it about the water?"

He breaks his gaze. "Oh. That. It's no big deal."

I stare at him. "Come on."

He loosens his grasp on my waist and turns to look at the soup. "Okaaay," he says. "When I was ten I was kayaking on a lake with my brother. There were two guys on Sea-Doos screwing around nearby, doing stupid stunts. One of them fell off and his Sea-Doo kept going for a ways after the motor cut, and the guy wasn't wearing a life vest or anything."

Sawyer stirs and shrugs his shoulders. "He was trying to swim to the craft but he was starting to struggle, so my brother and I glided over to try to give him a hand. I took off my life vest and threw it to him while my brother tried to reach out to him. The guy was starting to freak out, and he grabbed the side of the kayak. With my brother leaning out in that direction, the kayak flipped."

"Oh no," I whisper.

"Oh yeah. So basically I wasn't prepared. I panicked. My mind went blank. I was underwater, and when I finally had enough sense to realize the kayak wasn't flipping all the way around, I tried to get out. My leg got stuck. And the Sea-Doo guy was holding on to the bottom of the kayak, so I couldn't flip it upright again."

He pulls two bowls from the cupboard. "I sucked in some water and started to black out. And you know what's so scary about starting to drown? You stop moving. You can't struggle, because you go into shock, and you have no oxygen, so you can't make noise. You just go limp."

I can hardly breathe, listening to him. "What happened?"

"My brother got me out, and I coughed and puked and started breathing on my own again. And I was fine. But I never went in any body of water over my head again."

He gets spoons for us and ladles the soup into the bowls. "I'm not a strong swimmer, either. So." He shrugs and pulls a chair out for me, and we sit and eat our soup, even though I can hardly get it down after hearing that.

"You don't have to do this, you know. You can stay back on shore and help from there."

He smiles and draws his finger over the back of my hand. "And that's why I didn't tell you this before."

"I'm just saying—"

"I know. And I'm going with you, and I don't want to talk about it anymore. I'm dealing with it, okay? And this time I'm keeping my damn life vest to myself."

Thirty-Three

Tori calls every day. Things were better for a day or two after we met at her house, she says, but as the week progresses the vision is growing stronger and more intense. By Thursday afternoon she can't watch TV because it's just the vision on a loop, and on Friday it's reflected in all the windows in her house.

"Are you sure there's nothing more?" I ask. I'm getting impatient. We really need to figure out what day this will happen.

"Nothing," Tori says. There's an edge to her voice now, and I know she's suffering. "I'm looking at everything. I promise."

"I know." I don't know what else to say. "Be sure to tell me if . . . well, you know."

"Yeah."

"And e-mail me a detailed list of what all the drowning people look like and what they're wearing."

"Got it."

We hang up. I dig the heels of my hands into my eye sockets and yell out my frustration.

Rowan comes running into the bedroom holding a dish towel. "What? Did something happen?"

"No. I'm just frustrated." I fall back on my bed, and Rowan sits next to me. She checks her phone.

"I've been watching the weather. There's still a small chance of thunderstorms pretty much every day next week, but the highest chance is Monday."

"How big is the chance on Monday?"

"Forty percent, and windy. Ten to twenty percent on the other days."

I stare at the ceiling. "My gut says this is coming soon. It's getting really bad for Tori. And that's always been an indicator that we're either doing something wrong or the tragedy is imminent. And after doing this a few times, I'm feeling relatively confident that we're getting it right except for knowing the day. So that makes me think it's imminent."

"Like Monday imminent?"

"Like Monday imminent." I close my eyes, trying to really think it through. I muse, "Do we take a chance and get tickets for Monday's six a.m. voyage? If we're wrong, we'll miss school, and that'll be really hard to explain if we have to do it again later in the week. Not to mention expensive. And since none of us is working much at the moment, the money stash is definitely dwindling."

"How much is a ticket?"

"Like eighty-five bucks."

"Sheesh."

"I know, right? Not only do we have to save people, but we also have to spend big bucks to do it. This is getting outrageous." I turn my head to look at Rowan and smile. "We could always leave you home and save some money."

"No!"

"I'm kidding. We need you. Twenty-some people to save—heck, if we had any more friends I'd recruit them, too. We need all the help we can get." I size her up. "I wonder if they have children's tickets. If you can act like a little kid, we might be able to save money by getting you one."

She snorts. "Yeah, I'll tape my boobs down and wear my Burger King crown. That'll fool 'em. They see five-foot-seven-inch-tall, hippy eleven-year-olds all the time." She leers at me. "You, on the other hand . . ."

"Did you just call me short?"

"And, apparently, boobless."

"Sawyer doesn't think so. How about Charlie? Oh,

wait, he can't even tell because he's your fake Internet boyfriend."

"Shut your face, I hate you."

"I hate you, too."

That night Sawyer comes over with a diagram he somehow found of the ferry, showing the locations of the lifeboats and all the life vests. We study the diagram and Trey takes a photo of it and e-mails it to Ben so he can look at it too.

On Friday night we check the weather forecast. It's unchanged. Ben and Sawyer come over while my parents are out at some Friday-night food truck festival.

My phone vibrates. It's Tori with her daily call.

I hold my hand up to hush everybody, and answer. "Hey, Tori, how's it going?"

"There's something new," she says, almost breathless.

"Finally," I say. "What is it?" I cover the mouthpiece and whisper, "She says there's something new."

"Two things, actually. The first thing is inside the glassed-in deck. There's, like, a banner of some sort. Like a long birthday banner, you know? I can't read what it says, not even with my mom's binoculars, but I got to thinking that maybe on the first day of the season they might put up a banner of some sort, don't you think?"

I shrug. "Yeah, sounds reasonable."

"What?" Rowan whispers.

I kick her.

"What's the other thing?" I ask Tori. Rowan pinches me, Trey slugs her, and I realize I could probably just put Tori on speakerphone to avoid this situation. "Hang on, Tori—I'm going to put you on speaker." I snarl at Rowan and press the button. "Okay, go ahead."

"The other thing is that there's a new frame added on after the frame of the two buildings in the distance. I can see more buildings—tall ones. It's definitely a skyline. So I traced it for you guys."

"Cool, that's awesome! Downtown Milwaukee is right there, I think, so that makes sense that you can see the city from the water. Do you want to scan it and send it to Sawyer's e-mail?" I give her Sawyer's e-mail address. "Send him the victim list, too, would you? Then he can print copies for us."

"You got it."

"You sound a little better today," I say.

"I'm just relieved there's more. I feel like I'm not doing a very good job of this."

"Are you kidding me? You're doing great!" I say, and the others all chime in with their praise. We need to keep her going in these last few days.

"Okay," she says, like she's embarrassed. "Let me know what the plan is when you have one."

"I will," I say. We hang up.

"What was the first thing?" Rowan asks.

"Give me a second and I'll tell you, you little pain in the butt."

"Nose," Rowan adds.

I grin reluctantly. "Nice. Anyway, she said in the glassed-in cabin there's a banner hanging, like one of those kinds you see for birthdays and graduations, you know? She can't read it, but she suggests that they might use a banner like that on opening day of a new season." The more I think about it, the more sense it makes.

"Seems reasonable," Ben says.

"Yeah, I think it make sense," Sawyer says. He pages through the sketches, and then turns to his computer when it beeps to open up the files from Tori.

I look over his shoulder. "Well, they're not the most stunning revelations we've ever had, but it's progress."

Sawyer studies his computer screen as the others come around to look.

Trey takes a look at the skyline picture. He squints and looks closer. And then he shakes his head. "Guys?" he says. "That's not Milwaukee."

Thirty-Four

We all look at Trey, and then at the skyline *sketch*.

"Zoom in a little, can you, Sawyer?" Trey asks.

Sawyer expands the page and zooms in.

"If she traced this correctly, and I don't know how she could possibly mess it up, this is definitely not Milwaukee." He looks at me. "In fact, I think it's the north view of Chicago."

The room explodes in questions. We all talk over each other until Trey emits a shrill whistle with his fingers.

"Knock it off, guys," he says. "I don't know how the ferry could be this close to Chicago, but it is. That's the John Hancock building, and there's the Sears Tower. Or whatever they call that building now."

"Willis," Rowan mutters, but nobody cares. It'll always be the Sears Tower.

I'm so confused. "Why is the ferry this close to Chicago? Are we sure this is the Milwaukee ferry? It shouldn't be anywhere near here. It's almost a straight shot across the lake to Muskegon."

"Tori saw the ferry's website, including a picture of the ferry," Ben says. "She said she was sure that was it. Besides, our only other option for ferries on Lake Michigan is the one that operates even farther north than Milwaukee, and it's an old nineteen-fifties schooner type—nothing like the high-speed Milwaukee ferry."

"Okay," I say, "but Milwaukee isn't just the next town north of Chicago, you know. It's like seventy miles."

"True," Trey interjects. "But Tori's sketch shows the skyline quite far away. And Chicago is on the southwest curve of the lakeshore, so it's possible to see the skyline from quite a distance."

"But I don't understand how or why the ferry would venture so far off course." I know I keep saying this, but it doesn't make sense. And I'm getting frustrated.

"Maybe there's something wrong with the ferry," Ben says. "Maybe it's not just the storm causing this. Besides, I've been thinking about the storm a lot. And if the waves were really that enormous, no captain would take a passenger vessel out to sea. I could see them taking it out in

GASP

eight- or even ten-foot waves, but not much higher than that, or everybody would be yakking the whole trip. It must not be as rough as Tori made it out to be. I keep reminding myself that Tori's personal experience factors into her perspective."

I lie back on the floor and close my eyes. We've managed to come up with more questions than answers. And I'm starving. "Foooood," I groan.

Sawyer rolls over to me and rests his head on my stomach. "Yep, you're definitely hungry," he says. "And I think we can all use a break. Let's go get dinner."

"But we need to save our money for ferry tickets," I moan.

"I'm hungry too," Rowan says. "Hey, I know—we could go find Mom and Dad. They'll feed us for free. I think."

"They will," Trey says. "Well, maybe not Sawyer." He grins.

Sawyer shrugs. "I can pay. I'm not some jobless punk like you, you know." He straightens his collar. "I work with kittens." He pulls me to my feet and we all stagger to the not-delivery car and go in search of the giant balls.

While everybody chatters around me, I realize the thing that's so unsettling about the ferry within sight distance of Chicago is that it would take quite a long time for it to travel that far. And if Tori's spot of potential light low in the sky is actually the sun, I need to know how low in the sky it really is. And if it's possible for it to still be "low in the sky" if it takes a while to get from Milwaukee to the location in the vision.

Tori didn't draw the possible sun on the sketch. I text her. *What would you guess is the angle of that spot of yellow to the Earth?*

Sawyer peeks at what I'm doing. He nods. "Yeah, I was wondering the same thing."

Tori replies: *I was told there would be no math.*

"Oh, look," I say. "Tori's being funny for the first time in her life. She must be feeling better."

"I bet it's because we're figuring things out."

We wait, and in a few minutes she has an answer. *Around thirty degrees, I guess.*

I glance at Sawyer as Trey pulls into the parking lot for the Friday-night food truck festival. "You up for a little early morning research at North Avenue Beach tomorrow?"

"I don't start work until one," he says.

"Cool. I can probably get the car. I'll pick you up at five?"

"Oof, that's early. Yeah, sounds good. It'll be cold out there by the water."

"We can snuggle," I say. "I'll bring a blanket."

He wraps his arms around me and kisses the side of my head. "I like it. We can do more sexy time."

"You don't *do* sexy time. You have it."

"Yes, yes, I do," he says.

"Please stop now," Rowan remarks. "Gross. It's time to eat some juicy balls."

"Dot-com," I add. Hey, it's good to mix things up a little.

Thirty-Five

"There's probably a math problem that will tell us the answer here," Sawyer says. We snuggle together under a blanket on the beach facing the water, looking toward Michigan even though we can't see it, and watch the sunrise.

"Yeah, but any math problem that relies on the rotation of the Earth makes my head explode," I say. "Besides, this is more fun."

Sawyer rolls onto his side, facing me, and rests his hand on my stomach, his fingers tracing the stitching on my pullover. He nuzzles my neck. My skin tingles. I close my eyes and suck in a breath. My brain argues with my body, but my body wins. I turn toward Sawyer and slip my arm under his head, and my lips find his.

His hand travels to the small of my back and pulls me close, our legs entwining. In all our layers of clothes and blanket, we kiss, gently, softly. We touch our foreheads together and exist, for a moment, only in each other's eyes. I pull the blanket over our heads and we lie there, just kissing and touching and being close and safe and free of all the stress. I would lie like this forever if I could.

"I love you," I whisper.

"Yes, yes, you do." Sawyer grins and kisses me, and I grin too and our teeth click together. "Ow," he says, laughing.

The spell is broken. The brain wins round two. I pull the blanket off our faces and check the sun. Not quite there.

We wait and watch, mostly in silence amid gentle, somewhat absentminded caresses, cool fingers on bare skin, as the Earth turns us. As we focus on the task we're here to do, my mind moves to logistics. I think we're both trying to visualize this rescue and how it has to happen.

"We just need to put our life vests on first," I say at one point. "That's what's going to keep us alive."

"I know," Sawyer says.

"I wasn't telling you. I was just talking out loud."

He turns his face toward mine with the hint of a smile. "Oh."

Later, he says randomly, "Rope." He sits up. "Are you free tomorrow afternoon?"

"Duh." I shield my eyes from the sun with my hand. It's getting close to the thirty-degree-angle mark.

He pulls out his phone and sends a few text messages, then settles back down.

I pull out my protractor, scoot out from under the blanket, and set the tool on its edge on a mostly smooth portion of sand that looks like it's pretty level. Then I lie on my stomach and put my face in the sand next to it. I use a thin stick to project the thirty-degree line and wait.

"It's close. What time is it?"

Sawyer checks. "Eight fifteen."

I dig a little hole in the sand for my face, to make sure my eye is lined up with the protractor. My eyes water. "Should have brought sunglasses," I mutter.

"What exactly are you doing?" Sawyer asks. I can hear the amusement in his voice.

"I don't know! I'm just trying to think logically." I sit up and wipe the sand from my cheek. "The ferry leaves at six. It is now eight fifteen and the sun is in the position where Tori believes it to be behind the clouds. The question is, could the ferry get this far in two hours and fifteen minutes? I say absolutely yes, but only if it intended to, and at a reasonably high speed."

"But that is not the normal intent of this ferry."

"Correct. So what would have to happen to make the pilot of the ferry go so off course?"

We contemplate.

"All I can think of is the mafia," Sawyer says, half joking.

"Maybe it's hijacked. It can go wicked fast, you know. Or," I say, "I know—maybe there's a different vessel in trouble, and because the ferry can carry so many passengers, and because it's fast, the Coast Guard calls them to assist."

Sawyer drums his fingers on his thigh, considering. "That actually sounds plausible. Remember when that plane landed in the Hudson River in New York? Didn't the ferries come to help pick up people?"

"I don't know. But," I say, thinking of something new, "if the weather is too windy and the lake is choppy, a helicopter wouldn't be useful. Plus they can only rescue one person at a time."

We both think about it.

"And then," Sawyer says, "maybe in the act of saving the people on the other vessel and riding the crazy waves, the ferry smashes against a breakwall. It takes on water fast, plus the waves are getting higher and water rushes in over the sides, too, and in a matter of minutes, it's the *Titanic*."

"Man, that would suck for those people from the other shipwreck to be rescued and then immediately be in another one. Two shipwrecks in a matter of hours? Now that's a bad day."

"But the irony makes it feel right, doesn't it? I mean, unbelievably tragic shit like that happens all the time."

I stare out over Lake Michigan, which is deceptively calm this morning, with light waves washing ashore. I check the weather on my phone. The chance of thunderstorms has increased to 50 percent on Monday, and decreased to between 0 and 10 percent the rest of the week.

"Sawyer," I say, "based on the weather forecast and the banner Tori saw, I'm convinced this is happening on Monday. I think we should plan on being on that ferry in Milwaukee at six a.m."

Thirty-Six

We do a quick conference call on the way home from the beach. I explain my reasons for believing the ferry disaster is happening on Monday, and after a short discussion, everybody agrees. Ben, who has a credit card, buys five tickets for Monday at six a.m. We plan to pick up Ben at four (groan) and drive up to Milwaukee together.

Saturday night, after Sawyer gets done playing with kittens at the Humane Society, he and I meet up at Tori's to see how she's doing.

Her mom lets us in. "She's a wreck," Mrs. Hayes says fretfully. "Are you sure this will go away?"

"If we have all the clues right and we manage to save some people, it will go away." I'm still a little wary of her.

I don't need her obstructing things now. But she doesn't argue and she stays out of our way.

Tori is sitting in the same recliner as last time we were here. Her eyes are closed. "I'm awake," she says. "Just resting. Trying to get away from it for a bit." The vision must be playing out everywhere.

"How has it been?" I ask.

"A little better starting this morning."

Sawyer and I exchange a glance. Did we do something right today by deciding to buy tickets? Sure seems that way.

"Is there anything new?"

"No."

I take in a deep breath and let it out slowly. "We bought our tickets for Monday."

Tori nods slowly. "That makes sense to me." She opens her eyes. "I wish this didn't have to happen at all, but since it does, the sooner the better."

"We're going to need to be in touch with you," I say. "Call or text my phone if anything changes. I want you to watch the vision Monday morning starting at six, okay? Watch it like crazy, and send me a text now and then even if nothing's changing."

"I will, Jules. I promise."

"Okay." I look at Sawyer and he nods. I squeeze Tori's hand. "We're going to let you rest now. I'll call you if anything changes, but plan on this happening Monday morning."

"Thanks," she says. "And please be safe. I'd rather deal with this than have any of you get hurt. I mean it."

"We'll be fine," Sawyer says. But he kind of looks like he's going to hurl.

Mrs. Hayes walks us out and thanks us again.

On the ride home, I realize how exhausted I am from getting up early and thinking hard about this all day. Sawyer's tired too. I drop him off at Kate's, drive home, and go straight to bed.

Ben and Sawyer show up shortly after Mom and Dad go to mass on Sunday morning. Ben comes into the house carrying two thick garment bags. Sawyer arrives with duffel bags.

"Are you guys moving in?" Rowan asks with a grin.

Ben smiles. "Got a little surprise," he says. He opens the first garment bag and pulls out four wet suits. He eyeballs Sawyer and picks one, then does the same for Trey. "Try these on. They'll keep us warm if we end up in the water. Not commando, please—they're rentals. Here are instructions on the best way to get them on." He hands each of them a half sheet of paper. "Main thing is to take your time. They should fit tightly. Don't dig your fingernails in."

Sawyer looks at the wet suit like it might bite him. Trey takes both suits and drags Sawyer along with him, shoving him into the bathroom, and then continues to his bedroom.

"I can't wait to see your package in that suit," I call out.

"Thanks!" Trey answers.

"Not you!"

"Jules," Rowan says, disgusted.

"What? Might as well point out the obvious elephant in the room instead of stare and say nothing."

"I'm not quite *that* big," comes Sawyer's muffled response through the bathroom door.

Rowan rolls her eyes and turns to Ben. "Won't we look weird wearing them on the ferry?" Rowan asks.

"You can wear clothes over it. No one will even notice. These are top-of-the-line, superflexible, and you'll have complete range of motion."

"You're brilliant, Ben," I say. "How did you get these?"

"We rent them out at the marina. I woke up this morning and couldn't believe I hadn't thought of snagging some before. My parents are out of the country, so I didn't even need an excuse to grab a bunch of sizes I thought would fit." He unzips the other garment bag and pulls out a few more, then takes a good look at us and hands them over. "Let me know if you need a different size," he says, loud enough for the guys to hear too.

It takes forever to get them on. Once we have the right sizes figured out, we're exhausted. Ben then hauls out some green life vests that are so petite they look like they couldn't possibly hold us up in the water, but he assures us they are some of the best around. We practice getting into them, and then we have to take everything off again. We make plans to wear our wet suits from the time we get up tomorrow morning so we don't have to mess with them on the ferry.

Once we're back into regular clothes, Sawyer gives us an evil grin and holds up one of the duffel bags. "My turn," he says. "Get in the car."

Thirty-Seven

"Rock climbing?" I ask.

Sawyer leads the way into the gym. "It's a class. We're taking it."

"This is like seventh-grade PE all over again, when everybody called me gay," Trey grumbles.

"Me too," Ben says glumly.

"Clearly their taunts had no effect on either of you," Rowan says.

"I'm basically gay in defiance," Trey says. "Rowan, can you write me an excuse to get me out of this?"

"Because you're gay?"

"No, loser, because I *got shot* last month. Sheesh." He rubs his shoulder.

"Yeah, I thought about that," Sawyer says. "Just take it easy and don't overdo it, Trey."

Trey flashes a triumphant look.

"You're such a rebel." Ben slips his arm over Trey's shoulders and turns to Sawyer. "Now explain this. What are we doing? Is this the traditional day-before-disaster team-building event or something? Please tell me I don't have to do a trust fall. Because the last time I did a trust fall was in seventh-grade PE. Just saying."

"Yeah, what is this?" Rowan asks. "I don't want to mess up my hair, because I have to say good-bye forever to Charlie tonight in case I whiff."

"Oh my God," I mutter. "You and your hair."

"Nobody's going to whiff," Sawyer says. "We're invincible."

I shiver when he says it.

"We're here to learn the basics, mainly because I think rope might be our friend tomorrow. So we're going to learn how to tie knots and effectively throw ropes for rescue and use the belay apparatus just in case, and we're going to do a little practice climbing on the wall, too."

We learn the ropes (har har) of rock climbing for a couple of hours. We decide not to do too much because we don't want to be sore tomorrow, but the instructor shows us a lot of useful things that might come in handy in rescuing people from a sinking ferry.

The rest of the day we wander around our neighborhood and the elementary school playground, looking like your typical hoodlums, talking through our plan, enjoying the sunshine, and watching the clouds build in the west. "There's our storm," Rowan says. "It's causing flight delays in Minneapolis right now. Tomorrow morning's forecast for Milwaukee is now seventy percent chance of thunderstorms, occasionally heavy with gusty winds."

And while that scares me, it also reassures me, and pretty much guarantees that we're doing things right.

I sit on the swings and talk to Tori for a bit. "She's hanging in there," I report to the others after I hang up. "The vision has calmed down a little." I look at my shoes, dusty from the playground. "I think this is the most prepared we've ever been."

We go over the list of victims—now sitting at twenty-seven, according to Tori. We note what they're wearing and discuss our plan to find them in advance and split them up so we each have five or six to monitor.

When it starts to get dark and our stomachs are growling, we reluctantly part. Sawyer goes to Kate's, Ben drives back to UC, and we three Demarcos head inside our house, lured by the smells of something delicious cooking in the kitchen and the pleasant faces of two seemingly normal parents who are happy to see us and enjoying life. Bizarre.

All I know is that if anything happens to us now . . . it'll pretty much wreck everything.

Thirty-Eight

We all sleep terribly for about five hours, and are extra quiet getting ready so our parents don't wake up. Which they never do. Their body clocks are permanently on restaurant time, which means late to bed, late to rise. I see their faces before school so rarely I can count the number of times on one hand.

Shortly after three, we're off. Clad in wet suits and sweats, each of us carrying a duffel bag containing a life vest and rope, we are a glaringly obvious group of kids who are clearly skipping school and running away from home. Rowan, who can do Mom's voice best, remembers to call the absentee hotline and report us all absent so Mom and Dad don't get a call later.

We pick up Sawyer first, who is waiting at the

entrance of Kate's apartment building. He holds my hand in the backseat, not saying much, his face strained. By four, the rain has started. We reach the UC campus and Ben hops into the backseat next to me. He's wearing contacts today, not his usual glasses. He gives my arm a friendly squeeze and whispers, "We got this, kid," for which I am more grateful than I expect to be. The journey continues.

The wind picks up, blowing unidentifiable bits of floaty garbage across the highway, and the rain is steady. Occasional lightning streaks across the sky. There's not much traffic heading out of Chicago at four in the morning, and we make great time, reaching the ferry terminal before five thirty. Trey parks the car and we sit for a moment, listening to the rain on the car's roof and spraying the windows.

"I have to pee," Rowan says. It breaks the mood, and I'm glad she's here.

"Good luck with that," Trey says.

It might be our first mistake, putting these wet suits on at home. "I blame Ben," I say.

"Yeah," he says. "I forgot about that part. It's not as easy to pee in the suits if you're not actually in the lake."

I look at him. "Are you saying these suits have been peed in by strangers?"

"I'd say that's pretty likely."

I close my eyes as the giant wave of grossness washes over me.

"Why do you think I told you not to go commando?"

There is silence.

"We clean them, though, obviously," Ben adds.

I hold up a hand to him. "Okay, no. Let's pretend we never had this conversation." I take in a resigned breath and loop my fingers around my duffel bag. "Come on, guys. Let's do this. Are you ready?"

The murmur of agreement is soft but resolute. We have a plan.

Ben hands over our tickets and we board. The ferry is bigger than I pictured, and I imagine how monstrous and strange it'll look tipped on its side. I grip my duffel bag tighter.

I catch a glimpse of the vehicles driving onto the ferry and wince, wishing I could tell everyone to leave their cars on land. And themselves. One good thing about the weather this morning is that it's probably keeping people from using the ferry. But there are still plenty of passengers boarding.

We take a tour of our surroundings. There's a private room for first-class passengers. I peek through the open doorway, and hastily back out when a guy in a suit gives me a cool stare.

And there's the banner. WELCOME TO OUR 13TH SEASON, it reads.

"Lucky thirteen," Rowan remarks.

Glass doors and stairways lead to multiple open decks, which would be great on a sunny summer day, but everyone stays inside the glassed-in area today. There's a snack bar, where passengers line up to get coffee and breakfast. We seek out the location of the lifeboats and flotation devices, and assign a lifeboat to each of us to man—if things work out to enable us to man them. That's the thing. Who knows how this goes down? Who knows how hard that bump is when the ferry hits the wall? And what else happens that we don't know about? I know there's got to be something that puts people on the floor before the jolt.

Once we feel comfortable with the layout, we find a spot with a table by the window and sit around it, keeping our duffel bags close by.

"This feels weird," Trey mutters. He drums his knuckles on the table. "It's really different compared to the other ones."

I nod. "The others were high tension, counting down to an exact time, and then over in seconds. This one's going to feel like it's going in slow motion, I think."

Rowan and Sawyer study the list of victim descriptions and look around for matches. Ben pulls his list out too. "This could be heartbreaking if we let it be," he says. I follow his line of sight to a family with a baby coming on board.

And I know what he means. I'm glad he said it, because that means he's thinking the way you have to think when you are doing a job like this.

I text Tori, letting her know our status, and she replies immediately, saying things are getting crazy strong. As the ferry's engines rev and we begin to pull away, I can only hope the crazy strong vision is because it's imminent, and not because we're doing something wrong.

"We're moving," I say. I look around at the people who stand by the windows, watching us leave land, and everything inside me wants to scream, "Go back!"

Trey fidgets. After a moment he stands up. "I'm going outside to look for more life vests. I can't stand sitting here."

And I watch the time, knowing there's only so far we can go before the pilot—or whoever is sailing this thing—will take a sharp turn south.

Thirty-Nine

The minutes tick away, and soon we are past the pier and on the open lake. The ferry speeds up and flies over the choppy water. And damn, it's rough. People take their seats and try to keep their coffee from spilling. A few stumble to the bathrooms, and I see somebody puking into a white barf bag. I look at Sawyer, who is gripping the table with one hand and staring at his victim list with the other. He looks ill.

"You okay?" I ask.

"Yeah. Trying not to be sick. I'm not good with spinning rides at theme parks, either."

I smile and reach into my bag. "You'll do better if you look out the window rather than at the paper." I pull a box of Dramamine out and give him a dose, along with a small bottle of water. "Try this."

He downs the pills and looks out the window through half-slit eyes.

Rowan leans over, her sweet brown eyes troubled. "I only see one person who vaguely matches any of the descriptions of the victims," she says quietly. "That guy over there."

"We might need to move around a little to find everyone. And there's the first-class cabin—there could be people in there who we can't see."

"Some of the descriptions are pretty general," Sawyer says. He keeps his eyes on the horizon.

I check my phone for what must be the twentieth time, and then glance around, nervous. "We should be turning soon," I mutter. I stand up to see if I can keep my balance. The rocking is getting more and more pronounced, and hardly anybody is trying to walk around.

Ben looks at me, concern in his eyes. "Where's Trey?"

"I was just wondering that." And then I see him pushing open the door to come inside the cabin. The wind catches the door and he has to pull it closed. His hair is everywhere, and he looks damp, but not soaked. He makes his way over to our table like a drunk, staggering from side to side trying to stay level.

"Jesus futhermucker," he says under his breath, grabbing the table and swinging heavily into a chair. "There. Well, that was an adventure." He catches his breath and grins at Ben, who is looking rather stern.

"What's the status?" Trey asks.

"Rowan thinks she found one person on the list," I say. "That guy with the tie." Everybody turns, and I feel like we're in an episode of *Scooby-Doo*. "Don't all look at once, gosh." I duck when the guy looks at us and frowns.

"I don't know anymore," Rowan says. "He's a maybe."

"That's it?" Trey says.

"So far," she says.

I look at the time. It's been thirty minutes, and according to my compass app, we're still heading northeast.

"Hey, Sawyer?" I ask.

"Yeah, baby." He peels his eyes from the horizon and looks at me.

"Why aren't we turning?"

"I don't know."

I catch Trey's eye, and I don't have to say anything for him to know I'm getting anxious. "We should be turning," I say again.

Rowan bites her lip and stands up. "I need a new angle," she says. She walks forward like she's climbing a hill, and then suddenly lurches the rest of the way across the expanse of the ferry, grabbing the backs of chairs and whatever else she can reach. She disappears around a corner. I stare out the window at the rolling waves and whitecaps gnashing at the ferry. The sky gets noticeably lighter over the next few minutes. We have outrun the storm.

By the time Rowan returns with only one more possible match, it's six forty-five. The waves are growing calmer, and we are heading in the opposite direction of where the ferry sinks. There's no way we could get there now.

Everybody realizes it, but nobody says it. When Tori texts me, saying things are getting worse, I know it's not because the tragedy is imminent.

Another ten agonizing minutes pass in silence.

"It's not today," I say finally. I close my eyes and let out a sigh, and then drop my head into my folded arms on the table, thinking of all the problems I just triggered by getting the day wrong. A missed school day, which we'll have to do again once we figure out the right day. Another ticket home. And then another ferry ticket on the *right* day, if we can even figure out when that is . . . and then there's the whole emotional mess of getting psyched up for this all over again.

"Jules is not impressed," I say into my sweatshirt sleeves. "Not impressed at all."

Forty

Everybody tries to tell me it's not my fault, and they remind me they agreed with my assessment, but I feel terrible about it. I don't even have any money on me to buy a ticket home—I figured I'd just lose it anyway in the ferry disaster.

Ben has his wallet, though, already zipped up tight with his cell phone in the waterproof pocket of his life vest inside his duffel bag, and he says he has enough money in his bank account to cover everybody's tickets as long as we can pay him back this week.

The problem is, it's really difficult to get a decent cell phone signal out in the middle of Lake Michigan, and every time he tries to buy tickets for the ten fifteen ferry back to Milwaukee, he gets the gray wheel of death. Finally he gives up.

"We'll have to buy them at the terminal," he says.

When we get to the terminal in Muskegon, it's nine thirty local time, and once we disembark, there's a line for tickets.

Finally it's our turn.

"Two seats left," the woman says. "I can't give you five."

We look at each other, mildly panicked, unsure what to do.

"I've got five seats available on the four forty-five ferry," the woman says.

"Shall we take the two and then three of us go later?" Rowan asks.

"No," Trey says. "We only have one car in Milwaukee, so whoever would take this ferry would just be stuck in Milwaukee waiting for the rest of us. Let's all take the four forty-five."

"Yeah, good thinking," I say, relieved. "We'll just have to call Mom and tell her we're doing stuff after school today."

Ben buys the tickets, and then we go into the restrooms to peel off our wet suits and redress in our sweats. I wish I'd brought other clothes, but that would have been senseless if things had gone the way I expected.

We all find bench seats in the terminal to curl up in

and take naps, which should come easily after the night and morning we had, but I can't sleep. I lie there, eyes open, wondering where I went wrong. I text a bit with Tori, who is starting to lose it. She can't see her phone anymore to text, so her mother is doing it for her. After a few more messages, I step outside the terminal to call her.

Her mom answers and hands the phone to Tori.

"How bad is it?" I ask. "Tell me everything."

"Jules," she says softly, "it's so bad now that I can feel the water rising up around me."

Whoa. When we hang up, I check the weather forecast, and tomorrow looks to be a beautiful day. "Maybe it's a freak storm over the lake," I mumble to myself. "Or maybe I shouldn't put so much stupid faith in spring weather forecasts, since they're wrong half the time anyway."

By afternoon everyone's awake and starving, and nothing in the terminal looks appetizing. We decide to explore outside, and find a cool little hot dog shop nearby for a cheap lunch. Apparently we look old enough, or confident enough, not to be questioned about being there on a school day.

While we eat, we can hear thunder rolling in the distance. Sawyer takes a look out the window at the darkening skies and decides against finishing his second dog in case the ride to Milwaukee is rough.

Fat drops of rain hit the ground as we walk back to the

terminal. We go over everything we know for the thousandth time, trying to figure out where we went wrong and what obvious clue we're missing. I wish I could see the vision just a few times. It's so frustrating having to rely on Tori to look for all the clues. What if she's the one who is missing something? What if she doesn't know what to look for? What if she misinterpreted something? All I know is that we're either doing something very, very wrong, or this thing is happening tomorrow, or maybe the next day. Yet . . . we can't keep riding this ferry forever, trying to figure it out.

Rowan calls Mom to let her know we'll be home late tonight. And finally the afternoon ferry pulls in. We watch the stream of passengers get off, and then wearily we board the ferry for the two-and-a-half-hour ride to Milwaukee.

Sawyer takes his Dramamine before he feels sick this time, which should help him. He holds me close and I manage to fall asleep to the sound of driving rain hitting the windows. The rocking is almost soothing, since I know Sawyer won't let me fall. I drift into a hard nap and dream about Tori sinking under murky waves.

When I hear Rowan saying my name, and I feel her tugging at my arm, I have to struggle to wake up, and I can't remember where I am.

"Jules!" she says. And soon Sawyer is joining in.

I open my eyes and stare at the strange surroundings for a moment before I remember. "What's up?" I say. My voice sounds like it's far away. I sit up a little and see enormous waves rolling around the ferry, lightning streaking through the sky, and nervous passengers staring out the windows.

Everybody's looking at me. "What?" I say again. I look at Sawyer. "Are you sick?"

"Jules," Trey says, "did you hear the announcement?"

"What?"

"The pilot just came on the loudspeaker. He said there are tornado warnings in Milwaukee, and marine warnings for waterspouts all along the Wisconsin shoreline."

"Waterspouts?" I blink. "Okay. How far away are we?"

"We're an hour from Milwaukee and the storm super-cell is heading straight toward us, so the pilot says we're being diverted to a different port and buses will take everybody back to Milwaukee." His face is intense. "We're being diverted to Chicago, Jules. We're turning south right now, and we're heading for Chicago."

Forty-One

At first I can't comprehend what Trey is saying. The ferry lurches and rolls as the waves get bigger. "But the sun won't be right if it happens now," I say.

"I know, but maybe the ferry leaves from Chicago tomorrow morning," he says.

"Yeah," Sawyer says, sitting up. "That would put the ferry in the right place!"

"Hey, guys?" Ben says.

I close my eyes to concentrate. "But . . . but the passengers will still show up at the Milwaukee terminal—how would any of them know—"

"Because they can send an e-mail to everybody who pre-bought tickets to let them know of the change due to the weather," Trey says.

"Guys?" Ben says again.

I am still not sold. "Why wouldn't they just sail the ferry back to Milwaukee tonight after the storms pass?"

"*Guys,*" Rowan says this time.

We all look at her and Ben.

"What?" Trey says impatiently.

Rowan looks sidelong across the ferry and points her head in the direction she wants us to look. "There's the guy who is on the list. The one who rode with us this morning."

I narrow my eyes. "I thought you weren't sure."

"We weren't sure," Ben says, "until now, when we also spotted that girl sitting at ten o'clock to you, Jules." He shows me the victim list and points. "This girl," he says, "is her."

"And," Rowan continues, "I see two more. No, make that three."

I follow her gaze as I watch a woman lurch toward the bathroom. "No," I say, and then I grab the list and compare Tori's descriptions with the people Ben and Rowan are pointing out. A girl about thirteen with blond hair and a polka-dot headband. A black-haired woman in a red skirt and jacket. An older couple wearing matching sweatshirts from the Wisconsin Dells.

"Shit," Sawyer says in a low voice as he reads the list over my shoulder. "There's another one."

"But . . . the sun is wrong," I say weakly.

"Or maybe that light behind the clouds wasn't the sun," Trey says.

"Or . . ." My mind flies everywhere, combing over all the conversations I've ever had with Tori. "Or maybe Tori's sunrise is actually . . . a sun*set*?" I feel my throat close. "What time is it?" I scrounge around for my phone, finally remembering that I put it in my duffel bag. I grab it and check the time. It flips between six thirty-two and five thirty-two, depending on whether my phone is picking up a signal from the east side or the west side of the lake.

I see five new text messages from Tori, and I flip through them. *The water,* she says, again and again. *The water. It's rising. It's pouring into my mouth. It's flowing from my eyeballs. I can't breathe.*

While everybody waits for me to say something profound, I sit with my eyes closed, feeling sick and totally inadequate to lead this task. Trying to organize my crazy thoughts. Trying to figure out what to do first. Trying not to hyperventilate.

I suck in a deep breath, blow it out, and open my eyes. "Okay, guys." My voice shakes a little, which pisses me off.

I sit up straighter and start again, stronger. "Okay. This is happening. First, we take turns getting our wet suits back on without drawing attention to ourselves, which could be difficult with all the rocking and the pukers waiting for your stall. Rowan and Sawyer, you first, and when you get back, tackle the rest of the victim list."

Trey gives me the tiniest smile of encouragement, and I know he's proud of me.

"Ben, how are you with math?"

"Decent," he says.

"Good. See if you can figure out how fast we're going and how far we are from the disaster point so we can have a clue how much time we have."

"Got it." He pulls his phone out and starts working.

"Trey," I say.

"Yes?"

I blow out a breath. "First, don't die."

"Okay."

Ben looks up at us for a second, presses his lips together, and goes back to work.

"Second, I need you to use your amazing charm to try to talk to the pilot, or at least one of the crew, and try to tell them to steer clear of the low rock walls—"

Trey closes his eyes, a pained expression on his face.

"What?" I say.

"They won't listen, Jules. But I will try. I'll give it everything I've got."

"That's all I'm asking," I say. "Maybe you can convince them to ask passengers to put their life vests on." My throat hurts, and I know he's right—they won't listen to a teenager.

"I get it," Trey says. "I do. We have to try everything."

"Thanks."

Trey stands up carefully and aims for the nearest chair to grab on to, and he's on his way.

I sniff hard and pick up the victim list, staring blindly at it, thinking about the blond girl with the polka-dot headband.

I look out the rear starboard side of the ferry toward Milwaukee and see a gorgeous family of four waterspouts spinning like dust devils, connecting lake and sky.

Forty-Two

I point the waterspouts out to Ben as others on the ferry notice too.

"They're amazing," Ben says. "I've never seen one before."

I nod. I can't stop watching.

"You're doing great, Jules," he says. "I mean it."

I look at him, at the sincerity in his eyes, and I can see why Trey has fallen so hard for this guy. "Thanks. Thanks for helping us."

"How could I not?" comes his simple reply. "My life was saved in that music room. There's got to be a reason for that. I figure this is it." He looks at me. "What I can't figure out is *your* dedication to this phenomenon. You've never been saved from anything, yet you feel such a strong need to rescue others."

I shrug. It's too much to explain right now. As I spot Rowan making her way back to the table with her duffel bag, Ben turns back to his phone and says, "We've got about forty minutes."

I set the stopwatch on my phone. "Okay. Thanks. You change into your wet suit when Sawyer's back." I grab my bag and stagger toward the bathroom, pointing Rowan's attention in the direction of the waterspouts. And I'm amazed there is so much beauty in this carnivorous lake, and on this doomed ferry.

It takes forever to get my wet suit on. I bang against the sides of the stall and once nearly step into the toilet as I try to glide my second skin on without puncturing it with my fingernails. I grab on to the toilet paper holder and the purse hooks more than once as the ferry pitches from side to side, and slam against the stall wall, scaring the person next to me, before finally getting my wet suit on. Quickly I slip my life vest on and clip it into place like Ben suggested, and pull my sweatshirt over top. The vest is slight enough to fit underneath, I can move really well, and it'll save time later. I pull up my sweatpants, then replace my shoes and head back to the table.

Ben has already changed and beat me back to home base, and Sawyer's back too. Only Trey is missing.

"He's changing now," Ben says.

"Does everybody have their vests on?" I ask, though it's slightly obvious if you're looking in the right place.

"Yes," they all report.

"Timers set?"

Again, the answer is yes.

"Have we located all the victims?"

"All but five," Rowan says, "and they're all described as men or women wearing suits. So we figured they're in the first-class cabin."

"That makes sense," I say. "And since they're all grouped in one place, who wants to be in charge of them?"

"I will," Rowan says. "I've got their descriptions memorized. I'm going to accidentally go in there right now just to get a look."

She goes, and Trey returns from the bathroom with a bit of a bulge around his waist.

"Life vest?" I ask.

He nods.

"What did they say?"

He smiles ruefully. "Pretty much what you'd expect. I spoke to an officer of some sort, who assured me that the pilot has sailed these waters many times. He thanked me for putting my trust in the crew on this 'unusual' voyage."

I nod. "At least we tried. Thank you."

We divide up the rest of the victims based on where they're sitting, and assign a person to be on the lookout for them. It's the best plan we can think of, though there's sure to be chaos. Then we figure out where we're each going to get life vests from, and determine that the outside deck is the best place since no one will be out there to trample us until they start exiting to the lifeboats. And then we go over our final plan and make sure everybody knows what to do once the ferry makes contact with the breakwall.

Our valuables are put away in our waterproof vest pockets. Our duffel bags are unzipped so we can grab ropes quickly if necessary. We are as ready as we can be. And now all we can do is wait.

Ben stands and walks over to the window, better on his feet in these conditions than the rest of us. He looks for a moment and then beckons me to join him. Either the waves are not as bad now, or I'm getting better at this.

He points to the shore, where I can see buildings in the distance. "We're passing Waukegan. On a clear day you can see Chicago from here. Obviously that isn't today. But we're getting close. North Chicago is coming fast." He points at the sky. "See how it's clearing in this direction?"

I look, and there's the little spot of yellow behind thin clouds. It's not down quite far enough to match Tori's description of thirty degrees, but I'm sure now that this is Tori's sunrise—except it's a sunset. I'm disgusted with myself for not even considering it. She was just so sure. . . . I shake the negative thoughts from my head. No time to dwell on that now.

We watch the land grow closer. My phone vibrates from within the waterproof pocket of my life vest. I'm sure it's Tori. I hide my front from the passengers and reach in to get it.

SCENE CHANGE—now only 23 dead. You're doing something right! Also, NEW SCENE—big jolt right before smaller bump, then shot of ferry instrument panel covered with blood! Be careful!

Forty-Three

I text back in a frenzy, willing my fingers to hit the right buttons as we rock and churn: *Is there a clock on the instrument panel??*

And then I wait, frozen, begging her to narrow down the time of this imminent disaster. I show Ben, and he heads back to our table to tell the others about the big jolt.

Finally Tori replies: *6:38!!*

I look at the time. It's 6:35. "Shit," I mutter. And then something inside me explodes and kicks me into gear. I stagger over to the others. "Three minutes, guys. The big jolt is at six thirty-eight."

There's a split second when everyone takes in the news.

Then Ben calls 911, giving them the approximate

location as if we've already hit. Smart move. Every minute counts—especially when it comes to drowning.

"We should warn people to brace themselves," Sawyer says. "Most won't listen, but some might."

"Good," I say. "Yes. And remember—stay braced for two jolts. Then outside for life jackets, victims, lifeboats, rope. Everybody have their victim descriptions in mind?"

At 6:37, with no additional news, I shove my phone back into my waterproof pocket, seal it, and leave it there. We wait an agonizing thirty seconds, situating ourselves behind our table. Then Sawyer stands up and yells, "Brace yourselves! Everybody! Hang on!"

People turn to look at him, some in fear, others in annoyance.

"Hang on!" I echo, and so do the others. I grab the table, make sure Rowan is in a good spot. "I love you guys," I say. "See you on the other side of this one!"

Sawyer leans over and kisses me hard on the lips. "I love you."

"I love you, too," I whisper.

And then we hit.

Forty-Four

Five things that should never be airborne on a ferry:

1. A cat in a carrier
2. Golf clubs
3. Steaming-hot coffee
4. Any kind of coffee, really
5. Humans

The first jolt is a doozy, let me tell you. Not like the "run into a brick wall and stop" kind, but the "holy hell, that'll slow down a fast-moving ferry in a hurry" kind. My ribs slam into the table edge, which takes my breath away. Trey ends up on the floor, but he signals he's okay.

Everyone else in the ferry who wasn't bracing or

wedged behind a table is now on the floor. There's a second of weird silence, and I realize the engines have shut down, and then the cries of pain and the shouts begin, along with a muted chorus of honking horns and car alarms coming from belowdecks. I look out the window and see nothing but water, and a ways off, a harbor. "One more, guys!" I shout. And then my eyes widen as I see the massive wave of our own wake bearing down on us. And I realize it's Tori's giant wave she kept talking about. "It's after this wave!"

Trey crawls to the table and wraps his arms around the post.

It feels like we're on a roller coaster. The wave picks the ferry up and rolls us way to one side and then pushes us, like a surfer, toward the shore, throwing more people off balance and onto the floor or crashing into tables.

We spin and ride the wave, and when we reach the bottom of it we feel the second jolt, and hear the groaning, grinding, shredding sound from the starboard side as the ferry lurches and shudders.

There is mass confusion, an emergency alarm goes off, and then a voice on the loudspeaker says something nobody can understand.

"Everybody okay?" I ask, trying to talk over the noise.

They nod. And I'm not going to lie—they all look scared shitless. Which is exactly how I feel.

"Okay. Let's go!" I shout. "Now!"

We stay low to keep better balance as we step over and around people and luggage as the ferry continues to ride crazily over waves. As we move toward the door to the outer deck, we tell everyone who will listen to grab the flotation devices under their seats.

Once outside we can hear the emergency message directing people to put on their life vests and head to the lifeboat muster stations, but I know the people inside can't understand a word of the message with all that noise. We form a human chain, with Ben and Trey hauling the life vests out of the bench seats and shoving them down at me and Sawyer. Rowan, who stands near the glassed-in area, passes them by the handfuls to people who need them as they begin to stream outside. We try to talk in calm tones whenever the voice on the loudspeaker stops, trying to help keep order, but it's nearly impossible. And the ferry keeps lurching and rolling on the waves. But we manage to find at least a few of our victims from the list and get life vests on them.

Finally we grab armloads of the remaining life preservers from the front deck and go back inside to try to find our victims and make sure they have them. We figure that most of the drowning victims are the people who were injured at the first impact, thinking they may be unable to get to a lifeboat. But none of our victims are where they were just minutes ago. Crew members are in sight, some sporting obvious injuries but helping people to the lifeboats anyway.

We split up. Rowan peels away from the group and heads to the first-class cabin, and from my list I spot the older couple with matching sweatshirts and rush over to them. The woman is lying on the deck and the man is on his hands and knees beside her, trying to stay in one place.

"Put this on," I say near the man's ear, indicating the life vest. "And then we'll get you two out of here, okay?"

He's in shock or something, and the woman just stares up at me. Her wrist is twisted at a strange angle, and she says her hip hurts and she can't sit up or walk.

I put the life vest over her head and slide the belt around her back the best I can without hurting her, and I put her husband's on him as well when it's clear he's unable to do it himself. And then I look for help.

"Ben!" I yell when I spot him. He turns and sees me. Soon he's kneeling next to us. "She can't walk. And he's . . . not really responding to anything. What do we do?"

He looks around, his rain-soaked hair whipping and sticking to his face. "Ah. There's one," he says. He gets up and grabs a backboard from the wall and lays it on the deck next to the woman. "Help me lift her," he says. "On three."

We get the woman on the board and Ben straps her

down. I spy my duffel bag and crawl over to it just as all lights except a few emergency ones go out. A cry goes up. Luckily, it's not dark out yet, but the clouds are keeping any sunlight from shining in. I can still see, but not well. I grab the rope and sling it around my arm, and crawl back to Ben.

"You're going to get this man on the lifeboat," Ben says, "and then we'll come back for her once it's cleared out a bit and we can maneuver the board, okay? I see two of my people—I'll be back." He grabs his stack of life vests and goes.

I take the man by the arm and lead him to one of the lifeboat stations as the emergency alarm drills into my head over and over again.

When I turn around, I'm climbing uphill, and I realize that the ferry must be already starting to list to one side. Every few minutes I feel the ferry shudder, and I think the cars below us must be shifting as water pours in. I fight panic and strain my eyes trying to find the rest of my people. I don't see any of them, but I catch a glimpse of Trey getting some of his people out.

"Jules!" Rowan screams from behind me, in the doorway to the first-class cabin. I turn and run over to her. "I got four of them out of here, but this guy . . ."

I look beyond her and see a man facedown on the conference table in a pool of blood and glass everywhere. "Oh my God," I say. "Is he dead?"

"I think so. There's glass stuck all in his head."

"Let's go—we'll tell Ben. Lifeguards can probably tell if someone's dead or not, right? I still need to find three of my people."

"Which ones?"

"Brown-haired small man with blue-and-white pin-stripe shirt. Twentysomething woman with big earrings and hair in a bun. Light-blond, rosy-cheeked middle-aged man in a red Windbreaker."

"I saw Sawyer helping the woman with the earrings get into a lifeboat," Rowan says, peering around. "Let's check outside on the decks. They aren't in here."

The ferry shudders and tilts even more. We both instinctively drop to our hands and knees, slipping a little. A guy running past us totally biffs and falls over me. He gets up and keeps going, slipping and falling every few steps. Rowan looks at me. "We don't have much time."

We crawl at top speed to the outer deck. And there I see my little brown-haired man, without a life vest, jumping off the railing.

Forty-Five

"No!" I shout. I slide over to the railing and look out after him. "Shit!" I look at Rowan, knowing I need to go after this guy, but remembering the matching sweatshirt woman. "Ro! There's an older woman on a backboard not far from where we were sitting—Ben knows about her and will help you get her to the lifeboat. Don't worry about my red sweater guy. Just get the woman and then you get in that boat too, you hear me?" The ship groans and tilts more, and I slip on the wet deck and land on my back. "Shit." My panic shows in my voice. "Okay, Rowan?"

She can tell I'm freaked. "Okay, I promise! Are you going after him?"

"Yes, I have to. I'll be fine!" I whip my sweatshirt off

and toss my shoes aside, clip a life vest to one end of my rope, and then, without allowing myself to think, I climb the railing and balance there for a second, looking at the horrible scene below. Waves churning. The runaway empty lifeboat floating far away—we didn't even have a chance to try to save it. People struggling in the water and hanging on to the sides of the lifeboats, unable to climb in. It's a long enough drop to the water to give me pause.

I spot my little man in the water as the ferry shudders and tilts again. My foot slips off the railing, I lose my balance, and suddenly I'm falling. Before I can take a deep breath, I hit the water and keep going. The cold on my face makes me want to gasp, but I fight it, and before long my life vest has me popping up above the water again.

Wiping the water from my eyes, I get my bearings, and as a huge swell lifts me high, I see the little man. His head is tilted back and he's not yelling or trying to swim or struggling or anything, which Ben says is a major warning sign of drowning. I swim toward him as fast as I can, dragging my rope and extra life jacket with me. As I get closer, he bobs under the water and comes back up again.

"Sir!" I scream, unclipping the extra vest from my rope. "Take this!" I throw the life jacket at him and then swim the rest of the way as his head slips under the water again. I grab his shirt and lift him, and he grasps and clings to me and coughs, almost pulling me under the water. I thread the vest underneath his armpits to keep his face above the water, and I can only hope he can hang on, because I can't risk trying to get the thing on him the proper way.

My thighs burn and I'm out of breath. "Sir!" I yell in his face. "Hang on to this!" He manages a nod.

I strike out for the nearest lifeboat with the other end of the rope, checking over my shoulder every few seconds to make sure he's still there.

From here, the ferry looks huge and scary and completely misshapen as it sinks lower in the water, tilted at a strange, extreme angle. I can see the entire front deck, people crawling around trying to hang on. There's still one lifeboat attached to the ferry and being loaded, and as I push through the water I spot Rowan, Ben, and a crew member lowering the older woman on the board into the lifeboat using their ropes.

And then I see Sawyer on the rear deck railing, the blond girl with the polka-dot headband riding on his back. She must be injured. They're getting ready to jump. A wave of relief washes over me—she must be his last victim if he's going over the side with her. *Come on, Sawyer,* I think. *You can do this.* I send him all the mental energy I can muster to help him get past his fear and jump to safety.

I check on my guy, who is still hanging on. "We're almost there," I call out to him, and wind up with another mouthful of water as the tumultuous waves surround me. I am quickly growing exhausted. It's about all I can do right now to get to the lifeboat so the people in it can drag this man in. Finally I make it, and a woman grabs the rope from me and starts pulling. Others try to help me get in despite my protests, but the ferry groans and leans farther toward us, making everyone stop for a moment to stare.

And it keeps going, rolling slowly onto its side. "God in heaven," I whisper. I gasp and choke on water as the contents of the car ferry appear to shift drastically, the front end sinking faster than the back. The ferry tilts quickly now, to sixty degrees or so. The crew loosens their hold on the swinging lifeboat, and it drops sickeningly fast to the water. A second later, almost everyone else remaining on the deck falls too. I look around frantically for Trey and Rowan and Ben and Sawyer as the falling bodies surface. The water is dotted with a dozen passengers.

A woman in the lifeboat tugs at me. "No, I'm fine," I croak, not looking at her. "I'm going to help some of these people."

I search for the ones without life vests on, but it looks like everybody on my team did a fantastic job of doling them out, which gives me a surge of hope. I spy Trey in the water helping someone get to a lifeboat, and then I see that it's Rowan. My heart stops for a minute, but she is able to climb in on her own, so I think she's okay. She must have actually listened to me. Trey signals to somebody. I follow his gaze, and I see Ben swimming far out to save someone. As I ride up the next wave, I look for Sawyer, but I don't see him anywhere. "Sawyer!" I yell, but it's useless, because everybody else is yelling for people too.

I grab the rope and strike out toward a floating passenger, knowing we're still in a lot of danger. These people in the water don't have wet suits on. Just because they're not drowning at the moment doesn't mean they're safe. I sure as hell hope we're not relying solely on Ben's 911 call—there had to be others. Maybe somebody's fancy underwater car alerted OnStar. And of course there's the crew, who must have radioed for the Coast Guard. But I don't see anybody coming to our rescue. Lightning streaks across the sky and I realize it'll be totally dark soon.

I string two passengers together with the rope, and the woman in the lifeboat starts towing them in like a champ. Once I know they're good, I whip my head around, looking for anybody else who needs help, and I see the girl with the polka-dot headband. She no longer has the glasses she was wearing on the ferry. I swim toward her and she's just floating and crying, teeth chattering, in the water. "Come on," I say to her. "I'll help you."

I reach my arm out and she grabs on.

"What's your name?" I say. "I'm Jules."

"Bridget," she says. And then she mutters through her

tears, "As in, I wish there was a road from here to land so we could bridge it."

I can't help but smile. My mom would say this girl's got spunk.

I flip to my back and start kicking, pulling her with me, trying to get somewhere. But I'm losing steam. The rain pelts my face; it's warmer than the water I'm in. "We're headed for a lifeboat that has room for you. You doing all right?"

"I can't find my family," she says. "And I can't see very well. I lost my glasses."

I remember seeing her on board, and noting that the rest of her family was not on the victim list. "I'm sure they're fine. I'm positive, okay? I mean it. Hundred percent."

She nods, taking me at my word. "Okay."

"Are you hurt?"

"My ankle. It hurts really bad. I can't kick. That guy said it might be broken."

That guy. "That guy who was with you when you jumped?"

"Yeah."

"Where did he go?"

"I don't know," she says, her teeth chattering uncontrollably now. "He told me my job was to fight through the pain and swim to the lifeboat. And then he dropped me over the edge."

Sawyer, where the hell are you? My limbs are shaky and tired, and now that we're almost done here, I'm feeling the edge of the cold. My feet and face are getting numb.

I pull the girl toward the nearest lifeboat, where Rowan is, but the boat just seems to be floating farther and farther away in the waves. "Ro!" I shout. "Rowan!"

She turns and spots me. "Thank God!" she says. "We couldn't find you!"

"I'm fine, but do you have your rope you can throw us? She's freezing."

Rowan shakes her head, agitated. "It's with the lady on the board in a different boat." She looks around and apparently sees Trey on the other side of her boat. She calls to him, and a second later I see his rope flying through the air to her. She catches it, holds one end, and tosses the other one my way. I swim out to reach it and do my best to tie it to Bridget's life vest, but my fingers aren't cooperating.

It's when I'm stringing the rope through a fluorescent green loop on the vest that I realize it. My heart stops.

Bridget is wearing a life vest that looks exactly like mine.

"Where did you get this life vest?" I scream, my voice hoarse.

Bridget looks at me, scared. "The ferry was rolling onto its side and the guy made me take it. He said he could go back for another one."

I stare at her, my face in her face, and I have no words, only fear squeezing my lungs, suffocating me from inside my ribs.

Someone starts pulling Bridget to the lifeboat, and I flounder in the water as all light disappears, paralyzed in the murk.

I scream his name.

Scream it again, louder than the voice of the storm.

People in the boats stop to look at me.

Rowan stands up, and I catch the look of terror on her face, eyes wide in a flash of lightning. She joins me in yelling. "Sawyer!"

The woman from the first lifeboat yells for me too.

And then a man's voice.

Trey's voice.

But Trey is screaming a different name.

Forty-Six

Our screams are drowned out by thunder and groaning and engines and blades.

There are three full lifeboats and the one that got away. I don't know how many of the twenty-seven victims we saved, and I don't care. I am numb on the inside and hysterical on the outside.

"*Invincible!*" I scream. "You said!" I cry. "You said you wouldn't take it off!" But my voice is gone now.

What feels like hours later, I am lifted by strong arms and wrapped in a towel and put on a surface that doesn't move. We sit in a shadow. My sister holds my head and kisses it. Her tears drip on my tears.

My brother isn't screaming anymore on the outside. He leads us off the dock, away from the people. Even in our pain, we know we must be invisible. We escape cameras and paramedics and slip away to watch a helicopter shine a light on the water where a ferry used to be, searching for any signs of life. There are still people missing, the voices say over and over.

After a while, the light goes out.

We stare into the darkness, but there is no life out there.

Hours later, there is nothing we can do here. A bus takes my brother and sister and me to Milwaukee, and we get inside the not-delivery car with shaky hands and bare feet. When our doors are closed, Trey inserts the key, lets his forehead drop to the steering wheel, and sobs. And I cannot console him, because I am sobbing too.

And then we breathe, because we have to. And we hope, because there's nothing else to do.

We make a stop at Kate's because we don't have her phone number, tell her everything about the ferry disaster but not about the visions, and we let her decide what—and when—to tell Sawyer's estranged parents. We exchange phone numbers in case one of us hears something. And there's nothing we can do about Ben, whose mom and dad are in the Philippines visiting family.

It's well after midnight when we get home, and the lights are out. Rowan has taken care of Mom and Dad, bullshitting them about some major project we're apparently helping Trey with so he can win a scholarship. And they, tired from work and happy to hear we're so focused, have gone to sleep. We strip off our wet suits and dress in warm, dry clothes, and fall into bed, exhausted, phones in hands.

When I wake up with a start a little after five thirty, and then remember, the numbness inside of me is replaced by the most intense guilt, and I realize the extent of what I've done. Because I am responsible for this, too. I am responsible for all the world.

I crawl out of bed and knock softly on Trey's door, and then go in.

He's lying on his side in the dark, his face lit up by his phone, refreshing the news.

I stand in front of him. He doesn't look at me.

"I'm so sorry," I say.

His eyes twitch. His bottom lip quivers and then is still. Without a word, he opens up his arms, and I sit on the edge of his bed, and he holds me.

After a minute, he sits up and rubs his bleary eyes. And then he sighs. "It's not your fault."

I remain silent.

"If they're together, they're alive," he says after a while. "Ben is a lifeguard. Lifeguards don't drown. Even if that's not true, I have to believe it."

I swallow hard. I don't know how anybody could have

survived out there. "Ben has his phone, right?" I say. "Sawyer doesn't." *He broke his promise, and now he doesn't have his phone.*

"I think so." Trey looks at me. "What about Tori?"

I shrug. "I have a million texts from her. I haven't even started to read them."

"But wouldn't she know?"

"Know what?"

"Doesn't the vision change as the thing happens? Didn't you see body bags disappearing?"

I blink. And then I'm calling her, unable to breathe.

"Jules!" she says. "I'm so glad you're okay."

"Tori, listen to me. How did the vision change at the end? How many dead?"

"I texted you everything," she says. "Only three bodies."

"Who were they?" My throat constricts. I feel like I'm going to die if I don't get an answer immediately.

"I don't know—everything was dark in the vision at the end. I could only see dark shapes under the water."

"Can you pull it up and look at it? Get a closer look?" I ask, but I know the answer already.

"It's over, Jules," Tori says softly. "I can't. It's done."

Trey grips my hand.

"Sawyer and Ben are . . . missing," I say. "And I'm just wondering . . . do you think any of the bodies . . ."

She is silent. In shock. "I don't know. Oh my God, I'm so sorry. What can I do?"

I close my eyes. "Nothing. Just . . . send good thoughts. Or pray, or whatever you do."

She says something else comforting, but I don't comprehend it. "I can't talk right now," I say. I hang up. I never want to talk to her again. And then I look up at Trey.

"I don't know what to do," I say. "I'm just so sorry." The word drags itself from my gravelly throat and comes out like an oath. "I'm so *angry* . . . at myself. What was I thinking? How could I drag everybody into this? What the hell is wrong with me, Trey?"

He stares at a spot on the carpet for a long moment. And then he says, "You didn't drag anybody into this. We came willingly, knowing what could happen. You aren't in control of this thing." He looks up. "So if you're going to be mad at anybody, be mad at Dad. If he started it, then this is all his fault."

Forty-Seven

We want to stay home from school and stare at our phones, waiting for word, but we're already potentially in enough trouble. And really, if Sawyer or Ben calls, I have no problem barreling out of whatever class I'm in to answer him. So we go to school. By the time first hour is over, Sawyer and Ben have been missing for twelve hours.

I hear a few people talking about the ferry wreck, but there's no mention of Sawyer. People don't know he's missing . . . or possibly dead. And I don't want them to know. Because today, this grief belongs to me. And I don't want anybody infiltrating it with their fake-ass, disgusting bullshit.

After psych, Mr. Polselli asks me if I'm feeling all right. I don't want to cry, so I just nod and take off. At lunch Rowan sits with Trey and me at our usual table. We all look haggard and feel worse. My body is sore and I have bruises in weird places.

We can't seem to stay off our phones, checking the news, checking Chicago social media reports, seeing if Kate has heard from Sawyer, and both Trey and I get yelled at more than once in sculpting class. We accomplish nothing.

Trey checks the news once more in class and whispers, "There's a press conference scheduled with some new information. Three bodies pulled from the water."

My stomach drops. Before I can reply, Ms. White, the art teacher, walks over to our table and holds out her hands. "Hand them over."

I look up at her and feel all the blood draining from my face. "Please, no. We'll put them away, I promise."

"I've already asked you to put them away and you didn't listen." She sticks her hands closer. "Now, please."

Trey leans in. "We're having a little family emergency," he says in a soft voice. "I'm really sorry. You know we never do this otherwise. We're just hoping for some . . . some news."

The teacher hesitates, most likely because we look so horrible today, and finally relents. "Inside your backpacks, then. Don't let me see them again. You can check for news after class."

Phew. "Thank you," I say. "I'm sorry." We put our phones in our respective backpacks and fake like we're working on our vase projects as time slows down to a stop. I strain my ears, listening for my phone's vibration, but I don't hear anything. And I start to lose hope.

After class, there's nothing new. The press conference happens during last hour and reveals stuff we already know or suspected: The ferry was diverted because of the weather. On the way into the intended harbor, the ferry hit a sandbar, the engines cut, the pilot was injured, and the ferry smashed into a breakwall, which tore open the vessel. It began taking on water, and within forty minutes, the wreck had sunk. All but two passengers made it off the ferry. A third reportedly drowned while attempting rescue. They aren't releasing the names of the victims yet because families haven't been notified.

We three meet up after school. "One of them on the ferry was that guy in first class," Rowan says when Trey and I reach her locker. She shudders. "Ben said he was probably dead, and there was no time, so we had to leave him."

"So that's one of the three. But none of us saw Sawyer jump. The girl, Bridget, said he went back for another life vest . . . so maybe he never made it out. And I saw Ben swimming far off the rear end of the ferry. That's the last time anybody saw him. Could he be the third?"

Neither responds.

I want to die.

I think I really am losing my mind.

And speaking of that, I've put it off long enough. And I know what it's time to do. "I'm going to talk to Dad," I tell Trey and Rowan as we trudge to the car after school. "I don't care anymore what they do to me."

Forty-Eight

It was Food Truck Tuesday from eleven to one today at a nearby factory, which means Mom and Dad are home for a couple of hours to restock before heading out for the dinner hour. They're sitting at the kitchen table when we get home, having coffee and looking over some early sketches—plans for the new restaurant. It's still weird to see my dad acting like this. Like a normal human.

Trey and Rowan decide to stick by me, so I guess this is kind of an intervention. I can't even think right now. Part of me knows this is a bad idea, but I'm exhausted and sick and furious that my Sawyer is gone and my dad has done all these things to me, and I'm feeling reckless.

We walk into the kitchen.

Mom and Dad look up. "Oh, hi," Mom says. "I

thought you were our tomatoes being delivered." She smiles. "How was school?"

I stare at my dad. He looks nice today. His hair is smoothed back and his face looks healthy. Happy. My determination wavers.

But then I remember Sawyer, and how he wouldn't be dead right now if it weren't for my dad.

"I want to talk to you," I say.

My dad's face slackens. He looks at Mom. "She's pregnant," he says. He looks back at me. "You're pregnant?"

I have never hated him more than at this moment. "No!" I say, and I feel like I have no control over anything that is happening in my head right now. "Don't ask me that ever again!" My mouth screws up all weird and I fight hard not to cry.

"Oh, honey." Mom reaches out and touches my arm. She gives my dad a disapproving look, and he just sits there, probably trying to figure out why I'm falling apart. "He was kidding. Right, Antonio?"

My dad nods. "I'm sorry. That's not funny."

I don't even know who he is anymore. Since when does my dad joke? Since our house and restaurant burned to the ground, apparently. I can feel Trey and Rowan behind me, giving me strength.

I suck in a breath, trying to calm down. And then I say, "Can we talk about you and your, um, your . . . health problems? I want to know more about your depression and the hoarding and all that."

My dad leans back in his chair as if the questions threaten his personal space.

"Like," I continue, "I remember when it started—the hoarding—and I want to know why. I want you to tell me why it started. And if it's weird or crazy sounding, don't worry, just please tell me."

Mom frowns and lowers her gaze, turning slightly to look at my dad.

And he's got this strained, horrible look on his face, like I'm betraying him just by asking.

I refuse to look away.

Finally he nods toward Trey and Rowan and says in a low voice, "You told them?"

I stare. "What?" I have no idea what he's talking about.

He raises his voice a little, sounding stern now. "Did you tell them?"

I'm confused. Does he already know he passed the vision curse to me? "You mean," I say, my voice faltering, "about the visions?"

He leans forward, an intense, questioning look on his face. "The *what*?" He looks at Mom and back at me. "The *what*?" he repeats.

My lips part, then close again. "Wait. What are *you* talking about?"

"You're the one who has something to talk about," he says. "I want to know if you told them. If they know what you told me. That day you quit the restaurant."

And it hits me like a ton of bricks. He thinks I told Trey and Rowan about his affair. I press my hand to my eyes. And my hand slides away and I look at him again, at the hurt in his eyes. "No, Dad," I say softly. "That's not my story to tell."

I can feel the awkwardness penetrating the back of my brain as Trey and Rowan shift on their feet. When the doorbell rings, Trey hastily pulls Rowan with him to answer it.

Mom stands up. "That's probably our farmer with the tomatoes," she says like she's relieved to be squeezing past me and following Trey and Rowan.

When they're gone, I shake my head. "I can't believe this is what we're talking about, Dad. Is that really it? Your affair? That's what set off the hoarding and the depression? The years of us never knowing if we were going to come home to find that you killed yourself?"

He looks at me, pain washing over his face, making him look old again. "Depression is a disease," he says. "But the affair, the recipe that Fortuno stole—those things ruined my life."

I feel fury rising up so fast I can't stop it. "No, Dad. You own those things. That stuff didn't have to ruin your life. You just let it."

He takes it. And then he nods. "Maybe."

I let out a breath. "Okay."

He hesitates, and lowers his eyes. His big fingers lace together on the table and he taps his thumbs a few times. "So," he says, "you're seeing visions? What's that about?"

I stare at him. But before I can say anything, I hear the floor creak behind me, and my dad's gaze flits to a spot over my shoulder. Dad's eyes narrow the slightest bit, and then he frowns and says in rough voice, "What happened to you?"

I whirl around.

Standing in the kitchen doorway is a boy.

A boy with deep green eyes the color of the sea, and thick black lashes.

A boy with matted-down hair, wearing strange clothes, and wrapped in a blanket.

My lip quivers. "You're not the tomatoes." And when I throw myself into his arms, he collapses to the floor, and we lie there, sobbing together.

Forty-Nine

As my dad shakes his head and steps over us, apparently unconcerned, or mistaking our crying for laughter, Sawyer reaches up and holds my face with his cool hands and looks into my eyes. "Ben's here too," he rasps. His voice is gone.

I roll off him and my eyes threaten to start crying all over again. "Are you okay?"

He nods. "I am now."

"I'll be right back," I say, feeling heartless, but having to see for myself. I take off for the living room, where Trey and Ben are locked in an embrace that looks like it may never end. I wrap my arms around them both and kiss Ben on the cheek, and then I kiss Trey on the cheek too. And I have no words for how this feels right now.

Rowan, the come-through champion, is somehow giving Mom an explanation of what's happening. I have no idea if she's making up some story or going with the truth here, and I don't even care. I run back to Sawyer, who is still on the floor in the kitchen doorway. He smiles up at me through half-closed lids. He looks rough.

"Let's get you home to bed," I say.

"But I'm so tired. . . . I wanna sleep in your bed with you." He slings an arm over his eyes. "Please?"

"Um, somehow I don't think that's going to be okay with the parentals. How about the couch?"

He nods and strains to get up.

"Does Kate know you're okay?"

"Yeah, Trey just texted her for me. I don't have my phone." He starts crawling toward the living room.

"I *know* you don't have your phone, you big jerk. What happened to you promising not to take your stupid life vest off? We had a deal!"

"I just knew you were going to yell at me," he says glumly.

We round the corner and see that the couch is already occupied by Ben.

"Oh no." Sawyer says. He looks longingly at the cushions, then collapses on the floor and lies there. It's like he's drunk with exhaustion or something.

"So what happened to you guys?" I say. "Have you slept at all?"

"In the taxi."

"You took a taxi here? Why the heck didn't you call?"

"I don't know anybody's phone numbers. Tried to get people on the street to let me google your landline, but they pretty much took one look at the two of us and ran. When I finally got the taxi driver to look the number up for me, he just wrote it down and wouldn't let me use his phone at first. I guess we look like scary, drug-addicted homeless guys." He takes a breath. "Later I finally convinced him I wasn't going to steal it and I called, but I got the recording."

"But—" I sputter. "But what about Ben? Didn't he have his phone?"

"No," he says sadly. "It fell in the water because I'm a loser."

"You're not a loser, you just need to fucking learn how to swim," Ben says in a muffled voice from the couch. "It's really not that hard."

But Sawyer doesn't respond. A moment later, I realize he's asleep.

I look at Rowan and Trey, and we don't know what to think. Finally I shrug and go into our bedroom, pull blankets from our beds to drape over them, and give Sawyer my pillow. All we can do is hang around and wait and make up more crazy shit to answer our parents' questions about why Ben and Sawyer are crashed out in the living room.

When it becomes clear that Ben and Sawyer are down for the night, we three Demarcos go to bed early, since we're exhausted too, and everyone sleeps until morning, when we finally get to hear the whole story.

Fifty

Rowan and I get up at five to take showers and make some breakfast. When I tiptoe past Sawyer, he grabs my foot and scares the crap out of me.

"Hey," he says. He eases his way to his feet with a little help from me, and gives me a long hug. He follows me to the kitchen and sits by the table. "I just need to be near you," he says in his hoarse voice.

By six forty-five, all five of us are sitting around the kitchen table.

"I'm so hungry," Sawyer says. "I have never been this hungry in my entire life." He shovels a forkful of scrambled eggs and a biscuit into his mouth, and Ben chows down as well. While they eat, I fill them in on what happened on our end, and how Tori couldn't tell who the three dead people were, and how the news practically confirmed to us that it must have been Sawyer and Ben who had drowned.

"But I didn't give up hoping," Trey says. "By the way, information about the three dead was released this morning. They were the guy with the glass in his head, some woman I can't figure out from the victim list, and the pilot, who I don't think was even on Tori's list, unless he looked like one of the other passengers. I don't know what happened there."

"We must have confused something," I say. "I'm sad three people died, but that means we saved twenty-four. And our boys are alive, which means more than anything."

Sawyer squeezes my thigh under the table.

"So tell us everything," I say. "I saw you with the girl with the polka-dot headband up at the railing, but then I looked away and you were gone."

"Ah, Bridget," Sawyer says. "What a piece of work that girl is. I'm sure her ankle was broken but she was a total trouper."

"Yeah, I noticed that. I also noticed the life vest she was wearing." I give him a patronizing smile.

"Okay, look," Sawyer says, wiping his mouth with a napkin and sitting back. "What do you want me to do? Throw a thirteen-year-old girl with a broken ankle out into the water without one? The ferry was rolling onto its side, and there was no time, and I'd already given out all the ones I was carrying. I figured once I had her safely in the water, you guys would take care of her, and I could more easily get another life vest without her on my back. So I gave her mine. And I'm not sorry, because according to the death list, she's not on it."

"But *you* almost were," I say. "I'm not letting this one go. I have to be able to trust you."

He sighs. "Fair enough. Anyway, I dropped her down into the water and then tried to scale the deck, but the ferry tilted even farther until I felt like I was trying to climb straight up. And just when I'd almost made it to one of the benches with the life vests inside, the ferry shifted hard and rolled, and I lost my grip and slid down the decline, hitting the railing and flipping over it into the water." He scrunches his eyes shut for a moment and gingerly rubs the nape of his neck. "That sucked bad. Good thing I have such a hard head."

"I saw him go over," Ben says. "I was in the water on that end of the ferry. I thought he might be knocked out, because he hit the railing pretty hard. So I swam out there and saw him flailing and realized he didn't have his life vest on. So I grabbed him and started looking for debris to hang on to."

"But," Sawyer says, "it was almost dark by then, so we had to rely on lightning to see anything."

Ben continues. "I decided our best option was to try to

make it to the breakwall we'd hit, even though the waves were washing over it at the mouth of the channel. I could see the higher part of it, and that was closer to us than the lifeboats at this point. But then we got caught in a riptide that took us out even farther away from you guys, and honestly, I thought that was going to be the end of us. I was tired, hanging on to Sawyer, and trying to coach him on what to do without losing all of my energy talking."

"Never fight against a riptide," Sawyer says wisely. "Swim perpendicular to it, parallel to the shore."

"Very good," Ben says. "Now learn how to swim."

"Anyway," Sawyer says. "So by the time we get out of the riptide we're really far from the ferry and from you guys, and Ben's trying to conserve energy because he's got to keep my face above water, and I'm trying not to freak out and make it worse. *Then*," he says with a sardonic smile, "we make a brilliant decision to get Ben's phone out and call for help. So he tries to keep his life vest above water and I try to get it out, except my hands are numb. I manage to get the phone out without it getting too wet, and as I'm trying to hold it above the water and get to the phone page, I fumble it, and it bounces off Ben's vest and plops into the water. And I am a loser."

"Dude, seriously. I kinda figured that would happen. But we had to try. We weren't going to make it."

Sawyer nods. "It was pretty frightening." He pauses

and looks up. "I really thought Ben was going to have to let me go any minute. We were both freezing and exhausted and running out of hope."

Trey, Rowan, and I are spellbound. I'm gripping my fork so tightly my knuckles are white. "What happened?"

Sawyer leans forward. "But then there's more lightning. And poof."

"Poof," Ben says, nodding.

"Poof?" Trey asks. "What the hell does that mean?"

Fifty-One

"It means poof! The sky lights up, and there, not forty yards away, is that runaway lifeboat," Ben says.

"No way," Rowan says under her breath.

"Yeah way," Ben says.

"Hey, let's not bring God into this," Trey says.

I laugh because I'm a dork, but Ben ignores the joke and continues. "So then I have to decide if we should try to rest for a few minutes first by floating on our backs, and then strike out, or if we just go for it so it doesn't get farther away. And ultimately, I don't want to risk losing it, so I get Sawyer to kick his lazy-ass feet and hang on to my vest belt, and I flip over and start swimming breaststroke like my life depends on it, which it does, out in ten-foot waves trying to catch a lifeboat."

"It took us forever," Sawyer says. "I watched the helicopter leave—it never swept the light out as far away as we were. By the time Ben got us to the lifeboat, he was practically dead. I climbed in and hauled him up. He saved my life." He turns and looks at Ben. "You saved my life, man, and I will never forget it."

"Now we're even," Ben says lightly.

There's a quiet moment while *that* sinks in.

"But how did you guys survive the night?" I ask. "It was cold, and you were wet—how are you not frozen or hypothermic or dead?"

Ben and Sawyer exchange a glance and a small smile. "Body heat," Sawyer says with a shrug. "Skin-on-skin contact."

Trey stands up, his chair hitting the wall. "What?" he screeches. "That is . . . holy crap," he says, softer. "That's a picture, is what that is. Mmm."

"It was super-romantic," Sawyer says.

I bite my lip.

"Naaah, we're just kidding," Ben says after a beat. "The lifeboat had supplies in it. Blankets and hand warmers. Stuff like that." He grins as Trey sits back down. "But I did get to see his junk."

"Easy there, sailor," Sawyer says. "Don't spoil the surprise for the ladies."

Rowan laughs and then pouts. "I never get to see junk. Not fair."

"Fake boyfriend," I cough into my hand.

"Shut it," Rowan says. She turns to Ben. "So was there a flare gun or whatever? How did you get to shore?"

"Well, the helicopter was long gone by the time we got into the lifeboat. So we rested for a while first, and then we went into supersleuth mode and decided that we were out of immediate danger, and that life in general would go much smoother for Sawyer if his parents didn't ever find out he was on a ferry wreck on a school day. And my parents are out of the country, so I wasn't too worried about any news getting back to them very quickly."

Sawyer looks at me. "And I figured the last thing you'd do would be to go to my parents to tell them I'm missing, and that you'd go to Kate first to see what she thought, and she'd most likely want to wait to say anything until we knew for sure what was happening, because of the way my father tends to overreact."

"You know us pretty well," I say. "Though I'll bet Kate was on the verge of telling them when you guys landed on the doorstep."

Sawyer nods. "Yeah, I wouldn't blame her. Anyway, we decided the best plan would be to paddle to a pier or a jetty, put our wet suits back on, ditch the lifeboat, and walk to the beach like we were out just having fun."

"By then the rain had stopped," Ben says, "and the wind started calming down. It was just a matter of time before the lake would be easier to manage. So once we rested and got warm and ate some weird freeze-dried food and crackers we found in the lifeboat, the sun was coming up, so we could see where we were heading. We started paddling toward that bird sanctuary out there on the harbor north of Chicago. When we got close, we put our wet suits on again and I made Sawyer wear the life vest all the way into the park in case he fell headfirst into a bucket of water or something."

"Well played," Sawyer says, and they do some secret fist-bump handshake thing I've never seen them do before.

"We hailed a cab not far from the beach," Ben says. "Sawyer used the driver's phone to call your landline, but just got the recording that Demarco's Pizzeria is rebuilding and will reopen this fall."

"We didn't hook up the residential number when we moved here since we all had cell phones," Trey murmurs. "And those numbers aren't listed."

Ben nods. "I'm just glad I still had my wallet. It was a bit wet after the phone ordeal, but obviously the credit card still worked, and that's all that matters." He checks the clock on the wall and frowns. "The driver dropped us at my dorm and waited so we could quickly change into some clothes, and then took us straight here." He looks at Trey and reaches for his hand. "We couldn't wait to get here. It was so frustrating how lost we were, not having anybody's contact information memorized. I always had it there in my phone. And now it's at the bottom of Lake Michigan."

I notice Ben checking the time, and reluctantly I stand up, because we need to go. "Sawyer, do you want to go to school or just go home?"

"I want to go where you go."

Ben says, "My only class today starts in ten minutes, so I think I'm skipping one more day." He grins. "You want me to hang out here and wait for you?" he asks Trey. What a guy.

"Um, no." Trey looks sidelong at Rowan. "You wanna be Mom and call in sick for me?"

Rowan smirks. "How much is it worth to you?"

Fifty-Two

Trey drops Rowan, Sawyer, and me at Kate's. Sawyer brushes his teeth and grabs his backpack, and we take his car to school. Trey takes a sick day and spends it with Ben. Mr. Polselli checks in with me and I give him a bright smile. Lunch is intimate, just Sawyer and me, and we hold hands across the table as he tells me all the places on his body that hurt so I can feel sorry for him. In sculpting, Ms. White asks me if Trey and I got the news we were hoping for.

"We did," I say, and I can't stop smiling. I decide to work extra hard on my vase today to thank Ms. White for being lenient. And maybe I'll even pull off a better grade on it than Trey, which would rock.

After school, Sawyer drops Rowan and me off at our

house so he can go home, rest for a bit, and catch up on his homework.

And there's my dad, sitting in the living room with the shades drawn and the TV on at three o'clock in the afternoon.

Rowan gives me a look of doom. My stomach drops. The stretch of good times is over. Did I do this to him?

He looks up when we walk through the room on the way to our bedroom. "Girls!" he booms. "How was your day?"

I freeze. And slowly turn to look at him. "Fine," I say.

"Good. Rowan, your mother wants you to help her in the backyard. She's planting a garden so we can grow our own stuff for the food truck."

Rowan's eyes widen. "Oh. Okay." She drops her backpack in the bedroom and escapes out of here like a sidewinder.

Dad turns the TV off and reaches back to open the blinds behind the couch. "I was just killing time waiting for you to get here." He's shaved and showered and nicely dressed as usual for the past few weeks. "We never finished talking yesterday."

"Oo-kay," I say. I slide my backpack off my shoulder and lower my body to perch on the edge of the couch next to him.

"Your mother told me I need to communicate more,

and that I should tell you that we, ah, we like your friends. And that it's nice to have them come over, and at first we weren't used to having them in the house, but now it . . . it's nice. Because then we know where you are, and . . . well. She told me to tell you that."

I raise an eyebrow. "So you like Sawyer now?"

He shifts uneasily. "I . . . yes, I think he's okay. Your mom said he's not living at home."

I tilt my head. "Oh, I get it. He's having problems with his parents, so you like him more because of that."

"That's not what I meant. That's not fair. I tell you something nice and you throw it in my face." He fidgets with his hands and I can tell he's getting defensive.

I choose to let it go since he seems to be trying to be a better . . . whatever. "Okay. I'm sorry. I'm glad you like our friends."

"Also," he goes on, his face pained, "you told me I needed to own my mistakes, and I've been thinking about that. And even though your mother has been telling me that for years, hearing it from you seemed, well, different. It made me feel . . . ashamed."

I don't know where this is going, and I don't know what to say.

"I decided I'm going to go see somebody. A therapist," he says. "Your mom's coming with me."

"Oh," I say. "Oh. Well, that's great. I mean, I hope . . ." I trail off. What is the appropriate response to this statement? I don't know.

"Yeah," Dad says, his gaze drifting to the window, where we can barely see Mom laughing with Rowan and digging up the lawn. "I hope it's good, but I don't know. We'll see."

"Sure. Of course." I want to fall through this couch and through the floor and through the earth's crust and disappear. "Well, thanks for telling me." My body aches to stand and walk away, but my butt is glued to this cushion.

"And so, thank you. And for not saying anything to Trey and Rowan. I appreciate that. I—I think I'm going to tell them soon, but I want to ask the therapist first."

Who ARE you? I swear I am in an alternate reality right now. There's no way this can last.

"That brings me to my next question," he says. "Why did you ask me about the health stuff?"

My head grows light. "No reason," I say. I shift my weight farther onto the cushion, not because I want to relax and chat, but because I'm teetering on the edge of it and could fall at any time.

"Why did you ask me about visions?"

I glance at his face and see him looking earnestly into mine. And I still can't read his expression. Is he asking me because he wants to confess that he has seen visions too?

Or because he's worried that I have, and he wants to put me in an asylum?

"I don't know," I say, scrambling. "I guess I've seen you staring off into space, and you don't drive much, and we've got the whole mental illness thing in the family with Grandpa Demarco, so I thought I'd . . . ask."

He regards me thoughtfully. "Are you asking because of . . . anything personal that's happening with you? Do you need to talk to a doctor?"

Ugh. I wish he'd just answer. "Well, I'm not pregnant, if that's what you're asking."

He chuckles. "I said I was sorry about that. It really was a joke this time."

I feel the residual resentment boiling up again. "Yeah, well, you're very different lately and hard to read, and you're telling jokes now, so I guess I just don't know how to talk to you." I can feel my face getting hot.

He looks down. "I know. I'm sorry." He scratches his head and says softly, "Losing the house and the restaurant . . . losing all of that stuff . . ." He shakes his head. "I was suffocating at first. But then suddenly starting from nothing became this opportunity . . . I don't know. Like the chains came off my wrists." He rests his head in his hands for a moment. "I hated the hoarding, but I couldn't stop it. I was compelled to continue. I couldn't break the cycle." He reaches into his pocket and pulls out the thimble from the Monopoly game. He shows it to me. "This is what I chose to keep from the remains of the fire. The only thing."

I don't tell him that Trey and I watched him take it.

"When I was a kid, I used to play Monopoly with Mary and my dad. Whenever we landed on the income or luxury tax spaces, or had to pay to get out of jail, instead of paying the bank, we put the money in the middle of the board under the thimble. And if you landed on Free Parking, you won it—you got to take the money. It was the absolute best when it happened on your last turn before you ran out of money, facing all those houses and hotels in the Marvin's Gardens row. Hitting it just right—it gave you new life. A chance to change the game, my dad said." He looks at me. "All of that junk and the emotional baggage was dragging me down. And losing everything in the fire . . . well, that turned out to be my Free Parking. My chance to change the game. So even though it'll probably be really hard, I'm going to take it. I am taking it."

I nod, absorbing it all. It's amazing how much happens to the people around me when I'm not paying attention.

He reaches over and squeezes my hand. "I was a pretty good dad back before the dark days. I want to get better at being your dad again."

I had no idea my dad could speak so eloquently, and

I'm actually moved by this. Jules is reluctantly impressed. I place my other hand on top of his. "I just want you to feel good," I say. "Every day."

He leans over and kisses my cheek. "Me too."

And as we sit there, contemplating changes, the biggest question in my life remains. I still don't know for sure if he has seen a vision—he never answered the question. I still don't have any of the answers I need.

I am happy that he wants to be a better dad. But I am also tired, and I am sick of seeing people I love get hurt. I just want this trail of visions to end. I just want him to say no, he's never seen a vision, so that I can remove this responsibility from my shoulders and call it quits on this game of madness. Because if I don't find out for sure, I'm going to have to start trying to find the twenty-four people we saved and begin this stupid process all over. And I know I can't do this again.

So after all of that, I just say it. "Okay, well, back to the question, just to clear things up. Have you ever had a vision or not?"

Fear and concern flit across his face. And then he says, "I'm not sure why you're so fixated on this. But the answer is no, Julia. I have issues that I'm working on, but I'm not that far gone. I've never seen a vision." He hesitates and then frowns. "Have you?"

I look into his eyes, and I know he's telling the truth.

And I feel a surge of hope. Part of me feels a tremendous weight being lifted at the sudden realization: there is no Demarco vision curse.

But then I realize this only makes me look more insane. Does this mean that *I* am the true source of this vision curse? And does this make me even more responsible than before, now that I have no one to point to?

Before I can say a word to deflect his new concerns, my cell phone vibrates.

It's Sawyer—Sawyer's phone, rather—calling me.

Fifty-Three

"Of course not, don't be silly," I tell my dad, then point to the phone. "Mind if I take this?"

"Go for it. I'll be outside helping your mother," he says, which is so weird. He pats my hand and gets up.

I answer on the fifth ring. "Hello?" I say.

"Hi," comes a girl's self-assured voice. "Is this the Jules from the lake?"

I almost laugh. "Yes! Is this the Bridget with the sore ankle?"

"It's broken," she says, as if she's pleased about it. "I'm on crutches."

"Oh no," I say. "I was afraid of that. How did you figure out to call me?"

"Well," she says, "by the time I found my parents and

brother, I didn't see the guy anywhere to give the phone back to him. And by the time we got to our hotel from the emergency room, the battery was dead, and we don't own a charger to fit this kind of phone. So I had my brother buy one with the twenty bucks I also found in the pocket. And now, duh, it's working again."

"Wow," I say. "You definitely have spunk." This is quickly becoming an easy word to use.

"And," she rambles on, "I remembered how you pretty much screamed at me when you saw me wearing this life vest, and yours was just like it, so I figured you must know the guy. And I remembered you said your name was Jules. So I looked in the contacts and found you at the top. Are you his girlfriend or something?"

"Um, well, yes." I'm blushing.

"Well, can you tell him I've got his phone?"

I laugh. "Yes, I will tell him. How can we get it back from you?"

"One sec." She yells away from the mouthpiece, "Hey, Ma!"

I can hear muffled sounds of the mouthpiece against fabric, and then she's yelling something to her mom.

She comes back. "Where does the guy live?"

It occurs to me that she hasn't yet figured out *the guy's* name. "His name is Sawyer. We live in Melrose Park outside of Chicago."

"One sec," she says again. More hollering.

I walk over to the window to watch Rowan and my parents dig up the lawn for a garden. "What the heck is happening to us?" I mutter.

Bridget comes back. "Okay, my parents said we can bring it over tonight. Text me your address when we hang up."

I'm confused, and then I realize she means for me to text it to Sawyer's phone. "Sounds great," I say.

"Okay, bye."

Before I can ask if her family is okay, she hangs up.

I text my address to Sawyer's phone for Bridget, and then text Kate to see if Sawyer is with her.

A minute later Sawyer calls me from Kate's phone. "What's up?"

"Bridget is coming to my house to bring your phone back. Can you come over?"

"How excellent. I was just missing you enough to come over anyway. Yeah, I'll be there in a few."

I smile. "Cool. Also. My dad just told me he thinks you're okay."

"Well." He sounds pleased. "That's something."

When Sawyer arrives, we sit on the front steps waiting for Bridget. Rowan comes around the house and sits with us. Her hands are dirty.

"Dad thinks you need to see a therapist," she announces. She looks at her dirty fingernails and scowls. "Yick. What a mess."

"Great," I say. "Well, at least I finally got a straight answer out of him. He says he's never seen a vision."

Sawyer turns, a consternated look on his face. "Is he telling the truth?"

"I think so."

"Whoa," Rowan says.

"I know." I stare at the ants digging a home in the crack in the sidewalk. "So I don't know what this means, except that I really did start it. I can't blame it on anybody else." I pause, and then I say decisively, "But the ferry was the last straw. We're done. I'm done. It's too dangerous, and I can't go through this anymore." I sigh, thinking about the prospects. "Besides, I can't track down twenty-four strangers to see who might be next. I'm just . . . I'm so *fuh-rucking* tired of it," I say. My eyes burn and I press the palms of my hands against them. "I can't do it anymore."

Sawyer pulls me close and kisses the side of my head. "You're right," he says softly. "It's too dangerous. Whatever this is, it's bigger than us. It's out of our control. And contrary to my statement several days ago, after going through that ferry ordeal I no longer believe we are invincible."

"So . . . we're done?" Rowan says.

I nod. "We're done. I'm calling it. It's over."

It's a relief to say it. Rowan texts Trey to let him know our decision, and he replies: *Aw, shucks. I want to see how many more ways we can DIE.* Then he follows up with: *Secretly, good call.*

We sit in silence, contemplating everything we've been through, when a car drives up. It occurs to me that it would be awkward if my parents witnessed this exchange, so I stand up and walk to the car. Sawyer and Rowan follow.

The parents get out, and then Bridget does too, slower, using her crutches. She's wearing new retro cat-eye glasses.

"I'm Alan Brinkerhoff," Bridget's dad says. "This is my wife, Emily, and I think you know Bridget." Bridget waves awkwardly, acting shy in the presence of her parents.

He reaches out to shake our hands.

"I'm Jules," I say, deciding there's no need for last names on our end—anonymous is a better way to go. "This is Sawyer, and this is Rowan."

"We want to thank you," Mrs. Brinkerhoff says, "for helping Bridge. I still don't know how we got separated. When I realized she wasn't with us, I nearly gave up. Everybody was shoving and pushing . . ." She shakes her head, remembering.

"No problem," Sawyer says. "She was really brave.

I'm sure her jump into the water hurt really bad with that ankle."

Bridget's ivory cheeks turn red. She reaches into the backseat of the car and holds out Sawyer's life vest. "Here ya go," she says, shoving it at him. She reaches back in again and hands him his cell phone and the charger.

Sawyer looks puzzled. "I didn't have my charger with me," he says.

"I know," Bridget replies, "but you bought one later with your twenty bucks."

"I see," Sawyer says.

I grin. "Thanks for driving it all the way over here. Do you guys live nearby?"

"No," Mr. Brinkerhoff says. "We live in Michigan, but we come to Chicago every now and then."

"I have cancer," Bridget says matter-of-factly. "I go to the University of Chicago for tests and treatment and stuff. I've had it my whole life."

"Well, not quite," Bridget's mother says.

"I was born with it."

"You were five," Mrs. Brinkerhoff says. "Stop making things up."

Bridget grins at me.

"Wow, I'm sorry," I say. My head is spinning. *Cancer?*

Mr. Brinkerhoff continues where he left off, like he's used to Bridget's interruptions. "Normally, we drive around the lake to get here, but we thought it would be fun to take the car ferry once."

"Fun!" Bridget snorts. "And now we don't have a car," she says. "It totally sank. Probably has fish in it by now. So we got this rental. It's pretty cool. It has a plug for my iPod in the backseat."

"Cool," Rowan says.

"Yeppers," Bridget says. She bobs her head and looks around. "Huh. Nice little place you got here."

I stifle another laugh. This girl is a hoot.

"Well," Sawyer says to Mr. Brinkerhoff, "thanks for driving out here to bring it to me. That was really nice of you."

"It's the least we could do. We'd really love to do something more for you," Mrs. Brinkerhoff says. "Maybe take you out for dinner or something . . ."

Inwardly I recoil. They're nice and everything, and Bridget is mildly hilarious, but I don't really want to have a relationship with these people. "Maybe," I say. "But we only did what anybody would do."

"I don't think so," Mrs. Brinkerhoff says. "Did you miss all the pushing and shoving, and the people stealing other people's life vests? It was a nightmare. You guys and your calm process—not to mention helping others before yourselves—you probably saved a lot of people."

"Yeah," Bridget says. "It was almost like you knew

it was going to happen." She tilts her head and flashes a charming smile, then shoves a stick of gum into her mouth.

I freeze. Sawyer gives a hollow laugh. But the moment of panic passes.

Mrs. Brinkerhoff reaches out and gives me a hug. "Bridget wrote down your number—I hope that's okay."

I plaster a smile on my face. "Oh, how clever of her. Sure. Call anytime."

After another round of thanks, they get back into the car and Mr. Brinkerhoff presses buttons on the dashboard, probably entering their next destination into the GPS. We walk back to the step and watch them pull away. And then they stop.

The back door to the car opens and Bridget gets out, without her crutches this time. "Yo, Jules!" she yells. She hops on one foot across the yard toward us. I stand up and go toward her.

"What's up? Did you forget something?" I ask.

"Yeah, I forgot to give you a hug."

Kids these days. I try not to roll my eyes, and I lean down so she can hug me.

She wraps her arms around my neck and puts her mouth to my ear. And then she whispers, so softly I can barely hear her, "Guess what? I know about the vision."

Before I can say a word, she's hopping back to the car

and closing the door, and I'm watching them drive off, wondering, for the millionth time, if I'm losing my mind.

"She knows about the vision," I tell Sawyer and Rowan once their car is out of sight.

"What?" Rowan asks. "How?"

I think about it for a long moment. "She must have read our text messages on your phone, Sawyer. I wouldn't put it past her."

"I don't think anyone would believe her if she, you know, went to the media or something," Sawyer says. "Did she say it threateningly? Or what?"

"No," I say. "Just matter-of-factly, like she blurts out everything else."

"It probably just makes her feel cool," Rowan says. "I read your texts all the time. Makes me feel supercool."

I punch her in the shoulder. "You'd better not."

"Psh. Good luck trying to stop me."

Sawyer rolls his eyes. "Anyway. If she wasn't threatening, then I doubt we have to worry about it."

"Me too." I look sidelong at Rowan. "Do you really read my texts? That's gross."

She frowns. "Of course not. Don't be a douche."

Later, after Sawyer goes home and everybody is safe in their beds and Bridget Brinkerhoff is but a memory, my phone vibrates with a text message. I think it might be

Tori, so I scramble to check it because I forgot to tell her Sawyer and Ben are fine.

But it's not Tori.

It's a message from a strange number I don't have programmed into my phone. One I don't recognize. I open it and read: *Hey Julesies! Guess what? Now I'm seeing a vision too!*

Epilogue

Five weeks later.

It takes a four-eyed, hilariously blunt thirteen-year-old kid with cancer to point out the logic of the visions to me. And it's not until after we deal with her vision disaster that we realize we've hit a dead end.

As it turns out, Bridget Brinkerhoff is probably the best of all of us at solving the clues and carrying out the risky actions inside a vision. Maybe it's because she has to face death on a regular basis that she's so fearless. And maybe she's just faking bravery, like the rest of us. But Sawyer and I, Trey and Ben, Rowan, and probably even Rowan's not-fake Internet boyfriend, Charlie, would all agree that Bridget has a knack for figuring out what's in store for our little world. She's in remission now, by the way—a detail she nearly forgot to tell us after her last doctor's visit.

Bridget's vision? Stadium bleachers collapse at a graduation ceremony. At one point or another in the vision, she saw each of us dead, along with dozens of strangers.

But it's over now and here we are: Trey, Rowan, Sawyer, Ben, Bridget, and me. All still alive. We lie on our backs in the grass next to our garden, staring up at the stars.

"We could go try to get the graduating class list. Narrow down the possibilities to try to find the next person with the vision." It hurts my stomach to say it.

"It wouldn't help much, since none of the graduates were in those bleachers," Sawyer says. He holds my hand.

"Yeah, but maybe their families were."

"Extended families, friends," Trey says, "plus other students. Over a thousand of them. Face it, Jules. Unless the person finds us, we're done here. The vision curse moves on without us."

I close my eyes, wishing it to be true.

Bridget props herself up on an elbow. "So, I've been meaning to ask, who'd you get *your* vision from, Jules?"

"Nobody. I started it," I say.

Bridget snorts. "You did not."

I open my eyes and turn my head to look at her. "How would you know?"

"Ego much?" She grins.

I rip up a handful of grass and throw it at her face.

She laughs again and says, "No, come on. Really. Who'd you get your vision from?"

"I'm not joking," I say. "I really think it started with me. I haven't been in any tragedies."

"Well, when did your vision start?" she prods.

Rowan props up on her elbow too, on the other side of Bridget. "Yeah, when exactly did it start? Do you remember?"

Slowly everybody else shifts to look at me. "Suddenly I feel like I'm on a talk show," I say. I try to remember. "I don't know. I had my vision for a long time. Several weeks."

"If we work backward from the night before Valentine's, when the crash happened," Sawyer says, "where would that put you—first of the year, maybe?"

"Christmas," I say, thinking hard. "In fact, it was Christmas Day. We went to a movie—Trey, Rowan, and me. That first vision was in the theater."

"You're sure?" Ben asks.

I think harder. "Yes."

"So if it follows a pattern," he continues, "you would have been saved from some tragedy a day or two before, right?"

"I guess," I say. "But like I said, I wasn't—"

"Well, maybe somebody just did such a great job of saving you that you didn't even know you were saved," Bridget says.

Trey sits up. He starts to speak, and then he stops,

hand poised in the air as if he was about to make a point. And then he looks at me. "Wait," he says softly, closing his eyes, his face concentrating. "Wait a second." His eyes pop open. "When did you get mugged?"

Sawyer sits up in concern. "You got mugged?"

But I can't answer Sawyer because I'm thinking hard. "Christmas Eve, wasn't it, Trey? Or the night before that? But it was no big deal. Nothing really happened. The guy ran off when another guy came out of nowhere to help me." I look around the sea of faces, all wearing the same look. "Oh," I say.

I sit up as the details of that night flood my brain. The rush of footsteps in the dark. The guy shoving my pizza delivery bag at my face and grabbing me from behind, then pushing my face into a snowy bush. "He had a knife," I say. A shiver runs up my spine as I remember the click in my ear.

Everybody's silent for a second. And then Bridget says, "So there you go. You didn't start it. Next question?"

"So the guy . . ." I say, passing my hand over my eyes, trying to concentrate. It's like I can't quite put all the details together.

"The guy who saved you had a vision. He was waiting for you," Rowan says.

"Right," Trey says. "He saved you, and passed on the vision to you."

"And you passed it to me, and that guy probably got it from someone else, too," Sawyer says. "The point is, you didn't start it. You," he says, touching my shoulder, "are not responsible for this."

It's like somebody pulled a hundred-pound weight off my back. "I didn't start it," I whisper.

Rowan smiles. "You didn't start it."

"And," Trey says, "neither did Dad. You aren't hereditarily insane. Yet, anyway."

It's almost too much for me to take in.

I look at Bridget. "What the hell, Bridge," I say.

She shrugs, looking smug. "Logic," she says.

I think of all the risks we took. The crash. The school shooting. Nearly drowning. The graduation stampede. We all could have died so many times. And it wasn't my fault. It wasn't my responsibility. I can hardly comprehend it. All I know is that I feel true relief for the first time in over six months.

Later, when Trey and Ben take a walk in the school playground in the moonlight and Rowan goes inside to chat with Charlie, Sawyer and I drive Bridget Brinkerhoff back to her hotel. She's done getting treatments in Chicago for a while, and will travel back home to Michigan with her parents tomorrow—via land, of course. Maybe we'll see her again. Maybe we won't. That's how we leave it.

But when Sawyer and I drive back without her, it feels like a really long chapter of my life is over. There's just one thing missing. One thing I have to do before I can really close the door on this.

"Can we stop at that complex across from the Traverse Apartments for a minute?" I ask.

Sawyer glances sidelong at me. "You wanna have sexy time *there*?"

I laugh. "No." A wave of nerves washes over me. "I just want to go back to the scene of the crime. The incident."

"Where you got mugged?"

"Yeah."

He turns off to head in that direction, and soon he's pulling into the parking lot.

"There," I say, pointing to a parking spot.

He parks and we get out of the car. I walk to the sidewalk where I was standing when I heard the rush of footsteps. Walk up to the bush that had been full of snow. It's beautiful and green now, with a few extra-long spears sticking out of it.

"Where did the rescue guy come from?" Sawyer asks.

I tug on one of the spears. "I don't know. My face was full of snow. I didn't see. Somewhere over there." I look up and point. "I was so scared."

Sawyer pulls me close in a side hug and holds me.

"Do you want to knock on doors?" he asks, only partly teasing.

"Thinking about it," I say. "But what are the chances he actually lives here? The vision god isn't that thoughtful to make these tragedies convenient, you know?"

We stand for a few more minutes, Sawyer letting me take my time to process. And now I can't believe I never put the two incidents together. Like Bridget says, it's logic. I shake my head, deep in thought.

A door to one of the buildings opens.

Four twentysomething guys come out, talking a little too loudly for the time of night it is. Sawyer's grip on my shoulder grows noticeably tighter as the group heads toward us, but they are talking about going on a beer run and not paying attention to us.

"Hey," Sawyer says in greeting as they walk past.

They respond pleasantly. I relax a bit as they pile into a car nearby.

As the fourth guy opens the back door and puts his foot inside, he looks at us and nods once. The safety lighting from the building shines on him, and I see a raised scar down one cheek. With the door still open, his hand on the inside handle, ready to pull it shut, he pauses and looks at me. Hard.

Our eyes lock. I swallow and give a closed-lip smile.

He hesitates, and when the other guys start hollering for him to hurry up, a look of clarity washes over him. He smiles at me and nods. And I'm probably projecting, but it's almost like he's really pleased to see me. Alive.

My chest tightens.

The guy's fingers flit in an awkward wave as he sits down and closes the door.

The driver pulls out of his parking space and speeds off.

When they're gone, I look at Sawyer and he looks at me.

We shrug and grin together. "Do you think that was him?" Sawyer asks, incredulous.

"I don't know. I doubt it. Too much of a coincidence." I hesitate. "But maybe I'll just pretend it's him, and that we have an understanding now."

And then Sawyer plants a kiss on my lips, and we get in the car and go home.

Because it's over. For real this time.

All I know is that for a while there, we were invincible. And every now and then, when I see a news story about an ordinary hero saving people from an almost certain tragedy, I glance at Sawyer, and he glances at me, and we know the vision curse continues on without us. I think about the heroes and wonder how it happened for them—how they came to be saved, so that they, too, could rescue someone. I wonder about their stories and the people who have come in and touched their lives, and then disappeared again . . . or stayed in them.

But those are not my stories to tell.

Love the Visions series?
Check out Lisa McMann's
Don't Close Your Eyes

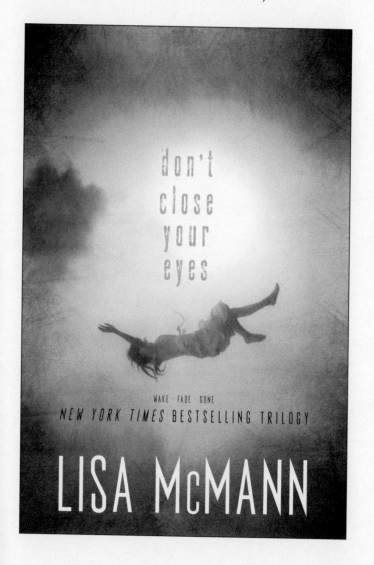

December 9, 2005, 12:55 p.m.

Janie Hannagan's math book slips from her fingers. She grips the edge of the table in the school library. Everything goes black and silent. She sighs and rests her head on the table. Tries to pull herself out of it, but fails miserably. She's too tired today. Too hungry. She really doesn't have time for this.

And then.

She's sitting in the bleachers in the football stadium, blinking under the lights, silent among the roars of the crowd.

She glances at the people sitting in the bleachers around her—fellow classmates, parents—trying to spot the dreamer. She can tell this dreamer is afraid, but where is he? Then she looks to the football field. Finds him. Rolls her eyes.

It's Luke Drake. No question about it. He is, after all, the only naked player on the field for the homecoming game.

Nobody seems to notice or care. Except him. The ball is snapped and the lines collide, but Luke is covering himself with his hands, hopping from one foot to the other. She can feel his panic increasing. Janie's fingers tingle and go numb.

Luke looks over at Janie, eyes pleading, as the football moves toward him, a bullet in slow motion. "Help," he says.

She thinks about helping him. Wonders what it would take to change the course of Luke's dream. She even considers that a boost of confidence to the star receiver the day before the big game could put Fieldridge High in the running for the Regional Class A Championship.

But Luke's really a jerk. He won't appreciate it. So she resigns herself to watching the debacle. She wonders if he'll choose pride or glory.

He's not as big as he thinks he is.
That's for damn sure.

The football nearly reaches Luke when the dream starts over again. *Oh, get ON with it already,* Janie thinks. She concentrates in her seat on the bleachers and slowly manages to stand. She tries to walk back under the bleachers for the rest of the dream so she doesn't have to watch, and surprisingly, this time, she is able.

That's a bonus.

1:01 p.m.

Janie's mind catapults back inside her body, still sitting at her usual remote corner table in the library. She flexes her fingers painfully, lifts her head and, when her sight returns, she scours the library.

She spies the culprit at a table about fifteen feet away. He's awake now. Rubbing his eyes and grinning sheepishly at the two other football players who stand around him, laughing. Shoving him. Whapping him on the head.

Janie shakes her head to clear it and she lifts up her math book, which sits open and facedown on the table where she dropped it. Under it, she finds a fun-size Snickers bar. She smiles to herself and peers to the left, between rows of bookshelves.

But no one is there for her to thank.

Evening, December 23, 1996

Janie Hannagan is eight. She wears a thin, faded red-print dress with too-short sleeves, off-white tights that sag between her thighs, gray moon boots, and a brown, nappy coat with two missing buttons. Her long, dirty-blond hair stands up with static. She rides on an Amtrak train with her mother from their home in Fieldridge, Michigan, to Chicago to visit her grandmother. Mother reads the *Globe* across from her. There is a picture on the cover of an enormous man wearing a powder-blue tuxedo. Janie rests her head against the window, watching her breath make a cloud on it.

The cloud blurs Janie's vision so slowly that she doesn't realize what is happening. She floats in the fog for a moment, and then she is in a large room, sitting at a conference table with five men and three women. At the front of the room is a tall, balding man with a briefcase. He stands in his underwear, giving a presentation, and he is flustered. He tries to speak but he can't get his mouth around the words. The other adults are all wearing crisp suits. They laugh and point at the bald man in his underwear.

The bald man looks at Janie.
And then he looks at the people who are laughing at him.
His face crumples in defeat.

He holds his briefcase in front of his privates, and that makes the others laugh harder. He runs to the door of the conference room, but the handle is slippery—something slimy drips from it. He can't get it open; it squeaks and rattles loudly in his hand, and the people at the table double over. The man's underwear is grayish-white, sagging. He turns to Janie again, with a look of panic and pleading.

Janie doesn't know what to do.
She freezes.
The train's brakes whine.
And the scene grows cloudy and is lost in fog.

"Janie!" Janie's mother is leaning toward Janie. Her breath smells like gin, and her straggly hair falls over one eye. "Janie, I said, maybe Grandma will take you to that big fancy doll store. I thought you would be excited about that, but I guess not." Janie's mother sips from a flask in her ratty old purse.

Janie focuses on her mother and smiles. "That sounds fun," she says, even though she doesn't like dolls. She would rather have new tights. She wriggles on the seat, trying to adjust them. The crotch stretches tight at mid-thigh. She thinks about the bald man and scrunches her eyes. *Weird.*

When the train stops, they take their bags and step into the aisle. In front of Janie's mother, a disheveled, bald businessman emerges from his compartment.

He wipes his face with a handkerchief.

Janie stares at him.

Her jaw drops. "Whoa," she whispers.

The man gives her a bland look when he sees her staring, and turns to exit the train.

September 6, 1999, 3:05 p.m.

Janie sprints to catch the bus after her first day of sixth grade. Melinda Jeffers, one of the Fieldridge North Side girls, sticks her foot out, sending Janie sprawling across the gravel. Melinda laughs all the way to her mother's shiny red Jeep Cherokee. Janie fights back the urge to cry, and dusts herself off. She climbs on the bus, flops into the front seat, and looks at the dirt and blood on the palms of her hands, and the rip in the knee of her already well-worn pants.

Sixth grade makes her throat hurt.

She leans her head against the window.

When she gets home, Janie walks past her mother, who is on the couch watching *Guiding Light* and drinking from a clear glass bottle. Janie washes her stinging hands carefully, dries them, and sits down next to her mother, hoping she'll notice. Hoping she'll say something.

But Janie's mother is asleep now.

Her mouth is open.

She snores lightly.

The bottle tips in her hand.

Janie sighs, sets the bottle on the beat-up coffee table, and starts her homework.

Halfway through her math homework, the room turns black.

Janie is rushed into a bright tunnel, like a multicolored

kaleidoscope. There's no floor, and Janie is floating while the walls spin around her. It makes her feel like throwing up.

Next to Janie in the tunnel is her mother, and a man who looks like a blond Jesus Christ. The man and Janie's mother are holding hands and flying. They look happy. Janie yells, but no sound comes out. She wants it to stop.

She feels the pencil fall from her fingers.

Feels her body slump to the arm of the couch.

Tries to sit up, but with all the whirling colors around her, she can't tell which way is upright. She overcompensates and falls the other way, onto her mother.

The colors stop, and everything goes black.

Janie hears her mother grumbling.

Feels her shove.

Slowly the room comes into focus again, and Janie's mother slaps Janie in the face.

"Get offa me," her mother says. "What the hell is wrong with you?"

Janie sits up and looks at her mother. Her stomach churns, and she feels dizzy from the colors. "I feel sick," she whispers, and then she stands up and stumbles to the bathroom to vomit.

When she peers out, pale and shaky, her mother is gone from the couch, retired to her bedroom.

Thank God, Janie thinks. She splashes cold water on her face.

January 1, 2001, 7:29 a.m.

A U-Haul truck pulls up next door. A man, a woman, and a girl Janie's age climb out and sink into the snow-covered driveway. Janie watches them from her bedroom window.

The girl is dark-haired and pretty.

Janie wonders if she'll be snooty, like all the other girls who call Janie white trash at school. Maybe, since this new girl lives next to Janie on the wrong side of town, they'll call her white trash too.

But she's really pretty.

Pretty enough to make a difference.

Janie dresses hurriedly, puts on her boots and coat, and marches next door to have the first chance to get to the girl before the North Siders get to her. Janie's desperate for a friend.

"You guys want some help?" Janie asks in a voice more confident than she feels.

The girl stops in her tracks. A smile deepens the dimples in her cheeks, and she tilts her head to the side. "Hi," she says. "I'm Carrie Brandt."

Carrie's eyes sparkle.

Janie's heart leaps.

March 2, 2001, 7:34 p.m.

Janie is thirteen.

She doesn't have a sleeping bag, but Carrie has an extra that Janie can use. Janie sets her plastic grocery bag on the floor by the couch in Carrie's living room.

Inside the bag:
a hand-made birthday gift for Carrie
Janie's pajamas
a toothbrush

She's nervous. But Carrie is chattering enough for both of them, waiting for Carrie's other new friend, Melinda Jeffers, to show up.

Yes, that Melinda Jeffers.

Of the Fieldridge North Side Jefferses.

Apparently, Melinda Jeffers is also the president of the "Make Janie Hannagan Miserable" Club. Janie wipes her sweating hands on her jeans.

When Melinda arrives, Carrie doesn't fawn over her. Janie nods hello.

Melinda smirks. Tries to whisper something to Carrie, but Carrie ignores her and says, "Hey! Let's do Janie's hair."

Melinda throws a daggered look at Carrie.

Carrie smiles brightly at Janie, asking her with her eyes if it's okay.

Janie squelches a grin, and Melinda shrugs and pretends like she doesn't mind after all.

Even though Janie knows it's killing her.

The three girls slowly grow more comfortable, or maybe just resigned, with one another. They put on make-up and watch Carrie's favorite videos of old comedians, some of whom Janie's never heard of before. And then they play truth or dare.

Carrie alternates: truth, dare, truth, dare.
Melinda always picks truth.
And then there's Janie.

Janie never picks truth.
She's a dare girl.
That way, nobody gets inside.
She can't afford to let anyone inside.
They might find out about her secret.

The giggles become hysterics when Melinda's dare for Janie is to run outside through the snow barefoot, around to the backyard, take off her clothes, and make a naked snow angel.

Janie doesn't have a problem doing that.

Because, really, what does she have to lose?

She'll take that dare over giving up her secrets any day.

Melinda watches Janie, arms folded in the cold night air, and with a sneer on her face, while Carrie giggles and helps Janie get her sweatshirt and jeans back on her wet body. Carrie takes Janie's bra, fills the cups with snow, and slingshots them like snowballs at Melinda.

"Ew, gross," Melinda sneers. "Where'd you get that old grungy thing, Salvation Army?"

Janie's giggles fade. She grabs her bra back from Carrie and shoves it in her jeans pocket, embarrassed. "No," she says hotly, then giggles again. "It was Goodwill. Why, does it look familiar?"

Carrie snorts.

Even Melinda laughs, reluctantly.

They trudge back inside for popcorn.

11:34 p.m.

The noise level in the living room of Carrie's house fades along with the lights after Mr. Brandt, Carrie's father, stomps to the doorway and hollers at the three girls to shut up and get to sleep.

Janie zips up the musty-smelling sleeping bag and closes her eyes, but she is too hyper to sleep after that exhilarating naked snow angel. She had a fun evening despite Melinda. She learned what it's like to be a rich girl (sounds nice for about a day, but too many stinking lessons), and that Luke Drake is supposedly the hottest boy in the class (in Carrie's mind), and what people like Melinda do four times a year (they take vacations to exotic places). Who knew?

Now the hushed giggles subside around her, and Janie opens her eyes to stare at the dark ceiling. She is glad to be here, even though Melinda teases her about her clothes. Melinda even had the nerve to ask Janie why she never wears anything new. But Carrie shut her up with a sudden exclamation: "Janie, you look simply stunning with your hair back like that. Doesn't she, Melinda?"

For the first time ever, Janie's hair is in French braids, and now, lying in the sleeping bag, she feels the bumps pressing against her scalp through the thin pillow. Maybe Carrie could teach her how to do it sometime.

She has to pee, but she is afraid to get up, in case Carrie's father hears her and starts yelling again. She rests quietly like the other girls, listening to them breathe as they drift off to sleep. Melinda is in the middle, curled on her side facing Carrie, her back to Janie.

12:14 a.m.

The ceiling clouds over and disappears. Janie blinks and she is at school, in civics class. She looks around and realizes she is not in her normal fourth-period class, but in the class that follows hers. She stands at the back of the room. There are no empty seats. Ms. Parchelli, the teacher, drones about the judicial branch of government and what the Supreme Court justices wear under their robes. No one seems surprised that Ms. Parchelli is teaching them this. Some of the kids take notes.

Janie looks around at the faces in the room. In the third row, seated at the center desk, is Melinda. Melinda has a dreamy look on her face. She is staring at someone in the next row, one seat forward. As the teacher talks, Melinda stands up slowly and approaches the person she's been staring at. From the back of the room, Janie cannot see who it is.

The teacher doesn't appear to notice. Melinda kneels next to the desk and touches the person's hand. In slow motion, the person turns to Melinda, touches her cheek, and then leans forward. The two of them kiss. After a moment, they both rise to their feet, still kissing. When they part, Janie can see the face of Melinda's kissing partner. Melinda leads her partner by the hand to the front of the room and opens the door of the supply closet. The bell rings, and like ants, the students crowd at the door to leave.

The ceiling in Carrie Brandt's living room reappears as Melinda sighs and flops onto her stomach in the sleeping bag next to Janie. *Cripes!* thinks Janie. She looks at the clock. It's 1:23 a.m.

About the Author

Lisa McMann is the author of the *New York Times* bestelling Wake trilogy, *Cryer's Cross*, *Dead to You*, the Visions series, and the middle-grade dystopian fantasy series The Unwanteds. She lives with her family in the Phoenix area. Read more about Lisa and find her blog through her website at LisaMcMann.com or, better yet, find her on Facebook (facebook.com/mcmannfan) or follow her on Twitter (twitter.com/lisa_mcmann).

love this **book**?
ready for **more**?